DAVID EBSWORTH is the pen name of ~~former~~ negotiator and workers' representative ~~& General Workers' Union. He was born in~~ in Wrexham, North Wales, with his wife Ann since 1981.

Following his retirement, Dave began to write historical fiction in 2009 and has now subsequently published twelve novels: political thrillers set against the history of the 1745 Jacobite rebellion, the 1879 Anglo-Zulu War, the Battle of Waterloo, warlord rivalry in Sixth Century Britain, and the Spanish Civil War. His sixth book, *Until the Curtain Falls*, returned to that same Spanish conflict, following the story of journalist Jack Telford, and is published in Spanish under the title *Hasta Que Caiga el Telón*. Jack Telford, as it happens, is also the main protagonist in a separate novella, *The Lisbon Labyrinth*. The third of his Jack Telford novels, *A Betrayal of Heroes*, takes Jack into the turmoil of the Second World War but through a series of real-life episodes, which are truly stranger than fiction.

Dave's *Yale Trilogy* tells the story of intrigue and mayhem around nabob, philanthropist (and slave-trader) Elihu Yale – who gave his name to Yale University – but told through the eyes of his much-maligned and largely forgotten wife, Catherine.

The eleventh novel, *The House on Hunter Street*, is a mystery set during the political turmoil of Liverpool in 1911 and, more recently, Dave has published a non-fiction guidebook of Wrexham history, *Wrexham Revealed*. It was his research for the guidebook which inspired him to write this current and twelfth novel, *Blood Among the Threads*.

Each of Dave's novels has been critically acclaimed by the Historical Novel Society and been awarded the coveted B.R.A.G. Medallion for independent authors.

For more information on the author and his work, visit his website at www.davidebsworth.com.

Also by David Ebsworth

The Jacobites' Apprentice
A story of the 1745 Rebellion.

The Jack Telford Series
Political thrillers set towards the end of the Spanish Civil War and beyond.
The Assassin's Mark
Until the Curtain Falls
(published in Spanish as *Hasta Que Caiga el Telón*)
A Betrayal of Heroes
(published in 2021)
The Lisbon Labyrinth
(an e-book novella, set during the 1974 Portuguese Revolution)

The Kraals of Ulundi: A Novel of the Zulu War

The Last Campaign of Marianne Tambour: A Novel of Waterloo
The Song-Sayer's Lament
Another political thriller but this time set in the time we know as the Dark
Ages, 6th Century post-Roman Britain

The Yale Trilogy
Set in old Madras, London and northern England between 1672 and 1721
The Doubtful Diaries of Wicked Mistress Yale
Mistress Yale's Diaries, The Glorious Return
Wicked Mistress Yale, The Parting Glass

The House on Hunter Street
A mystery set during the political turmoil of Liverpool in 1911

Wrexham Revealed
Non-fiction. A walking tour with tales of the city's history

BLOOD
AMONG *The*
Threads
A WREXHAM VICTORIAN MYSTERY

DAVID EBSWORTH

SilverWood

Published in 2023 by SilverWood Books

SilverWood Books Ltd
14 Small Street, Bristol, BS1 1DE, United Kingdom
www.silverwoodbooks.co.uk

Cover by Cathy Helms at Avalon Graphics,
featuring Wrexham Tailor's Coverlet image courtesy of
St Fagans Museum of History, Cardiff.

ISBN 978-1-80042-261-2 (paperback)

British Library Cataloguing in Publication Data
A CIP catalogue record for this book is available from the British Library

Page design and typesetting by SilverWood Books

Dedicated to the memory of Alfred Neobard Palmer as well as all family and friends in Wrexham. Our town. Our city.

For Ann Mary.

Author's Note

This is a work of fiction. But Alfred Neobard Palmer is a significant real-life character. He was born in 1847 and died in 1915, by which time he had become the author of ten major books concerning the history of Wrexham in North Wales and its surrounding areas. Those works remain among the most significant histories ever written on the subject. Palmer did not come to live in Wrexham until 1880, but I began to imagine "what if" scenarios, as authors of historical fiction are wont to do. So, what if Palmer had visited the town before, at the time of the Wrexham Art Treasures Exhibition of 1876? And what if there was some reason that the story of his time in Wrexham has had to be expunged from the pages of history? A matter of national security. From those two pieces of idle introspection came this yarn.

Blood Among the Threads

Chapter One

It was a death which had brought him here. Death by snake venom, of all things.

Palmer wiped his fingers across the grimed glass, peered out through the window, through the clouds of coal smoke which permeated the carriage with the stink of rotten eggs, and beyond the iron girders, down into the menace of serpentine, mud-stained waters below.

'This is the bridge which collapsed?' said Morrison, the carriage's only other occupant.

Palmer's images of writhing coils and vipers' fangs evaporated in an instant, subsumed by this older tragedy.

'The Dee Bridge,' he replied. 'I believe it must be so, though I have merely read the accounts. Can you imagine the horror of that event, Mr Morrison?'

Twenty-nine years ago, the year of Palmer's own birth. Faulty design. The collapse of a section which plunged the Ruabon-bound carriages into the Dee. Five innocents drowned.

'Engineers to blame, sir.' Morrison snorted, as the train trundled over the bridge – now, hopefully, rebuilt to a safer design. He took another swig of liquor from his silver hip flask. 'Engineers. Charlatans for the most part. Your new employer among them, I collect.'

He had been irascible since they boarded the train at Chester and discovered there were no first-class facilities for their onward journey to Wrexham. Morrison had been boorish enough all the four hours and more from Manchester but his pique at having to share the compartment with six other travellers seemingly knew no bounds. His most sustained complaint? No hat rack in which to hang his silk topper.

Yes, boorish, thought Palmer. Airs and graces. Monocle. A long face fixed in a permanent sneer. Expensive frock coat. Palmer had not been acquainted with him – apart from having read some of his acerbic pieces in *Reynolds's Newspaper* – before Morrison had inexplicably imposed his company upon him as they pulled out of Manchester's London Road station.

'Mr Low,' Palmer corrected him, 'has impeccable references. And the tragedy could hardly be laid at his door.'

Low had joined the Chester and Holyhead Railway shortly thereafter. As their Chief Engineer.

'Impeccable?' Morrison savoured the word. 'I wonder whether the investors in his Channel Tunnel escapade might share that enthusiasm.'

'Most of the investment, his own, was it not? Fifty thousand pounds, I understand. To purchase the necessary land at Dover and Calais.'

The land had been purchased and tunnelling commenced. A mile or two dug beneath the Channel, it was said, until the war between France and Prussia had brought a halt to the entire venture. Perhaps, Palmer mused, one day the project might be completed. And just imagine – the wonder of such a thing.

'Not entirely his own, sir,' said Morrison. 'The investment. Not entirely. Though I suppose you could be forgiven for failing to understand the finer points of economic liberalism. Where did you say? Thetford?'

Palmer tried to contain his anger. The change of trains at Chester, he had hoped, might provide the chance to be rid of Morrison. But his efforts had been thwarted, Morrison sticking to him like a limpet, despite his apparent poor opinion of Palmer's unsatisfactory education.

Alfred Palmer was taciturn by nature and believed firmly that there was virtue in being a man of few words. Yet he was plagued by his passion for discovery. Chimerical dreams of adventure which seemed to fly entirely in the face of his measured life as a chemist. And it was difficult to seek out the truth without asking questions. An enquiring mind trapped within an introspective character.

He had, at first, been intrigued by Morrison. Surely his journalistic profession must give them a shared interest in all things investigative.

But he had been disappointed. Worse, he had opened himself to the older man's churlish views.

'Yes, Thetford,' Palmer told him, defiantly – and not for the first time. 'The Grammar School, as I said. And afterwards, Minister Morgan's private academy.'

No university, then. Morrison had no need of the words – merely the dismissive twitch of his imperious nose.

The Grammar School had frequently been less than kind to Palmer and had forcibly rid him, to a large extent, of his East Anglian accent, though he clung stubbornly to a few idiosyncrasies of speech. He could never think of a pond as anything other than a *pit*, while he maintained a tendency to always think of his throat as his *stroop*. The word 'first' regularly succeeded in emerging as *fest*.

'And the academy,' Palmer announced, 'set me on the path towards pharmaceutical research.'

He offered his snuff box to the newspaperman. His only vice – every man was entitled to at least one, was he not?

'Truly?' said Morrison in a voice of practised *ennui* and shook his head to refuse the snuff. Then, 'Saltney,' he said in the same tone, as they pulled into the next station. 'How much more of this must we endure?'

Palmer took a pinch himself, gazed out onto the tops of trees, the track and platforms here elevated along higher ground. A forest of ferns. A haven for snakes, he decided, his thoughts returning to the very thing which occasioned his journey.

He reached into the travelling bag at his side, pulled out this month's copy of *Bradshaw*. Poor Bradshaw, he thought – a noted Quaker, yet dead from Asiatic cholera contracted during his travels in Norway. Palmer could have prescribed the perfect cure: the tablets of cocaine and creosote combination; then the morphine sulphate plus the tincture of digitalis; and, finally, the dilution of eucalyptus and camphor. But his mind turned, instead, to the ditty, now doing the rounds at the Music Halls, and a favourite of dear Ettie. The song about the young woman who could not recollect the station to which she was supposed to travel.

Birmingham and Sandringham, Ulverton and Wolverton,
Dorchester and Porchester, Rochester and Ryde;

Arlington and Darlington, Torrington and Warrington.
She said she'd sure to find it in my Bradshaw's Guide.

Palmer turned to page seventeen, which he had irresponsibly marked by folding down the corner. He smiled, recalling Morrison's tirade about the lengthy stop at Warrington. Intolerable, the newspaperman had whined. Comfort and refreshments? he had said. An oxymoron, surely. Though he had complained just as loudly, like old Mr Dombey, whenever the engine took advantage of those few stretches where it could hurtle them along at greater speeds. Fifty miles per hour? Sixty? To Morrison it was all hellish. The accelerated pace of modern life a curse.

'Beyond this,' said Palmer, 'four more stations before we reach Wrexham General.'

'And have you been to that God-forsaken backwater before, sir? Have you? No, you need not answer. For my colleagues tell me that if you have visited the place once, wild horses could not persuade you to return. Arts Exhibition, indeed. Can you imagine any place beyond the realms of heathens less suitable for such a thing?'

He continued in much the same vein all the way past Balderton, Pulfordsen and Rossett stations, until Palmer found himself forced to ask the inevitable question. This Kingston "Moggs" Morrison was, after all, the man who had covered the Mordaunt Affair and a dozen other salacious society stories.

'Then, if you can forgive the impertinence, Mr Morrison, since you have such a poor opinion of the town and its exhibition besides, might you not tell me your purpose in Wrexham?'

Morrison's smile was supercilious, cynical.

'All in good time, sir. All in good time.'

And as they pulled into Gresford Halt, with its fine two-storey stone-built station surrounded by trees, he added a further warning.

'Here, Mr Palmer. Draw your last salubrious inhalation here, if you will. For beyond Gresford you shall find nothing but pit wheels and coal dust, the stench of mediocrity.'

The tirade continued until they reached the outskirts of Wrexham itself. Through it all, Palmer clung to a determination that he would make his own judgement, yet afraid that, as his sweet Esther had warned him, he may have made a terrible mistake. It caused him to concentrate his mind upon the letter he'd received from her, just yesterday evening.

Dearest Neo, Ettie had written, exercising her own intimate salutation for him – Neobard being, rather than a rare Christian middle name, his mama's maiden name. And his parents, being somewhat European as well as somewhat modern in their outlook, had determined that Alfred should carry with him always the evidence of both his paternal and maternal lineage.

So...

Dearest Neo, I still pray that you might reconsider your rash decision. I fear you may have accepted this strange position in an effort to ingratiate yourself with my father and, in so doing, to escape me also. And yet I must assure you that such a sacrifice, such risk to your career, is unnecessary on each account. Even worse, I have been afflicted by such nightmare visions that I now truly fear for your safety.

She was correct. In part. Her father, Mr John Francis, a Welshman to the core, was Manchester's City Surveyor. Further to that, he was a patron of some Welsh bard, who would shortly be performing at Wrexham's Eisteddfod. More important, he was a close friend of this same William Low, the engineer with aspirations to dig a tunnel beneath the English Channel. William Low, who had helped dream up the idea for an Art Treasures and Industrial Exhibition, also to be held in Wrexham – the opening ceremony to take place on the following day. William Low, who seemingly possessed not one, but two museums – somehow suddenly and tragically lacking a curator.

Mr Francis, friend to William Low, also exercising considerable influence with Palmer's employer, so kindly securing Alfred a leave of absence from Levinstein's, that he might bend his skills, his fascination with history, to this purpose. Palmer was grateful for an additional reason – a relief to be away from Manchester, the filth and soot which so permanently filled the air and made his already weakened lungs much worse.

Mr Francis also had a further vested interest. He took a dim view, it seemed, of this pulmonary problem and had openly expressed his opinion that Palmer was not the man he would choose to marry his daughter. He would plainly see this post in Wrexham as a means of at least temporary separation. And, as it happened, Palmer welcomed it for similar reasons. Ettie was pressing him to marry before – in her words – they grew too old. Despite being a young woman of spirit, she had expressed a desire to be his wife, yet Palmer himself feared that marriage might consign his beloved to a role of subjugation. He considered himself inadequate to the task of preventing such a disaster and needed time to develop a formula to resolve his dilemma.

Ettie, meanwhile, had this tendency towards clairvoyance. Normally, her visions of impending doom, her imaginings, her dreams produced no tangible outcomes of any kind. Though, occasionally...

And, in this case, Palmer could not help thinking of the mysterious accident, the death by snake bite, which had deprived William Low of his original curator. The death which had summoned him to Wrexham.

Chapter Two

'An unfortunate accident, then,' said Palmer, as the kitchen maid – Harriet, he recalled from Low's introductions to his household – fetched the trays of sea kale and mixed vegetables to accompany the fine saddle of mutton.

'Unfortunate?' William Low's voice carried with it the very essence of the Scottish Highlands, the heather-laden voice blowing flurries of activity among the whiskers of his luxuriant white beard. 'Aye, that it was, Mr Palmer.'

Low, at the farthest end of the dining table, lifted his knife and fork, examined them for cleanliness, then turned to his son-in-law, the solicitor, John Bull. Yes, thought Palmer, John Bull, though he could not have looked less like his cartoon personification of England. As slender and parsimonious as Mary Louisa though, at about forty, he must have been a good ten years older than his spouse, Low's daughter.

'Well, Johnnie?' said Low, 'You found her. Poor wee woman.'

The solicitor glanced around the table. Nine of them, all told, seated for dinner, the Low's three youngest children – the girls both fifteen, and the boy just thirteen – already packed off to their beds.

'Yes, sir. I found her. Though it was Edward who treated Rose – or tried to do so.'

A hint of sarcasm there? Palmer believed so. Though the second son-in-law, Doctor Edward Davies, paid the inflection no heed.

'Yet perhaps,' said the doctor, 'not a tale entirely appropriate for dinner?'

He nodded discreetly in the direction of the two youngest members of the party – the Lows' daughter, nineteen, and the other son, two years her junior.

'I fear, Edward,' said Elizabeth Low, 'that my husband has already filled their heads with all manner of lurid details.'

Unlike Low himself, there was no hint of Scotland here. Some more local accent, thought Palmer.

Mr Low had already told him part of the story, how Rose Wimpole, a widow, had come to work for him at the Vron Colliery, which the Scotsman had owned and managed, among his many other engineering activities, for over twenty-five years. The pit, it seemed, was now the largest of those surrounding the neighbouring township of Brymbo – *Brum-bo*, as Palmer learned to pronounce the name. Low had steadily increased the number of bookkeepers associated with the mine's business and the Widow Wimpole had come highly recommended, previously having been in the employ of the Honourable William Cornwallis West, Lord-Lieutenant for this County of Denbighshire. And she had shown such acumen in the organisation of the colliery records that, when Low had determined on opening his museums within the other edifice he had so recently caused to be built in the centre of town, he had offered her the post as curator.

But the young people had been clamouring for Doctor Davies to continue.

'You shall be amazed, Mr Palmer,' the girl insisted. 'The rarity of this event. *Vipera berus*. Can you believe it?'

'The common adder?' said Palmer. 'I was astonished when I read of it. Responsible for a death?'

They had all stopped eating, food abandoned on their plates.

'She is correct, of course,' said the doctor. 'Rare indeed.'

'Though I have read of such cases,' said Palmer, 'cropping up from time to time.'

Doctor Davies used the interruption to extract a stubborn piece of mutton from between his teeth.

'But this one particularly unusual,' he went on. 'For, in this case, it seems the creature must have found its way into the widow's cottage.'

'Somewhat remote,' Mrs Low explained. 'Near the Red Bank farm – part of the Grosvenor estate. And not only into her cottage, but into her very bed.'

'We can never be sure precisely what happened,' said Doctor Davies, 'but we found the bed linen crumpled, the pillow upon the floor. And Widow Wimpole bitten upon her lips. The inside of her upper lip, to be precise.'

The Lows' daughter was beside herself with excitement, almost bouncing from the cushion of her chair.

'The farmer away from home,' she said. 'They say she may have tried to go there for help.'

'Perhaps, my dear.' The doctor smiled at her. 'Perhaps. But one way or the other, she eventually found her way to Brymbo Village itself. Such swelling to her face and neck that she was barely recognisable. By the time I reached there, it was quite impossible to help her. We arranged for her to be transferred to the infirmary, but she expired soon afterwards – the following morning.'

'A single bite?' said Palmer.

'Two sets of bite marks. Those upon her lips. And a second bite, precisely upon her jugular vein.'

'And the swelling – was it awful?'

'By the time I first saw her, it must have subsided somewhat, according to those who witnessed her desperate arrival. Still substantial but subsided to bruising. Around her neck and shoulders. Frightful.'

'I wish I could have seen it,' said the boy, and received a scolding from Mrs Low.

'Well,' Palmer murmured, stroking his own neatly trimmed beard, 'these are strange circumstances in which to procure an appointment. Strange, indeed.'

'Yet I trust it has not changed your mind,' said Mr Low, 'about accepting the post.'

The maid, Harriet, hovered in the doorway once more, a large silver tray dangling at her side.

'Shall I clear the table, sir?' she said to Low.

'Lassie, we have hardly done justice to Mary's fine dinner. And I cannot abide waste. Though, I fear it's all turned to rubbidge. But we shall make amends with her pudding, no doubt.'

Harriet bobbed a little curtsey, then came forward and began to gather their plates onto the tray.

'And a fine pudding it is, see,' she smiled.

'But you were saying, Mr Palmer.' Low turned to him. 'Not changed your mind, then?'

'Certainly not, sir. You have made me most comfortable.'

Indeed, they had. Roseneath House was elegant in the extreme, its building completed, Low had boasted in his gentle way, only twelve years earlier. In sixty-four, he had said, though another year to finish laying out the grounds – those terraced lawns with their flower beds Palmer could see through the French windows of the dining room. The grass was glistening, deepest bottle green in the dying light of the evening and the shower of July rain.

'I told you, Ma,' said Alison, wife to Doctor Davies and the eldest daughter. 'You could have given my old room to Mr Palmer.'

She was unremarkable, for the most part, and shared her mother's equally unremarkable features. Except for her hair. Copper red, and an inheritance, Palmer was sure, the same as the merest hint of an accent, from her father's Argyllshire ancestry. Perhaps his temper, besides. For a family argument erupted around Mrs Low's insistence on preserving each of her offsprings' bedrooms exactly as they had left them, despite the years since the older children had flown the nest. One of the sons, Richard, had been engaged as a surgeon in London, though now returned to Wrexham – a position at the infirmary and his own lodgings but, even in this case, the room was kept, in Alison's words, "as a sacred shrine."

'Truly,' said Palmer, almost having to shout above their clamour as a reminder of his presence, 'I am most comfortable. I have never before lived in a tower.'

His allocated third-floor attic room sat at the top of the square, ivory-wrapped turret which rose above the front entrance steps to the house. The views were attractive, far from the picture of the area painted for him by Morrison. A tower, yes. Perhaps some adventure here, after all. Something to rival the stories of Ballantyne and Captain Marryat which had so thrilled him as a boy. Before he became – a chemist.

'And, hopefully,' he pressed on, setting aside this foolish musing, 'this rain will subside before the opening.'

There was a brief and embarrassed silence, as the family recalled their guest and as Harriet returned with the Conservative steamed pudding.

'Aye,' said Mr Low, at last. He sniffed the air, causing another whisper of movement among those white whiskers. 'The weather should be fine on the morrow. An early start, though, Mr Palmer. For we've Bethan to meet. And I'm no' relishing the encounter.'

Chapter Three

Bethan Thomas glowered up at Palmer with her cataract-clouded eyes. But Palmer's own eyes were filled with wonder. Around each of the museum's walls, floor to ceiling glass cabinets, packed with antiquities and ancient manuscripts. Running down the centre, a tall, ebonised mahogany pyramid display case with bay-ends, full to overflowing with exhibits, which visitors might view from each side, and various angles.

'A waste,' she spat. 'To have fetched you here all the way from *Lloegr*. Eng-land.' She made it sound like somewhere in the mysterious Orient. 'Not needed, you're not.'

In the end, Mr Low had avoided the encounter, pleading the demands of some last-minute arrangement for today's opening celebrations. But he had warned Palmer what to expect – for most of the hard work to bring the museum's collection here had been undertaken by Rose Wimpole, with Bethan's assistance, although Low had now simply determined that it would be seemlier for the curator to be – well, a man.

'All the same,' said Palmer. 'Here now. I'm certain we shall get along perfectly well. You see? I have no idea why Mr Low should want me here, either' he lied. 'Though I should have travelled to visit the exhibition in any case.' Of course, he would. As a younger man, eight years before, he had been thrilled by the National Exhibition of Works of Art, in Leeds. 'So, a privilege to be here,' he assured her. 'And your collection, Mrs Thomas…'

'*Miss* Thomas, it is.'

He smiled at her, apologetically.

'Still,' he said. 'The collection. A fine example of the curator's art.'

She ignored him, continued to tidy the stacks of exhibition catalogues upon the desk, bent sideways through some limping weakness in her left leg as well as eyesight which, judging by the lens thickness of her spectacles, must have been seriously limited. Palmer knew the arrangement of the collection must certainly have been the handiwork of Rose Wimpole. Though he could instantly see the flaws in her design.

Outside the museum doors, outside the archway of Mr Low's Westminster Building, a queue was already forming at the turnstiles. The town full of people, the atmosphere positively electric. Beyond the opposite, northern end of the arch, a covered walkway of timbers clad with zinc roofing sheets, and skylights. At the farthest end, a window of stained glass. This covered area led towards the main exhibition hall – of similar but significantly larger-scale construction. To Palmer it all seemed so – temporary. And this sense was somehow heightened by the nervous, skittish anticipation among the liveried servants waiting at their various posts, the cloakrooms, the refreshment and reading rooms, to receive the first guests.

'No danger of the crowds getting wet, I see,' he said, and once again received no response.

Perhaps, he thought, a touch of deafness besides her other afflictions.

'And this.' He gestured towards the vaulted ceiling, though he intended the movement to embrace the entire building. He spoke more loudly, as well. 'Mr Low tells me it represented a dowry for his daughter, Alison.'

No answer.

The building stood proud upon Wrexham's Hope Street, newly built, shops below, office accommodation and lodging rooms above, the archway here through the middle. The rents, Palmer assumed, must provide a tidy independent income for Alison and her husband, Doctor Davies.

'Then I shall begin to rearrange the display,' he said, as quietly as he was able.

'You shall not!' She spun about, waved one of the catalogues in his face. 'Bad enough to have the Wimpole woman meddling with everything.'

The Wimpole woman? Palmer was taken aback by this lack of respect for one so recently deceased.

'I shall not be a-meddling, Miss Thomas. But I sense some friction between yourself and the Widow Wimpole. For my part I simply hoped we might be colleagues. Partners, so to speak, in this enterprise. I imagine that, when the crowds begin to arrive there shall be more than enough work for two pairs of hands. And when the exhibition is over, the crowds subside, I shall be gone again, back to Manchester – this domain all your own, once more.'

In truth, he had no idea about Low's plans once the show was done, though he doubted they would include poor Miss Bethan Thomas. He also dreaded the prospect of a return to Manchester. Ettie was one thing, but the dun haze of smoke nuisance which played such havoc with his lungs was quite another.

'Didn't know her, see, you didn't. High and mighty madam, she was. Always wanting to interfere, as well. Brought her down in the end. Change, see. You people always want to change things.'

'I prefer to think of it as bringing order to the world. Like this...'

He pointed to a wooden drinking bowl, a mazer, with a silver rim and foot, this latter inscribed with the date *Anno Domini 1597*.

'It was contributed, I see,' he said, 'by your Reverend Jones. Yet I could not help noticing that the good reverend had also loaned some other items from his collection across...'

He pointed to the opposite side of the archway, the other half of Mr Low's museum.

'Dates,' she told him, as though he were the village idiot. 'Arranged by dates, they are.'

She nodded her head towards the late-sixteenth century Hebrew prayer book sitting alongside the mazer.

'Yes, I understand. Though dates are not the only way of achieving order, Miss Thomas. And order is – well, crucial. Is it not?'

'If you says so.'

'Without the correct understanding of order, Miss Thomas, there can be no laws. No predictability in research and investigation. You see?'

'Oh, Bethan sees well enough.'

'Different forms of order,' Palmer pressed on. 'Those dictated by the natural world we see around us. And the entirely distinct form of order within the human mind. Our aim here should be to educate, do not you think?'

Bethan, it seemed, had been struck by yet another attack of deafness.

'And to educate the human mind,' he said, rather for his own benefit, 'we must provide hooks upon which to hang our memories. Connections.'

Connections and collections, he thought.

From outside, a church bell began to toll the hour, the sound borne upon that breeze which, he'd noticed, in Wrexham seemed to permanently carry the olfactory reminders of the town's many tanneries, the stink of dead hides, and its equally numerous breweries, the heady aroma of hops. Palmer checked his pocket watch. Ten o'clock. The turnstiles now also ringing. The exhibition about to open, and the first guests, all dressed so elegantly for the occasion, filling the archway with the echoes of their festive pleasure. Five shillings for a seat, two shillings to stand, at the official opening in just four hours' time. Then at five o'clock, and thereafter, the public to be admitted for just one shilling. Cheap, thought Palmer. Perhaps too cheap?

But the catalogues were selling like hotcakes, as the Americans might say.

Art Treasures Exhibition for North Wales and the Border Counties,
22nd July 1876.

'Forgive me, Miss Thomas,' Palmer shouted across to her when the initial rush had died down. 'But did I hear you correctly? You say that the Widow Wimpole's interference brought her down in the end? The serpent, did you mean?'

It had worried him, somewhat. And, miracle of miracles, it seemed her hearing was perfectly restored.

'Adder?' she chortled. 'Whoever heard of adders bothering folk in their own homes?'

Yes, he had thought the same thing.

'But interference,' he said. 'You mean interference with the adder? Disturbed it, perhaps. It had bitten her in some other way? Some other location, rather than in her bed?'

'She was bit, to be sure. And interference, yes indeed. But back then, see. Before. How she came to be at the colliery, instead of all those airs and graces at Ruthin Castle. Not that it's any of my business, mind. Just saying, like.'

'And whose business might it be, then?'

'You could ask Mr Low. He must know, I suppose.'

Chapter Four

'Really, Mr Palmer?' said William Low, as he waited to take the stage. 'Now?'

He turned and waved at his family. Already seated, among a hundred other privileged guests, on the slightly tiered chairs towards the rear of the platform, just in front of the exhibition organ. Only the front rows were still empty, reserved for those of even greater prestige and still to arrive.

'There was no urgency in the question, sir,' Palmer replied. 'Mere curiosity, piqued by my assistant – if that is the correct way to describe Miss Thomas. I find myself somewhat uncertain in that regard, though it is early days, as they say. And I merely asked by way of passing the time.'

It was true. Mr Low seemed afflicted by a fit of stage fright and Palmer had sought only to distract him.

Not an inch of space left within the body of the hall, every one of those seats occupied and so many standing that they constantly encroached into the seating area, disputes and even a few actual scuffles breaking out as folk were jostled, or their view of the performance platform impeded. Attendants rushed to protect the glass cabinets separating each partitioned side gallery from the hall itself. Besides the carnival capering, excessively colourful language filled the air and, in Wrexham he had discovered, such language was employed equitably across the entire social spectrum. Yes, he had decided, by just his second day in town – so many things in Wrexham indeed seemed equitable.

A determined but badly outnumbered cordon of red-uniformed soldiers and blue-clad policemen still struggled to keep a central passageway clear for the imminent arrival of the platform party.

'No love lost between Bethan and poor Rose, laddie. But her heart's in the right place, to be sure.'

Palmer was far from convinced, and then the strains of a military marching band reached them from somewhere in the distance.

'The Widow Wimpole came to you from Ruthin Castle, did Bethan say?' shouted Palmer, as the noise grew louder.

'Her previous post was with the major, to be sure. With the wife, anyway.'

Low infused the word 'wife' with more contempt than Palmer would have thought possible. Interesting. And the major in question? None other than the Lord-Lieutenant of Denbighshire himself, one of those most responsible for bringing this project to fruition. Major William Cornwallis West, chairman of the exhibition's organising committee.

'A falling-out of some sort?' said Palmer.

'Aye, perhaps. It would be easy enough wi' that one. Though, tittle-tattle – a dangerous thing, is it not? Still, the major asked if I could find wee Rose a position and, whatever had passed between her and the major's woman – well, their loss was Low's gain. Eh, Mr Palmer?'

The adder's bite, though, Palmer thought. He could not quite shake Bethan's comment from his mind. Still, he kept it to himself.

'And now a loss to you also, sir,' he said.

But here came the band. Still not properly in sight, though the pomp and pride of their brass section, their drums, echoing around the walls of the covered approaches, heads craning among the crowd near the main hall's entrance – another archway – for a first view. *Men of Harlech*, naturally.

Mr Low's response – if he made one – was lost amid the applause as the leading ranks turned into the hall's central aisle, which now miraculously cleared itself, people falling away to the sides, like the parting of the Red Sea, before the pounding rhythm of polished boots, the swagger of a drum major at their head, the rainbow-infused twirl of his ceremonial mace. Trombones, trumpets, horns, and drums. Black headgear with silver spikes.

'The Thirtieth,' Palmer shouted. Familiar numbering on gilded helmet plates and belt buckles. 'I'd expected a Welsh regiment.'

'Home service,' Low replied. 'Visiting, so to speak.'

Palmer almost felt at home. The Three Tens. The Fighting Cambridgeshires. As a boy, back in Thetford, they had been very much the local heroes. Oh, the battle honours, the tales of Salamanca and Waterloo, of Inkerman and Sebastopol. Recently? Their actions in Canada against the Fenian Brotherhood, Irish Republicans raiding across the American border.

After they passed, the procession of dignitaries behind a banner proclaiming the exhibition, each of those worthies named by Mr Low.

'His Grace,' he said. 'And the Duchess, Lady Constance.'

The Duke of Westminster, Hugh Grosvenor, would have been fifty or thereabouts, Palmer guessed. Extensive sideburns down to his throat, a prominent nose thrusting forward like a railway signal, so that it extended even beyond the brim of his grey top hat. A huge bow tie, almost a cravat, which spilled over the lapels of his morning coat.

'A fine patron of the arts,' said Low. 'Hospitals. Architecture.'

'And horse racing, is he not?' Palmer smiled.

'Aye, horse racing too.'

At Grosvenor's side, the Duchess. Younger than her husband? It was hard to tell. She looked a little like the queen. A summer coat of green silk, hair braided above and at the nape of her neck, beneath her ribbon-trimmed bonnet.

'The good major himself...' said Mr Low.

Major Cornwallis West, then. His name was on everything concerning the exhibition. But he was not exactly as Palmer had expected. Forty or so, but attired as a far younger man might be. A double-breasted Newmarket jacket of grey Scotch stripe, the edges bound with narrow braid and the long tails hanging from his hips. Crimson cravat with a sparkling diamond pin. The tight-fitting trousers almost white. A waxed Imperial moustache and oiled black hair.

'And, of course...'

It seemed that Low could not bring himself to even name her. But, at the major's side, upon his arm, one of the most beautiful women Palmer had ever seen.

'Great heavens,' he murmured. 'His wife?'

Half her husband's age, at best. A finely striped coat, almost in the Regency style. The same material as the major's jacket, with contrasting flounces around the substantial bustle. Matching bonnet. The skirts, just below the coat's hem, were lifted high enough to see her buttoned boots beneath. Skipping alongside her, a child, a little girl, perhaps three years old, and swinging a parasol. Their daughter? Palmer wondered. And, just behind, another lady, older but equally arresting.

'Aye, wife,' said Low, with almost the same venom as before. 'And her mother, married to some Irish buffoon – a parson, over at Warren Hall. Fitzpatrick.'

The younger woman's languid eyes turned towards a place somewhere above and behind Palmer's head. He turned as well, drawn to follow the direction. Classical wooden columns supported the ornately fashioned roof trusses at the end of each of the side gallery partitions. And the lower section of each square column displayed its own marble bust. Yet more exhibits. One of them, Palmer had earlier been pleased to see, represented John Wesley. Palmer had, himself, served God as a local Methodist preacher during his time in Bury St. Edmunds and elsewhere. But Wesley's likeness sat among those on the other, western side of the hall. At Palmer's back, the sculpted likeness was that of His Royal Highness, the Prince of Wales. Not especially remarkable, yet by the time Palmer had returned his gaze to the major's wife, he found her staring at him. Expressionless, though staring.

Palmer felt the heat rise in his neck and cheeks. He determined to recover himself.

'Ah, here is somebody I recognise,' he said.

William Chaffers, the exhibition's General Superintendent. A famous antiquarian, who had been prominent in the organisation of the Leeds exhibition which Palmer had visited. But others besides. At Manchester, South Kensington, and Dublin. Probably more. Though a sorry sight, old and bent, leaning heavily on his stick. Still, here all the way from London.

And not the only ancient present, still barely living among all these other relics of the past. For here came an old and cadaverous fellow in a bath chair. Curls of rampant white hair on the sides his face and erupting from an oversized top hat.

'Penrhyn,' said Low quietly. 'Damn his eyes. Makes me ashamed to be a Scot.'

Famous, of course. Infamous, perhaps, might be more correct. His name inseparable from the Welsh slate industry but achieving notoriety, not too many years ago, when he had dismissed eighty of his Penrhyn Quarry workers because they had failed to vote for his son in the General Election. Palmer could not remember the son's name, but he could have been any one of the half-dozen fellows among Lord Penrhyn's escort – though a few of them could easily have been bodyguards.

The band had by now mounted the stage and struck up yet another popular tune. It seemed to have quickly become a favourite for military bands. He knew it as *Land of My Fathers*. But in Welsh? He was determined to learn. Around him, folk began to sing, some of them, indeed, in the Welsh language. And a cheer went up at the same time for the next fellow in the procession's line. This rotund gentleman raised his arms, waved his hands in the air to acknowledge the crowd. Florid face. Smokey sideburns stuck out from the sides of his jawbone as though he had just seen a ghost or been subjected to an electric shock. His belly may be restrained by his waistcoat, but it still protruded through his jacket as though it might burst its restraints. He could have provided a model for Samuel Pickwick, Palmer decided. A woman, presumably the wife, waddling alongside.

'Sir Watkin,' Low told him. 'Williams-Wynn.' Then he lowered his voice. 'Fancies himself the King of Wales,' he murmured. 'Old fool.'

Next, a veritable muddle of lord mayors and their lady wives – from Wrexham, naturally, but also from Denbigh, from Liverpool, and a half-dozen more besides. Gold chains galore.

Behind this mayoral gathering – well, Palmer heard the names, score upon score, and in his normal methodical manner must have filed them in his memory, though he was hardly aware of having done so. No, he was more concerned by the lack of punctuality. How he despised retardation. For the official opening should have commenced at two o'clock and, by half-past the hour, the Duke of Westminster had still not spoken.

Palmer was not excessively anxious to hear the speech, and Mr Low had now joined that substantial platform party, but he could not bring himself to return to the museum until, at least, after the National Anthem – Her Majesty being, after all, the exhibition's patron.

As the final notes died away, the band marched into the wings, and the crowd's standing reverence turned to the noisy resumption of seating and conversation, Palmer took a last look at the stage – where Major Cornwallis West, as chairman of the exhibition committee and these proceedings – prepared to make his opening address, one hand tucked inside his double-breasted jacket, the other holding a page of notes at his side. A little further back, the Duke of Westminster, also standing, with his wife sitting alongside, already clutching a bouquet of flowers. And behind the duke and duchess, those other rows of notables, including Mr Low and his family. Though it was the major's wife upon whom Palmer's gaze fell, in the end. And, once again, he found her regarding *him* in his turn.

He spun away, confused, looked towards the art gallery's archway so he might escape. Yet the throng was now so dense he doubted he could easily push his way through. Instead, he turned left, through the side gallery housing the Chinese and Japanese exhibits, at the farther end of which another doorway led into the Industrial section. He was reasonably certain that, from there, he could more easily find his way back to the museum though, in any case, it seemed to offer the best chance to escape the woman's scrutiny. What was her interest in him? Or was it merely his imagination?

He paid scant regard to the Japanese lacquered furniture, screens, and sweetmeat boxes, nor to the Chinese blue and white porcelain, the enamelled platters, or the huge cloisonné garden vases but, rather, passed through the wide doorway into a long avenue, twenty feet wide, running the length of the exhibition building's eastern edge. He turned right, passed between displays of textile manufacturing and shoemaking, of clocks and watches, of more modern pottery. To his delight, at the end, where another door – as he had calculated – would allow him to pass behind the crowd and reach the hall's main entrance, an exhibit to warm his heart, to distract him fully from thoughts of the major's wife.

An advertisement, *Frederick Cooper and Sons, Coachbuilder.*

He helped himself to a pinch of snuff and thought about his father's business, back in Thetford, Palmer's younger brother John now plying the same trade. Palmer himself owed a great deal to his father and the family enterprise – for his education, apart from all else. And, without wishing to feel ingratitude, though the practice of chemistry might hardly be adventurous, it was several steps removed from the tedium of the spokeshave.

And then there was Catherine, his sister – how was she managing? Their mother was ailing, and Catherine had taken responsibility for her care. Not long past twenty and the burden was great. There was the verse, from Psalm 144:

That our sons may be as plants grown up in their youth; that our daughters may be as corner stones, polished after the similitude of a palace.

Yes, that was Catherine, now the cornerstone of the family. While John – and he himself, also, Palmer hoped – would surely and diligently follow the respective paths upon which the Lord had set their feet.

For now, he set his steps around the rear of the crowd, which was gifting a round of applause to His Grace, the duke. He headed diagonally across the entrance hall, but as he turned the corner into the covered passageway, he glanced across at the window of the first-class dining room. Just inside, at one of the tables, Kingston "Moggs" Morrison. Palmer hoped to avoid him, but their eyes met for a moment and the newspaperman beckoned to him. Palmer hesitated, wished he could ignore the summons, yet it would have been churlish to do so.

'Well, Mr Morrison,' he said, as he approached the table, 'I thought you might have been among the platform party, taking a record of the event.'

'Care to join me in a snifter?'

A bottle of Pattisons Whisky stood on the table, but Palmer declined with a shake of his head, though he accepted the chair which Morrison also offered.

'And I already wrote my piece about this mediocre affair,' Morrison went on.

'Mediocre…?' Palmer began to protest.

'In any case,' the newspaperman cut across him, 'it is not this poor excuse for an exhibition in itself that intrigues me, nor brings me all the way here to the Wild West. You did not think so, surely, Mr Palmer?'

Palmer had certainly wondered about this. The pursuit of the Mordaunt Affair, the queen's son cited in a divorce case, of all things. It had been in his mind again when he saw the bust of the Prince of Wales in the exhibition hall. Then the scandal upon which Morrison had reported, involving America's Reverend Beecher, just two years before. Last year, the Prince of Wales in his sights once more. This time his undignified behaviour during the visit to India, his participation in pig-sticking and other barbarous activities. Yes, Moggs was a man, in the best traditions of *Reynolds's Newspaper*, for upsetting the apple cart, for displaying radicalism alongside sensationalism.

'Then what, Mr Morrison?' said Palmer. 'What brings you to Wrexham?'

'Ah!' Morrison raised his whisky tumbler and his eyebrows at the same time, haughty and cynical. 'For that, you shall have to wait. A pity, however. It was Mr Low's bookkeeper I had hoped to ensnare. And now – this nonsense about snake bites…'

Chapter Five

The article, when Palmer finally managed to read it the following morning, offered perhaps some hint of the line Morrison was pursuing. After their encounter in the first-class dining room, the newspaperman had left him and hurried away to one of the town's telegraph offices so he could dispatch his composition to London.

'I tremble to think how much these new telegraph stamps will cost,' he had said. 'Still, I have kept it short and – well, perhaps a little less than sweet.'

At five o'clock, the turnstiles had indeed permitted members of the public to attend the exhibition for just a shilling and Palmer had expected that, with it being half-day Saturday, many more people would have availed themselves of the opportunity. In reality, however, he judged the attendance to be disappointing.

He had worked late, urging Bethan Thomas to perhaps hear some of the evening's entertainment: an organ recital by Mr Best from St. George's Hall in Liverpool; the Birkenhead Choral Society; several vocalists; a harpist; and, naturally, more martial music from the band of the Thirtieth Regiment – in town, Palmer now discovered, as part of a recruitment exercise. The soldiers were encamped at the pleasure of that same florid-faced rotund gentleman, Sir Watkin Williams-Wynn, out on the local racecourse, which he owned. Apart from the obvious, the ground was also frequently in use for cricket matches and for football, Sir Watkin being a great supporter of Wrexham's football club and recently elected as President of the newly formed – also here in Wrexham – Football Association of Wales.

Palmer had been able to hear some of the music from the museum, while he continued to curate Mr Low's exhibits: beginning the process of arrangement by contributor; noting those items needing some measure of cautious cleaning and listing the chemicals he might need for the task; drafting the texts for identification and information cards; seeking inspiration for collectors who might supplement some of the displays; considering inventive ways in which he might help publicise the establishment; and wondering how he might pose the possibility of employing further assistance.

'More help?' snarled Bethan when he later explained his thinking. 'For this place?' she cackled.

'We can talk about it tomorrow.'

He hoped to buy some time, but she snapped back at him straight away.

'Tomorrow? Don't work on Sundays, see, I don't. Sabbath, it is.'

She had collected her shawl, wrapped it around her hunched shoulders and bid him a curt goodnight. So, his final task of the evening, writing a small placard for those times, on the following day, when he might need to leave the museum unattended.

Back within the hour.

He ate supper with the servants at Roseneath House, but he did not sleep well. Friday's travelling finally getting the better of him. He tried to read by the light of his bedside candle – *Dombey and Son*, of course, which he had brought with him, and the reason Dickens's character had been so on his mind during the journey. Though it was thoughts of Major Cornwallis West's wife which filled his head, distracted him from the story, during those spells when he lay awake. Those languid eyes – and yet, in the moments before slumber finally took him, they became the deadly eyes of a venomous serpent. A viper.

The following day, with Mr Low's permission, he was present at the museum for the opening of the exhibition's second day, then hung his sign on the door before taking himself off to chapel. A choice of two, in fact. The Wesleyan Methodist Chapel near St. Mark's Church. Or the Primitive Methodist Chapel, near the school at the rear of the Beast Market, close to the tannery and its stench, towards the top end of Farndon Street. He chose the latter. Each of them half a mile distant from Roseneath.

Primitive, Palmer reminded himself, in the sense of seeking a restoration of Wesley's revivalist teachings, of the first Methodists.

The encouragement of women preachers. Their affinity with workers in struggle. Affinity with trades unions.

The chapel was small but packed with worshippers who welcomed him into their fold and invited him to preach when they discovered he had been ordained as an itinerant minister. He preached, of course, about art and beauty, about how each might calm our fears and lift our spirits. About how God is the master artist. Example followed example. Gospel quotations poured forth. For Palmer had the gift. The ability to see art and beauty through God's eyes.

He hurried back to the town centre, acutely aware that he had exceeded the hour but anxious, as well, to discover whether Morrison's column might have appeared in *Reynolds's Newspaper*. Newsagents aplenty, naturally, and reading rooms available above some of the public houses, within the Liberal Working Men's Club, at the Conservative Association and a dozen other locations. Yet he preferred to see whether the paper might be available at the exhibition's own reading room.

And there it was. Among salacious penny weeklies and the more efficacious reading. The Welsh language papers and children's religious publications. The *Sunday Times*. A copy of yesterday's *Wrexham and Denbighshire Advertiser* among the mass of other local and weekly broadsheets. The three big Sundays: *The News of the World, Lloyd's Weekly* – and, of course, *Reynolds's Newspaper*.

This wonder of the modern age, that even London-printed newspapers – thanks to the miracle of sorting carriages and news guards on express trains, and the wholesale delivery agencies of W.H. Smith and Sons, as well as others – could, for this past year or so, now be on breakfast tables across the nation, as well as simply in London itself.

Reynolds's Newspaper lay upon the table of the exhibition's reading room. Though it was impossible to get close for the gentlemen already pressed all around.

'The cost of the building,' one was saying, peering closely through a quizzer. 'Thirty thousand – can that be correct?'

'And this,' said another. 'I know a few who won't be happy with this: "*The numbers attending are unlikely to satisfy the expectations of investors.*" Just glad I'm not one of them. Look at the place this morning. Almost empty.'

'But this is disappointing,' laughed a third. 'Plenty of mention for Cornwallis West, though I'd rather hoped for a picture of that wife of his. Good gracious, did you see her?'

The fellow slapped his neighbour upon the back and a couple of the men made comments which Palmer considered somewhat lewd. He decided to return later. They were correct in one respect, however. There were far fewer visitors today. Though it was Sunday, after all. Hopefully, the other fine folk of Wrexham at their devotions.

Still, he thought, a chance for him to explore the exhibition in more depth.

He did so, working his way through the various galleries of the main hall. Antiquities and Illustrated Manuscripts – where he spent some time, first, examining the Precious Pebble of Owen Gwynedd, and then that astonishing silver harp belonging to the Mostyn family. The Art Bronzes and Metal Work included a crucifix attributed to John of Bologna. In Plate, Bijouterie and Watches, he admired the Grace Cup of St. Thomas à Becket, the gold rosary and crucifix of Mary, Queen of Scots, as well as the alarm watch given by Charles the First to Sir Thomas Herbert when going to the place of the king's execution.

Palmer skipped quickly past Arms and Armour, before coming to the final gallery on the western side, just in front of the orchestra stage. Paintings, by Velasquez, Murillo, Tintoretto, Castiglione, and Canaletto. Then Van Dyck and all the other German, Flemish or Dutch masters. The colours and forms dazzled him. Among the British, Turner's *Battle of the Nile* and several of Gainsborough's landscapes. Simply too much to comprehend, the walls crammed with oil paintings, then watercolours and miniatures, hundreds more in the partitioned salon opposite, on the eastern side of the hall.

He studied them with a chemist's eye, calculating the formulae and pigments needed to produce this depth of Cobalt blue, or that luminosity of Cadmium yellow, though he finally decided that, with luck, the reading room might now have emptied – or, at least, that interest in the *Reynolds's Newspaper* may have abated.

Palmer chose to return there by a somewhat circuitous route, returning to the Plate, Bijouterie and Watches section where a door at the back led through into the western gallery, that portion of the industrial exhibition he'd not yet had a chance to visit. Agricultural machinery, elaborate foundry work, a display of mining industry safety equipment, and a fine collection of locks, keys, and door fittings. And still more textiles.

He stopped, taken by one particular exhibit. A patchwork of pieced needlework, about seven feet by eight, perhaps a little smaller. Alive with vivid images. The object label declared that it was Industrial Annexe Exhibit Number 46, a Table Cover, produced by the hand of military master tailor James Williams, College Street, Wrexham, using four and a half thousand separate fragments of cloth.

'Astonishing,' he said, rather for his own benefit, and was surprised when his comment received a response from a woman he had not noticed at the time he spoke. She was standing back, almost in the shadows.

'You think so, *señor*?' she said. 'Yet there is blood among those threads.'

The English was perfect, though heavily accented. Spanish, of course, though whether from the Peninsula itself, or from some portion of South America, he could not tell. She was wrinkled, though perhaps simply the result of hard living, for she did not seem especially old. Small and dark. Fierce eyes. A black lace scarf upon her head and shoulders which could have come straight from one of the Murillo paintings.

'Blood, you say?' Palmer murmured, somewhat confused though, for the sake of appearances and to avoid seeming rude, he peered more closely at the coverlet – specifically at one of the many scenes it portrayed, Jonah and the Whale.

'Each piece of cloth,' she said, 'from the uniform of a *soldado* – a soldier.'

'You know its history then, *señora*.'

He took the snuff box from his pocket and opened it, but before he could take a pinch, she had made some snapping gesture with her fingers, stretched out her hand towards him. Palmer reluctantly handed over his precious supply of Wilsons, watched her snort the powder, first up one nostril, then the other, before pointing to the name, James Williams, of College Street.

'It is hanging in his workshop, many years. Everybody in Wrexham know this thing.'

She handed back the box and then, she was gone, in a flurry of dark silk skirts and not a by-your-leave, nor further explanation. Blood? Palmer wondered. If this Williams was a military tailor, he would surely only be fashioning new uniforms for officers and gentlemen to replace their worn attire, or to supplement their wardrobes. Hard to imagine that any of their discarded clothing would be tainted by blood. Yet it played on his mind even as he studied Morrison's article, back in the reading room. Page two, below the edition's review of new books.

The Wrexham Art Treasures Exhibition. *The industrial town of Wrexham in Denbighshire has opened an Art Treasures Exhibition, with the principal support of the county's Lord-Lieutenant, Major W. Cornwallis West.*

Details of the construction contractor. The hall's dimensions. A broad description of the art treasures by simple category. Mention of the industrial section and entertainers, the procession, the main speakers.

But then the sentences which had attracted the attention of those gentlemen in the reading room earlier.

Receipts, we are given to understand, are already expected to fall far short of expenditure. Expenditure already far in excess of the original intention and promise, the calculation of final expenditure now standing at a figure of thirty thousand pounds.

Many questions are asked by the good people of Wrexham about financial probity in the award of contracts, in the cost of decoration, and in the lavish extravagance of the entertainments.

Finally, if we may judge by the poor sale of season tickets, the numbers attending are unlikely to satisfy the expectations of investors.

Hints of a scandal, and Palmer wondered whether he had been wise to accept his part here.

That evening, an angry Mr Low alleged plagiarism, insisting that the substance of the piece had simply been lifted from a large notice in the *Wrexham Guardian* earlier in the month.

'But this.' He stabbed at the final paragraph. 'The major will nae be best pleased. Nor His Grace, neither. You know this fellow, don't you, laddie?'

'Only from the train, sir. On Friday.'

'Well, it won't answer. Nothing must spoil the Exhibition. Nothing. Too much at stake.'

Later, over supper, Palmer asked Harriet, the kitchen maid, whether there were many Spanish folk in town – and one in particular. He described her.

'That?' said Harriet. 'A witch, that one. The Blackstone woman. Mistress of the workhouse.'

She and Mr Blackstone had only held their positions for a couple of years, it seemed. Before that? Harriet couldn't say. But those with dealings at the workhouse spoke of dark things, the Mistress muttering curses in that heathen tongue of hers.

Palmer filed away the inadequate information and, next day, Monday, he returned to his work at the museum.

Monday, and Wrexham livestock auctions at the pens he had seen the day before near the chapel, drovers herding their cattle through the town's streets in time for Monday's Beast Market. A busy day for Wrexham's markets in general.

'*Duw Annwyl*,' said Bethan. Good Lord. 'What else can you expect?' she asked him, when he remarked about yet another day when attendance at the exhibition was mediocre, to say the least. 'Market day, see?'

Morrison's fault, as well, perhaps? He could hardly be entirely to blame, surely.

But when Palmer returned to Roseneath House late on that Monday evening, he found Mr Low in sombre mood.

'You've not heard, laddie?' said the old man. 'Another accident. Morrison – he's dead.'

Chapter Six

The preliminary inquest took place two days later, on the Wednesday, but was adjourned pending a *post mortem* examination – a family affair, thought Palmer, since it was carried out, on the Wednesday, by Mr Low's recently returned son, the surgeon, Richard. And he was assisted in this gruesome business by none other than Low's son-in-law, Alison's husband, Doctor Edward Davies.

The inquest reconvened on the Saturday at the lime-rendered Talbot Inn, its two dormer windows and large gable on Hope Street by now a familiar landmark for Palmer. The hearing itself took place in the dark interior of the half-timbered dining room running almost the length of the Talbot's white and wide-windowed flank on Queen Street. It was overseen by the Coroner, Mr H.B. Thelwall and a jury, for whom one Mr Evan Evans served as foreman.

Evidence was to be taken from the surgeon himself, from two other witnesses, and from Police Inspector William Wilde. Mr Low strongly suggested that Palmer should also make himself available, in case – as the newspaperman's "friend" – he should have anything to add. Besides, it was Palmer who had been called upon to identify the body.

Also in attendance were Deputy Chief Constable Bradshaw, a reporter – he had introduced himself to Palmer earlier in the week as Hancock from the *Wrexham and Denbighshire Advertiser* – several spectators, and Morrison's grieving widow. At least, Palmer assumed so. She was small, plump, and veiled, her widow's weeds of the darkest purple, like a damson plum, he thought, a damascene, *Prunus domestica*.

After some delay, and the preliminaries over, the coroner invited Mr Low's son to present his evidence. The young surgeon read from his notes, his Scottish accent almost as strong as his father's.

'I made a *post mortem* examination of the body of the deceased on Wednesday, the 26th instant. On examining the body externally, I found there was one large bruise on the inner side of the right leg, five inches long by one inch broad. I found a second bruise on his shoulder of a similar size. There were no other external marks of violence. On opening...'

'A moment, Mr Low,' said the coroner, pausing from his recording of the account. 'A moment, if you please. You say no *other* marks of violence. You mean to say...?'

'No, sir. A person may incur violent bruising without the violence having been inflicted by another person. If you would allow me...'

'By all means, yes. Continue.'

Richard Low went back to his notes, found his place. He coughed, and then began again.

'On opening the body, I found the lungs to be congested with water, but all the other organs were healthy...'

'Drowned, then?' Mr Thelwall interrupted him again.

The surgeon sounded impatient, irritated by the distraction.

'No, sir. A person may ingest water into their lungs at or near the point of death, even though drowning itself may not be the cause of their demise.'

'I see. Pray continue.'

'On making examination of the head, I found an extensive comminuted fracture of the bones at the back of the skull.'

This time, the surgeon was ahead of the coroner. He had seen Mr Thelwall's head rise, and his mouth begin to open.

'Comminuted, sir,' he said, forestalling the obvious question. 'Broken in at least two places.'

Thelwall smiled and waved his pen, so that Richard Low might continue.

'After removing the brain – '

There was a cry of anguish from the distressed lady.

' – and making an examination of the bones of the neck, I found dislocation of the spine.'

Another cry, followed by continuous sobbing. Palmer could not bring himself to look at the poor woman.

'And there was,' the surgeon concluded, 'sufficient cause of death in the fracture of the skull posteriorly. Death must have ensued within a minute, and during that minute, water was ingested into the lungs of the deceased.'

Richard Low was excused, and his place taken by Grufydd Griffiths, who had been on duty on Sunday night at the Feathers, where Morrison had been staying. The newspaperman had taken supper in the commercial room at the inn – there was a lot of irrelevant detail about the nature of the meal – and then left the premises a little after ten o'clock.

'Last I saw of 'im, it was, Your Honour,' said Griffiths, almost with glee. He was young, a mop of unruly hair, and the infuriating habit of hopping from one foot to the other. And his voice! Palmer had become accustomed to the profusion of ways in which the Queen's English was spoken in Wrexham: the lilting singsong of those who were natural Welsh speakers; the gentle tones of those with little or no *Cymraeg* but whose Welsh accent resonated more with the Marches borderlands, with neighbouring Shropshire; and then the somewhat coarse and nasal Welsh inflection of those who spoke no Welsh at all. Griffiths fitted firmly into this latter category.

'Left after ten o'clock,' said the coroner. 'His destination?'

Griffiths laughed. He actually laughed.

'Your Honour,' he said, 'how would I know, like? Only the Lord Jesus knows where 'e ended up after 'e kicked the bucket.'

There was a scream of pain and shock from the woman. And a protest from the Deputy Chief Constable.

'Mr Griffiths!' said the coroner. 'If you please. I rather gather that we have the widow of the deceased in our midst. Respect, sir. Respect.'

Griffiths grinned, the mockery of an apology, while the Widow Morrison continued to sob in the background. It took Mr Thelwall a few moments to compose himself again, but finally asked Griffiths to continue, to answer his question with more decorum. But the man had no idea where Morrison might have been heading.

'Offered 'im a lantern, see? But didn't want it. Said 'e had only a short step to go and knew the way.'

'And when he failed to return?' said the coroner.

'Just assumed he'd found himself some company for the night. Know what I mean?'

The fellow had the temerity to turn towards the spectators and winked his eye. Thelwall dismissed him without further ado and declared a brief recess. Ten minutes, he said, and they all filed out into the small parlour which, today, served as a waiting room for the inquest.

Palmer watched Griffiths making himself scarce, out through the door onto Hope Street.

'Disreputable fellow,' said Hancock from the *Advertiser*. 'Things have never been the same at the Feathers since poor Anderson passed away.' They had met on Tuesday, at the Floral and Horticultural show, taking place in one of the fields adjoining Grosvenor Road. Palmer, against his better judgement, had been persuaded to assist with some of the judging.

'But here,' Hancock took his arm, and led him across the room, 'let me introduce you to Mrs Morrison.'

She was being consoled by the Deputy Chief Constable. Hancock was plump and round as the widow, while Bradshaw – old enough, Palmer thought, to be near or past the age when he should have been retired – towered above them, painfully thin, white-haired, his eyes grey and piercing. His accent, when he spoke, was southern. And Bradshaw – such a coincidence. He heard his sweetheart Ettie once more, gaily humming the tune to that Music Hall ditty about *Bradshaw's Guide*.

'In truth,' Palmer told the tearful woman, after Hancock had also described him as her late husband's friend, 'we merely travelled together on the train from Manchester. And then a brief discussion on the following day. But my sincere condolences, all the same. A terrible accident.'

'I do hope so,' she sobbed. 'An accident, I mean.'

'No reason to believe otherwise, dear lady,' said the Deputy Chief Constable. He sounded almost amused, though Palmer saw Hancock prick up his ears, as though he sensed a story.

'Poor Kingston was always meddling in one thing or another,' said the widow. 'Manchester. And then – well, here…'

I never asked him, Palmer thought to himself. Never asked him what had taken him to Manchester.

'All the way from London, I assume?' he said.

'Chislehurst, Mr Palmer. We live – lived, perhaps I should have said. For, poor Kingston...'

She broke down again, pressed her face into the frock coat breast of an embarrassed Deputy Chief Constable, while Palmer searched his memory, recalled Chislehurst's more recent significance. Of course, the French connection. It was the place where exiled Napoleon the Third had settled with his family. The Empress Eugénie. The handsome young Prince Imperial. So, the recent war between France and Prussia had put an end both to the French Empire *and* to Mr Low's dreams of a tunnel beneath the Channel.

'You have been staying at the Feathers also, Mrs Morrison?' Palmer asked, by way of finding something – anything – to change the subject.

'I could not bear to do so,' she said. 'The Wynnstay. But the people at the Feathers have sent me...'

Her next words were lost in the outpouring of her grief. His effects, Palmer supposed. They would have delivered Morrison's personal effects.

'And we have a few things at the Bridewell,' said the Deputy Chief Constable. 'Pen. Pocket watch. Notebook. If you should care, ma'am...'

'Perhaps better,' Palmer cut across him as they were ushered back into the inquest, 'if one of us collected them and delivered them to the Wynnstay?'

Bradshaw was grateful for the suggestion, plainly assuming it would be Palmer who would undertake that duty. Mrs Morrison thanked him also. She touched his arm before they resumed their seats, while the coroner called the next witness.

Aled Pierce was a cattle drover, weather-beaten, drooping grey moustache, and eyes like slits from too many years glowering against the cruel winds of Wales and time alike. An Anglesey man, lodging at the Horns Inn, alongside the bridge, after herding his cows to the Beast Market pens. Pierce admitted, without the slightest shame, that he had been drinking at the inn until late, when he had stepped outside to relieve himself in a side alley.

'Heard a shout, I did. And when I looked round the corner, there was this creature on the bridge. Black as night. Wings spread. Big as an eagle. Bigger.'

The inevitable questions about precisely how long and how much had Pierce been drinking that night, and whether he had ever seen such Gothic apparitions in the past, though fundamentally it transpired that he could not swear to having seen Mr Morrison himself at all, and neither had he crossed to the bridge to discover the source of the shout he might, or might not, have heard.

Finally, Inspector Wilde was called. Not yet forty, Palmer decided. A chinstrap beard, like those pictures of American President Abraham Lincoln. Indeed, he rather resembled images Palmer had seen of the assassinated president in his younger days.

'At about six o'clock,' Wilde read from his notebook, 'last Monday morning...'

The accent was English. Slightly rural?

'You were working at that hour, Inspector?'

'There have been disturbances in town of late, sir. It has been necessary to ensure the Bridewell is manned around the clock, and on Sunday night...'

'Yes, yes, I understand.'

'Last Monday morning – yes, here it is. Last Monday morning, I received certain information...'

'Certain information, Inspector? What was that, precisely?'

'A boy, sir. From the Horns Inn. He brought a note. The innkeeper had been up early, about his business, and under the bridge...'

'Very well.'

The inspector completed his evidence, with the coroner holding up his hand at the end of each sentence to slow him down, so that his pen could keep up with the details.

'I proceeded to the bridge, sir, and climbed down to discover the body of a man lying wedged against some rocks of the bank, a little under the bridge itself. On reaching him, I found the deceased, though he was quite dead, the body cold and a great quantity of dried blood around his ears. I found nothing else and, after closely examining the spot, I concluded that the deceased must have fallen from the top of the bridge, where the parapet is somewhat collapsed and been awaiting repair for a considerable while. There are rocks in the stream, just below this point, and I believe the deceased must have fallen upon them, incurred his injuries and been precipitated by the flow underneath the bridge.'

It was all perfectly sufficient. Mr Thelwall summed up the points he had heard. Lucid enough. And the jury, without needing to retire, ultimately returned an open verdict.

'An open verdict,' the coroner repeated, wrote these final words, and signed his name upon the page with a flourish. 'Found...dead.'

No more? Palmer thought as they left the Talbot. Found dead? It seemed so terribly inadequate. And he, himself, had not been asked to say a word. He was glad, for what could he have told them? That Morrison had hinted at something afoot? That he had hoped to ensnare – yes, that was the word Morrison had used – Mr Low's bookkeeper? That he had dismissed Rose Wimpole's death by viper bite with ridicule? That he had hinted at financial irregularities surrounding the exhibition? How might any of that be relevant to his demise?

'Did they not then believe,' Mrs Morrison murmured, 'that this was an accident?'

It had begun to rain, and not a napper between them.

'It simply means, ma'am,' said Deputy Chief Constable Bradshaw, 'that your late husband's death was a sudden one, and that there is no specific witness evidence relating to the incident in which he met his tragic end. Had there been any suspicion in the minds of the jury or Mr Thelwall to the contrary, they would have said so. The matter would have been referred to the police. To investigate. An accident, therefore, yes, of course.'

It made perfect sense. So, why did Palmer have this itch in his thumbs? This nagging desire to study Morrison's notebook.

Chapter Seven

Palmer found the blood on his way to the Bridewell, though with some difficulty.

He had stopped at the bridge, the bottom of Town Hill, where the road crossed the Gwenfro before climbing again and leading out of Wrexham to the south. He had stopped with a twinge of guilt, hoping that Bethan Thomas was coping without him at the museum. Yet he was somehow pleased, as well, to be fulfilling this duty.

There, on the farther side, just to his left, stood the Horns Inn – a favourite among the visiting cowherds, drovers like Aled Pierce, whose beasts presumably gave this hostelry its name. And, therefore, the bridge as well. The Horns Bridge.

It was busy. Another Saturday afternoon, yet a steady flow of traffic, a couple of landaus, a coal cart, and a horse-drawn omnibus. Congestion here, for there was work in progress on the road, tracks being laid for the tramway system due to open later in the year – though the workmen's half-day now at an end. Still, the jangle of harness, creak of leather, the hammer of shod hooves and clatter of wheel rims on cobbles, the smell of dung. And the hops. The sickly smells hanging over the place from the several breweries and malthouses up ahead.

The parapet was indeed badly damaged and plainly neglected, as Inspector Wilde had described, many of its stones tumbled down into the stream below but some still here, scattered along the edge of the cobbled surface.

It had rained, of course, since Sunday night. Rained several times. But Palmer scattered the debris with the toe of his shoe, turning over a few pieces with no true intention, simply in a distracted way as he gazed down into the sluggish waters, dyed a shade of stinking olive drab by, he assumed, some industry or collection of enterprises upstream. He thought, inevitably, about Morrison. What an end to one's days! And he was about to continue his journey when he happened to see that one of the upturned stones was darkly stained.

He picked up the small rock. Bigger than his fist. Perhaps twice that size and, from its shape, the corner of a coping stone. Palmer rubbed at the dark brown discolouration and some of it came away on his thumb. Could it be?

He remembered a chemistry lesson at Morgan Lloyd's Academy, based on the studies of Second Century Chinese doctor Hsu Chich-Ts'si, in which the boys were all invited to test a variety of stains, all similar in appearance, by heating them and then applying distilled vinegar. If this resulted in a brown liquid, the stain was proven to have been blood, the acetic acid in the vinegar having reacted with the blood's own chemicals to form brown haematic crystals. Simple. Further experiments using a microscope to differentiate between human blood and, for example, its bovine counterpart.

Palmer determined to take the stone to Inspector Wilde, simply to confirm whether this was, indeed, a bloodstain – though whether there might be any connection to Morrison was, of course, an entirely different matter. And even if it were so, might the poor fellow not simply have bashed his head on the parapet as he fell? Could some curiosity have caused him to see something in the waters below, and then simply to lose his balance as he peered over the wall? Or to trip perhaps on these very piles of rubble?

He held up the stone to the light and there – what was it, precisely? Something matted into the stain. He thought of Morrison and that, in turn, caused him to think of *Reynolds's Newspaper* – or to be more precise, the paper's proprietor, George Reynolds, among whose considerable and varied attributes was his talent as a writer of wonderful penny serials, which Palmer had subsequently read as complete volumes. *The Mysteries of London.*

Palmer wondered what Richard Markham – the closest thing to a hero in the stories – would have made of the stone. Or, indeed, of Morrison's demise in general. And, during the inquest this morning, that ridiculous statement from the Anglesey drover – about some dark creature on the bridge – had already put him in mind of the story's villain, the Resurrection Man, Tidkins. It plagued him all the way to the Bridewell.

From this angle, the place seemed unimpressive. Yet that was perhaps a deception. At the top of the hill, then a turning to the right and past some meagre dwellings, another malthouse, where Palmer crossed a small, cobbled square to reach the Bridewell's entrance. It was built into the narrow eastern extremity of the building. A half-round sentry box stood next to a reinforced door and a single window, two more barred windows on the first floor. A solid perimeter wall stretched away twenty yards to his left, and ten to his right, before each turned westwards, along the Bridewell's full length. Inside, there was a desk and a long corridor stretching ahead of him. He asked for Inspector Wilde and was duly escorted to a central staircase, which he climbed to reach the office with Wilde's name stencilled across its glass panel.

There were hurried pleasantries, the inspector perhaps keen to pursue other duties but, more likely, Palmer considered, he simply wanted to get away, back to his family.

'But here are the deceased's effects,' said Wilde, and took from his desk drawer a small linen bag. He tipped the contents onto the green leather writing surface and checked them off rapidly against an official typed list. Once again, Palmer was struck by the Abraham Lincoln similarity.

'Pocket watch, fob, and chain. Pen. Ring, one, gold. Hip flask. Wallet. Coin pouch.'

It all showed signs, naturally, of having been immersed in water. Stained. Damaged. Still damp, so far as Palmer could discern.

The contents of the wallet and pouch were detailed separately.

'Train ticket, one. Postage stamps, two. Banknotes – one ten pound note, three fivers.' He counted them out. 'Coins – three half-sovereigns, five silver shillings, six pennies and three farthings.'

Wilde collected the money together again.

'And one notebook,' he said.

A pocket-sized journal, leather-bound and fastened with a ribbon of hide, but also water-damaged.

'Anything interesting, Inspector?'

'In what way, sir?'

Palmer could feel the stone's weight, its presence, in his pocket, pulling down that side of his jacket. Uncomfortable. But he now experienced a sense of foolishness about producing his evidence. Evidence of what, precisely?

'I was simply intrigued,' he said, 'to know whether Mr Morrison may have had some reason to be on the bridge. Whatever his business on this side of town, it plainly brought him to his misfortune.'

The inspector pulled out his own watch, replied with some impatience.

'I rather fear the foolish fellow from the Feathers may have been correct.'

'You mean...?'

Yes, Palmer remembered. The implication that Palmer might have been seeking some lewd assignation.

'Best for the widow not to be taken down that road, Mr Palmer.'

'Indeed, Inspector. Indeed. And the clothes...'

Wilde quickly collected the effects back into the small sack.

'Transferred from the mortuary along with the corpse, sir – after the *post mortem*. Collens in Church Street. Funeral furnisher. The good lady must have the details, I imagine. And now, sir, if you please...'

Palmer had not given the matter any thought. The funeral, yes. But there was still the stone, and Wilde was busily ushering him back towards the door, pressing the linen bag into his hands. Palmer determined it was now or never.

'Inspector,' he said, and pulled the stone from his pocket. 'You see? Blood, I think. Found it on the bridge. On it rather than under it, you understand?'

Wilde gave a sigh, deep with disappointment and *ennui*. He took his hand – with which he'd been guiding his visitor back towards the corridor – from Palmer's arm and clasped thumb and fingers around his own forehead, massaging the temples.

'Lord, give me strength,' he said. 'Another one.'

Palmer felt utterly stupid, but he was unable to stop himself.

'Forgive me. But might it not at least be worth some investigation? See, might this not be hair, matted into the blood?'

'It's been sitting in your pocket, sir?'

Palmer saw the folly, that he could, himself, have contaminated the thing. Yes, that was foolish. Beneath him as a chemist.

'But this is dried – and, if this is indeed hair…'

'Mr Palmer,' said the inspector, 'do you have *any* idea how many permutations there must be to explain that, even if this *may* be blood, and even if it *may* belong to Mr Morrison… That *is* where you're heading with this, I take it?'

Palmer nodded, and looked again at the stone. It all seemed so pitiful now.

'And you perhaps have some suspicion that your friend might have been the victim of violence by a party or parties unknown? This, the murder weapon, I suppose.'

There was a tone of mockery now, which Palmer was beginning to find irksome. But Wilde had at least taken the stone from him and was turning it over and over.

'Mr Morrison was not my friend, Inspector. An acquaintance, no more. And it was simply – you think such a thing unlikely here?'

'There's a tendency for everybody to now consider himself a detective, sir. The penny dreadfuls, I'm afraid.'

George Reynolds, thought Palmer, with a twinge of guilt. *The Mysteries of London.*

'Wrexham?' said Wilde. 'We have our share of trouble to deal with. Drunks and vagrants. The odd stolen cow now and again. But mayhem and murder? Not in my time, Mr Palmer. A couple of cases in the records, but those were more than ten years ago. And I'd like to keep it that way. Don't want a repeat of Denbigh. Not here.'

In a seemingly absent-minded manner, Wilde lifted his hand, stroked his fingers through the hair of his own head.

Palmer was curious, but this was not the time to ask about Denbigh.

'I think I've taken up enough of your time, Inspector,' he said, retreating now towards the open doorway.

Wilde turned, set down the stone on the corner of his desk. And perhaps it was just Palmer's imagination, but he thought he saw some wistful expression on the inspector's face, the fellow's eyes resting on the small rock for just a second, the corner of his mouth twisted in a moment of reflection.

'Mind how you go, Mr Palmer. Maybe see you at the funeral.'

Indeed, thought Palmer. He turned to leave, then stopped.

'Though, perhaps one last question, Inspector? Just now.' Palmer checked himself, making sure he recalled the words correctly. 'You said, "Another one", did you not? What did you mean?'

Chapter Eight

Palmer was intrigued by the accordion file folder, which the Widow Morrison had brought to their reunion.

'Mr Murless has been so kind,' she said, and began to pour the tea so recently delivered to their table by one of the Wynnstay's serving girls, her face badly scarred by smallpox. 'And a true benefactor. He provides some employment for such as that poor unfortunate young woman – the town's most destitute.'

It was a small and private dining room – officially, the Ladies' Room – a broad window looking out along the High Street, with the Town Hall at the farther end of this busy thoroughfare.

Palmer had dutifully handed across her husband's effects and she had spent some time lingering over each of them in turn, the memories conjured by them playing like a magic lantern show in her eyes. With every item's impact upon her, Palmer was forced to revise his own perhaps hasty opinion of the man. Surely, nobody could be as boorish as he had thought Morrison to be, and yet also invite such love. But it was the ring had brought her to tears. Morrison's signet ring. Then she had carefully replaced everything in the linen bag. Everything except the notebook.

'And might it be an intrusion,' said Palmer, 'if I looked inside?'

The journal still lay on the mahogany surface between them. He had been tempted to take a peek on his way back there, to the hotel, though he had resisted. A matter of privacy. Respect. In any case, he had been preoccupied with Wilde's response to his question. Another one?

The inspector had brushed the thing aside.

'Miss Thomas,' Wilde had said. 'Bethan. Wanted us to investigate poor Rose Wimpole's death. Refused to believe it was a simple accident. For Heaven's sake...'

That had been the end of it, Wilde's door kicked shut behind him. It was all very strange, Palmer decided, as Mrs Morrison slid her late husband's journal towards him.

'If you can decipher Kingston's shorthand,' she said, dabbing at her tears with a kerchief, 'you are most welcome.'

Even so, he was reluctant. He fumbled in his jacket pocket until he found the snuff box.

'And would you mind?' he said, holding up the ivory container.

'By all means, Mr Palmer. Feel free. And that is elegant in the extreme.'

Elegant, indeed. The lid carved with an oriental scene, a fisherman in a conical rice hat, the image of a bamboo house, exotic foliage, all in tiny miniature. A gift from Ettie, discovered in one of Manchester's many curio emporiums.

'From your sweetheart,' said Mrs Morrison, perceptively.

Indeed. Dear Ettie. What would she make of all this? He would have to write back to her, of course. But how to answer her charge? The charge that he was there, in Wrexham, to escape her marital inclinations. For now, he took a pinch of the powdered tobacco and put away the box, at the same time picking up the notebook.

Palmer flicked through the pages, saw them filled with symbols and squiggles which he did not recognise, though there were occasional words of plain English, locations and dates for the most part. But the rest...

'I see what you mean,' he said, and took a sip of his tea. 'Not Pitman, then.'

Minister Lloyd, such an impressive preacher at Thetford's own Primitive Chapel, had insisted that students at his academy should have a fundamental knowledge of the Pitman system. Essential, he believed, for anybody with aspirations of employment in so many different fields. Yet we must take care, the minister would caution them, never to think or speak in shorthand, for in shorthand we are prone to lose the beauty and colour of God's creation.

'Kingston always boasted that, like Mr Dickens, he was self-taught about the finer points of grammar and style.'

'And if he had designs to become a writer, a journalist, the shorthand would also have been essential. His own invention, perhaps?'

'He told me he had once attended a lecture – something of that sort – at which Mr Dickens spoke of his own system. Kingston was working for the *Kentish Mercury* at the time. Before he joined George.'

George Reynolds, Palmer assumed

'I remember reading something about Dickens's passion for shorthand,' he said. 'Gurney's, was it not? His own variant. But I have no idea how to decipher it. I shall ask Mr Low. For now…'

He turned carefully to the pages containing the final entries. A few legible words, at least. The previous Saturday's date and the word 'Deadline', followed by single number, '4'. That would make sense. Just about the time Morrison had left him to find the telegraph office. A short section of the shorthand again before Sunday's date. Another number, '2' – the time again, he supposed. Then this: 'FB (puta)' followed by 'Fs'. A meeting at Morrison's hotel, perhaps? At the Feathers? More shorthand. And, finally, this: '10' and the words 'Town Mill, P-F'. Nothing further. Just more of the stains left by the Gwenfro's encroachment into the paper.

'Do you believe, Mr Palmer,' she said, with great deliberation, 'that there might be some clue here?'

The question caught him by surprise and he almost answered with excessive haste, though stopped himself just in time.

'Clues, ma'am? To what, pray?'

He heard his own words emerge in some dissembling voice he did not recognise as his own. The widow's turn to pause now, her teacup poised to her lips.

'There is a gleam in your eye, sir. I have seen it, the same, with my late husband many times. Always when he pursued some quest, some obsession. I am guessing you think Kingston may have had some other reason to be there, upon the bridge. And perhaps some suspicion…'

She did not complete the sentence. There was no need. Palmer wondered whether, like Ettie, she had some power of clairvoyancy, knew about the stone he had upturned. And these final entries in the notebook. It could not do any harm, surely, to discover just a little more about Morrison's planned meetings for that fateful Sunday afternoon and evening.

'I simply need,' she was saying, 'to be satisfied that my husband's death was, indeed, no more than an accident. Natural enough, I think. But you, Mr Palmer – your interest in this seems…'

'Less than natural?'

'If you like. For my part, I have some cause. Kingston's life has, after all, been threatened in the past. The Mordaunt business, you know?'

Palmer wondered whether this accusation – this entirely justified accusation, since she was correct, and Morrison's death was none of his affair – might be the prelude to his dismissal from her company. What right did he have, after all, to risk bringing her further grief through his meddling? But she lifted the accordion file from the table and passed it to him. It was tied with green silk ribbon.

'These are the documents he left behind,' she said. 'When he left for Manchester. His current project, he called it.'

Manchester, thought Palmer. I must remember to ask…

He unfastened the file and lifted out the first collection of papers, also tied with emerald ribbon. His thumb riffled through the tops of the pages. Many were hand-written in that same unfamiliar shorthand, but there were enough official documents for him to realise the subject matter.

'The case is closed, surely?' he said. 'Mordaunt finally got his divorce and the unfaithful wife is locked away in an asylum. It hardly feels like justice, but…'

The case had been in the public eye for – how long? Five years? Only settled the previous summer. Five years of readers poring over every salacious detail. Hardly a day gone by without some new revelation. It had subsumed almost everything else. Only settled the previous March.

Sir Charles Mordaunt had filed for divorce when his wife gave birth to a daughter whom he had plainly not sired, being himself out of the country. The file for divorce was contested, initially with success, on the grounds that Lady Mordaunt was insane – and therefore unfit to plead or answer charges of her infidelity. To make matters worse, Sir Charles discovered that one of his wife's suitors was none other than the queen's son, Albert Edward, Prince of Wales. In the end, some cove had accepted responsibility as the child's father and the case concluded.

'There is little justice for women in this world, Mr Palmer. Whether we are sane or otherwise.'

'Your husband wrote some scathing articles on the subject, ma'am. But a current project? It cannot be this?'

The door opened just then, the serving girl returning to ask whether they needed anything further – more tea, perhaps, or a slice of *bara brith*. Mrs Morrison thanked her, no, and after she had gone the widow composed herself before answering Palmer's question. She seemed unsure whether or not to continue.

'You may remember that the Prince of Wales was on the stand for no more than seven minutes. And no cross-examination. Kingston wrote one of his most sardonic pieces about it. Hinted at conspiracy. That perhaps this fellow Lord Cole might have been handsomely rewarded for accepting the paternity. My husband could not go any further, naturally, but the following week, he was attacked on the street. Perhaps coincidence. Perhaps some royalist fanatic. Perhaps some more sinister motive. In any case, there were no further incidents.'

'Then his continued interest in the case?'

'I have no idea, Mr Palmer. Not really.' Palmer wondered whether she was telling him the whole truth.

'Though he did once say to me,' she went on, 'in one of his unguarded moments, that he wondered how much greater the scandal had the child proved to be of royal blood.'

Palmer flicked through the rest of the bundles, one set of papers all related to the exhibition, many of them also in shorthand. Yet here was a *Wrexham Guardian* cutting from a few weeks ago, with all the details of the opening. It would certainly have helped Morrison write the background to the piece which so disappointed Mr Low and dismayed those gentlemen in the reading room. The alleged excessive expenditure. The hints about financial probity. The promise of another scandal.

Pinned to the cutting, a piece of writing paper, with the words *Mrs Wimpole* scrawled across, and Palmer remembered the last words Morrison had spoken to him.

'*It was Mr Low's bookkeeper I had hoped to ensnare,*' the newspaperman had said. '*And now – this nonsense about snake bites…*'

The widow had said not a word while Palmer studied the file's contents, simply gathering together their tea things or gazing out at the traffic along the High Street's gathering gloom, but now she reached across and touched his arm.

'Well, Mr Palmer?'

'Ma'am?'

'You are a methodical man, it seems. Might you not explore my husband's papers a little further? Give me the assurance I mentioned – that I may rest somewhat easier in the knowledge that this was, indeed, an accident?'

'I thought,' he said, 'you considered my curiosity to be less than natural. And I am certainly no detective – as I have already been reminded this afternoon.'

She looked quizzically at him, but he chose not to explain. He would have been forced to mention the stone, and already felt foolish on that account.

'It was no consequence,' he smiled. 'But truly, I think Inspector Wilde may be the better person to consult, do you not think? Besides, I have badly neglected my duties on behalf of Mr Low and his museum.'

Mrs Morrison seemed crestfallen.

'Kingston had few friends, Mr Palmer. I simply hoped…'

There it was, again. He had not been Morrison's friend. Far from it. Yet he now believed he may have judged the fellow unfairly. After all, *Reynolds's Newspaper* was itself known for being a fearless and uncompromising supporter of popular principles. It was hard to imagine that one of its most noted correspondents would not have shared its aims.

'As I say,' he murmured, 'I do not believe myself qualified in that direction.'

He stood to leave, straightened his jacket.

'But there is one thing, ma'am. I never had the chance to ask your husband what he was doing in Manchester.'

She stood also, stretched out her hand so he might shake it, though with a look of disappointment on her face.

'Oh, something else, I think,' she said. 'The registers are kept there, I believe, for the industrial schools, the workhouses, and so on. He was following another story, perhaps.'

Indeed, Palmer decided. Something else, then.

'And I regret, dear lady,' he said, as he took her proffered hand, 'that I cannot help. But is there anything else, ma'am, you might wish for?'

To his surprise, she squeezed his fingers, set her other hand on top of his own. There was another tear. Then she released him, turned to pick up the accordion file folder, thrust it into his arms.

'At least,' she insisted, 'promise me you will study this whenever you have time. Return it to me in Chislehurst in due course. And I wish only, Mr Palmer, that you might have a care for your own safety.'

Only days later, he had cause to recall her warning.

Chapter Nine

He feared as much. He had brought to mind his schooldays once more. Their adventures in Latin, a light relief from so many more painful experiences. The self-mockery of their teacher, Mr Venables, who chose to use Leigh's *Comic Latin Grammar* as his principal textbook. *Derideo magistrum*. I laugh at the master. And all those schoolboy jokes. Discovery of the word *putta* for a young woman. Its supposed connection to the French, *putain*. Whore.

He had no idea whether Morrison had been a student of the Spanish language, but when he ventured to the Feathers Hotel – careful to ensure that the obnoxious Grufydd Griffiths was nowhere to be seen – his supposition of some Spanish connection had been confirmed in a meeting with Mrs Anderson, the flustered widow of the late licensee. But she recalled Morrison's visitor to the establishment perfectly well.

The previous Sunday. Not this Sunday just gone, but the one before. Afternoon. Yes, about two o'clock – that would be about right. Poor man.

'Walked in, bold as brass, she did. That foreign woman, like. Never took to 'er, I 'aven't.'

Mrs Blackstone, Mistress at the Union Workhouse. And it had been the simplest of enquiries to discover her Christian name, Faustina.

'Spanish, by any chance?' Palmer had asked her and received a shrug of the woman's shoulders by way of a response.

'Foreigners is just foreigners, like. All the same to me, see.'

And did she have any idea what they discussed? Of course not.

Palmer had purchased his own notebook by now – Tuesday, the first day of August. Pages of random scribbling. Purely his curiosity about the code, of course. Not an investigation. Certainly not that. But now, as he took a break from the museum in the exhibition's second-class refreshment room, he turned to a clean page. He wrote Morrison's words afresh. *2 FB (puta)* and *Fs*. Then, his own interpretation. *Two o'clock. Mrs Blackstone. Workhouse.* Finally, the word *puta*, which he underlined several times before adding three neat question marks.

'Bethan...' he said, when he returned to find her busily rearranging one of the displays – restoring it, so far as he could see, to the way it had been before his arrival.

'Well?' she snapped, without even turning her head.

'Never mind,' he sighed. 'But I wanted to ask you about Mrs Blackstone. The Mistress at the workhouse, I believe?'

'What about her?'

'A small, dark lady. Spanish, I suppose. Have you seen her here?'

'Been a few times, like. Season ticket.'

He could sense the distaste in her voice and was about to ask her the reason, but then realised that Bethan would likely have applied the same tone to just about everybody of her acquaintance. There could, of course, be more than one such foreign person within the rich tapestry of Wrexham's population, but he was certain this could only be the same woman who had so shamefully shared his snuff, his precious Wilsons, on the opening Saturday. Blood among the threads? Weren't those the words she'd spoken?

'There's an exhibit in the industrial annexe,' he said. 'A large table coverlet. You know it?'

'Jim Williams's patchwork? Of course, I know it. Who doesn't?'

'Mrs Blackstone has some connection to the piece?'

She turned for the first time to peer up at him.

'Why?'

'Curiosity. Mere curiosity. I saw her admiring the thing. Nothing more.'

'Killed the cat, curiosity did.'

He should have expected that.

'And has she been here long – in Wrexham?'

'Long enough. Lordie, a lot of questions, isn't it. You don't mind, like?'

'Mind?'

'Me. Doin' this.'

She flapped a hand at the display.

'If you think it looks better that way, Bethan, then who am I to argue?' She sneered – though it could perhaps have been a smile. 'And the Town Mill…' He changed tack. 'Am I correct in thinking it stands on Pentre-Felin?'

'Where else would it be?'

Palmer had assumed as much. The other entry in Morrison's notebook. Somebody the fellow was intending to meet at the Town Mill at ten o'clock. That would certainly have taken him across the Horns Bridge. But who was he planning to meet? Certainly, nobody had come forward, so far as he was aware, with any information that the newspaperman had missed an appointment. And ten o'clock at night? He determined on a visit to the Union Workhouse. Perhaps *señora* Blackstone might shed some light.

The day passed pleasantly enough. Palmer and Bethan Thomas had reached some unspoken accord. She, principally arranging exhibits housed in the eastern half of the archway and Palmer himself in the other. Visitor numbers seemed, once more, to be less than expected, and he said so, that evening, to Mr Low.

'No cause for concern, laddie. Still three weeks before the Eisteddfod and we originally planned for the two things to go hand in hand. All the visitors over this past month – just a bonus. Great success for the town. Aye, great success.'

Palmer wanted to ask him about Morrison's article again. About the expenditure. About the return on investments. And about whether there was any connection between Rose Wimpole and the accounts. Otherwise, for what reason could the newspaperman have wished to "ensnare" her, as he had described it? Her name scrawled on that piece of paper pinned to the *Wrexham Guardian* cutting. Now, her name had appeared again on another item in the accordion folder, this one a receipt, three years old, relating to the household accounts of Major William Cornwallis West. The Lord-Lieutenant, Palmer had recalled, when he'd found the thing yesterday evening – the folder now in his room and being dissected, page by page. Yes, the Lord-

Lieutenant. The one whose good lady wife had regarded him with such hypnotically languid eyes.

Again, he told himself, mere curiosity.

Yet, in the end, it was not about the article, nor about the major's wife, that he posed his question to Mr Low. It was, rather, about libraries in the town – whether there might be a collection which included a copy of Gurney's *Brachygraphy*. He had even invented an excuse. For Low's own manuscript collection already included a first edition of John Byrom's *Universal English Short-Hand*, printed in 1767 – though written fifty years earlier, in Manchester – and a copy of Taylor's 1786 *Universal System of Stenography*. Neither had been any help in deciphering Morrison's notes, though Palmer did not share that particular snippet with his host. It would be interesting, he suggested, instead, if a contributor might be found who was willing to loan a copy of Gurney for the duration of the exhibition. Without hesitation, Mr Low suggested the Grammar School's headmaster, Thomas Kirk, for that fine establishment must be certain to possess such a volume.

Another visit to be arranged. Tomorrow evening, perhaps.

For the next morning saw him at Kingston Morrison's funeral, the widow having either decided or been persuaded to have him buried there in Wrexham.

There was a new cemetery, out on the road to Ruabon, though its grim elegance was shrouded today by the rain sheeting in from the open countryside beyond. August, yet it was windswept, dark clouds driven across the heavens, as they processed from the Anglican chapel to the graveside. It could not, Palmer decided, have been more Gothic.

'I am the resurrection and the life, saith the Lord,' intoned the clergyman, protected by a brolly held aloft by the cemetery's sexton.

'He would never have forgiven me,' cried Mrs Morrison, clinging to Palmer's arm beneath the umbrella they shared, 'had I not arranged a first-class plot.'

Perfectly normal, of course, for cemeteries to be divided according to class, the requirement by the wealthiest for a tomb with a view, but it sat uncomfortably beside Palmer's Methodism.

'We brought nothing into this world,' quoted the parson, 'and it is certain we can carry nothing out.'

'Surely his reputation?' said the widow. 'Must we not carry with us the account of our deeds in life, that we may be judged for eternity?'

'The Almighty already knows those who have lived in His image, dear lady. So, fear not. Your husband's reputation is already a matter of record. I believe that Paul was here instructing Timothy on the dangers of obsession with material wealth.'

She seemed not to hear him.

'Mr Collens is taking care of the monument,' she said, 'and I shall return to see it installed.'

Mr Collens had seemingly ensured that no expense should be spared in celebrating the newspaperman's demise. The white hearse, a framed daguerreotype image of Morrison in eternal repose, the featherman, the carriages, the service. Everything so finely organised, nothing missing from the ceremony – except Morrison himself. The clergyman had barely mentioned his name. Perhaps, Palmer thought, I have allowed Dickens to excessively jaundice my opinion of our rituals – though rituals they were, indeed. At least, High Church rituals, with few adherents to these new fashions among his fellow Primitive Methodists.

He had carefully declined Mrs Morrison's invitation to bid her late husband farewell, at his rest in Collens's commodious funeral parlour. For the last time, she had said, before we are all reunited in the glory of God.

At the graveside itself – a suitably first-class location at the junction of two pathways and upon a slight rise – the mourners' impatience was palpable. The weather. The one thing for which the undertaker could not extract a price to guarantee. It seemed, to Palmer, like a protest from the Almighty Himself. A reminder that His blessings are beyond the reach of even the most prominent funeral furnisher, beyond the means of the wealthiest purse.

'Man, that is born of a woman,' recited the clergyman, still protected by the umbrella, though the sexton fighting with it against the wind, 'hath but a short time to live, and is full of misery. He cometh up, and is cut down, like a flower.'

'You see?' murmured Mrs Morrison. 'Cut down. Shall you not reconsider, Mr Palmer? A simple investigation of the circumstance?'

As the minister's prayers battled the elements, Palmer wondered how she could press him so, and here, in this place. He struggled to prevent the umbrella being blown inside out and was forced to keep his free hand pressed against the top of his derby. The other sombre figures gathered about them fought similarly to maintain their decorum. Mr and Mrs Low. Their daughter Alison and son-in-law, Doctor Davies. Inspector Wilde. Hancock from the *Advertiser*. A dozen others he did not know.

How was Palmer to answer her? Perhaps promise a few simple enquiries, he thought. Little harm in that, surely. Yet he could hardly admit, even to himself, that investigation was precisely the activity in which he was engaged. Why else the accordion folder's contents scattered across his room? His list of intended lines of enquiry. Palmer had no real expectation of discovering anything untoward, though perhaps an ulterior motive. He felt that he should like to know this town better. And if, in the course of his education…

He heard the first shovelfuls of wet earth splatter upon the lid of the coffin.

'We therefore commit his body to the ground,' shouted the clergyman. 'Earth to earth, ashes to ashes, dust to dust.'

The rest of his words vanished somehow in the storm, and Palmer could scarcely remember the Lord's Prayer being recited with such reckless speed and so little vocal coordination between worshippers. The final blessing, he thought, was delivered with unseemly haste.

'I shall consider your request,' he found himself shouting into Mrs Morrison's ear, as they all began to hurry back towards the shelter of the chapels, and she was taken into the minister's care. 'If I find anything…'

'Yes, Mr Palmer,' she called back. 'You may write…'

He felt a hand on his shoulder, turned to find Wilde at his side.

'I understand you've been asking at the Feathers – about Mr Morrison, sir.'

'Is there anything wrong with that, Inspector?'

The distraction caused him to lose control of the brolly, the black canopy reversing itself into a blaring trumpet, the ribs and stretchers exposed to the elements. Wilde helped him to bring the beast back to its proper form.

'You would not wish to interfere with police business, Mr Palmer.'

'I rather thought you were done with it,' Palmer replied, but the policeman said no more, marching away as the Lows caught up with him.

'First-class,' said William Low from beneath their own rain napper. 'Aye, first-class.'

Palmer assumed he meant the service, or perhaps it was, indeed, some simple two-word eulogy to the manner of Kingston Morrison's lifestyle and journey to the afterlife. Into the Bosom of Abraham, he thought, though his mind was also somewhat focused on the inspector's warning. Was it – a warning? He took shelter in the spired archway between the twin chapels, watched as the other mourners hurried to their carriages, realising just too late that there might not be any conveyance left to carry him into town.

He looked back through a veil of rain. What had Bethan Thomas said so disparagingly about this very epitome of modern fashion, the garden cemetery. Some words of Welsh. *Cae'r Cleifion.*

'The Field of the Sick,' she had explained. 'Lepers' Land, see.'

Palmer smiled, and would have turned to leave. But something caught his eye. Movement.

There. Many of the cemetery's trees and hedges were newly planted. Saplings carefully arranged. But older trees as well, which the designer – an associate of Mr Low, he thought, another Scotsman – had so carefully incorporated into the plan. Among them, a venerable yew. Sheltering beneath its branches, pressed against the trunk, almost hidden from view, some person.

His imagination? Somebody regarding him? And what was it, about the indistinct form which brought to mind the Spanish woman, *señora* Blackstone, Mistress of the Workhouse?

He would have the chance to find out that very evening – a little while before his own careless accident.

Chapter Ten

He had determined to find out more about the connection between *señora* Blackstone and Kingston Morrison by visiting the Union Workhouse. Five o'clock and yes, some time before misadventure laid Palmer low.

Earlier still, he had paid a visit to Mr Kirk, the Grammar School's headmaster. He had felt guilty about the deception – though he eased his conscience with the conviction that, as soon as he had decoded Morrison's shorthand, satisfied himself that the journal hid no secrets, he would indeed include the precious copy of Gurney's *Brachygraphy* among Mr Low's exhibits.

Back at the museum, he carefully turned a few of the fragile pages before locking the volume away and venturing onto busy Hope Street to find a cab.

The hackney carried him out across the second smaller bridge over the Gwenfro and onto the rutted road they called Pentre-Felin, to the leaning, half-timbered mill marking the very edge of town, with the sluice from a waterlily-strewn pond – a pit, to Palmer's mind – powering its wheel.

The vehicle trotted them between open fields and hedgerows, where Palmer looked back through the lowered window to see the tower of St. Giles rising above the rest of Wrexham, and then out past a huge flour mill alongside the railway.

Beyond the railway, above a buttressed outer wall, the workhouse itself, where the cabbie dropped him at the main entrance.

'Want me to wait, like?' asked the driver, but Palmer declined. The storm had passed and the weather was warm again. He would walk back to town. The cabbie looked as though he must be insane, but with a click of his tongue, a flick of his whip, he turned the horse about and was gone.

'Mr Alfred Palmer to see the Master,' he told the porter. This fellow looked like an old and flea-bitten bear, long past its prime, with a shambling gait. Simple-minded, but looming above Palmer when the man emerged from his lodge and reared to his full height as though just emerging from some winter's hibernation.

Palmer was relieved of his hat, and the umbrella he had brought against any eventuality of the storm's return, then found himself ushered into the reception hall, leather-cushioned benches lining the walls. A polished wooden panel, as well, listing the names of previous Masters and Matrons inscribed in gold leaf, beneath the legend *Wrexham Poor Law Union Workhouse*, and the date, *30th March 1837.*

'Wait,' growled the porter, and Palmer waited.

On both flanks of the hall, further rooms, one with the sign *Men's Searching Room*, the other similarly designated for women, and Palmer wondered whether he would himself have to go through this indignation before being permitted to enter. A groundless concern, however.

'Here,' the doorkeeper told him and showed him through a further set of double doors with barred windows. A long corridor, gated staircases on each side, then another door. *Master's Parlour*, the nameplate announced, and the great bear left him upon the threshold.

'Come.' A woman's voice when Palmer knocked.

He found *señora* Blackstone waiting within. She looked surprised to see him, eased herself from a rosewood armchair when he entered.

'You, *señor*. I did not recognise your name when Edward told me we have a visitor. You are welcome, of course. But allow me to ask the purpose of your visit?'

She offered a gloved hand, fragile black lace. For a moment, he wondered whether he was supposed to bow, to kiss the fingers, but he resisted the temptation, shook the hand instead – though with the refinement he thought it deserved. He could still not quite determine her age. The lined face made her seem older, but the fire in those eyes convinced him she could be little more than fifty, less than sixty.

Señora Blackstone was dressed as any woman of her age and social standing might be – though perhaps with some additional elegance, a dress of deepest autumnal green, the bodice, sleeves and skirts all layered, trimmed with more black lace. The difference, of course? A silk *mantilla* draped over a high shell-shaped comb. Gold rings in her ears. A closed fan in her other hand.

'To be honest, *señora*,' he replied, 'I am no longer certain. Our nation's workhouses are the subject of such varied opinion that I have sought the opportunity for some time now, to view an institution such as your own for myself, so to speak.'

He could hear that dissembling voice yet again, knew it sounded false.

'But your more pressing purpose, I think,' she smiled at him, her hands all the time making a dance in the air, 'would be to discover the nature of my discussion with your friend, *señor* Morrison. No?'

A neat enough trick, but he had no intention of giving her the satisfaction of asking how she knew. She gestured for him to sit, picked up a brass bell by its wooden handle from the occasional table at her side. She shook it vigorously.

'That,' said Palmer, taking a matching chair on the opposite side of the parlour, 'and other matters. Were you, by any chance, at his funeral today?'

'And why should I have been?'

A maid entered in answer to the bell. No more than a child, really, and *señora* Blackstone beckoned her across, murmured an instruction in her ear. Palmer took the opportunity to reach for his snuff box, rose and offered it to his host while the servant retreated once more from the room.

'You had a liking for my Wilsons blend, I recall.'

Her head tilted quickly to one side, a birdlike gesture of acceptance. She thanked him. *Gracias, señor.*

'But I can think of no reason,' Palmer went on, 'why you might have been there. Though perhaps that shall become clear if you could, indeed, tell me the reason for your visit to Mister Morrison at the Feathers Hotel.'

'There is a reason why I should tell you?'

The hands again. Never still. Like fluttering birds. An affectation, perhaps, he wondered, of Spaniards in general?

'None,' said Palmer, and she smiled once more, that slightest flick of her head again before she took a pinch, closed the lid and, after wiping the excess powder from the sides of her nostrils, she ran a finger along the design, nodding in admiration before handing it back. She waited for him to resume his seat, watching him carefully as he enjoyed the Wilsons himself.

'Well,' she said at last, 'there is no secret, *señor*. I visited your friend because he invited me to do so. We are old – what is your word? Acquaintances. From London.'

She spoke the words in a coquettish way, dripping with innuendo and Palmer regarded her afresh. He remembered the word from Morrison's notebook. *Puta.* So simple? He felt bile rise from his stomach. Surely, this woman was old enough to be Palmer's mother. He pushed away the images which rose upon the bile, while *señora* Blackstone lifted her eyebrows, the ghost of a smile on her thin lips, many fathoms of pride in those dark eyes. Pride and mockery.

'I see,' he said. 'Acquaintances, yes.' To say he was ill at ease with this turn in the conversation would have been a euphemistic understatement. He was shocked and appalled, struggling to change the subject. 'And when we met at the exhibition,' he stammered, 'you spoke about the table coverlet. If I remember correctly, you said, "blood among the threads." What did you mean, *señora*?'

The enigmatic smile remained and, for an awful moment, he thought she might ignore this question and continue with a more salacious response, but in the end she waved her hand in the air, as though to dismiss the previous exchange.

'The *sastre*,' she said. 'The tailor, *señor* Williams. He made that entire thing from pieces of army uniform. You knew?'

Yes, he knew.

'And some of these uniforms,' she went on, 'saw fighting in my country. Fighting and bloodshed.'

The maid returned. A small silver tray, two miniature drinking glasses and a quart-sized bottle of cut crystal containing a pale ruby liquid.

Palmer remained trapped in horrendous reverie of Morrison and his assignation at the Feathers, but at least there was some respite among these new visions of Wellington's armies, the great battles of the Peninsular War, but he forced himself back to the present as *señora* Blackstone poured the drinks and the young servant disappeared again.

'I fear,' he said, 'that I am a teetotaller.'

'It is nothing but a fruit cordial,' she laughed. 'From the berries of the blackthorn tree. *Endrinos*, no?'

Blackthorn, he thought. Sloes, surely? And he took the glass, sipped at the ice-cold liquid. Not unpleasant, something of the linseed, liquorice and chlorodyne lozenges he favoured whenever he suffered from his frequent bronchial congestions. Yes, not unpleasant at all.

'But the fighting you mentioned,' he said. 'Against the French. It would be – more than sixty years ago?'

She raised her glass.

'*Salud*,' she said. Good health. 'And no, *señor*. Our civil wars. The Carlists. *Sabe usted?*' You know?

Yes, he knew. Should have remembered. Two – or was it three? – separate conflicts, supporters of the liberal Queen Isabella on one side, her reactionary Catholic rivals, the Carlist fanatics, on the other. The most recent only just concluded. And the first? Four decades past. He wished he had studied the subject in more detail, for it was pleasant, he found, discussing history with this woman, harlot though she might be. He looked around the walls. The paper, he realised, though patterned, was almost the same shade as this cordial, and the framed paintings, the clock on the mantle shelf, each of the room's many curios, every piece of fine porcelain on the table, all spoke of Hispanic exoticism. He was reminded of illustrations he had seen in an edition of Washington Irving's *Tales of the Alhambra*.

'Your husband,' he said, suddenly wondering how the fellow fitted into this strange picture now filling his head. 'He is Spanish also? Or did you meet him in Spain?'

'I met my husband here, in England,' she told him, without any hint of embarrassment. 'Also in London.'

'And is he here? I should have enjoyed speaking with him as well.' The words came forth almost as a threat. An unintended threat. The implication he might expose her secret – if a secret it was, indeed.

73

'Perhaps,' he hastened to add, in a placatory tone, 'to see a little more of your establishment.'

If she had heard any intimation of threat, she certainly rose above it.

'Frederick is away. Business, you understand. But I can arrange to have you shown around. When we have finished our cordial, perhaps.'

He would be glad of the opportunity to escape, even though he now had more questions than answers. And she had ventured across the room, replenished his glass, came dangerously close so that he smelled the perfume upon her *mantilla*. Heady orange jessamine. The word again. *Puta*.

'That would be most kind,' he said, sipping again at the cordial to regain his composure. 'But the uniforms.' Yes, he thought, as she resumed her own seat. Focus on the uniforms. 'English soldiers fighting in the Carlist War?'

'Volunteers, of course. Queen Isabella asked for help from England, and the English king allowed volunteers from your army to fight for her. Ten thousand volunteers, *señor*. A British legion of volunteers. Many of them did not come home. And many who did...'

It was intriguing, and he determined to find out more. To satisfy his own curiosity. A helpful distraction, as well. But this was not helping him with Morrison's death. What, if anything, was *señora* Blackstone's connection to the Carlist conflicts? And the relevance to Morrison?

'I hope you do not mind me asking but, during your...' He was forced to search for the word he needed. 'Your... visit to the Feathers Hotel. Did Mr Morrison mention another assignation? Later that night, at the Town Mill?'

She laughed at him.

'No, *señor* Palmer. He did not. And it is curious, but you have not told me the reason for all these questions. About your friend. About the day of his accident. It *was* an accident, of course, no?'

Palmer thought for a moment before he answered.

'What is curious, *señora*, is that you have not asked earlier.'

She laughed again.

'Well,' she said, 'if we are done with the questions, allow me to have you shown around.'

She rang the handbell again, this time a more protracted summons, while another bell, somewhere else in the building, tolled the hour. Six o'clock. A surly fellow entered, an Irishman called Wicklow, who was charged with guiding him on his tour of the premises. He had wanted to ask about Rose Wimpole. A connection there, as well, perhaps? But there was no opportunity. He rose from his seat, set down the cordial glass, and found his vision suddenly blurred, a moment of dizziness. He had risen too quickly, that was plain.

Indeed, he later recalled little of his remaining time there. Something of a fug as Wicklow sped him through the visit: the workhouse infirmary; the playground; the work rooms; the kitchens; the piggery; the slaughterhouse; the preparation room for the dead; the separate yards for the boys, girls, women and men respectively; and, finally, the upstairs dining rooms where those same groups separately ate their suppers of bread and cheese. He managed to spend a few moments studying the wall charts listing the various dietary classes within the place: the homeless employed; those without work; the feeble infirm; the working infirm; the children; and the seriously sick.

Almost before he knew it, he was returned to the reception hall. No sign of the shambling porter, and no *señora* Blackstone to bid him farewell. It was Wicklow who returned Palmer's derby and umbrella.

He now regretted his earlier dismissal of the cabbie's offer to wait for him. It was a fair stretch back to Roseneath House and he was still somewhat unsteady on his feet. The cordial? Surely not.

But still a couple of hours before dark, so he set off towards town, almost taking a tumble when he tripped on the railway track. There was little traffic along the lane, a couple of carts, a tinker carrying his wares upon his back. Palmer rested, to recover a moment, outside the brick-built enormity and pungent aromas of the corn mill, then pressed on, swinging the umbrella and puzzling over the enigma of *señora* Blackstone. A lady of ill-repute? An improper liaison with Morrison? Yet Mistress of the workhouse. Something was amiss.

Something…

His presence had disturbed the many green plovers in the neighbouring fields but now they had fallen silent again. Even the summer's insect hum had stilled, and Palmer found himself almost walking on tiptoes to avoid disturbing the deathly tranquillity.

He had just rounded a bend in the road when he first heard the horse, though he paid it little heed. Another cart trundled past, heading in the opposite direction, and he could see the other mill now – the Town Mill – down the slope ahead of him. Marshy ground below him, to his left.

The horse again, behind him. At the canter. He could feel the vibration beneath his feet, hear the rhythm of its hooves, sense the moment when it broke to a full gallop.

Palmer turned too late to get out of its path. He smelled the beast's hide, heard the snorting of its flared nostrils as it hit him. At first, he felt nothing. Only the falling. Down that grassy embankment. Then a jolt of pain as he hit the ground, bounced, and hit again. Rolling now through the weeds and wildflowers. Some strange elation as he splashed into the quagmire. He had survived. Except, then the pain began in earnest.

The reckless rider had not even stopped. And Palmer needed help. Needed it badly. For this was a hurt such as he had never felt before. His back, his arms, his head. Oh, how his head pained him. The only part of him without pain was his legs. No, he could not feel his legs at all.

It became dark much faster than he had expected, but before the evening's light was extinguished, he had one final view of the horse, galloping down the road. Upon its back was a creature. Black as night. Wings spread. Big as an eagle. Bigger.

Chapter Eleven

The creature came to visit him many times over the following days. Nightmares in which Palmer was attacked upon the Horns Bridge by some monstrous apparition. Sometimes he was taunted at the same time by a lascivious *señora* Blackstone. Sometimes he was alone and sometimes in company with Morrison. Sometimes even his poor ailing mother shared their fate. And sometimes Ettie was present as well, scolding him, reminding him of the times she had warned him against the perils of a visit to Wrexham. But always the outcome was the same. Falling, falling, falling. Onto the ragged rocks of the Gwenfro where his back was broken. And always the waking, the stifled scream, the awareness of this paralysis in his legs.

'I have told you, sir,' said the surgeon, Richard Low, in his now condescending Scots lilt, 'that your back is not broken. Compression of the nerves in your lower spine, yes. A Cauda Equina Syndrome. But broken? No, Mister Palmer, most certainly it is not.'

A less than sympathetic sister propelled Palmer's bathchair along the corridor of this infirmary. Towards the surgeon's personal torture chamber, a room filled with fiendish mechanical devices of which the Inquisition would have been proud.

'It was your father, I suppose, who recommended my admittance?'

'Lord, no,' replied the surgeon, striding along at his side. 'You have here a progressive establishment, Mister Palmer. Accident patients accepted with no recommendation at all. And even regardless of their place in society. Is that not a wonder?'

The fellow mocks me, thought Palmer. Even in my dire adversity, he mocks me.

Yet the surgeon was perhaps entitled to his moment. For Palmer had seen the quality of the man just the previous day. One of the town's rat catchers had been delivered to the hospital's entrance having suffered some apoplexy during the performance of his noxious duties. Naturally, he did not possess the necessary letter of recommendation from the Committee of Benefactors, and nor was he on the list of approved potential patients provided by any of the individual benefactors themselves.

Richard Low had vociferously insisted that the fellow be admitted in any case. A public argument with the matron.

'For pity's sake,' he had said, 'the poor man will be dead by the time we wait for a decision by the Committee.'

There would be repercussions, Palmer was certain.

And he now privately hoped they would be severe, as the surgeon supervised his crucifixion. The attendants strapped the leather corset below his armpits and then fastened a stiff collar about his neck, padded below his jaw so that it forced his chin upwards. They entirely ignored his cries of pain when they jostled the broken arm – already reset by Mister Low junior – and hauled upon the pulleys to lift him out of the chair and suspend him from the ceiling. No end of protests about the weakness of his lungs, and the potential impact upon them, was to any avail. He could not speak and was thus forced to hear the surgeon's regular diatribe yet again.

'You see, Mister Palmer? The simple use of corsets alone in such cases is purely wishful thinking. It is necessary to relieve the spinal column of its weight-bearing functions entirely and thus also relieve the nerve bundle. The Russians, you know, are far advanced in these treatments and, to your singular benefit, I had the honour of working with a colleague in London who studied them in Odessa.'

Palmer tried his best to make some intelligent response but failed dismally.

'Quite so, Mister Palmer,' the surgeon smiled, 'we wish only to make you better. Our hospitals are now, after all, places of healing rather than merely the gateways to death. Oh, and I have brought those papers from my father's house, as you requested.'

If he could have spoken, Palmer would have agreed. This infirmary was a far cry from the hospital in which he had been confined for so long as a boy. Pneumonia. It had almost killed him, left him with this pulmonary weakness.

There had been a letter, also. From Morrison's widow. Her return to Chislehurst, she wrote, and the infirmary had prevented her from visiting him beforehand. But thanks again for his kindness and yet another exhortation for him to explore the circumstances of Kingston's demise. Especially now, she said. And had she not begged him to have a care for his own safety?

The thought had been much upon his own mind.

Later that day – it was Sunday, five days after he had been knocked from the road – he received his first visitor. The attendants had eventually returned him to his bathchair, wheeled him to chapel for the noon service, then settled him outside the French windows at the end of his ward, where he might take the air in the modest paved garden with its potted shrubs and pair of damson trees. They had also allowed him a small occasional table and upon it, now, lay just one sheaf of papers from within the accordion folder.

'You don't look ill, see,' said Bethan. Slung across her back, a crocheted sack bag. She limped across to study him, until her face was on a level with his own, and refusing his offer that she might sit on the bench just outside the windows.

'And you, Miss Thomas, you took the trouble to apply for a card?'

The rules were strict. Sundays, two o'clock until half-past three. Wednesdays, three until four. And only visitors in possession of the appropriate authorisation paper, a valid visitors' card.

'Wanted the book, isn't it?'

She unslung the bag, reached inside, and set Gurney's *Brachygraphy* on top of Palmer's papers. He had sent the message but never expected she would deliver the book in person.

'Well, most kind. And the exhibition – how goes everything at the museum?'

It was a disparaging account, a few mumbled comments, mingled with a scattering of Welsh, by which Palmer was given to understand that she expected the whole venture to be an abject failure. Just her opinion, he knew. And Bethan Thomas could certainly be no authority on the exhibition's finances. But might it be possible? Some financial scandal in the wind?

'You think,' he said, 'Mrs Wimpole also believed so? That the exhibition might fail?'

She had been flitting about him like some small bird, but now she stopped, suddenly on her guard – suspicious, Palmer thought.

'Why you asking, like?' she spat at him.

'Nothing, really. I seem to have become the custodian of poor Mister Morrison's papers. And among them I found mention of Mrs Wimpole. Perhaps he had reason to meet with her. I wondered if you might know why that should be.'

'Lordie, how would I know such a thing?'

'Morrison knew she was Mr Low's bookkeeper. I simply thought…'

In the ward behind them, a man was groaning loudly, shouting for help. Bethan lifted her nose, nostrils flared, as a strong faecal odour wafted through the doorway, mingling with the ever-present aroma of carbolic and overcooked food.

'Not just for Low,' she said. 'The major's before, like.'

'Major Cornwallis West. Yes. Mr Low told me the same.'

He conjured an image of the major's wife. Her beauty. Those languid, hypnotic eyes.

'Then how did she come to be…?'

Morrison had hoped to ensnare her, Palmer recalled. Those were his words. Though maybe this was not about Low, after all. But Bethan had no answer for him.

'You went to see Inspector Wilde, Miss Thomas. He told me you wanted him to investigate Mrs Wimpole's death.'

'Well, seems plain to me, see. Not natural. All this nonsense about snake bites. Then him from the newspapers. Now you.'

It had been there, in Palmer's head, since he regained his senses. By then he was strapped to a fire brigade litter and being wheeled past the town's well and up the hill beyond. Some passing carter had spotted his body in the quagmire and sent for help. Accident? Surely that maniacal rider must have seen him – at least known there had been a collision. Left him there. It was inhuman, certainly. But was it deliberate? That was another matter entirely. And Mrs Morrison's words were there again. *Have a care for your own safety.*

'And the arm,' said Bethan. She fluttered around him once more, pointing at his sling. 'How's the arm, like?'

'It will heal. Indeed, it will. The nurses are most attentive.'

He hated to admit it, but since this morning's session upon the surgeon's rack, he had also been able to wriggle his toes, the first sign of sensation returning to his lower limbs.

'Then you could do it, see. When it's healed, I mean.'

She had stopped in front of him, her head moving quickly, though almost imperceptibly, from side to side, like a nervous tic.

'Do what, Miss Thomas?' Of course, he knew precisely what she meant.

'Investigate, isn't it. Got the mind for it, you have. Up here.'

She tapped a finger to her forehead.

The mind for it, he thought. Yes, an obsession with formulae. With rationality. Though there seemed nothing rational about any of this. Rationality, he had long since decided, could not help in understanding the chaos of the human mind, with its frequent degradations. He was not certain that the scriptures could help in that regard, either. And formulae? Rationality? What had happened to his boyhood dreams of adventure? Formulae and rationality were not the characteristics of adventurers. Yet, perhaps for an investigator...

'I shall consider your suggestion, Miss Thomas. Though I shall need an assistant.'

He tried to remember whether Richard Markham had such an associate in *The Mysteries of London* but, to his shame, all he could bring to mind was "the old hag" who appeared so often in the stories alongside the awful villain Tidkins, the Resurrection Man.

'Don't mind helping, I don't.' It was little more than a snarl. He was not entirely certain he had been offering her such a position but now, it seemed, he was stuck with it.

'Then, if you might be prepared to help me in this way,' he said, 'perhaps your first task might be to visit your friend, Mr Williams in College Street. Ask the tailor for anything he might be able to tell us about uniform pieces within his coverlet from soldiers who fought in Spain?'

She did not question him, merely shrugged her agreement.

'And might I crave a further favour, Miss Thomas?' he asked, in this spirit of truce which seemed to have descended upon them.

*

81

There were no more visitors until the following Wednesday and, by then, he hoped his letter to Ettie would be well on its way to Manchester.

My dearest Ettie. You will have gathered that this missive is not penned by my own hand. Rather, by my colleague at the museum, Miss Bethan Thomas.

He suspected the sentence would arouse some suspicion or jealousy in Ettie's mind, but he could think of no way to explain the relationship without further offending Bethan herself.

You see, sweet girl, that I have suffered a minor accident, precisely as you might have predicted. My right arm broken, though now considerably on the mend.

Yet it is hard to credit the indignities inflicted upon one's person, the impossibility of everyday ablutions, the complexities of basic cleanliness, simply by being deprived of this one limb alone. My beard, as the most facile of examples, is now substantially unkempt, the barber's abilities here being more suited to the Shambles than to the tonsorial parlour.

There was more in the same vein, though Palmer apologised for the letter's brevity, pleading that he did not wish to excessively abuse the good offices of Miss Thomas. Though, of course, it was the best possible excuse for avoiding the question about which he had promised to write her – Ettie's insistence that he should give the proper consideration to their marriage.

Still, he added a postscript, asked whether Ettie might visit Manchester's registry office for the northern industrial schools and workhouses. A simple enquiry about whether they recalled a visit from Mr Kingston Morrison, the nature of any intelligence he may have sought from them.

And if Bethan Thomas saw any significance in those short closing sentences, she certainly did not remark upon them.

By Wednesday – the ninth day of August – he had also gained some success in his first attempts at applying Gurney's *Brachygraphy* rules to the page within Morrison's papers which most intrigued him.

It was a page plainly containing a list of some sort, the letter symbols, abbreviations and arbitrary characters slowly coming together to form meaningful words, each entry with numbers alongside which must surely represent the relevant year. But what was the connection between the words? He had managed to write these with his left hand, so they were barely legible. Yet he had now pored over them so many times, he knew them by heart.

Cliff	*Den*	*61*
Skit	*Less*	*62*
Tempest		*65*
M		*68? 69?*
Be Nanny		*68*
<u>*Pat*</u>	<u>*Sea*</u>	*70*
Jay	*Rome*	*72*

The ciphers for *Pat* and *Sea* were heavily underlined.

He was still struggling with the puzzle when Inspector Wilde found him, more or less in the same spot where Palmer had been visited by Bethan. Only, today, his bathchair was stationed just inside the French windows, for it was raining.

'Bloody fools,' the inspector fumed, and shook his umbrella out through the doorway. 'Fools and their rules. I said to them – I said, what if some poor soul had been murdered here on a Monday? Have to wait until Wednesday afternoon, would I, before I could get in? And you know what that damned matron says to me?' He made an imitation of matron's voice. 'Yes, she says. Yes. But only if you have the requisite visitor's card. Can you believe it, Mister Palmer?'

Palmer could believe it quite readily.

At Wilde's request he provided an update on the condition of his treatment. The inspector, in turn, taking a chair from the ward, apologised for not visiting earlier. Unfamiliar drovers in town over the past couple of weeks, he said. Ruffians among them. Carousing. Causing a riot. Trouble on the streets.

'Worse than Denbigh?' Palmer asked, recalling their earlier conversation.

The inspector took his pipe and tobacco pouch from a coat pocket, filled the bowl.

'Denbigh,' he said. 'Nearly died. Went to arrest this young poacher. Billy Jones. Found him at home with his ma and pa. Tried to cuff him but the old man hit me with a poker.' Wilde touched a hand to his head, as he had done previously. 'Got knocked to the floor and then they all start booting me. Stroke of luck one of the neighbours sent for help. Tudge, my inspector, turned up. Saved my life, Mister Palmer.'

'All's well that ends well, I suppose, Inspector.'

Wilde remembered his pipe, glanced surreptitiously back along the ward and, satisfied the coast was clear, lit it with his matches.

'You think so? Know what happened next? I end up in court, that parcel of rogues trying to sue me. For smashing up their property. For attacking *them*. I don't think the Bench bought all that, but in the end they only fined Billy a pound. A pound! Breach of the peace, said the Beak. After that, the threats began. Anonymous, of course. Said they'd kill my girls. So, here we are. In Wrexham. Gets a bit rough now and then. But safe, Mr Palmer. Know what I mean?'

It sounded to Palmer like an apology, a plea to let sleeping dogs lie.

'Am I to understand,' he said, 'that there is nothing further on Morrison?'

'The stone? Cow's blood, nothing more.'

'And my own accident?'

'The report says you were visiting the workhouse.'

'Indeed, though purely from curiosity,' Palmer lied. 'You are acquainted with *señora* Blackstone and her husband, I suppose?'

'I am, though not closely. They arrived in Wrexham just before me and Martha Jane. From London, of all places. There were a few strange stories about the workhouse back then – though just gossip as it turned out. But this accident of yours. Horse and rider - but no description?'

'I was unable to provide one, Inspector.'

Had I done so, thought Palmer, as Wilde took another puff upon his pipe, blew the smoke out into the rain, what would I have said? A creature, black as night, wings spread? And strange stories from the workhouse? He would have liked to hear what they might have been, though the inspector was keen to press on.

'Almost certainly one of the drovers I mentioned,' said Wilde. 'Drunk, I'm guessing.'

'I have seen the cowherds' mounts often enough,' Palmer replied. 'Stocky hill ponies, are they not? But this beast? It was big. Sixteen or seventeen hands.'

'You know horses, Mr Palmer?'

'Only a little. Enough to know the difference between a Welsh cob and a full-grown hunter. You know, of course, that Morrison's life was threatened also? After the articles he wrote about Lady Mordaunt.'

He had no sooner said the word than the letter *M* from the ciphered page sprang to his mind. *M* for Mordaunt. And 1868 or 1869? Yes, that would fit. But the other gibberish?

'I did not know, Mr Palmer.' Wilde tapped the pipe's bit against his teeth. 'But why should Lady Mordaunt have anything even remotely to do with Morrison's accident?'

It was a good question.

'And how many fatal or near-fatal accidents would you normally expect to happen in Wrexham, Inspector? Three in almost the same number of weeks, perhaps?'

'You're counting your own mishap?' Wilde seemed genuinely surprised. 'Did you take refreshments there, at the workhouse?'

'A cordial of sloe berries, only.'

'Sloes? You mean sloe gin?'

'Indeed not, Inspector. Sloes – and liquorice, I believe. I am firmly for temperance. A teetotaller as we now seem to be described.' Yet he had wondered several times about the subsequent blurring of his vision, the unsteadiness, and the fug which had surrounded him during his later tour of the place. He suddenly felt foolish, finding himself speaking a little too harshly when he returned to the original point. 'And what else should we say about my accident, do you suppose? Coincidence?'

Palmer watched as Wilde took the pipe from his mouth and regarded him, almost as though he were seeing him for the first time.

'Interesting,' said the policeman, finally. 'My old inspector, Tudge, used to drum it into us. No such thing as coincidence, my boys, he'd say. No, indeed.'

Palmer could almost hear the man's brain making some calculation.

'Something else I should know, Inspector?'

'Another piece of news which brought me here. Perhaps I should have mentioned it at the beginning. Almost forgot. All that nonsense about visitors' cards. But last night. Mr Low's house – Roseneath. Unusual, even for Wrexham. Housebreaker, it seems.'

Chapter Twelve

'A week ago,' William Low told the major. 'While we slept. Could have been murdered in our beds. Aye, indeed.'

The garden party had been arranged to celebrate his daughter Alison's twenty-ninth birthday.

'Much stolen?' the major asked, flicking some of his cheroot's ash from the lapels of a Promenade jacket, dark indigo-blue check. Palmer had already determined it would have better suited a much younger man. 'I am astonished, sir,' said the major. 'Astonished.'

'My study ransacked. Some items of silver taken. A gold watch – it once belonged to my father. And papers missing from the room of Mr Palmer, here.'

Palmer leaned against the terrace's balustrade, the walking cane resting at his side, so he might use his one free hand to accept a glass of lemonade from the maid, Harriet, as she passed among the guests. It was a fine evening, but little consolation for the loss of Morrison's precious files. All that were left, now, were those pages he had studied at the infirmary.

'The rogues,' said Major Cornwallis West, sipping at his champagne. 'And while you slept, you say? Rest assured, Mr Low, I shall move Heaven and earth to have them brought to justice. Did you hear this, my dear?' he called to his wife. 'Housebreaking. While they slept.'

Mary Cornwallis West gave him the merest pretence of a smile in acknowledgement, then returned to watching her children play, out upon the terraced lawns: the same girl, about three, Palmer had seen with her at the exhibition's opening – and enjoying a game with Alison's own daughter; a boy, perhaps a year younger; and a baby, just walking, in the care of its nanny. The Lows' older children were further away, towards the orchard, and playing raucously at Blind Man's Bluff.

'Indeed,' said Low, pursing his lips and frowning. 'Well, it was a great matter for my family, anyways.' He stressed this final word as a riposte to Mrs Cornwallis West's display of disinterest. 'And we must allow nothing to despoil next week.'

'Gracious, no,' replied the major, though his gaze was fixed upon his wife – murder in his eyes, Palmer thought. 'Nothing. At least,' the major added, 'nothing *more*.'

The National Eisteddfod, due to commence on the following Tuesday, upon the field adjacent to St. Marks. The first time in Wrexham and already beset by tragedy. The winning entrant in the competition for the most respected form of Welsh poetry – the *awdl*, Palmer now knew – had died before he could be awarded, as was the custom, his own unique and ornate bardic chair. A legend already, this Taliesin o Eifion – in everyday life, and less lyrically, Llangollen's Thomas Jones, apparently – for his final deathbed words: "Was the poem delivered safely?" Yes, indeed, it had been. And now the bardic chair must be presented posthumously.

'And you, Mr Palmer,' said the major. 'Not the best of welcomes to Wrexham. Your accident. The theft. Was there some intrinsic value to the papers which might have caused them to be stolen? Rare manuscripts, perhaps?'

Palmer set down his glass upon the balustrade, then fiddled in his pocket to find the snuff box.

'No obvious value, sir. Simply some documents left in my care by Mr Morrison's widow.'

'Morrison?' the major growled. 'I should not speak ill of the dead but damn the fellow's eyes. That piece he wrote for his dreadful rag. The implications. Cost of the pavilion. Numbers unlikely to satisfy our investors. Great Heavens, the time we had to spend pacifying a few of them. And His Grace...'

Palmer had heard the same grumbling within the Lows' household both before, during and after Morrison's funeral.

'Still,' he said, 'I shall have some difficulty explaining to the dear lady that they are lost. Though, by coincidence, one of those still in my possession relates to yourself, Major. Indirectly, at least.'

'You say so?'

The major's voice rose to an even higher pitch, and he tugged at one end of his waxed moustache, winced as he did so.

'A cutting,' said Palmer. He could at least use the fingers of the hand within the sling to hold the ivory box, while taking a pinch with the other. 'And no,' he said, to forestall the further outburst he saw forming on the major's lips, 'not the one from *Reynolds's Newspaper*. This from the *Wrexham Guardian*. About the prospects for the exhibition, but with Rose Wimpole's name written across the paper. I understand she worked for you at Ruthin Castle, sir – before she came into Mr Low's employ.'

'Housekeeper.' The major was suddenly attentive. 'For a while. My wife tired of her.'

Palmer turned to find Mrs Cornwallis West staring at him. As she had done during the procession at the exhibition's opening. Expressionless, though staring. And now as then, he felt himself flush, redden. Yes, perhaps the most beautiful woman he had ever seen. Guilt now added to his embarrassment – his admiration of this lady's allure somehow a betrayal of his own Ettie. All yellow silk and black lace as she spun about, lifted her skirts and returned to the house. Both Mr Low and the major seemed relieved to see her go.

'And your interest in Wimpole?' said the major.

'Morrison's widow, Major,' Mr Low answered on Palmer's behalf. 'Some curiosity about her husband's final days.'

'Morrison, it seems,' said Palmer, 'had hoped to speak with her, and the widow asked me to see whether there was any unfinished business with which she needed to deal.'

'They tell me,' said Mr Low, 'it is a natural phenomenon among the recently bereaved. Some comfort in being able to recreate the ultimate movements of their loved one. A chance to share those lost precious moments.'

It was almost biblical. A gentle breeze stirred Mr Low's beard. A vision of Moses, but the old gentleman faithfully reproducing the yarn Palmer had fabricated to explain his possession of the papers. It was a gentle enough deception, he believed. And the more important question was how anybody else had known he had them. For, like Wilde's old inspector, Palmer's scientific mind did not believe greatly in coincidence either. Somebody knew he had the files – and believed them important enough to arrange the house-breaking. But who?

'If you wish to know about Wimpole,' said the major, looking about him for somewhere to deposit the end of his cheroot, 'you had better speak with my wife, Mister Palmer.'

Palmer felt as though he had been dismissed. But the major's suggestion was not entirely unwelcome, some racing of his pulse at the excuse for interviewing the elegant Mrs Cornwallis West. He drank the last of his lemonade, set down the glass and, picking up the cane, he limped after her. He found her in the Lows' library, across the reception hall from the dining room, where she was running her fingers idly along the mantle shelf, studying the examples of pinned lepidoptera in the glass case above.

'Moth to the flame, Mr Palmer?' she said, without even turning her head. Her accent, he discovered, was Irish. Very pleasantly Irish.

'Your husband suggested I might speak with you about the Widow Wimpole, ma'am.'

'You needed his permission?'

He decided that jocularity might be his best defence, knowing even as he spoke the words that it was not his greatest skill.

'Is there not, such a requirement within Holy Scripture? *"For the husband is the head of the wife, even as Christ is the head of the church."* Ephesians, I believe. Though, in truth,' he smiled, 'the major made the suggestion without any need on my part to seek such authority.'

Palmer regretted the reference at once. It was the very thing he feared about marriage. This expectation of blind obedience in a wife. Poor Ettie. How could he subject her to such slavery? Yet, now, Mrs Cornwallis West swung about, the yellow silk rustling, the faintest perfumed scent of roses reaching him where he stood, leaning against Low's favourite leather armchair, and her eyes – green, he could now see, as the light from the library windows touched them – ferocious as some wild creature.

'And does this lesson in Holy Scripture have something to do with the Wimpole woman? What had she been saying?'

The venom in her words would have been sufficient to kill Rose Wimpole afresh, and Palmer found himself retreating a step, almost stumbling across the walking cane, his chest tightening and resulting

90

in a brief fit of coughing, which left him as breathless as Manchester's smoke nuisance.

'Saying?' he wheezed. 'No, ma'am, you misunderstand. As you must have heard me say, Mr Morrison, the newspaperman, had scribbled her name and told me he was keen to speak with her.'

'And this involves me – how, exactly?'

'I was simply intrigued. And since she had some experience with accountancy, both for Mr Low and, earlier, for yourself, I assume, I merely wondered whether you might shed some light on the matter.'

'Light?'

'Some information about the Widow Wimpole's character, for example.'

It all sounded so terribly weak. A fishing expedition, he knew. He had already probed old Mr Low on the same theme with no tangible result. Yet Morrison's concerns about the financial probity of the exhibition, his need to speak with Rose Wimpole – surely, they must be connected.

'You were intrigued, Mr Palmer? Intrigued, you say? And in what capacity, might I ask? You are a museum curator, I believe. Sometimes, a chemist.'

'I have the honour to be both, yes.'

'Yet here you are, intrigued by the lives of folk far above your station.'

Something stirred within his Primitive Methodism.

'Are we not all one in Christ Jesus, madam?'

'You truly believe that a lady of breeding could possibly have the least concern about those trivialities which intrigue you? You – with your painful accent, like some country bumpkin. And the look of one with consumption, Mister Palmer. Is it catching?'

Palmer was a man who rarely took offence. He was aware of his own deficiencies. Brutally aware. It was the reason he broadly shared the concerns of Ettie's father about his lack of suitability as a potential son-in-law and suitor. Yet there was a level to Mrs Cornwallis West's attack which cut him deeply. In the main, he had been welcomed here in Wrexham, had begun to think of it as home, somewhere perhaps that he might one day settle. But perhaps this was all just illusion. A foolish fantasy.

He chose to respond as diplomatically as possible.

'I seem to have offended you, ma'am,' he said, merely offering her a curt nod of the head, and backing out of the room, as best he was able with the walking stick.

He needed some air but could not bear to be in her husband's presence either. There would be questions, he assumed. So, he crossed the hallway, carrying with him the vivid impression of the hatred in her eyes, and opened the front door, closed it behind him and eased himself down upon the entrance steps outside.

Palmer reached for the snuff. One thing was certain. He had touched a nerve, as the saying went. But how?

He was still trying to make sense of the thing when another hackney swung into the driveway and a flustered Hancock from the *Advertiser* alighted.

'Late,' he said, and shook Palmer's left hand. 'I'm supposed to be interviewing the major about the Eisteddfod. Have I missed much?'

'Plenty of food left, I think. But otherwise…'

Missed much? Palmer thought. Well, it all depends on your point of view, I suppose.

'And you – recovering, I hope? You still look as though you've been in the wars, Mr Palmer.'

The wars. Oh, how he wished he had been fit to serve as a soldier. The adventure it would have brought.

'How do you manage, Hancock? Your job, I mean. I just tried to put the most innocuous of questions to Mrs Cornwallis West and almost had my head bitten off. I suppose it must happen to you every day.'

He immediately regretted this intimacy as well, prayed that Hancock would not repeat his comment – though he was no longer entirely sure he cared.

'To find the truth requires resolution,' Hancock smiled. 'Be wary of all truths presented to us on a platter.'

Yes, that was pretty much Palmer's philosophy also.

'And the major's wife,' said Hancock. 'Formidable, is she not. The formidable Patsy Cornwallis West.'

'Patsy?' Palmer repeated. 'I thought I had seen her name as Mary.' He could not quite recall where. One of the newspaper reports. For she and her husband were mentioned often enough. Almost daily.

'Her maiden name,' Hancock explained. 'Irish, as you might have gathered. Fitzpatrick. So, in her younger days, the high society circles in which she mixed, she was known to the world as Patsy.'

Palmer thought for a moment. He remembered the *Brachygraphy*. A flaw. No system for adding inflection, the stresses with words which lend them correct pronunciation. And so, within the riddles on that page with the list.

<u>Pat</u>   <u>Sea</u>   *70*

The ciphers for *Pat* and *Sea* heavily underlined. *Pat Sea*. Patsy!

Chapter Thirteen

'The lady has made a formal complaint, Mr Palmer,' said Inspector Wilde.

Pat Sea. Patsy. Palmer still wondered whether it had truly been a eureka moment.

'Is this the time or place, Inspector?'

It seemed less than professional, Wilde raising this in front of his wife, Martha Jane.

'Lady?' said Ettie, at Palmer's side as they queued before the turnstiles on St. Mark's Road. The proceedings of the Eisteddfod's opening day had run so far beyond the official programme's finishing time that those waiting for the evening's concert had been forced to wait for the grounds to be cleared before they could take their seats.

'I had no time to tell you, my dear. My curiosity about Morrison's accident – Mrs Cornwallis West has seemingly taken offence. But no crime committed, surely?'

They edged forward, the ticket office turnstiles operating at last. He still needed the walking cane, though he had discarded the sling.

'Depends on your point of view, sir. But a complaint of public nuisance. Disorderly conduct, she says.'

'My Alfred?' Ettie laughed and could hardly stop. 'Disorderly?'

She had arrived in Wrexham just after noon with her father, Mr Francis, and a whole contingent of Manchester's Welsh community, but since Bethan had insisted on attending that Tuesday's initial ceremonies, Palmer had been forced to shoulder the burden of attending to the museum alone.

'All the same,' said the inspector, 'do not be deceived, Mr Palmer. This lady has it within her power to see you bound over. You know it. Should you ignore my warning, I should have to consider your behaviour refractory. Keep your distance, sir. Keep your distance. And leave this investigation nonsense alone, if you please.'

They were separated at the turnstiles, the inspector and his wife presenting their complimentary tickets and Palmer extravagantly paying for the three-shilling seats, picking up a programme, before they joined the crowd heading down the lane and beneath the triumphal entrance arch of evergreens. *Croeso.* And *Welcome* in English, as well.

'That policeman, Neo. Does he not bear a resemblance to…?'

'Abraham Lincoln? Yes, my dearest.'

'How intriguing. But keep your distance? Whatever were you doing?'

'You could have let me know you were coming.'

He so hoped that he could avoid sharing the details. But his heart had been gladdened when she had appeared at the museum. It was gladdened now, as they sought their places. She had only turned twenty the previous month, a week before Palmer had left for Wrexham. So replete with summer vitality. Indeed, she was.

'Was it not a worthy surprise?' she beamed up at him. Almost ten years younger than Palmer, though she bore herself as somewhat older. Her eyes were a little too dark, a little too widely spaced, and the brows placed a little too high upon her forehead so that she wore a permanent expression of astonishment, her other features just a little too sharp, the mouth a little too pursed. And this evening? Oh, so fine she looked. Two-piece walking dress, beige silk and wool trim, a smart matching bonnet.

Yet how on earth, sweet girl, he thought, did you come to choose me?

'Worthy, indeed,' he said, and pointed at the programme. 'Now, what are we promised?'

'These fellows first, of course.' She lifted the programme towards the stage, where members of the scarlet-uniformed militia band were tuning their instruments. 'An operatic selection, apparently.'

'A good audience, at least.'

There must have been five thousand people in the pavilion, though many of these three-shilling seats around them remained empty. The pavilion's canvas walls were draped with banners bearing shibboleths defining the principles of the Eisteddfodau. *Without God, Without All.* And *Our Armour is Knowledge.* This one as well, among a dozen more: *Who Slays Shall Be Slain.*

Yes, that one played upon his senses.

'And I am minded to ask,' he murmured, eyes fixed upon the maxim and reaching for the snuff box, 'whether you had a chance to visit the Manchester registry. You see?' he brandished the ivory container. 'My constant companion.'

'As I could be, also, Neo, if only you might reconcile yourself to marriage.' She waited for a response, sighed when no such response was forthcoming. 'But yes,' she said, at last. 'And Mr Morrison *had* been there. Examined the details for the Wrexham workhouse. The clerks remembered it quite clearly. The entry, it seems. Normally, there would be substantial records and references for the appointed Master and Mistress. But, in this case, almost nothing. Their names – Blackstone, would that be right? Frederick and Faustina Blackstone?'

'I have met the woman,' said Palmer. Another tale he preferred not to share. '*Señora* Blackstone. And Faustina? Yes, indeed.'

He was puzzled, however. Morrison must surely have had some foreknowledge of them, some earlier connection. Else, why the enquiry? And that word, *puta. Señora* Blackstone's intimation of carnal pleasure? It did not fit.

'Yet only some sort of letter from a royal equerry,' Ettie went on. 'From Marlborough House, I think they said.'

The military band struck up Rossini's *William Tell.* And Marlborough House? Why in Heaven's name would the royal household be interested in Wrexham's workhouse?

'Another puzzle,' he said, struggling to prevent himself from humming aloud to the music.

'Puzzle? Were you not instructed to abandon this investigation?'

'So long as I stay away from the major's wife, I should be safe enough.'

Ettie stared at him as though he must be quite mad. But she sat through the rest of that first part of the concert in silence.

Against the strains of more Rossini, *The Thieving Magpie,* then Mozart's Overture to *Figaro,* and finally Handel's Largo from *Xerxes,* Palmer pondered the connections – if connections, indeed, they were. "Patsy" Cornwallis West. *Señora* Blackstone – Faustina. Rose Wimpole and adder bites. Morrison's encryptions. Marlborough House. And a creature with black, widespread wings.

There was an intermission, time to visit some of the stalls arranged around the interior margins of the pavilion.

'Your father,' he said to her, when they stopped to admire some jars of locally produced heather honey. 'I fear he may be avoiding me.'

'He is simply busy,' she replied. 'Remember? Ceiriog – Mr Hughes. Tada has responsibilities as his patron. Performing tomorrow, I believe. And why should he be avoiding you?'

'You know very well,' said Palmer. 'He believes I would make an unsuitable husband. And that, my dear, is an end to it. Why else do you suppose he would have had me exiled to these foreign parts?'

They had moved on to a table displaying carefully carved love spoons and sugar tongs, walnut chain links, elaborate eating bowls and goblets in beechwood, sycamore or stag horn, inlays of tinsel-edged glass or mother-of-pearl.

'You do not like it here?' Ettie bent and sniffed at the sylvan and beeswax fragrances wafting from the collection.

'I like it a great deal, my dear.' It was true, though his affection for Wrexham had certainly and absurdly paled after Mrs Cornwallis West's outburst. 'Good for my health. But exiled I have been, regardless,' he said. 'And look, somebody else you should meet.'

Bethan Thomas had at least been pressed, this evening, into presiding over the sale of programmes for the Art Treasures Exhibition – Mr. Low being insistent that those visiting Wrexham for the Eisteddfod should not miss the opportunity of enjoying the town's attractions to the fullest. Palmer made the introductions and Bethan responded by sniffing at Ettie in her turn.

They moved on quickly.

'She is not...' said Ettie, hugging Palmer's still weakened arm and causing him to wince.

'What you expected? Your clairvoyancy must be failing you, Esther.'

He always reserved her full Sunday name for moments of gentle admonition. But as they returned to their seats for the second portion of the concert, he rather regretted his failure to ask Bethan whether she had been able to visit Mr. Williams the military tailor. His coverlet. *Blood among the threads*. Soldiers who fought in Spain?

It all played on his mind through the Lord Mayor's excessively verbose introduction to the sacred music which followed. Pieces from Handel's *Messiah*. Mr. Edward Lloyd the tenor. The inimitable Madame Edith Wynne with *I Know That My Redeemer Liveth*. A South Wales songstress he did not know – Miss Harries. And the choir's *Hallelujah* Chorus.

A further interlude, and Hancock from the *Advertiser* waiting behind them in one of four refreshment lines.

'Astonishing, is it not?' said Hancock. 'So good for the town.'

More introductions, and Palmer experienced something akin to jealousy as the fellow took Ettie's fingers in his own and kissed them. Palmer's own age, he supposed, and tending towards the portly, but with a handsome, pleasant face now displaying the most open and unseemly admiration for the young woman's charms.

'Astonishing, indeed,' Palmer snapped. 'Yet should you not be at your scribbling, Mr. Hancock?'

'All done for the day, sir. And such a day!'

They were a captive audience as Hancock regaled them with his recollections of the morning. The procession of bards in their druidic robes, the finery of Wrexham's aldermen and other dignitaries, as they followed the marching band from their *Gorsedd* meeting to the Eisteddfod ground. The speeches. The competitions. The prizes.

'But it was the choirs,' Hancock told Ettie. 'Always the choirs, my dear, as you will most certainly understand.'

Palmer now the outsider. Hancock, Welsh. Ettie, Welsh. And me, he thought, the bumpkin from Thetford.

'I wanted to ask, Mr Hancock,' he said, 'whether you know anything about the background of the Master and Mistress at the workhouse.'

'I was here for the choirs,' Ettie cut across him. 'Tredegar. Quite extraordinary.'

They had reached the front of their refreshment line, a whole ensemble of sweating and flustered helpers brewing and serving tea from brown muggen pots, hot water boiling behind them on a pair of braziers.

'I do not envy them the task of cleaning up,' said Hancock. 'And yes, Tredegar. They so deserved their prize. But the workhouse, Mr Palmer? I have never had cause to consider the question. Blackstone and his wife – foreign, I believe – arrived a few years ago. From London? Gossip at the outset, as always, when outsiders arrive in town, but...'

'Gossip?' said Palmer, taking his cup and saucer before they moved away from the tables. He saw the newspaperman glance in Ettie's direction, though she was looking elsewhere, focused on the performers taking the stage for Part Three.

'I cannot recall just now,' he said, hastily, and shaking his head at Palmer by way of warning not to pursue the point. 'Perhaps for another occasion.'

'Then,' said Palmer, 'in the course of searching your memory, something else?' He took from his pocket a piece of paper upon which he had pencilled those deciphered words from Morrison's documents. 'These. You see? I have reason to believe they may represent names. Tempest, of course.' He pointed at the words *Cliff* and *Den*. 'Clifton, perhaps? Though this has me somewhat confounded. *Skit* and *Less*.'

'What are these?' said Ettie, peering at the page.

'Probably nothing at all,' he told her. 'And I shall explain later. But I was wondering, Mr Hancock. Names? Some connection? Notoriety?'

Hancock shrugged, sipped at his tea.

'I once knew a family,' he said, 'Skittles by name – though this was in Berkshire. Still, I shall consult the *Advertiser*'s archives for you. Ask around, so to speak.'

The third, secular, element of the concert passed pleasurably enough, though Ettie pestering him at every change of performer, every round of applause, to explain himself, to remind him of Wilde's warning. A pianoforte solo of *Morgan's March*; songs in Welsh by Miss Edwards; the raucously amusing *Selling the Welshman*.

They all stood for *God Save the Queen*, but Palmer noticed the pair of policemen who had entered the pavilion in haste yet hesitated in confusion as the anthem was sung. They seemed to be arguing about whether they should proceed. Or to wait until the end. To remove their helmets or leave them upon their heads.

But some crisis, that much was certain. Ettie had noticed it as well.

In the end, they had made so much commotion that Wilde, though down towards the front, must also have seen them, edged from the row of seats, strode back to encounter his two subordinates. Whispered conversations, heads turned among the nearest audience members.

Palmer mouthed the final patriotic words and dragged Ettie, as well as her protests, from their places. He was certain – insanely certain – this must have some relevance to the mystery in which he now seemed embroiled. He knocked over the last of the chairs in his desperation to find out what was happening.

'Inspector…' he began.

'Not now, Mr Palmer. Not now. No concern of yours. A self-murder, it seems. A suicide.'

Chapter Fourteen

'Yes, hanged himself,' said Ettie. Her finger followed the print on page four of the *Western Mail*, spread across the small table in the Wynnstay Hotel's reception hall.

The rumours had been running wild all through the previous day, gossip flowing like gravy in the dining rooms of the Art Treasures Exhibition.

'Or so their correspondent supposes,' she said. 'No indication of foul play.'

The hotel was crowded this morning and they were jostled every few moments by the excited guests. Thursday. Chair Day, the third morning of the Eisteddfod. And the Wynnstay about to play its own small part in the proceedings.

'Does it give a name?' said Palmer, standing over her and leaning on the cane. 'For Heaven's sake, Esther, I have asked twice already.'

Rumours? Yes, of course. But all the previous day trying to ascertain some facts – it had been tortuous. Not a single response from his messages to Wilde.

'Wait,' she said. 'Wait! I am getting there. And do not scold me so. I shall not suffer you to scold me. Not until we are married, at least.'

'That is the strangest piece of pre-nuptial chastity, my dear. But very well – just…'

'Here it is,' she said. 'Wicklow. James Wicklow.'

I knew it, thought Palmer. I knew it. The Irish fellow from the workhouse. Ettie looked up at him, must have seen the smile of triumph on his lips, but as he opened his mouth to explain, the entire reception hall exploded with a roar of cheering, a thunder of applause.

Coming down the stairs, surrounded by his family, was the gentleman he had last seen at the exhibition's opening ceremony.

'God bless the King,' Palmer murmured, recalling Mr Low's scorn for the old fellow. *Fancies himself the King of Wales.* Though perhaps it was not so fanciful after all. Member of Parliament for Denbighshire and had already been so for thirty-five years. Among the greatest land and property owners of the Principality. The family's great Wynnstay mansion out at Ruabon. President of the Football Association of Wales. Master of the Hunt – a duty he still fulfilled, it was said, on at least four days of every week. And Palmer had absorbed all this without ever once asking a question. It was almost as though Sir Watkin Williams-Wynn – proprietor of this hotel, among so many other possessions – was simply part of the air that one breathed if you resided in Wrexham Abbot or Wrexham Regis, this town of two halves.

'He looks like…' said Ettie, standing from the table and allowing the newspaper to slip to the tiled floor.

'Yes,' said Palmer as Sir Watkin passed them. 'Samuel Pickwick. I know.'

At the same moment, the sound of a brass band, *Men of Harlech* just audible above the clamour here, inside the hotel. Palmer had agreed with Mr Low that the museum might be closed today, and he had been up early, hurrying from Roseneath House so he might escort Ettie to the Eisteddfod grounds. But he had not quite expected *this* level of excitement.

'Well, shall we join them?' he laughed, and they pushed their way into the revellers, followed them out past the enormous hall mirror.

Palmer caught a glimpse of them both, Ettie's pretty face, his own sallow skin, the beard, the puffiness beneath his sad Spaniel eyes. Yet in the reflection he also caught sight of the Ladies' Room, the serving girl within, clearing the tables. The same girl with the smallpox scars who had waited upon Mrs Morrison on the day…

They were outside now, Yorke Street sloping down sharply to their left and, from their right, along Chester Street – the same route Palmer had followed to reach the hotel from the Lows' house – a mighty procession. The band. The crowd of druidic bards. The red robes of Wrexham's aldermen. All here to escort the town's very own Samuel Pickwick towards his duties as President of the Day.

'The papers,' he said, as the swelling column turned along the High Street with Sir Watkin at its head. 'The girl was there!'

'My dear?'

'The serving girl. She saw the accordion file on the table, between myself and Morrison's widow.'

The revelation excited him, though it was plainly all beyond Ettie's comprehension. He must make time to explain all this. But first he had to disentangle the thing. For the Pickwick reference had created an absurd kaleidoscope confusion in his head. Morrison. *Reynolds's Newspaper*. George Reynolds. And Dickens. Palmer had, of course, enjoyed the *Pickwick Club* stories as a youngster. Yet, strangely, long after George Reynolds had appropriated the Pickwick character for his own novels, *Pickwick Abroad* and *Pickwick Married*, and Palmer had discovered them, he had enjoyed them far more than the original tales. If he was honest, he preferred Reynolds's writing.

'Neo!' Ettie scolded him. And not for the first time, he realised. 'I said – oh, never mind.'

They had turned right between the Town Hall and the elegant Dutton's *Sig-Ar-Ro* grocery stores, along Hope Street. His back bothered him, and his mind churned in turmoil. Wicklow. Could it have been Wicklow who had ridden him off the road? But why? The workhouse. The cordial.

'I am most dreadfully sorry,' he told her, hoping to alleviate the huff into which she seemed to have descended. 'I promise to explain it all later – after I have explained it to myself, of course.'

It raised a smile, at least, and they both basked in the joy of the moment. The crowded thoroughfare with its busy shops. Past Mr Low's Westminster Building, its archway entrance to the exhibition and the museum, a queue already formed at the turnstiles. Then Regent Street, the band raising the morning's early heat still higher as their playing reached a crescendo with *God Bless the Prince of Wales*.

The procession turned into St. Mark's Road, the church and its high roof, its impossibly tall spire.

'You know, my dear,' he shouted, 'that the town claims the tower of St. Giles as one of the Seven Wonders of Wales?'

'Of course, I know.'

'But see? Is this not a more appropriate candidate to fit the poem? Wrexham Steeple it says, not Wrexham Tower. And such a steeple.'

'Really, Neo? You speak to me in riddles about mystery and mayhem and have no time to explain any of it – yet you invite my enthusiasm for a contest between two church towers?'

She was correct, of course. But he needed some respite from his obsession.

'I can hardly do the matter justice in the midst of such a throng, Esther. And how can one not be intrigued by the history of a place like this?'

A throng? Indeed, it took half an hour to press their way past the entrance booths, the arch and into the pavilion. A capacity audience today. Eight thousand, at least. And in all that half-hour, they spoke little. Palmer, in particular, had sunk back into his normal reveries.

Nor did they rise above their respective and occasional mere murmurs of approval for the welcoming address, for the President's reply, or for the competition performances and prizes. A Welsh translation of *As You Like It*. A Welsh essay on *Hamlet*. Then, time for the Chairing of the Bard.

'Oh, Neo.' Ettie took his hand as a mournful silence fell upon the pavilion.

At last, something momentous enough to distract him. It seemed to Palmer as though the sun must suddenly have vanished behind a storm cloud, for the light failed also, as one of the adjudicating panel stood before the oak-carved throne and stammered his declaration of the winner. Taliesin o Eifion, of course. Thomas Jones of Llangollen.

The words, half-strangled by the speaker's emotion, rang from the sounding board above the stage to a respectful bowing of heads, an occasional sob, as the bards retired, the entire platform party with them.

Palmer, Ettie and the other eight thousand stood in their places, observing the silence for two minutes, three or four, until the band – somewhere hidden from sight – began to play Handel's *Dead March*, while Sir Watkin and the rest solemnly took their places again. Each of them now wore a black crepe armband, and the chair was draped in black cloth, the bards all gathered about and several weeping openly. Though, in Palmer's mind, they wept not only for Taliesin o Eifion, but also for the Widow Wimpole, for Morrison and, now, for Wicklow. And how nearly might he, Palmer, have been added to the list.

Madame Edith Wynne took the stage as well and began to sing a Welsh lament but got no further than the second verse, broke down in tears, and Sir Watkin, sobbing himself, attempted to comfort her.

'The saddest thing I have ever seen,' said Palmer, later, when they had gathered before supper, with Ettie's father as Mr Low's guest of honour. The maid was serving a dry madeira for the purpose of stimulating the diners' appetites.

'Sad indeed, laddie,' Low agreed. 'But that old fool blubbering like a wee babe, was he not? A president needs more decorum. And all this Prince of Wales nonsense.'

Ettie looked up from the game of Lotto in which she was engaged with Alison, Mary Louisa and young Jane.

'It was affection, sir, I think,' she said.

The very end of the day, and a bold attempt to set aside the earlier sadness. Closing speeches and Madame Edith Wynne returned to the stage, leading the choir, and then the entire audience, everybody standing – eight thousand voices.

'I had not understood the significance,' said Palmer. 'In the morning, when we arrived at the pavilion. The last tune the band played.'

It had been *God Bless the Prince of Wales*, had it not?

'Aye,' said Low. 'Maybe more significance than you might realise. All this that we have done, and not a sign of royal presence nor support.'

'Apart from the Queen, papa,' said Alison. 'She is our patron, after all.'

'It's presence that counts, my dear. And that blasted old ninny supposed to be using his influence to have the *real* Prince of Wales attend here. Nothing. Not even a message of support from Marlborough House.'

Marlborough House again, thought Palmer. But he was remembering the singing. To that same tune. *God Bless the Prince of Wales*. Yet their own words. And each of those eight thousand – apart from himself and Ettie, it seemed – familiar with them, filled them with a different sort of emotion. And if any in the audience shared Mr Low's poor opinion of the fellow, it was far from evident.

Of all the chiefs of Cambria,
Sy'n byw y dyddiau hyn,
There's none who love the Cymry
Like Watkin Williams Wynn.

There, in the midst of it all, savouring the moment – yes, like a veritable Pickwick, waving his hands and those absurd sideburns splayed out as joyously as his fingers – had stood Sir Watkin.

Ettie's father, however, showed no interest in this turn within the conversation. He still held their host's own copy of the *Western Mail*, turned to the appropriate page.

'Knew this fellow, did you?' Mr Francis hurled the question like an accusation. He was a younger version of his friend, Mr Low. A sturdy Welsh engineer, built like a pit pony. An equally bushy beard, though all the shades of autumnal leaves. The antagonism in his voice excited a tightening of Palmer's chest, a brief fit of coughing.

'As Esther must have explained,' Palmer wheezed. He cursed himself for this weakness in front of her father. 'Briefly. I had made a visit to the local workhouse. Wicklow was employed there. He showed me around.'

'Coincidence, then?' snapped Ettie's father. 'That so soon afterwards, this same rogue chose this very house as a target for his felonious activity.'

Coincidence again.

Inspector Wilde and his force had visited the cottage occupied by Wicklow when not on duty at the workhouse. They had recovered Mr Low's stolen watch and found a note confirming he had – as thieves' cant might phrase it – "fenced" the silver at one of the town's several pawnbrokers.

Wicklow himself, the *Mail* confirmed, had hanged himself from the railway viaduct at Cefn Mawr, just a mile from his cottage. But Morrison's documents? All burned, it seemed. Only the remains of the accordion file. And a message scrawled in ash across an interior wall. *CULPABLE.*

Chapter Fifteen

'Yes, Neo. It was *you* on trial, my dear.'

He pointed the way with his walking cane and led her into the main exhibition hall, where she stopped to admire, in one of the antiquities cabinets, the gleaming though cracked crystal pebble which had once been a talisman for Prince Owen Gwynedd.

'You see?' said Ettie. 'The stone foretells death – when the crack widens.'

'Superstition, Ettie. Irrational. I simply wish you were not going.'

'And I wish you would pay more heed to my foreboding.'

'It was a dream, sweet girl. Nothing more. You said so yourself.'

She peered into another cabinet. The gleaming portion of a gold corslet, found near Mold.

'Yet now I am no longer so certain. A waking dream perhaps. But there you stood, in the dock – and that word writ large upon the panelling at your back. *Culpable.* I saw it, plain as day.'

Palmer hated to corroborate her faith in augury, but he had experienced similar dreams himself since the discovery of Wicklow's body. Dreams in which Palmer himself stood accused. Of what? He had no idea. His main concern now, however, was that Ettie would be returning to Manchester with her father this very afternoon. His secondary concern? If Wicklow had been responsible for the house-breaking, was it on his own initiative, or at the behest of a third party?

The Eisteddfod was over, its grand pavilion in the process of demolition even now, and the town suddenly seemed so empty. This morning, at the exhibition's turnstiles, barely a trickle of visitors. Though another Monday. Maybe they were all at the Beast Market.

'But come,' he said. 'The Irishman must have daubed the word himself. A confession of his own guilt rather than accusation of another's blame, surely. And I need to show you the object about which we shall meet its maker.'

Yet he still needed to establish the links between Wicklow and Morrison's papers, though he now had a plan, at least. For later.

He led her past the Art Bronzes and Metalwork exhibits and into the Plate, Bijouterie and Watches section, where Ettie came to an abrupt halt before a further display case.

'Wait,' she snapped. 'I refuse to be dragged about like some piece of baggage. And this – the watch mentioned by Mr Buddicom?'

The silver watch and cranking key once belonging to King Charles the First again. Old Buddicom had also been a guest of Mr Low, a former associate, another railway engineer, now retired to Nannerch.

'The same, Esther.'

In the care of his family, Buddicom had boasted, since his great-grandfather had wed the daughter of Sir Thomas Herbert, to whom the ill-fated monarch had gifted his timepiece. It had been a fine yarn to spin over yet another Roseneath House dinner.

'But please,' said Palmer. 'Our own time together, I fear, is short.'

She pouted but followed him out into the industrial annexe and straight to the coverlet. Exhibit Number 46.

'Gracious,' she said, studying the object label. 'That *is* impressive. And you are certain those are the words she used? Blood among the threads?'

'The very words.'

'And some connection to Spain?'

'Indeed. Though only one of several connections I do not yet quite fathom.'

'Spain – and this woman from the workhouse?'

'Indeed. A letter of credentials for *señora* Blackstone and her husband from Marlborough House, of all places. Then, there is Wicklow and the workhouse, as well.'

Ettie stood back and tilted her head.

'You know, Neo, that you sometimes have an unhealthy obsession with analysis. With the supposition that all things in life may be reduced to a chemical calculation.'

'I believe it was beaten into me,' he replied, and instantly regretted the indiscretion. She looked at him, aghast.

'Beaten?'

'A figure of speech,' he lied. 'I have told you, my dear, a study of chemistry freed me from the prospect of a lifetime spent in coach building.'

Yet, he had dreamed of adventure. At Thetford's Grammar School, the dreaming had made him an inattentive pupil. And at Thetford's Grammar School, a lack of attention – especially under the mathematical and chemistry disciplines of Mr "Potash" Porter – was rewarded with severe beating. Perhaps they were deserved. Perhaps their agonising application had been more efficacious than detrimental. But they had caused him to protect himself from further punishment behind a scholarly wall of perfect familiarity with formulae, of excessive rationality, of an end to adventurous ambition. An end to beatings.

'A study,' she said, 'which sometimes prevents you seeing the wood for the trees.' She pointed to the bottom left-hand corner of the coverlet. 'Is that not a serpent?'

He saw that it was.

'Well, of course...'

'And here,' said Ettie. 'This beast with horns or antlers – a deer, do you think?'

She had no need to prompt him further. Palmer peered at the small panel. Upon its back, attacking the poor animal, some large predatory creature, black, like an eagle with widespread wings.

'The thing upon the Horns Bridge?'

'Coincidence only, I am sure,' she said, but the fingers of her right hand flickered towards the other side of the patchwork. 'This? The galloping horse – perhaps the very one which struck you?'

'This is absurd, Esther. You are trying to have me believe this coverlet is somehow responsible for all these incidents?'

'Have you never heard of such things, my dearest? Material objects somehow infused with evil. Possessed by the devil himself.'

'You just accused me of an unhealthy obsession with analysis. And now wish me to consider...'

But even as he spoke, his gaze wandered upwards. From the snake. From the black winged creature. From the horse. The next panel above them. It was a neat representation of a railway viaduct.

The viaduct at Cefn Mawr. The viaduct where Wicklow had seemingly hanged himself.

'Yes,' she said, 'I see it too.'

They spoke little when they left the exhibition, except to say a curt farewell to Bethan Thomas. So few visitors today, Palmer was comfortable with leaving her in charge. Besides, he had asked her several times whether she had been able to speak with Mr Williams the tailor, but each time an excuse until, at last, she told him that, if he was desperate, perhaps he should just do it himself. And now, after this further examination of the coverlet, it seemed even more imperative that he should do so.

It was only a short step to College Street, though stinging whips of foul weather were lashing the town. So, Ettie picked her way through the puddles, kept them sheltered beneath Palmer's rain napper while he hobbled along beside her. Back past Hope Street's shops, where water cascaded from the edges of striped awnings, customers huddled beneath the meagre shelter provided by the canopies and planned their next move. Splashing past the Talbot, to the junction where the Town Hall jutted out into the High Street. It may once have been a glory, but it was now long past its best, serving as a meeting place only on its upper floors, with wine merchant Thomas Williams below, the place stinking of liquor fumes and oak barrels. Today, of dog-damp decay, as well. Just inside the building's front doors, Palmer knew, a town centre desk for the police.

He wondered whether Wilde might be inside, but they needed to get out of this downpour.

'This is the quickest way,' he said from beneath the umbrella, and pointed across to the gates of St. Giles, at the farther end of half-timbered Church Street, less than a hundred yards away. 'And the most sheltered.'

They dodged through a line of carts, avoided a mound of steaming dung, turned right at the railings, along the narrow confines of Temple Row, negotiated the dog stile, then down the steps into the lane beyond. Narrow, yet a fine coach, the rain pattering upon its roof, had been reversed from the alleyway's farther end to stand outside number eight, their own destination.

'We shall be soaked,' said Ettie, realising the impossibility of reaching the shop's doorway with the brolly still deployed. Indeed, they were already wet by the time she had closed the apparatus and begun to squeeze past the single bay window.

Palmer had an impression of the window's shower-streaked glass panes on one side – a hazy display of clothed tailors' dummies within – and, on the other, some half-perceived livery upon the door of the carriage, the muttered curses of the driver above, huddled in his cap and cape, and the snorting discomfort of the horses, uneasy, equally complaining in their jingling traces.

The bell above the shop's door jingled too, when they pushed their way inside. Palmer removed his hat, shook water from the brim and Ettie found the pottery urn in which several other dripping umbrellas already stood.

'Heavens, you must be drenched.' Palmer assumed the speaker to be Mr Williams. Perhaps sixty, tall and thin, his head almost devoid of hair, though still a reckless spread of mutton-chop whiskers filling the sides of his face. And bandy-legged, he saw, as the old fellow manoeuvred with a tape around his customer, who stood with his back to Palmer, each arm raised to ninety degrees from his body, elbows bent so that the fists touched his chest.

'Walter,' cried the tailor, as he applied his measure to the fellow's scarlet back, checking the fitting. 'Make this gentleman and his lady comfortable, will you? With you shortly, sir.'

Palmer would not have guessed from the outside that the interior could be so large. The younger man – Walter, he supposed – rose from his place at a cutting table, which he had been sharing with a somewhat junior assistant while, behind them, an apprentice teetered on a ladder, arranging bolts of cloth on shelves filling each wall but one. That one white wall conspicuously empty.

'The coverlet,' said Ettie, as Walter helped her out of her coat. 'It normally hangs there, I suppose?'

'Indeed, miss,' Walter beamed, and Palmer could see the family resemblance between Williams and the two younger tailors. Cut from the same cloth, he thought, and smiled at his own wit. 'You've seen it, then?'

'The very reason for our visit,' Palmer explained. He saw the customer turn his head.

'Mr Palmer!'

Major Cornwallis West, of all people.

'Major,' Palmer replied and felt his chest tighten. 'How good to see you again.'

'Mr Palmer must know your quilt intimately,' the major told his tailor. 'Low's curator at the exhibition museum.'

Ettie crossed to the window, examining the mannequins, several of them with scarlet or blue uniform tunics, others with gentlemen's tweed sporting jackets.

'Yet not strictly a quilt, I think,' she said, and earned an appreciative smile from old James Williams.

'Quite so, Miss. Quite so, indeed.'

'New uniform for a special occasion, Major?' said Palmer, shrugging out of his own summer mackintosh.

'Why, yes,' said Cornwallis West, over his shoulder. 'A regatta, of all things. Along the Menai Straits to mark Trafalgar Day. You must join us, Palmer. Yourself and…?'

Palmer apologised and introduced Esther. Her Sunday name again. It seemed appropriate, though he struggled, as always, to find a suitable title for her.

'My…' he coughed.

'His young lady,' said Ettie. 'And sailing? It sounds wonderful.'

Wonderful it might be, thought Palmer. But impractical, surely. And then there was…

'Delightful,' cried the major, then shouted a stentorian command. 'My dear, you must come. See who is here.'

Palmer was filled with dread, paid proper heed for the first time to the doorway leading deeper into the dwelling. A parlour, perhaps. Or another workshop. Now, framed against the interior, was the major's wife. In her undergarments. A shocking display of laced ankle boots, stockings, pink satin corset, ruffled bustle and petticoat flummery. But holding the single emerald sleeve of an unfinished dress in place upon her right arm. Flustering behind her, a seamstress – perhaps Williams's wife – clutching another fold of the same material. Behind the seamstress, an older woman, elegantly dressed and almost a twin of Mrs Cornwallis West — but more senior. Striking. Palmer remembered seeing her at the Exhibition's opening.

The younger woman's immodesty caused a familiar heat to rise from Palmer's neck to his cheeks. He saw the younger tailors avert their gaze, heard Ettie's strangled gasp.

'Mary!' The major's chiding tone had little effect.

Patsy, thought Palmer. *Pat Sea.*

'Young lady? Fiancée?' She inspected Ettie from head to toe. 'No, I doubt he has had the temerity to go so far. Whatever do you see in the dull fellow?'

Ettie opened her mouth to respond, but Mrs Cornwallis West allowed her no opportunity to do so.

'And you, Mr Palmer,' she raged. 'Not here to pursue me further, I trust?'

The major cast a reproachful glance in her direction but said nothing.

'Palmer?' said the older woman. Palmer supposed she must be Patsy's mother. Irish accent, like her daughter. 'The ubiquitous Mr Palmer?'

There was no introduction, though it seemed none was necessary. Ubiquitous, indeed?

'Pursue?' said the major, as his wife and her mother retreated once more into the back room.

'A misunderstanding,' Palmer stammered. 'You may recall, sir. You suggested I might speak with your good lady wife about the Widow Wimpole. I fear I may have put my questions badly...'

Thankfully, the major smiled.

'It takes very little,' he said. 'Irish, you know? Famous for it, I fear.'

Palmer was not quite certain what "it" might be, but he was relieved that the major seemed blissfully unaware of his wife's complaint to the police. Relieved, also, that Mrs Cornwallis West had returned to her own fitting.

'And the quilt, you say?' the major went on. 'Well, here is the very fellow to tell you all you might wish to know. Fire away, sir. Fire away.'

He patted James Williams on the shoulder.

'It was myself, in truth,' said Ettie, coming to link Palmer's arm. 'Alfred is very far from dull, gentlemen. But there is a limit, even to his own considerable talents. He tells me that much of the coverlet is made from fragments of military uniforms – but I was intrigued by how those may have been acquired.'

Between the various phases of adjusting the major's tunic – pins here, a chalk mark there, white basting thread unpicked somewhere else, and regular interruptions from Major Cornwallis West – Williams related how, after his marriage to Beth, thirty-six years earlier, he had left his father's business and opened his own shop. On Pen-y-Bryn.

'Very often,' he told them, 'gentlemen would bring their old and badly worn uniforms so I might use their parts as patterns. The tunic overall might no longer be serviceable, yet there were always sections of material almost as good as new. Occasionally, I might also be asked to exchange a military coat for a civilian jacket. Say, for example, where somebody had completed their period of duty.'

And an ambition, he said.

'We started work on the coverlet. Evenings, like.'

'An admirable way to pass the time,' said Ettie.

'Quite so, miss. Beth drew the designs. And we calculated how long it might take to finish. Ten years, I said.'

'Ambition, to be sure,' Palmer replied. 'Why, in a decade the entire world could be shaped anew.'

'Made myself a promise,' said Williams. 'By the time it was done, I would be established as the finest military tailor in Wales. Beyond Wales, even.'

'And so you are, Mr Williams,' laughed the major, while the tailor helped him out of the uniform jacket. 'So you are. And *here* you are!'

Yes, thought Palmer. These fine premises in College Street. The framed parchment scroll proudly proclaiming his guild membership. The displayed letters of recommendation including one, he saw, from Sir Watkin. James Williams, Military Master Tailor.

'And might you recall,' said Ettie, 'any such exchanges from soldiers who had served in Spain?'

'I do, miss. Clear as day, though it would be – what? Around the time I married my Beth. Must have been. The Crick brothers – well, Edward anyhow.'

'Brothers?' said Palmer.

'Local lads. First Royal Dragoons, both of them. Volunteered to go fight in Spain. The younger brother, Alfred, died there. But Edward? Rough rider.'

'Horse trainer?' Palmer asked him.

'Aye. Big lad. Stayed until the very end. Some last battle. Can't remember the name, now. But their whole legion almost wiped out. Edward captured it seems. By some bunch of papist fanatics.'

'Carlists,' murmured the major, now being assisted into his own coat. He peered out of the window at the rain. 'My goodness. Summer, what? But yes, they would have been Carlists, surely. Something of a legend in the army. The volunteers of the British Legion were seen by the rebels as the most odious of all Spain's loyalist soldiers. Mercenaries. Heretics. If they fell into the Carlists' hands…'

He paused, glanced at Ettie, as though reluctant to proceed. Though the tailor, James Williams, setting the major's basted tunic back on its own mannequin, had no such restraint.

'Tortured the boy,' he said. 'Bad, like.' He made a slight gesture with his chalk-stained fingers, down towards his own nether parts. 'Know what I mean?' he grimaced. 'Lost more than that, though. The best part of his wits too, when he came home.'

'Home to Wrexham?' said Palmer, sensing that he might be on the verge of an epiphany.

'He did, sir. But not for long. Disappeared to London. Still had just enough reasoning to exchange his poor uniform for some everyday clothes before he went.'

'Poor man,' murmured the major. 'And are you almost finished, my dear?' he shouted, pulling forth his pocket watch and waving it impatiently. 'But you will remember my invitation, Palmer?' It was little more than a whisper, perhaps so that his wife might not hear. 'The regatta. The Straits. Twenty-first of October. I shall send a reminder.'

'October, major?' said Palmer. 'Yes, of course. I had not thought…'

He felt foolish. The exhibition was not due to close until late in November. Yet he had somehow failed to quite reconcile himself to being in Wrexham so long.

Meanwhile, the promise of revelation had vanished as quickly as it appeared. Elements of Edward Crick's uniform within the coverlet. And Crick's Spanish connection. Blood among the threads? Indubitably, but how might *señora* Blackstone be linked to all this? And the images – mere coincidence that they somehow reflected these recent events, accidents or otherwise? He heard Wilde's words again. No such thing as coincidence.

'And you mentioned, Mr Williams,' said Ettie, 'that your wife designed the images. But after poor Edward Crick had gone to London, I assume.'

"Patsy" Cornwallis West had emerged from her own appointment, now fully dressed, thank goodness, in her outdoor clothes, a jaunty Parisian tam fastened to the side of her hair. She glowered at him, so that he almost missed the tailor's reply.

'That's right, Miss. Yet he loves to study them.'

James Williams saw that he had confused her.

'There I go again,' he laughed. 'Telling half a tale. Came back, you see? A few years ago. Since then, whenever he had the chance, while it was hanging here,' he pointed at the blank wall, 'before the exhibition, Edward used to come most weeks to stare at it. From the workhouse.'

'Workhouse?' said Palmer.

'Indeed, sir. Crick is the porter there.'

Chapter Sixteen

'A shambling fellow,' said Palmer. The rain had stopped and the sun shone down upon the burial ground of St. Giles Church where they had paused on the way back from the tailor's emporium. 'And yes, big. Like an old bear, as I recall...'

He paused in mid-sentence, distracted by the sound of running feet, turned to see Mr Williams's boy apprentice near the gates behind them, presumably off on some errand for the old master tailor.

'Yes, big,' Palmer went on. 'Harmless enough, however. Or so he seemed.'

'I imagine even an old and toothless bear can be a dangerous creature.'

Ettie peered at the substantial chest tomb just below the tower. Sandstone. Old, very old. Though the panels on each of the longer sides were entirely new.

'Not Crick. Not dangerous, I am certain.' Though he was not – certain. 'And this famous chap.' He pointed at the poem inscribed on the side of the tomb farthest from the church. 'I must make some effort to discover more about him. Sounds like a rum devil, does he not?'

He studied one of the lines.

Much good, some ill, he did.

'Quite a confession,' said Palmer, and crooked his arm so that Ettie might link it in her own.

'I have a confession also,' she said. 'For when Mr Williams told the tale about Crick and his brother, I needed no sybil's crystal ball to foresee you in danger once more should you pursue this passion you possess.'

They passed through the elaborate wrought-iron church gates with their gilded decoration. Church Street again.

'Really, Esther? More foreboding? How could one not be impassioned by this mystery? And the poor wretch, mutilated in that way.'

Tuesday's edition of the *Western Mail* had carried two horrific articles – alongside, on the same page, a lengthy and far less disturbing piece about the opening of the ninth trades unions' congress in Newcastle. They concerned, first, the war in the East, between Serbia and the Ottomans, with details of atrocities committed by the Turks – though Palmer imagined that, in such conflicts, barbarity must rarely be simply one-sided. Second, more news from America on the latest in the Sioux War, that massacre of General Custer's soldiers back in June, and further accounts of the way in which the troopers' bodies had been mistreated.

'And war itself, my dear,' he said. 'How incompatible with the teachings of our Lord Jesus Christ. It fills my heart with despair. Shall we never learn?'

He had preached on this very theme at the Beast Market chapel on the previous Sunday.

'Even so, Neo,' she said, as they turned onto the bustling High Street, the hotel ahead of them, 'I beg you to take care. This thing about blood among the threads. Let it not be your own. At least,' she squeezed his arm and smiled up at him, teasing, 'not until we are wed. I should so hate to fail so miserably in life that I might not even attain widowhood.'

If he was honest, he was pleased to be distracted by her dark sense of humour. For the mystery was becoming just somewhat too confusing. How did this all fit together? Or did it, indeed, fit together at all? Was it not easier to let things stand? Rose Wimpole and the serpent, a bizarre accident. But an accident indeed. Morrison the same. Palmer's misadventure with the horse, simply a misadventure. And Wicklow, a self-confessed and guilt-ridden house-breaker – his theft of the papers yet another chance twist of fate?

No, by Heaven, none of that would answer. And nor would this.

From across the road, past the broad stone-built entrance to the Butchers' Market, a couple of drunkards staggered from the Golden

Lion's alleyway and tried to cross to this nearer side, cursing like troopers, in Welsh, at the drayman who almost crushed them beneath his team's hooves. By their shapeless hats, by their dirty, ankle-length waxed coats, and by their mud-splattered leather gaiters, Palmer guessed they might be drovers.

'Neo.' She gripped his arm tighter. 'Those men. Why…?'

They were still yelling, yet their shrillness had now taken a ribald tone. Palmer spoke no Welsh, but Ettie certainly must have understood their words. He looked into her eyes and saw only fear.

The two men were in front of them. Shouting. Gesticulating. Stinking of beer. Stinking of horses and manure. One of them leaned forward, pressed his face close to Ettie's own. He murmured something. It sounded lascivious. A gap-toothed grin.

Palmer felt afraid. His Methodism committed him to a life of peace. But, more than any form of philosophy, he knew himself to be no fighter. Not physically. He trembled at the very thought of it. Yet now he saw himself – as though watching some other person – raising the stick, prodding Ettie's assailant in the chest and causing him to retreat by just a step, turning his ire towards Palmer himself.

Ettie screamed. Unpretentious. But a scream, all the same. Shock, he supposed, and felt himself gripped by his coat lapels. The second rogue, pressing him back against a lamp post.

People gathered to stare. From doorways of the nearest establishments on each side of the High Street. From another public house just to their right. Yet they stared in that offended, defensive way which made it clear they would offer no assistance.

The drunkard's growling words of Welsh echoed in Palmer's ears. A filthy fist, raised to punch him, filled his vision. The stench of ale and foul breath assaulted his nostrils. Protest and reasoned argument rose in his throat and stuck there. And pride, respect for dear Ettie filled his mind when she landed a kick on the shin of her own assailant – the last thing he saw before closing his eyes and waiting for the fist to strike.

A shout, strident and clear above the clatter of horses and carriage wheels on cobbles. The terrified bleating of sheep.

No blow struck. His lapels released.

He opened his eyes cautiously, to see a shepherd trying frantically to bring his small flock back under control, scattered by the carriage which had come to such a precipitous halt alongside. Major Cornwallis West jumped from the open door, brandishing his own stick, pulling at the ivory handle to reveal several inches of the gleaming blade concealed within.

'My dear fellow,' said the major, after the wretches had taken to their heels. 'And Miss – Francis, is it not?' He tipped his hat and bowed. 'What can I say? I sometimes wonder… But you are not hurt, I hope? Please, my carriage is at your service.'

Palmer glanced at the liveried coach, from the shadows of which the major's wife regarded him with contempt – a contempt matched only by that which shone from her mother's Irish eyes.

'We thank you, Major,' said Ettie, before Palmer himself found his voice. Her own still trembled. 'But our destination lies just there.' She pointed at the Wynnstay, directly ahead of them and no more than a stone's throw distant. 'Simply a couple of foolish cowherds, I think. A little excess after their time on the drovers' trails, I suppose.'

'All the same, miss. Such lawlessness is not to be tolerated. Not in my county. No, indeed. But if you are sure…'

Palmer thanked him and they followed as the carriage drove away, disappearing around the corner at the Feathers into Chester Street.

'You see?' he said, taking her arm. 'Your father is quite correct, my dear. What a useless fellow I am. But you, Ettie. Tell me you are unharmed.'

'Quite unharmed. But not here, Neo. Not now.'

She was distraught. Understandable. But something in her manner. Something else. Not just the attack.

They continued those final forty yards in silence, entered the Wynnstay also in silence and were met by Ettie's father, waving an impatient hand at the hallway clock.

'Can I not trust you, sir, to even have my daughter here on time?'

'Tada…'

'No, my dear,' said Palmer, 'your father is quite correct. Remiss of me. My apologies, Mr Francis. And I trust your journey will not be excessively arduous.'

Their cases were all packed, waiting there on the tiled floor.

'And where, pray,' Mr Francis demanded of poor Murless the licensee and entirely ignoring Palmer's poor attempt to seek forgiveness, 'might the omnibus be? Do you not know the hour, sir? Twenty minutes until our train. Twenty, see?'

A flurry of activity. Mr Murless begging their pardon. The potman dispatched to whistle up the hotel's omnibus. The maid summoned to help with the baggage. The same maid with the scarred cheeks, forehead and chin, as Palmer had hoped.

It was almost a theatrical performance, but as the young woman picked up one of Ettie's travelling bags, Palmer played his card, laid – he hoped – his trap.

'And, my dear,' he said to Ettie, perhaps somewhat too loudly, 'I simply thank goodness that the stolen papers were not crucial. The only ones which signify still in my possession.'

Ettie was puzzled.

'Papers, Neo?'

He raised his voice to make sure he was heard. 'Safely under lock and key in my desk at the museum.'

Her father grumbled at another servant, urging him to hurry with the cases.

'Yes, dearest,' said Palmer. 'The papers. In my possession and sequestered at the exhibition museum.'

He allowed himself a cautious glance at the maid. He was certain she had heard. Hopefully, she had heard.

'It's here, sir,' shouted the potman, appearing once more in the vestibule. Behind him, out on the street, the Wynnstay's yellow omnibus, proudly sporting a coat of arms, two foxes in each of the white quarters. Three eagles in each of the green. Sir Watkin's escutcheon, Palmer supposed.

'What game are you playing?' Ettie hissed at him as he helped with the cases.

'I shall write,' he told her. 'Write and explain.'

'Yet you put yourself in harm's way. I fear for you, my love.'

She seemed to be genuinely afraid. But there was no time now to pursue her concern. On the street, the pair of white horses harnessed to the omnibus were literally champing at the bit. And so was Ettie's father. Not even a word of farewell as he clambered aboard, the luggage now all safely stowed in the rear boot.

'Tell me, Ettie,' Palmer whispered to her through the open window, once she was also safely inside. 'The scoundrel who frightened you – what did he say?'

The omnibus driver plied his reins, a flick of the whip, to keep the horses in their place on the severe incline of Yorke Street, until Mr Francis shouted for him to proceed. Not the easiest task, the team having to be coaxed up the remains of the slope before they might make the turn along the High Street. The conveyance was barely moving, the horses snorting and straining at their traces, and Palmer keeping pace, his hand still upon the open window, almost pushing the vehicle on its way.

'Tell me,' he said again as the omnibus gathered pace and Mr Francis yelled for the driver to make haste. 'Please!' said Palmer. 'And I shall – take care.'

Ettie thought for just a moment, her features distraught.

'It was this,' she told him. '*Dywedwch wrtho! Dim mwy!*'

'What?' he shouted, almost running now. 'I don't understand.'

He fell behind, breathless and panting, and Ettie poked her head through the window.

'It means "Tell him!" And the rest? "No more!" It was a warning, Neo. No chance encounter. Take care, my love.'

Chapter Seventeen

'I tell you, Inspector. It was no chance encounter. And the details I gave you – how many drovers in town that day who might have met my description?'

Wilde rolled open the slatted top on Palmer's desk at the museum for at least the sixth or seventh time.

'Forced,' he said, peering at the damage, the splintered mahogany, around the lock. 'These too.' He opened and closed each of the drawers in the single pedestal. 'A jemmy, of course. Small one, by the look of things.'

'So, Wicklow not the only house-breaker at large, then?'

Palmer aimed for sarcasm, but his arrow seemed to miss its mark.

'Apparently not, sir. Nothing taken, you say?'

'I've explained. I merely wanted to set a trap. The girl at the Wynnstay – Maudie Meadows, I believe. I made it as plain as day. Important papers hidden here in my desk. As I suspected, the very next night – this!'

'Yet nothing taken?'

'Of course not, Inspector.' Palmer reached into his pocket. The snuff. He badly needed a pinch of snuff. This was all too much. 'I wouldn't have risked losing them. A ruse. To flush out those who...'

Those who – what? He was still unsure.

Wilde produced a pipe and tobacco pouch from his own jacket and gazed through the doorway to the expectant crowd gathering out on Hope Street.

'And these papers – part of the same dossier we found in the ashes at Wicklow's cottage?'

'The very same. Except, I had some of them with me at the Infirmary when the rest were stolen from Mr Low's house.'

'Important, then?'

'Well…' Palmer hesitated, unwilling to share too much even of his own absurdly limited intelligence. 'Morrison's papers, as it happens. His widow had asked me to study them. All enciphered, you see? His own version of Gurney's shorthand system.'

The inspector lit his pipe, blew a cloud of smoke towards the ceiling beams.

'She asked you – why, exactly? Still not convinced it was an accident?'

A question, Palmer determined, which did not warrant a response.

'The girl, Inspector. Has she even been questioned? Perhaps then we should have some answers. Plainly she could not have been spying for Wicklow alone.'

'Spying – truly?' he regarded Palmer as though he was addressing a ranting lunatic. 'Perhaps you might start by telling me what you discovered – in these so-called coded pages, like.'

'Random words,' Palmer lied. 'Names, perhaps. I could make neither head nor tail of them. Though Hancock from the *Advertiser* agreed to have a look, see if they hold any significance.'

'Hancock?' Wilde sneered. 'Tied up in this, as well? Why am I not surprised? But *this* is more Hancock's style, is it not?'

He waved his pipe out towards the street. The circus coming to town today. Lurid posters plastered everywhere for the past two weeks. The *Pinder Continental Circus and Lion Show*. And the event had also brought an early press of visitors to the exhibition. Bethan's half of the museum, on the opposite side of the archway, was already busy. Here, just a gentleman and his blushing companion wishing to purchase a copy of the catalogue. Palmer served them and bade them a pleasant morning, hoped they would enjoy their visit.

Privately, he cursed Hancock for his lack of diligence. Nothing. He had heard nothing from the newspaperman whatsoever. And there had been precious little time for Palmer himself to do much work on the single piece of Morrison's papers which still remained to be fully decoded.

'Hancock seems a decent fellow,' said Palmer, more for the sake of appearances than duty to defend the man. 'But these drovers – they have not been apprehended either?'

'A couple of tosspots on Market Day? Needle in a haystack, wouldn't you say? And if not a chance encounter, how precisely might they have known you would be in that precise place? At that precise time.'

It was a good question.

'I have no idea, Inspector.'

It was true. No idea, at all.

'More than my own share of paperwork to plough through, as well, Mr Palmer. This further complaint from the major's good lady wife. Harassing her during a dress fitting, she says. Is that true, sir?'

Mockery in his voice.

'Her husband, the major, was a witness to the very real assault suffered by Miss Francis and myself.'

'All the same, you must take this as a final warning, Mr Palmer.'

'For Heaven's sake, I was there with my young lady to speak with Williams – the tailor, you know?' Of course, Wilde knew. 'And what, precisely, is likely to be my fate should Mrs Cornwallis West happen upon me once again and determine that such a chance encounter constitutes further harassment?'

'Hauled before the Beak for a breach of the peace, I suppose,' said Wilde, as Bethan – her side of the museum now empty of customers – shuffled across towards them.

'Nothin' better to do with your time than botherin' decent folk, Mister?'

'The inspector,' said Palmer, 'is about to solve our crime, Bethan.' He pointed to the damaged desk.

'*Duw*. Miracle, that'll be. Asked the girl, has he?'

Yes, Palmer had shared that much with Bethan, at least.

'Won't be wasting police time on this, Mr Palmer,' said the inspector. 'With this lot in town? Circus – always trouble.'

He waved his pipe at Palmer, wrinkled his nose in the general direction of Bethan Thomas, and left.

A fanfare of trumpets out on the street. The crowd cheering – or, at least, that portion of the crowd Palmer could see framed by the archway and beyond the turnstiles.

'Goin' for a look, I am,' shouted Bethan from the doorway. He had not seen her so enlivened in the two months since his arrival in Wrexham.

'And would you mind if I joined you?'

Her shoulders shifted imperceptibly, almost horizontally, as if to say that she could not give a tinker's damn, one way or the other, though he imagined he saw just the hint of a smile.

A great clatter of hooves as he followed her out into the sunlight. An entire cavalcade of horses. A juggler performing his act while balanced upon the back of a prancing pony. A whole team of acrobats, men and women, transporting themselves by somersaults, by cartwheels, from mount to mount in a dizzying display. Oriental tumblers spinning and cavorting along their flanks.

Then a red and white caravan, with Pinder's slogan painted upon the side and, behind, a chariot. A gleaming, silver Roman chariot drawn by four pure white stallions. At the reins, a Nubian charioteer, garbed in a classical toga.

'An' the lions, see,' Bethan hissed, pointing to the wheeled cage with its six ferocious beasts, one of them almost as black as the Nubian.

'I once saw the great Maccomo, Bethan,' Palmer recalled. 'In Thetford. With the Manders Menagerie. The year before he died.'

Quite a show. It would have been six years ago. And then that poor one-armed fellow who succeeded him. He had been Irish, as well, had he not? What was his name? McCarthy? McCartee? Something of the sort. Mauled to death, of course.

'Who's this, then?' she said.

More equestrian entertainers, and he named them all for her, as best he was able. Dick Turpin. Joan of Arc. Bonnie Prince Charlie. More circus caravans and, bringing up the rear, another troupe of riders – but these were fine operatic singers, extracts from *Madame Angot's Daughter* unless he was much mistaken – whose horses danced elaborate quadrilles in time to the music.

Ettie would have enjoyed this. He missed her. And they had taken as much advantage of the town's entertainments as possible. The town had a proud tradition of theatricals though all seemed disappeared now. The Theatre Royal still stood near the Beast Market chapel but currently converted to a Temperance Hall. All the same, at the Public Hall's theatre on Henblas Street they had twice gone to see Chester and Lee's *Imperial French Marionettes*.

At the exhibition itself, there had been Mr Forbes-Robertson's lecture on the *Old Masters of the Continental School* – though only to a meagre audience. After the lecture, an astonishing concert by the Rhos Choir.

And then, all the time they had spent admiring the actual exhibits – her fascination with Bellini's *Portrait of Dante Alighieri*.

They had even been enticed, one rainswept afternoon, to the racecourse, where they had watched Wrexham's very own football club field a team of sixteen in a muddy match against the Volunteer Fire Brigade.

But her greatest amusement had come watching him stumble around on a pair of Plimpton's American patent roller skates out on Chester Road while Ettie herself glided with such grace around the Rink itself.

Palmer recalled Morrison's criticism of the town. Yes, its local industries could sometimes make the air a trifle difficult to breathe. Yet compared to Manchester this was indeed a veritable Eden, as the Swan of Lichfield, Anna Seward, had once famously described the place in her poetry.

'Well, there,' said Palmer. 'It looks like we've already seen the show. Shall we?'

He led Bethan back through the turnstiles and into her own half of the museum.

'You know,' he said, 'I like what you have done in here.'

It was just noon, the first of the twice-daily organ recitals beginning in the exhibition hall. The opening drama of Bach's *Toccata and Fugue*. Amusing. It sounded almost as though the music emphasised his praise for her efforts.

'An' what is it you want, like?' she said.

He had learned that she could see through him like a window. But now that everything was running smoothly, there seemed little point in remaining here. If Mr Low could be persuaded, there was no reason Bethan Thomas should not take over the whole curatorship. By now, Palmer had catalogued the collections, renewed every identification card, negotiated with collectors from Denbighshire and Flintshire, from Shropshire and Cheshire. The collection was extended and there were regular advertisements for the museum in every pertinent periodical.

'I expect, Bethan, that you shall be pleased to see the back of me – once my time here is at an end.'

She peered up at him, seemingly trying to fathom precisely what he might actually want from her.

'Need help, I would.'

It was hardly an enthusiastic response, but from Bethan one had to be grateful for small mercies.

'Then I shall speak with Mr Low. But the circus, Miss Thomas. Life's treasures bring little joy unless they may be shared. Perhaps you would do me the honour of joining me to see the show tomorrow evening.'

Bethan muttered something in Welsh, and he decided it might have been a thank you. She turned to go, and Palmer went back to the book he had been studying before the inspector interrupted him.

'What's that, then?'

He started with surprise, thinking she had gone but also taken aback by her display of interest.

'This?' said Palmer. 'Kirk. At the Grammar School. He had a copy.'

He closed the volume but used his finger to keep the place while he scrutinised the green leather spine, gold lettering. *A History of the British Legion and War in Spain.*

'Somerville,' he explained. 'Did you know, Bethan, that some of Mr Williams's coverlet is fashioned from the uniforms of our soldiers who fought in Spain?'

'Edward Crick?'

'You knew.'

'Of course. The family, like.'

'The other brother – the one who died there?'

'Alfie – aye. Sweet boy, 'e was.'

'And Edward? Sweet, also?'

She cackled at him.

'Reckon 'e came back not a man, they do. Wethered, like.'

Palmer knew the word. Common enough in Thetford as well as Wales.

According to Somerville, most of the volunteers had returned home in July 1837. But some had remained – many buried in Spanish soil, others to continue the fight, and Crick apparently among them. In September that year there had been a final battle, this New Legion almost totally destroyed at a place Somerville named as Andoain. The dead had been left in heaps upon the field. And those taken captive by the Carlists? There was a quotation from one of the few who had escaped.

"To our foes, we of the British Legion were the most odious of all; strangers, mercenaries, heretics, scoffers, polluters of their sacred soil; so they did term us. For us there was no quarter; in the heat of battle, or by cold judicial form, it was all the same: to fall into their hands was certainly a tortured death."

'No,' said Palmer. 'Not a whole man, it seems. Mr Williams told me Crick only came back to Wrexham for a while and then to London. Have you any idea, Bethan, how a fellow like that, injured so badly, might have made his way in London?'

'London,' she spat. 'Sodom and Gomorrah, see. Can't have been anything respectable, like. Not in London. Better go and ask him, you had.'

Yes, he supposed he must. But the idea haunted him through the rest of the afternoon and into the evening. He worked until eight o'clock, when the Exhibition Band struck up their own second performance of the day. An American medley so that, still thinking of the workhouse, of *señora* Blackstone, of Edward Crick, and of blood among the threads, he was drawn once more to Williams's coverlet.

He studied the panels afresh, hungry for his supper. Those he already knew: the serpent and other creatures; the railway viaduct; Noah's Ark; Jonah; Cain and Abel. But his eyes were drawn to the image at the patchwork's very heart. The wild beasts and Adam among them.

"And Adam gave names to all cattle, and to the fowl of the air, and to every beast of the field."

Adam. And that creature to which Adam seemed to stretch his hand. Black as night. A mountain lion, perhaps.

In the background, the band played *John Brown's Body*.

Chapter Eighteen

The following morning, the circus came to the exhibition. In the form of that Nubian lion tamer, at least. Though not a Nubian at all, as it turned out, but Senegalese. And his stage name, César, not his own, either.

He caused quite a sensation, arriving with Mr Chaffers to give a lecture and demonstration involving some of the weaponry on display in the hall. Quite an expert, it seemed, having served as a *zouave*, a Turco in French General Faidherbe's regiment. And in the uniform of that gallant band, he was attired. His stage costume. Red tasselled cap. A short and open-fronted green jacket, braided with gold. And baggy *sirwal* trousers in a lighter shade of green.

'Théophile Léon, *monsieur*,' the African introduced himself.

'Léon?' said Palmer as they shook hands at the museum entrance.

'Extraordinary, is it not?' William Chaffers smiled, despite the pain which so obviously afflicted his bent back. Palmer knew the old gentleman quite well by now. His duties as General Superintendent brought him to town frequently from London. And Palmer had enjoyed the antiquarian's own publications, his books on hallmarks and ceramic marks. 'Léon by name,' said Chaffers, 'and now lions are his trade.'

There were photographs. Laings from the High Street who had their own and exclusive portraiture studio adjoining the main gallery. Photographs of the lion tamer displaying the use of a pair of Chinese Tartary swords, an Indian tulwar, Spanish and Italian rapiers. And an interview. Hancock from the *Advertiser*, naturally, there among the other newspapermen.

'Apologies,' he shouted to Palmer. 'I have news. As soon as I'm finished here...'

News? Well, that was something. Still, it seemed Palmer must be patient a while longer. Anyhow, he had his own findings to share with Hancock. The remaining page of Morrison's encrypted notes, though he remained unsure about them. Unsure about his translation. Unsure whether he should divulge his incomplete calculations at all.

He wandered back past the busy refreshment saloons and entered the cloak room, where he had invested in a locker box to keep those papers and possessions he no longer deemed safe either at Roseneath House nor in the museum. There, he collected the thin file and returned to his desk, ready to roll down the top should he be disturbed. But he had not counted on Bethan's capacity for stealth.

'What's this, then?' she said, and startled him yet again. Perhaps too absorbed in the paper, but he had not heard her approach. And it was too late to slam down the slats.

He sighed, supposed he needed to show *somebody* else. Even Bethan. Though she had caught him with the *Brachygraphy* often enough to know what was afoot.

'Morrison's coded page,' he said. 'It has taken far longer than I should have liked. And still makes little sense. But here it is.'

He trundled his winged office chair to one side, so she might have a better view. Difficult for her, at times. The bent back. The thickly lensed spectacles. He admired her tenacity.

'You see?' he said. 'First line. Seems to read *GR*. Then this forward angle bracket. Then *List Ladies Inn Tree G.*'

The words were plain enough. But the meaning? The intent? Palmer had no idea.

'*GR*?' said Bethan.

'Good point. I shall return to that. At first, I mistook it for numbers. Easy enough with this form of shorthand. But now – anyway, the next line...'

She read it for him.

'*Man Pleasures 1860 Miss F Café Royal.* What's that mean? Café Royal in London, like?'

It was famous enough, Palmer had to concede. But a connection to Wrexham? It seemed unlikely. And followed by the words *Broth* and *All.*

'*Broth*?' he said. 'Why, for pity's sake?'

But she was already peering at Palmer's subsequent bit of scribble, comparing it with Morrison's original.

'You sure?' she murmured. He saw she was studying the words *Young Wales Ebon Rock* and *Agent*. 'Could be Blackstone at the workhouse, see.'

He had been tempted to think the same thing.

'It would certainly fit with this section,' he admitted. 'If I have it correct, that is. *Man Chester Work House Wreck Sam.* Manchester to check the workhouse records for Wrexham? I believe so. And the rest clear, as well. Almost, anyway. *GR.* That forward angle bracket again. *Check Rose Whim Pole Link. Pat Sea.*'

To check on Rose Wimpole's link to Patsy – Mrs Cornwallis West. Though the reference to *Pat Sea* appeared to ring no bells with Bethan. But GR. Yes, initially, he had mistaken the letters for numbers. GR? George Reynolds, surely. He should have thought of it before. Why would Morrison be working alone, without the knowledge of the newspaper's proprietor? Did Reynolds hold the key to all this?

'Rose Wimpole,' said Bethan. 'Told you, I did. No accident. You believe me now?' Palmer had no doubt about it. 'An' that so-called inspector,' she sneered. 'Trust him, do you? Incomer, see. Foreigner, like.'

It was another good point. And Palmer decided not to remind her that he, himself, was more an incomer than Wilde. Presumably, however, he did not count, given the temporary nature of his time in Wrexham, whereas the inspector...

She had, of course, touched a nerve. He had wondered about Inspector Wilde himself. The over-eager warnings on behalf of the major's wife. His refusal to conduct even cursory investigations. But, by then, Hancock had come blustering into the museum.

'What's this?' he said. 'More coded messages from beyond the grave?'

With regular interruptions from Bethan Thomas, Palmer went through the page again. No response from Hancock. Simply a blank expression on his otherwise affable face.

'Well?' said Palmer, impatiently, when he had finished. He had expected *something* from the newspaperman by way of constructive comment. 'News, did you say?'

'Nothing that will not keep,' Hancock replied, with theatrical nonchalance.

Bethan turned her head upon its side so she could stare malevolently up at him.

'See how the wind blows, I can,' she snapped. 'Take the hint, see.'

She flounced off to her own domain, across the passageway.

'I have offended her,' said Hancock.

'Truly, it takes but little.'

'I had no idea, old fellow, to what extent you might have embroiled her in this affair.'

Embroiled. Yes, thought Palmer, perhaps he had. And misfortunes seemed so regularly to befall those who became entangled. Did he need to worry about Bethan as well? Or Hancock, if it came to that. This was the very devil! Becoming complicated.

'Very little,' he said, and reached for his snuff box. 'But your news?'

'I wonder whether it might have some connection to this part.' He ran his finger along the words *Ladies Inn Tree G* and looked about him to make sure they were not overheard. 'You remember we talked about the major's wife? Her younger days and high society circles?' Of course, Palmer remembered. 'Well, there was another entry on that same list which struck a chord with an old friend of mine. Remember, *Cliff Den 61*? Before our time, but this friend, he recalled a hint of scandal. A story about a woman called Nellie Clifden. Irish as well, as it happens. Some questionable relationship with...' He glanced around again, his voice dropping to a whisper. 'With HRH.'

'The...'

'Yes, the same. And it would have been about fifteen years ago. 'Sixty-one, you see? The Prince himself, of course, still a young man. But my friend used that same phrase to describe the Clifden woman.'

'Phrase?' said Palmer.

'Great heavens, man. *Ladies Inn Tree G*. Ladies of intrigue. Do you not know...?'

'Yes, yes. Of course, I know. I had simply not associated the thing. But then, on the list...' He rummaged in the file, found the other sheet, the one he had copied for Hancock. 'Here. *M*. And this.' He pointed to the numbers which followed. 'I thought about this a while back. *M* for Mordaunt. And 1868 or 1869. That would indeed fit. Lady Mordaunt, a lady of intrigue and accusations concerning...'

Palmer paused, calculating the implications.

'HRH,' murmured Hancock. 'Indeed. So, this list...'

'And the major's wife?' said Palmer. 'But these others. If Morrison was indeed investigating some royal scandal, the rest on the list – I suppose Reynolds must know.'

'You shall write to him?'

Write? It would be an excessively long missive. And could he be sure the contents would be secure?

Good grief. HRH. The Prince of Wales. This must surely be some foolish misunderstanding. And even if Morrison's pages justified the implication, how did this all fit here? How did it fit Morrison's demise?

No, a letter would not answer.

'I believe,' he said, at last, 'that I shall seek some purpose to justify a journey to London. Easier to explain in person, do you not think?'

There was something else. It seemed to him a good thing that any villains in the piece should believe Morrison's papers to have burned in Wicklow's cottage. But the wider any knowledge might spread that some of those papers were still in existence, the greater, surely, must be the danger among those who were a party to this intelligence. The widow herself, for example.

'I take it you have no immediate plans to travel?' said Hancock.

Palmer shook himself free from the dark place into which his mind had begun to descend.

'There will be things to arrange,' he said. 'And besides, I have promised to escort Miss Thomas to the circus – this very evening.'

'Then you shall see me in a considerably different light, Mr Palmer. But here. I shall leave *monsieur* Léon to explain.'

The lion tamer, with Mr Chaffers and a whole band of eager followers, had emerged from the covered passage and were now gathered within the archway.

'*Le voici!*' Here he is, shouted the African. 'My assistant for tonight.'

Palmer saw Hancock preen himself.

'I must admit to a modicum of trepidation,' the newspaperman smiled. 'He assures me I shall be safe in his hands, of course.'

'Safe?' said Palmer.

'Indeed,' said the lion tamer. 'My show always includes a volunteer from the audience. Tonight, it shall be *monsieur* Hancock. And then he shall write about the experience in his newspaper.' He slapped Hancock heartily on the back and smiled. A broad and beautiful jester's smile. 'That is, of course, if he survives to tell the tale.'

Chapter Nineteen

The mechanical calliope played the final notes of *Old Black Joe*, and Palmer wondered whether there could possibly be a better place than this for a carefully arranged accident.

From their seats on the topmost tier of benches, beneath the red and white circus tent canvas, he experienced a strange chemical blend of anticipation and dread. Excited by the prospect of the performance, fearful in the certainty that Hancock must surely suffer some dreadful fate.

'I begged him, Bethan. Not to be so foolish.'

'What's writ is writ,' she replied.

At least she had a decent vantage point up there and she applauded with wild abandon, along with five hundred other spectators, when the ringmaster appeared. Scarlet hunting habit and whip in hand.

'Roll up! Roll up!' he bellowed through a speaking horn, loud and resonant as the bells of St. Giles. 'Ladies and gentlemen, the greatest show in all the world.'

The Beast Market field had been transformed, the striped marquee at its centre, like some mighty paladin's pavilion, surrounded by a defensive perimeter of caravans and wheeled cages, the approaches lined with coconut shies and carousels.

'Your friend, the policeman?'

'Not my friend,' said Palmer as the first horses cantered into the ring. Exquisite. Their bestial smell. The wind they stirred, whispering against his cheeks, even so high up. 'And I begged him – begged him, to be here, to watch over Hancock.'

Ettie would have seen it more clearly, he knew. The threat. The danger.

He fretted about it all the way through that first part of the show. Those bareback acrobats again, the La Perche Brothers. And where was Hancock anyway? Hopefully, he had decided to stay at home. Yes, hopefully.

Next, the Oriental Jing-Ling Jumpers. Chinamen able to fold themselves entirely in half and insert their bodies into very small barrels.

'Well, 'e's here, anyhow,' said Bethan, and pointed across to the front row, directly opposite.

There, indeed, was Inspector Wilde. A whole gaggle of children. Small children. Three boys. Two girls. And then his wife – Martha Jane, was it not? With an infant girl on one knee, a tiny baby on the other. At the circus, after all, though plainly not for Hancock's protection.

'I tried to persuade him that Hancock might be in danger. Seems like it fell on deaf ears.'

'What did 'e have to say, like – when you was on your own?'

'Hancock?' The Chinamen had left the ring, to be replaced by the renowned Nellie Daniels, a specialist in striking ballet poses and steps – upon the back of a pure white stallion, naturally. Scissor split leaps and pirouettes, *assemblés* and attitudes, while the calliope whistled and tooted a medley from *La Sylphide*. 'Very little,' Palmer murmured. 'But he has suggested I might go to London. To see Morrison's editor – the proprietor of his newspaper, in fact.'

Nellie Daniels had put him in mind of Nellie Clifden. A supposed liaison with the Prince of Wales – though he decided not to share that with Bethan.

'Reynolds?' she said.

'George Reynolds, yes. You read his paper? His books, perhaps?'

'Don't need to read no papers to know what goes on in the world. It's what men do – read about politics. Have to study it, you do. But women, we live it, see. Every day. Live it an' breathe it.'

Miss Daniels had just completed a complex *penché* arabesque, and brought the audience to its own feet. Palmer remained seated, however, still fretting for Hancock but wondering, as well, how Bethan's strong opinions about women and politics might sit against her staunch Welsh Presbyterian upbringing. Further niggling doubts, as well, about Wilde – his failure to question the girl from the Wynnstay and to investigate the attempted robbery at the museum, or the attack they had suffered at the hands of those drovers.

'Well,' he said, 'if I'm to travel to London, you shall have to care for the whole thing.'

He had already spoken with Mr Low, having wired several gentlemen in London who, through their Welsh connections, might be happy to loan exhibits from their collections to Wrexham. And he had, of course, also wired George Reynolds though, so far, without response.

'But who,' Bethan smiled up at him, 'will care for you in that sinful place?'

It was something to contemplate. Yet, for now, they enjoyed the rest of the show in companionable silence. Matthews and Sattelle on the Horizontal Bar. Pageants – Dick Turpin's Ride to York and the Maid of Orléans. Comic opera performed on horseback – and more of those equine quadrilles.

'Well, here it is, at last,' said Palmer, feeling the bile of brooding apprehension rise in his gorge.

A troupe of clowns cavorted around the arena while circus hands rapidly erected the sides and top of an iron-barred enclosure in the centre of the ring. Within the enclosure, five circular three-legged stands, of differing heights, and some form of treadmill. It took several minutes, while an elegant Whiteface, Italian by his voice, and a wild Auguste, the butt of his companion's japes, kept the crowd amused. A third jester worked among the audience itself, a character clown, with all the usual face paint but dressed remarkably like Sir Watkin. Another Pickwick, but with sleight of hand.

Anarchy, until the ringmaster appeared once more, and the clowns scampered away.

'And now, ladies and gentlemen, the finale of this evening's performance.'

The circus hands heaved a wheeled cage into the entrance and secured the front of the wagon to the rear of the enclosure. In the cage, Théophile Léon's five beasts, the darkest of them roaring, precisely on cue. Perhaps not roaring, thought Palmer, to whom it sounded more like the deepest and most terrifying cough.

'Pinder's Continental Circus is proud to present, for your edification, our new Lion Show. And here, in a demonstration of skills which shall astonish you…'

The introduction continued while the Great César, still in his green *zouave* uniform, strode into the ring also. Yet now he carried a whip and, in a shoulder holster half-hidden beneath his jacket, a revolver. Applause, as he took up a stance near the enclosure's bolted gate.

'*Mesdames et messieurs*,' he began. 'The creatures you are about to see are among the most deadly predators on earth.'

His English, though heavily accented, was perfect.

'The claws of a fully-grown lion are three inches long. Razor sharp. Its jaw, when open, is more than twelve inches wide. Wide enough to take the whole of a man's head. And yes, a bite strong enough… Ah, but I see we have some children in the audience so perhaps I shall not elaborate. Enough to say that these are dangerous beasts.'

Yes, thought Palmer. And poor Hancock…

'I may carry a whip,' the African was saying, 'but I use it only to mark my own space from that of my beasts. I carry a pistol, but it is loaded only with blank cartridges. Because, you see, though you may call me a lion tamer, I think of myself only as their trainer.'

'Still, a dangerous business,' Palmer murmured.

'I read, see,' Bethan replied. 'Four times more dangerous to 'ave a babe than work down the pit, it is. An' work down the pit's a sight more dangerous than this, like.'

Palmer thought of those who might disagree. The one-armed Irishman, McCarthy or McCartee, mauled to death. Or the tale his father had told him about the girl, Ellen-something, a lion tamer at the age of seventeen, and killed by a tiger. And Bethan Thomas – had she? Ever had a child? Palmer had never even thought to ask. Still, he was sure she must be correct. About the relative dangers in all these things. Though, at the moment, the danger from the circus lions seemed clear and immediately present.

'But now,' César shouted, 'allow me to introduce you.'

He marched to the back of the enclosure, climbed the wagons steps and pulled back the large metal bolt securing a door in the wooden wall of their cage.

The door fell open and, one by one, the creatures sprang out, sprinted around the enclosure but, at a single crack of the whip, each leapt up onto its own circular platform.

César took a bucket from a hook on the steps and approached the first lion. He lifted a thick chunk of meat from the bucket, gripped the meat between his teeth and offered his face up to the creature. It regarded him a moment, then stretched its neck, bared its huge fangs, and took the beefsteak in its own ferocious mouth to a riot of acclaim from the audience.

'Elsa,' said César. 'A five-year old female from my own Senegal.'

More applause, as he repeated the trick with each of the others, coming finally to the largest of them all. Almost black, with an enormous mane. It was huge, yet it took the meat from César's mouth as meekly as all the rest.

'Mahmoud,' he told them. 'A ten-year old Barbary male from French Morocco.' Cheering, and some in the crowd chanting the creature's name. '*Eh bien,*' he continued. 'You know, there are those who say we blunt the teeth of these fine animals. Or that we pull their claws.'

And there are those, thought Palmer, who say, that exhibitions of this sort are nothing more than a gratuitous impertinence towards a noble animal. But César's monologue was captivating, he had to admit.

'So,' said the performer, 'allow me to demonstrate that this is a lie. And to help me, I have a volunteer – a respected writer from your newspaper, the *Wrexham Advertiser*. Please welcome... *Monsieur* Herbert Hancock!'

Hancock was led into the arena by the ringmaster. Further applause, though Hancock himself seemed petrified, having almost to be dragged towards the enclosure's entrance grille, to the discordant calliope rendition of *Cheer, Boys, Cheer!* And the lions greeted him, as well, each growling and shifting on its raised dais, while the dark-furred Barbary jumped down, stretching its legs before it and turning its gargantuan head to display those brutal fangs. It required another crack of César's whip to persuade the creature back onto its platform.

'Do not fear, *Monsieur* Hancock,' cried the lion tamer. 'We must never show fear to these fellows. But respect? Yes, indeed. Help me to demonstrate.'

Leaning against the bars of the cage was a wooden board, perhaps three feet square and, somehow, César – Théophile Léon – persuaded a quaking Hancock to hold the thing in his outstretched arms before the same black Barbary. A single whistle from the Senegalese and Mahmoud the lion reached out its paw so fast that Palmer barely saw the movement. Yet Hancock was suddenly standing with the board sliced neatly in half. He dropped the pieces as though they must be made of molten metal, while César took his trembling arm, drew the newspaperman back away from the lion's reach and offered him a military salute, which occasioned a further ovation from the audience.

The applause continued through all the minutes during which Hancock, his legs barely able to keep him upright, was escorted from the ring and to a place of honour in the dignitaries' box – where he joined Chaffers and several of the town's aldermen. And when the clapping had died, César continued with his act: the creatures encouraged to jump through hoops; the Senegalese riding about on the Barbary's back; and one of the females trotting inside the treadmill, causing the drum to turn, while a second of the beasts leapt onto the upper and outer part of the drum, against the direction of its rotation so that, effectively, it was running on the spot.

'Safe, then.' Bethan nudged Palmer with her elbow. 'Your friend.'

'It seems so.'

It seemed, also, that Palmer had his own lions to be tamed. What on earth had he imagined might happen? An accident befalling Hancock here in plain view of the audience? The fellow eaten in front of so many onlookers? It hardly fitted with the pattern of his mystery so far. But he noted that, with each piece of César's act successfully completed, the audience reaction became more muted. Becoming bored, perhaps? What did they truly want – a display of the African's undisputed skills, or the thrill of seeing him fail? As he was already brutally aware, the cruel death of lion tamers in the ring was hardly unknown.

And there was the lesson for Palmer, as well. He supposed that, if you wished to tame lions, even metaphorical ones, you must face the risk of being hooked by your unpredictable demon's claws, brought under its control and then having your throat crushed by its fangs. The price you paid for disturbing ferocious beasts.

'Madman, he is,' said Bethan, as César began to demonstrate his final act of faith. He stood in the centre of the enclosure, calm and composed, while Mahmoud the black Barbary raised itself behind him, rearing up to its full height, front paws resting on the lion tamer's shoulders. César staggered briefly, then regained his stance, while the audience gasped.

'Enormous,' Palmer observed. And so it was, towering above the Senegalese. It lowered its great shaggy head, opened its jaws wide and caused César's head to disappear entirely from view.

Chapter Twenty

'Well, Mr Palmer. Looks like you were right, sir. Death follows where you tread, sure enough.'

Their paths had crossed on Town Hill, Palmer on his way to the Post Office – sending his latest letter to Ettie – and Wilde... Well, Palmer had no idea where the inspector might be heading.

'No, Inspector. Mr Hancock is perfectly safe. No thanks to your good self, of course. But at least I hope your lady wife and beautiful children enjoyed the show.'

Wilde managed to ignore the implied criticism, his attention drawn instead to the tinker who was loudly cursing the half-starved dappled nag struggling both with the gradient and its clattering load of kettles and blackened cookpots.

'We did, aye,' said Wilde, turning back to face Palmer. 'But not Hancock. No, it was the girl from the Wynnstay.'

'The girl...'

'Forgotten already, sir? Her name was Maudie Meadows, though you may not have known it.'

'Maudie – yes, I had forgotten. But died...'

'Simple accident, Mister Palmer. Fell down the steps at the Tiger. Broken neck. But great Heavens...'

The packhorse had stumbled to its knees, then collapsed entirely onto its side, the load scattering across the road, causing all carts and wagons to grind to a halt on the cobblestones. The inspector went off to do his duty – to bring some order to the chaos, Palmer assumed. He himself went into the Post Office on the corner of College Street, where they weighed his lengthy missive to Manchester. A full ounce and a tuppenny blue applied to the envelope. The rest of his correspondence, letters of introduction to various collectors in London, required only penny reds.

The Tiger Inn, Wilde had said. Palmer knew the place well, for it stood on the corner of Farndon Street, just across from the Beast Market Chapel. He passed it every Sunday.

'Adam naming the animals,' Palmer murmured, as he came out onto the street again. 'Beast Market. The Tiger. How could I be so stupid? I thought – the circus, it seemed so obvious. Yet...'

'Beg pardon?' said Wilde. He was waiting outside the Post Office door while two of his constables – presumably summoned from their desk in the Town Hall building – berated the tinker, forced him to pick up his goods and directed the traffic around the obstacle while they waited for the knackerman to come and remove the sad animal.

'Another accident, Inspector. Does it not make you wonder? Simple coincidence? Oh, but I forgot – drummed into you, was it not? No such thing as coincidence?'

'It would be a rare week in Wrexham, sir, without an inquest into one untimely demise or another.'

'You see no connection here?'

He had tried to put those pieces together in the pages he had written to Ettie. News of his planned journey to London. Rather, to Chislehurst, for Reynolds was living – and working from – Herne Bay in Kent. Chislehurst was a happy compromise. Possibly a visit to Mrs Morrison as well, then.

'None,' said Wilde. He paused, shouted some instructions to his men. 'Except your own misplaced interest,' he spoke again to Palmer. 'I could almost imagine you feel personally responsible for each of them.'

Culpable, thought Palmer, as they both headed up the hill. Culpable – was that not the word scrawled on Wicklow's wall? *For none of us liveth to himself, and no man dieth to himself.* Or, as Dean John Donne had preached, *No man is an island entire of itself.*

'Are we not all responsible for each other's life and death?' he said. 'Yet for poor Morrison – yes, I suppose it may be true. I hope to renew my acquaintance with his widow shortly. You were asking about her, Inspector. Did you have a reason? Some responsibility of your own?'

'There are times, Mr Palmer,' the inspector growled, more than just a hint of menace in his voice, 'I could almost swear you think I have some part to play in your fantasies. You'll tell me that's not so, will you not?'

He did not wait for Palmer's answer, though he did not truly expect one, Palmer knew. More a warning than anything else. Not even a word of farewell as Wilde headed for the Town Hall's entrance.

But the exchange churned at Palmer's innards as he walked the next few yards along Hope Street. The inspector had plainly bristled at mention of the Widow Morrison. Yet Wilde had asked about her, wanted to know if she still believed her husband's death to be other than an accident. Could she – possibly, be at risk?

He stopped at the books and music seller to collect the copy of Mr Gladstone's *Bulgarian Horrors* pamphlet he had ordered. From Miss Priscilla Jones, the proprietor. Spinster, with a penchant for alluring attire of yellow and black, as waspish as her ways. She flattered him on each occasion he patronised her establishment – something he now did with a frequency which caused him considerable guilt with regard to dear Ettie and despite knowing that a fellow might find himself badly stung should he pursue such a liaison.

But Ettie was in Manchester. Otherwise, he suspected he would have feared for her, as well.

At the turnstiles, he found Hancock making a point of brandishing his pocket watch.

'Did we not say eleven o'clock?' he said.

Indeed, they had, but Palmer had carelessly lost track of the time – matters at the museum to be set in order. It was an important day, for the proprietor of the Broughton Ironworks had purchased tickets to the exhibition for his entire workforce. Then the Post Office to visit, and his words with Wilde. Now, therefore, he readily agreed they should take a hansom cab out to the workhouse. In any case, it had threatened rain all morning and he had left his rain napper at Roseneath House.

'You are certain?' he said, when they were on their way towards the workhouse. 'They will not think it strange – me, arriving with you? Unannounced?'

'Strange? Perhaps they shall. But perhaps that might give us the edge. Unbalance them, perhaps. You need answers, do you not? And surely you have conjured some cover story to explain you being there?'

Cover story? Good point. He would give the thing some thought. When Hancock had told him the reason for his own visit, Palmer had simply decided to join him. But, for now, more immediate matters.

'One or two answers from you, also, Hancock.' He heard the patter of rain on the window. 'There, do you see? As we thought. A shower.'

'From me?'

'Indeed. When we first met, you hinted at some scandal relating to the place.'

The hansom cab jolted and bounced over the potholes along Watery Lane.

'There are always rumours,' Hancock smiled, 'about the immorality of the workhouse. It was no different here. Salacious stories about the girls who worked there providing inappropriate entertainment for some of the local lads. Night-time visits, if you catch my drift.'

Yes, that was pretty much the story Palmer had eventually heard from Bethan as well.

'But the Board of Guardians investigated,' said Hancock, 'and decided there was no substance to the tale.'

The Board of Guardians. Now, there was something to ponder. The very reason for Hancock's own visit. One of the reasons. Three meetings at the workhouse on the same day. The Board itself. An inquest. And a meeting of the Rural Sanitary Authority. Each of the proceedings needing to be reported in the *Advertiser*.

'And you are sure they will have dealt with the matter thoroughly?'

'I will most certainly not be challenging the outcome. I should rather face that Barbary lion again. Great Heavens, the size of that brute's paws. I shall never forget it, Palmer. Never.'

They arrived at the workhouse just before noon. The courtyard outside the main entrance was busy with other cabs and private carriages, coming and going. Hancock was astonished that the inquest was already over. Fortunately for him, Mr Thelwall the coroner was still there, though just leaving. They passed each other at the porter's lodge.

'Death from natural causes,' said the coroner, as he collected his coat and donned his hat. 'Old fellow. Sixty-nine. Been in the care of Surgeon Low for the past year. If you need more details, Hancock...'

Palmer watched the porter – Crick, he now knew – that shambling, ruined bear of a man. Edward Crick. And by that name, Palmer addressed the fellow.

'Mister Crick,' he said. He removed his hat and saw a spark of animal intelligence flash within those otherwise listless eyes. 'I should like to see the Master and the Mistress, if you please. My name is...'

'Wait.'

Palmer waited, sat himself on those leather-covered benches, watching as Hancock shook hands with some newcomers. He recognised them. Captain Griffith-Boscawen, chairman both to the Board of Governors *and* the Rural Sanitary Authority. Formerly with the Fusiliers. Fought at Sebastopol. Local magistrate now, along with the first of his companions.

This gentleman was the elderly Wilson Edwards – prominent landlord and a neighbour of Mr Low. A prominent dissenter, like so many others in Wrexham. A remarkable town, with the Catholic St. Mary's at the northern edge, the High Church Anglican St. Giles at the southern end, each serving their respective congregations. But between? Every shade of dissenter and nonconformist. Baptists. Quakers. Methodists, like Palmer himself. And the Bible classes of Alexander Wilson Edwards were a legend. Palmer had heard him at the Baptist Chapel on Chester Street. Remarkable.

With these two notables, Rowland the pharmacist. Each of them acknowledged Palmer with a nod of the head and Hancock told him he would be back when the meetings ended.

'Are you sure?' he said. 'About...'

'I shall be fine,' Palmer confirmed, as Griffith-Boscawen led his party – Hancock included – through the double doors to the interior, and towards the staircase beyond. Plainly, the fellow was at home here, the lord of this particular manor.

'*Señor* Palmer?'

Faustina Blackstone appeared in the doorway as though by magic but turned to look up the stairs before Palmer could acknowledge her.

'My husband,' she shouted to the chairman, 'is already in the boardroom.'

Griffith-Boscawen thanked her, allowing her to pay full attention to Palmer yet again.

'My apologies, *señora*, I should have realised – that your husband would also be at the meeting.'

The noon dinner bell rang throughout the building and, almost at once, the staircases were filled with their respective lines of men and women. Palmer recalled a snatch of some ironical penny ballad.

> *Of their uniform, too, you something shall hear,*
> *In strong Fearnaught jackets the men do appear;*
> *In coarse Grogram gowns the women do shine,*
> *And a ninepenny cap – now won't they be fine?*

'You wish to speak with my husband?' said Faustina Blackstone.

'Both of you. I am interested in the history of the workhouse – for the museum, you understand.'

She laughed – laughed at him, quite openly. Her attire was similar to his previous visit, though the dress today was deepest purple, and the lace trim all cream. But the *mantilla*, the fan, the gold earrings all the same. Her hands were bare as well, and he saw they were as aged as her prematurely lined face.

'You know, *señor*, that we have much to do. The meetings. And the cow – she is giving light to…'

She struggled for the word.

'I promise not to take too much of your time. Or I could wait. It seems I shall be here for a while, until Mr Hancock…'

'Not only the cow. Since you came here – the last time – there has been fever. Then the man Jones.' She crossed herself. 'Tried to kill himself.'

Palmer had read about the incident in the papers. The fellow had attempted suicide on the railway line but only his leg had been crushed, smashed to smithereens by the engine and the wheels of six carriages.

'It was very… ugly, *señor*. After that, a girl drowns in the mill race.'

'No fever now, I hope.' He was suddenly troubled. The weakness in his chest made him rather susceptible.

Señora Blackstone gave a sigh of resignation, gestured for him to follow.

'*Vale*,' she said. Very well. 'Perhaps, you might take more of the cordial?'

He politely declined. She led him to the Master's Parlour, but he was intoxicated again by her familiar scent of orange jessamine as he brushed past her in the doorway, where she stood aside to let him enter.

Then he froze, immediately afraid.

Just across the room, at the fireplace, loomed the porter. Crick, with a blackened poker in his hand. He looked as though he might pounce at any second. Growling. Teeth bared.

'Eduardo,' commanded Faustina Blackstone, moving to stand in front of Palmer. 'Go now.'

She spoke the instruction as she might have done to a faithful hound. And – Palmer thanked Heaven – Crick obeyed, set down the poker in its stand on the hearth and, with head bowed, loped from the room.

'You meant *his* uniform,' he said. 'The first time we met. Blood among the threads – you remember?'

She offered him a seat, as previously, and sat opposite, rang the handbell.

'Perhaps, this time, some tea, *señor*?'

'Tea would be pleasant. But last time, it seems, I asked the wrong question. About how you met your husband. I *should* have asked whether you met Crick there, in Spain. Edward – Eduardo?'

He could rarely hear the name Edward without thinking of Maryatt. *The Children of the New Forest* again. Edward Beverley, the lad to whose fictional heroism young Palmer had so greatly aspired and so spectacularly failed to attain.

'I was just a girl when they came,' she said, and her fingers seemed to act out the scene. 'To San Sebastián. So fine, those *soldados*. To fight for us. I saw him there. Eduardo and his horses.'

The child-like maid knocked on the door and *señora* Blackstone told her to bring tea. When she had gone, Palmer offered his hostess another pinch of his snuff. There had been passion in her eyes when she had spoken about Crick. But was it really Crick she recalled so fondly? It did not seem possible.

'I see the thing you are thinking, *señor*.' She closed the snuff box lid, handed it back. 'The same man – can it be? Oh, but he was different. Then. So very different.'

'Forty years,' said Palmer, 'is enough to change us all.'

'No,' she said. 'I think you do not understand. He promised to bring me to England. And I followed him. To Hernani and Vitoria. To Bilbao. To Oriamendi and Irún. And then...'

She stopped and gazed at a framed pencil sketch, one of the many pictures adorning her walls. It was simply executed with broad lines of shading but, now Palmer studied it, there could be no mistake. Faustina as little more than a girl.

'Then,' he said, 'Andoain. And did Edward Crick draw that?'

She was about to answer when the door opened. The maid, the tea – and, by his bearing, his air of authority, surely the Master, Frederick Blackstone.

The fellow brushed imperiously past the girl, so that she almost spilled the contents of the silver tray.

'Palmer, sir? You is Palmer?'

He wore a uniform jacket. Blue, like a naval pea jacket, a bridge coat. A naval beard to match, a similar hint of blue among the black whiskers – whiskers which failed to conceal a large purple birthmark, a port wine stain, covering much of his neck. Was there a formal attire for workhouse Masters? Palmer had no idea.

'Indeed,' he replied. 'And I presume...'

'Master here,' Blackstone told him. 'Master. Understood? You want...'

Unless Palmer was much mistaken, Frederick Blackstone must be somewhat younger than his wife. He remembered the line from Morrison's shorthand. *Young Wales Ebon Rock Agent.* Young? Wales? And agent – for what? For whom?

'I believe I have some right to be here, Mr Blackstone. Robbed, you see. My property discovered in the cottage of your man, Wicklow. I wondered...'

He allowed the words to hang in the frozen scene. *Señora* Blackstone standing at her chair, head high, like a proud vixen. The maid, dithering in the doorway, uncertain how to proceed. And Blackstone himself, one hand behind his back, the other thrust inside the breast of his coat, a veritable Bonaparte.

'Mary,' said Faustina at last, breaking the web, 'please set down the tray. I shall pour.'

A sigh of relief, and the maid settled the tea things on the ivory-inlaid occasional table.

'But Wicklow?' said the Master. 'Never knowed, we didn't – when he'd be here and when 'e would not. Some is that way, sir. That way.'

'It seems that the rogue…' said *señora* Blackstone, filling the cups – only two cups, Palmer noted – while the maid slipped away. 'That the rogue was stealing from us also.'

'My friend Hancock tells me neither of you attended the inquest.'

'I believe,' the woman reproached him, 'you wished to know about the history of this place.'

Palmer considered himself corrected but, at her invitation, he took his seat again and accepted the proffered oriental-patterned cup and saucer. She also sat, though Mr Blackstone remained standing. Awkward, for Palmer was forced to crane his neck in order to address his next question.

'A military man yourself, Mr Blackstone?'

'Had that honour, to be sure.'

There was no pride in the man's voice, however. No, suspicion – that's what Palmer heard.

'I only ask, Mr Blackstone, by way of understanding how one might aspire to be Master of such a worthy institution. You must have been highly recommended, I imagine.'

Palmer sipped at his tea, then instantly regretted his stupidity, recalling the effect of the previous visit's cordial. He found himself sniffing at the cup, for any hint of noxious ingredient.

'Marlborough House,' said *señora* Blackstone. Her husband coughed, a warning that she was dispensing too much information. But she was astute, Palmer knew. She would have calculated that he already knew their connection with the royal residence. 'My husband,' she went on, the hands performing their own dumb show again, 'had seen service there for a while. He was due to retire and discovered the vacancy here. His former employers were happy to provide a reference.'

Interesting, Palmer thought. Military pension. And his Master's salary – sixty pounds per annum, he knew. And his wife, the Matron, forty pounds more. A fair income.

'And Crick,' he said, specifically to Faustina. 'At Marlborough House also? He came with you from London, I think?'

He had not seen it so plainly before. Almost forty years had elapsed since she had met Edward Crick in Spain and here they were, still together, despite her marriage. How? Where?

'My wife were proprietor of a fine establishment in London. Crick, 'er servant.'

A fine establishment? Palmer thought about it. Then, Morrison's word, *puta*? Her own innuendo about being an old acquaintance of Morrison.

'A piece of good fortune, then, that besides the vacancy for Master and Matron, Crick was also able to find the position of porter open.'

'An accident, *señor*,' she said. 'The old porter.'

'I should have known,' Palmer smiled. 'And since he came back to Wrexham, Mr Williams the tailor says Crick has been a regular visitor at his premises. Renewing association with his old uniform. Blood among the threads – is that not what you told me?'

'Accidents 'appen,' said Frederick Blackstone. He rubbed unwittingly at that port wine stain around his neck. Perhaps, thought Palmer, not a birthmark after all. 'Happen to the careless, they does. Had one yourself, did you not? Bad fortune follows you, don't it?'

Almost the same words as Wilde had employed.

There was a knock at the door, and Hancock appeared. He apologised for the interruption, wondered whether Mr Palmer might be finished.

'It seems,' said Palmer, 'to be a curse we share, Mr Blackstone. The former porter. Then Wicklow. Not to mention – well, let me not take up more of your time.' He set down his cup and got to his feet. 'I very much appreciate the insight you have given me. But tell me,' he said, 'the branch of our armed forces which took you to Marlborough House?'

'My husband,' said *señora* Blackstone, 'served with Major Best Jervis.'

'Faustina!' her husband snapped at her, though it meant nothing to Palmer.

'I am sorry,' he said, 'but…'

'Best Jervis,' Hancock told him, from the doorway. 'Directorate of Military Intelligence.'

Chapter Twenty-One

'It sounds,' said George Reynolds, 'as though you have kicked the hornets' nest.'

He held the six playing cards close to his wire-rimmed spectacles. The rheumy eyes behind the thick lenses flickered back and forth between the hand and the scrimshaw cribbage board. They had been fortunate indeed to find an empty booth at the Bull's Head, for the Chislehurst coaching inn was already busy, noisy, filled with tobacco smoke. But at least they sold a decent botanic beer.

'I took it as a threat,' Palmer told him. *Accidents happen to the careless.* 'But yes, that is all the story I know, sir. You say Morrison received a note – from Ruthin?'

He had already discarded two cards – a queen and a nine – from his own hand for the old fellow's box. At least his luck seemed to have turned, though he had a lot of ground to make up. And at a penny a point...

'I know only that he had received intelligence. A colleague at the *North Wales Chronicle.* Some questionable liaison with the postmistress at Ruthin.'

'Wait, let me guess. About a local housekeeper. The Widow Wimpole?'

'I have no recollection of the name, but letters regularly dispatched on behalf of her employer.'

'To Marlborough House,' Palmer suggested.

'You are well-informed, Mr Palmer. And, in particular, to none other than His Royal Hellspawn. The Prince of Wastrels himself.'

There was bitterness in his satire as he set two cards of his own on top of the pair already laid face-down by Palmer. He ran a hand through the tumble of boyish waves and curls spilling across his left temple, though the hair purest white, like bleached parchment. He was clean-shaven as well which helped Reynolds fight against the outward evidence of his own autumn years.

'The housekeeper,' said Palmer. 'By the time he tracked her down, she would have been dismissed and gone to Wrexham. And if Morrison wished to speak with the Widow Wimpole about the letters from Mrs Cornwallis West to Prince Albert, he must surely have been pursuing the same line of enquiry during the rest of his time in Wrexham.'

Including, perhaps, the renewal of his acquaintance with Faustina Blackstone.

'Knowing Moggs,' said Reynolds, 'he would have encrypted his information. In the destroyed paperwork, we must assume.'

Palmer played the opening card in the pegging round.

'But letters to the Prince of Wales – for what purpose?'

'Moggs would most certainly,' said Reynolds, matching Palmer's six and scoring two points for the double, 'have suspected either blackmail or a demand for favours.'

'Blackmailing the prince? And – eighteen,' he declared, setting down a third six and pegging six points on the board for three of a kind.

'Mr Dicks and myself upbraided him most regularly for the jealous way in which he guarded his leads.'

Dicks had already featured in their conversation – the publisher and printer on the Strand where Reynolds would spend each Saturday editing the content before the paper was put to bed, and before returning each Sunday to his home in Herne Bay.

'And did he similarly guard the secret of his connection to *señora* Blackstone?'

'Now, with that one,' Reynolds smiled, 'I am familiar. Moggs had come across a story. It came out of the work we had done on the Mordaunt Affair. You see? The Prince of Wastrels again. But this time, a rumour of an establishment in which ladies of a certain sort...'

'Ladies of intrigue,' said Palmer, recalling his epiphany with Hancock's help. *Ladies Inn Tree G.*

'Indeed. Ladies both married and unmarried. So they might be introduced to gentlemen of means and there to consummate their respective libidinous desires. He had discovered it in *The Man of Pleasures*. Latest edition. You know it? No – and I should hope not. An illustrated pocketbook. Details of every den of iniquity in London.'

They had finished pegging. Time to tally the cards in their hands. Past sixty, Reynolds remained upright in his bearing, his outward attire meticulous, like an ancient tome which has been cherished while, within, the pages become increasingly frail. It seemed to Palmer you could almost hear the rustle of his innards each time he moved, and he carried with him the distinct odour of printer's ink. He was, indeed, the body and soul of literary excellence.

'And this place led him to Faustina Blackstone?' said Palmer, dealing the next hand, then sipping at his temperance beer.

'Yes and no, Mister Palmer. The pocketbook entry which interested him, from memory, went something like this. *Miss Faustina. Church Street, Soho. On the left hand, next door to the fruiterers.* But when he tracked down the place, they had moved. To Regent Street, near the Café Royal. It seemed your friend, *señora* Blackstone, had rather come up in the world.'

It fitted. Morrison's encryption translated. *Man Pleasures 1860 Miss F Café Royal.* And *puta*. He supposed she must have been. Yet it flew in the face of the workhouse Master's description of her premises as a fine establishment. The impression of a very different enterprise. But the connection between this establishment and Patsy Cornwallis West? Ladies of intrigue – could it be?

'And do you know what happened – when Morrison went there? The only thing which appears certain is that, at some point, she married Frederick Blackstone. A man who had served, it seems, with the Directorate of Military Intelligence. And, at some time, at Marlborough House.'

Reynolds smiled.

'Do you know the reason, Mr Palmer, I so enjoy a game of cribbage?'

'Because you always win, sir?'

Reynolds was now a full street, thirty points, ahead.

'It is because Dickens plainly has no idea of the way in which the game functions. Truly, how it functions. Its depths and complexities. You have read it, I assume? His *Old Curiosity Shop*?'

Of course, Palmer had read it. He recalled the scene. The Marchioness at her cribbage.

'Less than convincing?' he suggested.

'If Dick Swiveller had really taught her to play,' Reynolds scoffed, 'he either did not understand the rudiments himself, or the Marchioness had failed to attend him.'

Palmer's turn to smile, though he wondered whether he himself was being played. His own box, and he knew he had chosen badly.

'Military Intelligence,' Reynolds mused. 'Marlborough House. It seems that all our roads lead to Rome, sir. To Rome. With His Royal Hellspawn. Someday, Mr Palmer, that privileged fool will ascend to the throne and their whole corrupt dynasty shall generate itself afresh yet again.'

Dickens? Trollope? Thackeray? No, here was the true literary legend of the age. George William MacArthur Reynolds. And not literature alone. Palmer had never heard Marx or Engels speak but he had read transcripts of their speeches. He did not agree with all the doctrines they proclaimed but there was enough to chime with much of his Primitive Methodism. Yet, before Marx, before Engels, there had been George W.M. Reynolds. Palmer's father introduced him to Reynolds's writings alongside Thomas Paine's *Rights of Man* – for had Paine not also been a son of Thetford? Synergy.

'Did I hear you insult the Prince of Wales, sir?'

It was a fellow from the booth just behind them. A heavy-set man, ruddy-faced, dressed all in tweed. Something familiar about him. Reynolds peered up at the rogue but did not respond.

'Were you a younger man, sir,' said the fellow, 'I should see you horsewhipped.'

'And were you a brighter man, sir,' Reynolds finally replied, 'I might enlighten you about the questionable heritage of this royalty you admire so much.'

'Yet here you sit, bold as brass, on this fine thoroughfare we proudly named the Royal Parade.'

'The good folk of Chislehurst named it so because the French Imperial family now resides here. They reside here in exile, sir. Because the French, as a nation, know how to deal with their feudal monarchies.'

Palmer had harboured a foolish desire to actually see them. But yesterday's copy of Reynolds's own paper – Palmer's companion on the long journey there from Wrexham – confirmed that the now widowed Empress Eugénie and her son, the Prince Imperial, Louis Napoleon, were now in Florence, with plans to winter in Rome. But Palmer thought he might at least pay a visit to Napoleon the Third's tomb in the local Catholic church.

'I can do no better, sir,' Reynolds was saying, 'than recommend you try to purchase a copy of yesterday's *Reynolds's Newspaper*. A concise account of the Empress Eugénie's misguided legal proceedings against a certain French journal. Misguided because, in her efforts to prove that she is, indeed the daughter of a Spanish nobleman, she will simply succeed in strengthening the views of those who already believe her legitimate father to be none other than George Villiers, the late Earl of Clarendon.'

Well, he should know, Palmer mused. One of Reynolds's most successful penny dreadfuls, *The Empress Eugénie's Boudoir* – salacious goings-on in the court of Napoleon the Third. Though their adversary was unlikely to recognise this level of expertise.

'*Reynolds's*? That rag?' growled the man. 'And you are, I suppose, one of those who also defame the good lady's parentage?'

He had begun to attract five or six others, gathering at his back. A magnet as such fellows can often be. It reminded Palmer... Could it be? Earlier that morning, at Charing Cross. His journey yesterday had been tiresome. Twelve hours from Wrexham by way of Shrewsbury, Birmingham, Leamington and Oxford. From Paddington by cab to the Charing Cross Hotel where he had slept badly. And he had still been only half-awake when he went to catch the Chislehurst train. He believed he had been followed, but with the crowds, it was difficult to be certain. When he had turned, at times, to confront his pursuer – if, indeed, there had been such a person – he had caught mere glimpses of some elusive shade. Yet something about this rogue...

'Perhaps I might assist,' said Palmer, and took from his travelling bag the copy of yesterday's paper. 'You may have mine.'

The man regarded him with disdain.

'But you,' the fellow said. 'You the same? Another traitor? Well, you're certainly not too old for a good hidin'. An' what sort o' folk,' he shouted to the barmaid, 'are we servin' here these days, Louisa? Mr Wain?' He called to the gentleman behind the bar who, Palmer assumed, must be the proprietor. 'This one a-sippin' at his teetotaller's piss. An' this one without a whisker to 'is name. Sodomites, you reckon?'

Yes, there was a certain class of fool that associated a man's lack of facial hair with some flaw in his masculinity. But extending this absurd labelling to include abstinence from alcohol? Extraordinary.

'It is always pleasurable to engage in intelligent debate,' said Reynolds, 'but I have to tell you, sir, that I find your demeanour threatening and, unless you desist, I shall have no alternative but to send for a constable. Mine host!' His turn now to engage Mr Wain. 'If you please. This fellow has rather spoiled my game. Perhaps you would be good enough to send young Louisa to find a policeman?'

The man had clamped a hand on Palmer's shoulder and squeezed.

Palmer reached up, gripped the rogue's wrist, but he could not shift it. He tried to stand, and the fellow slammed him down again onto the bench. It brought on a fit of coughing.

Wain had emerged from behind the bar, a wooden cudgel – actually a belaying pin – in his hand.

'No need for that, sir,' he said. Palmer was unsure whether Wain's response was aimed at Reynolds's demand for a policeman or the rogue's assault upon them. 'This is a reputable establishment.' Wain pushed his way through those five or six spectators, leaned forward to murmur in the fellow's ear, spoke his words quietly but with supreme authority. 'You'll be leaving now, sir. And please do not trouble to return.'

The man loosened his grip on Palmer's shoulder, clenched his fists, turned to face Wain, and the muscles in his neck stiffened, seemed to swell.

It appeared certain they must fight, but Mr Wain never flinched. An entire half-minute went by while the rogue's supporters drifted away. The innkeeper, it seemed, had a certain reputation.

Finally, the man pushed past him, turned briefly to scowl first at Reynolds and then at Palmer. He lifted his right hand, the fist balled, but the index and little fingers extended, hooked slightly, and stabbing towards them.

A threat of some sort, Palmer was certain.

But at least he was gone, and Mr Wain offered them an apology. He had never known such a thing in the Bull's Head, not in all his years.

'It is Mr Reynolds, is it not?' he said. 'I thought so, sir. From your image on the cover of the old *Miscellany*. How I loved some of those stories. But I took the liberty of a dining room for you, gentlemen. Not the quietest place – next to the skittles alley, see. But private. None of this…'

He had no need to finish.

'That would be excellent, Mr Wain,' said Reynolds. 'And as for you, sir,' he turned to Palmer, glancing down at the cribbage board, 'thirty-six points. Three shillings. Dinner at your expense, I think. But at least we shall endeavour to solve your particular conundrum.'

Chapter Twenty-Two

Mr Wain's private room at the Bull's Head had a fine view out onto Chislehurst's Royal Parade. October, and autumn had come early, leaves of red and amber already blowing along from the common.

'That fellow,' said Reynolds, applying his spoon to the russet beef stew Louisa had brought them. 'Strutting about like John Bull himself.'

'John Bull...' repeated Palmer, though he was thinking more of Mr Low's son-in-law, the solicitor bearing the same name. There was a rumble, like distant thunder, followed by the crack of lightning-smitten timber. The skittles alley adjoining their chamber.

'Remarkable, is it not?' said Reynolds. 'That our nation should go about the world, garbed in Union Jack waistcoat, insisting we are more exceptional than all the rest, claiming our British values superior to those of everybody else when nobody has ever been able to explain to me precisely how *our* values differ from those of any decent citizen of France, or Russia – or Timbuktu, for that matter.'

Palmer reflected on the fact that he had never met a single person, decent or otherwise, from any of those places. But he supposed Reynolds must be correct. Love for one's family. Pride in one's country. Passion for liberty. Respect for the rule of law. Surely these must be universally valued in any civilised society. And yet...

'Russia,' he said, chewing on a piece of meat. 'I am not certain that Russia under the Czar stands firmly on the side of democracy, sir.'

He applied the clean white napkin to his mouth, spat a piece of gristle into its folds. His coat was draped about his shoulders, for the room was cool. Too late in the year for natural warmth, too early for the fires to be lit. The windows rattled in their frames and the green drapes flapped in the invading wind.

'Russia, my friend, is an insecure child which has not truly found its place in the world – and perhaps shall never do so. Pulled one way by its European mater and the other by a harsh Asian papa. But make no mistake, Mr Palmer, we may maintain the pretence of democracy here, yet we are governed almost entirely by the same levels of unaccountable and inherited privilege as you may find anywhere in St. Petersburg.'

Palmer pondered Reynolds's republicanism. His depictions of royalty in his novels were at times portrayals of the dissipated, the greedy, the depraved.

'Is monarchy truly such an abhorrent part of our system?' he said.

'The crowned miscreants and harlots of Europe's royal families? Surrounded and sustained by tier upon tier of aristocrats with their obscene wealth. Wealth possessed simply because they are descended from the whores of Charles the Second. Or because their forebears were professional plunderers and despoilers. Hereditary aristocracy which breeds our passion for privilege over merit. How does it feel, Mr Palmer, to be a subject rather than a citizen? For there, my friend, is the fly in their anointment.'

Reynolds beamed at his own jest.

'From my own limited studies, sir,' Palmer replied, 'I believe the election of the American Republic's presidents to be an equally imprecise way of selecting a head of state.'

A cheer and raucous laughter from the skittles alley as the ninepins were scattered once more.

'Of course,' said Reynolds. 'Yet that election itself has a symbolic value, does it not? The will of the people. In Britain, it is not the individual members of the royal family with whom I find fault but the system they represent. Inheritance? Inherited privilege? And our present monarch seems praised essentially for her neutrality in matters of politics.'

'Does that not run entirely contrary to your defence of democracy, Mr Reynolds? I do not disagree with you in that regard, either. But if we elect a government by the will of the people, should they not be allowed to govern without interference from an inherited crown?'

'A neat tautology, my friend.' He slammed his hand on the oak tabletop in delight. 'For what, then, is the point of a head of state who presides over such poverty and pain as we see among the working people of our great cities – and lifts not a finger from her gilded throne to help them?'

They spent a pleasurable hour finishing their food and debating the other causes so often espoused by Reynolds in his writings and editorials. Universal suffrage as a protection against despotism. The conviction that the cause of Chartism would one day prevail and bring an end to false systems and corrupt institutions. His pity for the white slaves of England in its factories and fields. The fiction of Britain's glorious constitution. The dream of a federal union of democrats, first in Britain, then across all Europe. The way that steam power had annihilated time and distance – and how much more those demons could be reduced should plans for the canals at Suez and Panama come to fruition. And his contempt for Disraeli's stance on the Eastern War, the Prime Minister's continuing advocacy for the Sublime Porte – for the Turkish oppressors of the Balkans – despite the plain wishes of the British people to the contrary.

A knock at the door. Louisa begging their pardon and wanting to know whether they might have room for some Cabinet Pudding and custard. Indeed, they did.

'Even Czar Alexander,' said Reynolds, when she had gone again, 'now obliged to allow Russian volunteers to go and fight in support of Serbia against the Turks. Just as the queen was obliged to allow Englishmen to fight alongside Garibaldi for a united Italy. Indeed, as the Crown was obliged to allow British volunteers to fight for Liberalism and Isabella in Spain.'

'Then monarchies may – at times, at least – become a force for good? Though strange that you should mention Spain. For my conundrum, as you named it, seems to have that country at its heart. And the Wrexham Union Workhouse, of course.'

'The workhouse,' Reynolds mused, 'to which the destitute, the aged and the friendless hasten to lay down their aching heads – and die!'

'You wrote that, did you not?' Palmer laughed. '*The Mysteries of London*, if my memory serves me well.'

More celebration from the ninepins alley.

'Indeed, Mr Palmer. But upon the Wrexham Union Workhouse, its Master and Matron, and your mysterious Edward Crick, I fear I am unable to shed light. Yet – another Edward. Like our Prince of Wastrels. Albert Edward. Did you know that his family and friends call him Bertie?'

Palmer did not.

Louisa arrived with their pudding, a jug of custard and fresh drinks. She asked whether they required anything further, then left them.

'Better with a white brandy sauce, is it not?' said Reynolds

'And the Prince of Wales fits within this puzzle, you believe?'

Between spoonsful of sponge and cherries, between Reynolds's encyclopaedic knowledge and the deciphering already completed by Palmer, they soon had a picture. *Cliff Den 61*. Nellie Clifden, with whom – according to that hint of a scandal he had discussed with Hancock – the Prince of Wales had enjoyed some liaison in that year, 1861. *M*? Lady Mordaunt, of course. The accusation of a relationship with Bertie. And, again, the year matched.

'The others?' said Reynolds. 'I recall another story. About His Royal Hellspawn and a paramour, Catherine Walters. A courtesan and noted horsewoman. It seems she and the prince shared a degree of – well, riding. Together.'

'Walters?' said Palmer. 'There is no name of that sort on Morrison's list.'

'Indeed there is, sir. For she was known in society circles by her pseudonym. Skittles, Mr Palmer. The world knew her as Skittles.'

Skit Less 62.

'So,' said Palmer, 'there *are* such things as coincidence after all. Skittles.' He laughed as, on cue, they heard the rumble of the ball from next door and the clatter of pins. 'And the rest?'

'Ladies of intrigue, Mr Palmer. *Tempest*? Lady Susan Vane-Tempest. *Be Nanny*? Giulia Beneni. *Jay Rome*? Unless I miss my guess, a certain Jennie Jerome.'

'If Morrison had Clifden and Mordaunt on his list – and the words *Young Wales* in his notes...'

'We can be reasonably sure he was investigating an entire series of adventures involving the Prince of Wastrels with those various ladies of intrigue. Perhaps more. A whole harem. And Bertie, only married these three years past? Three. Yet a string of coquettes before, during and after.'

'Including Patsy Cornwallis West,' said Palmer.

And there was a recollection. He saw the scene again. The procession down the exhibition hall's central aisle. The scarlet band of the Thirtieth Regiment playing *Men of Harlech*. Mrs Cornwallis West in her finely striped grey Regency coat. The contrasting flounces, the bustle, and the buttoned boots. The child skipping at her side. Patsy's languid eyes. They had been fixed on a place somewhere above and behind Palmer's head. Those marble busts which adorned the hall's columns. The sculpted likeness of His Royal Highness, the Prince of Wales.

'Morrison's death may, of course,' Reynolds sighed, 'simply have been an accident after all. Though, on the other hand, if it was known that this was the line of his investigation...'

'You said we could be *reasonably* certain. Yet you gave him the assignment, I had assumed,' said Palmer, and he ladled the last of the pudding and custard from his bowl.

'I did not *give him the assignment*, as you put it. But, indeed, I was generally aware that Moggs was working on a story which would show Bertie – His Royal Highness, Prince of Wales, next king of this Sceptr'd Isle, soon to be Emperor of India, and all the rest – to be a serial philanderer and a moral degenerate.'

'Do you not think, sir, that might have been just enough to get him killed?'

'Indubitably.'

'Then perhaps it is you, Mr Reynolds, who is culpable for his death.'

Reynolds appeared stricken, and Palmer instantly regretted his words.

'I mean...' he began. But Reynolds raised his own spoon, wagged the implement at him, a warning frown creasing the old fellow's face.

'No, Mr Palmer. No, sir. You are correct. Do you imagine I have not tortured myself with the same thought ever since I heard the news? In truth, I chose to believe it must indeed have been an accident. But now, with the rest of your strange tale…'

'Morrison's widow?'

'I will watch over her as best I am able, Mr Palmer. Widowed myself. Eighteen years gone, but not a day when I do not feel the agony of her loss.'

There! Palmer thought. The other reason. The skeleton in the closet. Marriage to Ettie? Surely better to live with a permanent modesty of loneliness than forever in the fear of that crippling tidal wave of grief, deprived of a lifelong companion. The thought of having to face such a catastrophe himself filled Palmer with a profound dread. The thought that being wed should inflict such a fate on dear Ettie was entirely intolerable.

Yet perhaps a chance to confront this confusion soon. For his most recent letter to her had included a reminder of the invitation they had received from Major Cornwallis West himself – the regatta upon the Menai Straits to mark Trafalgar Day. Indeed, now he came to think about it, the regatta might provide an opportunity to confront one or two other puzzles.

'My sympathies, Mr Reynolds,' he said. 'And I shall visit Mrs Morrison myself before I leave. I fear I owe her an apology.'

'The fire?'

'Her husband's lost papers, yes. But would you still publish – if I am able to piece together the rest of the puzzle?'

Louisa again, to collect their empty plates, to ask if they needed anything more, and to provide their bill. Four shillings each, and Palmer settled the account for both of them – the price of losing so badly at cribbage.

'If you do so, Mr Palmer – piece together the puzzle,' said Reynolds as they put on their coats, 'it would be a matter for the authorities. Yet I doubt they will dare to deal with it. Still, your duty to report any malfeasance – and in the event there is some prosecution, the newspaper's duty to publish, indeed.'

True to his word, Palmer persuaded the hansom cab's driver to stop and wait that evening on his way back to the station. He might have walked, since the Widow Morrison's cottage on Watts Lane would have provided a reasonable place to break the one-mile journey.

But it was raining again when he took his leave of Reynolds, who intended to travel home to Herne Bay the following morning. And, the wind blowing so hard, Palmer knew his brolly would provide little protection.

Still, he was satisfied he had learned all he might from Mr Reynolds. He had begun to thread together some of the remaining scraps of intelligence, and his visit to Mrs Morrison was less painful than he had imagined. Some tears, naturally, but she was generally pleased to see him and brushed aside his apology for the loss of the file. She offered him tea, which he declined, for the cab was waiting and the fare would be mounting. Though he did take advantage of her privy. An excess of botanic beer and he doubted there would be a gentlemen's convenience at the station. One's journeys had to be so carefully planned, though it was promised that last year's Public Health Act would lead to a flowering of public toilets all across the nation – albeit, according to an outraged Reynolds, principally only for gentlemen.

'How much?' he asked, when the cab had reached the bottom of the hill and halted in the rain-slashed light of the station building's lamp.

'Five shillings, if you please, guv'nor.'

Palmer objected, cited the regulated London cab fares – though it seemed the regulations did not apply this far outside the city, and then there was the wait to be considered. He was obliged to pay the thief. In any case, he needed to get out of this wind and wet.

He had no need of the ticket office in the platform's main brick-built structure, for he had his return ticket already. So, he hurried over the crossing to the opposite side. There were so far no other passengers for the one-hour journey back to London. Nobody but the station master, some distance away, loading packages onto his trolley.

Palmer glanced at his pocket watch, his other hand holding the derby to his head. The waiting room on this platform was locked, and while there was shelter from the rain, at least, beneath the station's canopy, the wind was relentless. But the northern end of the wooden building on this side of the tracks offered sanctuary, and he pressed himself against the cream-painted clapboards. Beyond the passing line to his left, beyond a row of thrashing saplings, trucks in the goods siding glistened in the gathering darkness. A miserable fifteen minutes to wait for the train. Cold. Damp. His cough. The last thing he needed was to catch another chill.

Time passed slowly, his thoughts plagued by those links they had made, himself and Reynolds, but each time he thought he might be making sense of it all, the whole house of cards came tumbling down. All those unanswered questions. Blackstone, an agent? His service with Military Intelligence? Marlborough House? Edward Crick and *señora* Blackstone? The workhouse? Patsy Cornwallis West?

The monotony and frustration relieved at last by the ringing of a bell from the opposite platform and the clang of an unseen semaphore signal carried on the wind, followed a few minutes later by the arrival of the train from London on the "down" line. It sidled into the station, all coal smoke and billowing steam, silhouetted passengers preparing to descend or peering through rain-streaked windows at nameboards, checking whereabouts they might be on their journey southwards. A first-class coupé saloon. Two second-class carriages. One third-class. A single carriage truck with a landau loaded aboard. Behind, a horsebox – with its own compartment for a groom. Finally, the brake van with a birdcage roof. A five minute halt, before the whistle, the hiss of steam once more, the anvil clash of the couplings, and the slow *chug, chug, chug* as it gathered pace.

It had barely left when the whole process began afresh – his own London-bound train. He held his hat tight upon his head as he risked a glance around the corner to watch its approach.

Palmer was about to venture forth of his own volition when he felt himself propelled forward. It took a moment to realise…

A hand pressed against his shoulder. Another gripping the collar of his coat, lifting him onto the tips of his toes.

He glanced to his right.

'Help!' he yelled. Or, rather, he *tried* to yell. 'Help!'

The station master was there, but twenty yards away, busy with his flag and his parcels trolley. But the wind carried away whatever might be left of Palmer's ineffectual cry for assistance. And the engine was coming closer. Ever closer. A noisy monster, hungry for his blood.

He tried to turn his head, caught the whiff of rum on the man's breath, tobacco on the tweed jacket.

'Why?' Palmer shouted. 'No...'

Florid, stubbled cheeks. The same rogue – from the Bull's Head?

Their feet became entangled. Palmer's assailant stumbled, released his collar. Released his shoulder as well.

Now free, Palmer tried to stop himself, but the wretch had come up ahead of him. Palmer stabbed at him with the rain napper, as the wind caught at his derby, sent it spinning along the platform.

The fellow had seized hold of Palmer's umbrella, one hand gripping the tip, the other further along, fingers folded about the black fabric. The man heaved at the thing, trying to swing Palmer around, past him, to the platform's edge and over, into the path of the train – and Palmer had not the wit to simply let go.

Chapter Twenty-Three

'So, Mr Palmer,' said Inspector Wilde, 'you involved yourself in a brawl in a public house and the fellow chose to continue his vendetta when you took yourself off to the station. Is that not correct?'

Palmer sneezed, blew his nose into his kerchief. His voice was hoarse. The laryngitis.

'No, indeed it is not. I did not involve myself in anything of the sort. And the wretch plainly followed me to Chislehurst all the way from Charing Cross. Does that not speak of an assassin, rather than some alehouse blackguard?'

'And how exactly would this so-called assassin have known you would be at Charing Cross in the first place, sir?'

'Well…'

Palmer flapped his arms in exasperation, for he had no answer, and the question had plagued him throughout his return journey to Wrexham.

His interrogator tapped the stem of his pipe against teeth beginning to yellow through too many years chewing upon the briar.

'You opened the brolly,' said the inspector, and took the pipe from his mouth, rubbed his knuckles into the whiskers on his cheeks. There was incredulity in his voice.

'I have told you this,' Palmer groaned. 'Three times now. Four?'

'Rather than merely releasing it?'

'I know it makes little sense in the cold light of day,' Palmer croaked. 'But I had already lost my hat. And the weather… You must believe me. I bore this fellow no ill will. Except, of course – yet I still have no idea why I am here. Of all places, here!'

A cell in the Bridewell. Not even Wilde's office. He had been directed straight to this whitewashed cell.

'Tell me again, sir. The sequence of events, if you please.'

'Very well! I opened the umbrella. And the wind – well, the wind did the rest, I think. The fellow yelled. And he fell. There was a scream. A terrible scream. I saw his hand... And then the engine rolled past. Came to a halt further along the platform. I could not move. How long? I cannot recall. But then there was the station master. Shouting at me to get aboard. It took a long time – to make him understand.'

But, in the end, he had understood. For where the wheels of the tender then rested upon the rails, down in that gap between the sleepers and the platform, resting upon the dark ballast, was a single amputated foot. After that? It was all very much a blur. The engine driver – or perhaps it had been the fireman – persuaded to climb down and investigate. To confirm the nightmare.

It could so easily have been me, thought Palmer. And he shivered. The recollection. The fever, as well.

Afterwards, the delay. The rain.

'Soaked to the skin,' said Palmer. 'Before they finally unlocked the waiting room. A policeman came. Took a statement. It must have been an hour before another train arrived. They brought it up on the passing line and transferred all the passengers. I asked whether I could ride in the brake van. There would have been questions, would there not? From the curious. The rumour-mongers. I could not face them.'

An hour to London, in those wet clothes. A miserable night at the Charing Cross Hotel.

'And you were in Chislehurst for what purpose, Mr Palmer?'

'No! First, tell me why I am here.'

'A gentleman from London, sir. Wishes to speak with you. Sir Patrick Something-or-Other. My superiors have made it clear. You're to be detained until he gets here.'

'And when, pray, might that be?'

Wilde shrugged his shoulders.

'Then I should like to speak with Deputy Chief Constable Bradshaw in person, Inspector. I am the victim here, not the perpetrator. And why, in Heaven's name, should somebody from London need to speak with me about this?'

But he thought, perhaps, he knew the reason. The very same as the purpose of his visit to Chislehurst.

'Besides,' he said, 'it was more than a week ago. And when might this Sir Patrick get here? Who is the fellow? Why detained? Why?'

He stared frantically around the cell. Make a run for it? He imagined himself hunted down by dogs somewhere in the wilds of North Wales.

Wilde took a notebook from his pocket and turned the pages.

'Sir Patrick – MacDougall, sir. And I've not been given a date for his visit.'

'But on what charge am I to be imprisoned, Inspector?'

'Imprisoned, Mr Palmer?' Wilde was confused, then smiled. 'Why, sir, you misunderstand. My office – being painted, at last. Instructions were simply that you should be detained here in Wrexham – rather than leaving for, say, Manchester or some other place. So that Sir Patrick knows how to find you, like. There'll need to be an inquest, of course. An' you'll be called as a witness, naturally. But after Sir Patrick speaks with you, I expect.'

But Palmer still felt like a felon released from custody when he left the Bridewell. He headed down Pen-y-Bryn and stopped briefly at the Horns Bridge, gazed down into the waters of the Gwenfro and wondered what Morrison would have made of it all.

Sir Patrick MacDougall – whoever he might be – coming all the way from London to interview him about some rogue? Yet a rogue who had apparently tried to kill him. Why? Surely not just the incident at the Bull's Head. Though he had wired Reynolds in any case. It had seemed a proper precaution. After all…

He coughed and wheezed all the way up Town Hill and made a stop on the High Street – at Mr Scotcher's where he knew the surgeon dentist Mr Maurice sometimes practised. He was certain that one of his lower teeth had been loosened in the scuffle. It hurt like the very devil. But Maurice seemingly had business elsewhere and Palmer scribbled down the days, listed upon a flyer in the stairwell, when the fellow might be in Wrexham.

Next, to Mucklestone's in the arcade, for yet another new hat. The replacement derby he had purchased in such haste near Charing

Cross had, according to Bethan Thomas, sat too small upon his head – like a pustule, she claimed.

From there to the pharmaceutical chemist near the Museum to purchase another package of Voice Lozenges, manufactured on the premises by the pharmacist himself and, Palmer had found, highly efficacious in soothing his throat, uvula and tonsils. He also contemplated the prominent advertisement for Joy's Cigarettes – *Cigares de Joy* – which promised such instant relief from affliction by asthma, wheezing and winter coughs. But, in the end, he settled for the lozenges alone.

Finally, to the Museum itself.

'Well?' said Bethan when they were alone, the last of the present batch of exhibition visitors safely on their way to the main hall or for refreshments. 'What did he want, then? That foreigner? Had to tell him the whole story, did you? *Duw Annwyl.*'

He had, of course, made the mistake of reciting the Chislehurst tale to her – well, as much of the tale as he felt might be discreet.

'Warned you, I did,' she said, yet again, as she had done so many times in the days since his return. 'London, see. Sodom and Gomorrah, like. Fool, you are. Bad as that friend of yours. Him with the lions.'

Palmer felt the tickle in his sinuses, the warning signs of another sneeze, dragged the handkerchief from his pocket just in time to contain the beast. But Hancock. Yes, he must track down Hancock and share all this with him.

'And the rest?' Bethan hobbled a couple of steps away from him as though he were diseased, a lazar. She peered up at him, head tilted to one side.

'Rest?' he replied.

'Know what I mean, you do. Blackstone at the workhouse. The woman. Another foreigner, she is. All those stories. Filth, see.'

She opened one of the cabinets, adjusted the position of an Etruscan plate.

'No,' he said. 'That part – the Board of Guardians investigated. No substance, apparently.'

'Board of Guardians?' Bethan snorted, and closed the cabinet once more. 'Be the worst, they would. An' what about *Pat Sea*, then?' It was almost coy.

Palmer tidied the diminishing stack of exhibition catalogues on the desk. Time to order a fresh supply, though they had not gone as quickly as he would have hoped.

'You know?'

'Worked it out, I did. Not hard. Thought about Rose Wimpole. Asked a few questions – two and two, like. Mrs High-and-Mighty Cornwallis West.'

'Bethan,' he said. 'Better keep that to yourself.'

'Not denying it, then? One of *those* women? And you going there again, like? The workhouse, is it?'

Indeed, it was. But when he got there, later that same afternoon, he found Faustina Blackstone alone – well, alone apart from the two hundred and thirty inmates and two dozen attendants.

'You must pardon me, *señora*.' He stood in the Master's Parlour, his new hat in one hand, kerchief in the other. 'But I needed to speak with your husband. Or with Mr Crick?'

'My husband is not here.' The hand gestures were dismissive, irritated. 'He has business. Somewhere else. And Eduardo has gone with him. But perhaps you knew. Before you came.'

The sibilance in her accented words was serpentine. Temptation. It brought back thoughts of Rose Wimpole yet again. A nest of vipers.

'Indeed, madam, I did not.'

'Yet you seem drawn here, *señor*. And what other purpose could you have for so many questions?'

If she thought to act the temptress, she had counted without the monastic effects which the common cold might inflict upon a fellow. Still, for her age… Another *mantilla*, but today her whole attire spoke of Spain. A black-trimmed bolero vest of red cloth, over a blouse of scarlet silk. Skirts of charcoal grey.

'Curiosity, *señora*,' he said, and wiped his nose, as though to dismiss her advances. 'Simple curiosity. We established during my previous visit that your husband was an agent of the Crown. The Directorate of Military Intelligence? And that he served for a while at Marlborough House. I simply wondered…'

'Will you not take a seat, at least? Perhaps some…'

She reached for the hand bell.

'I thank you, madam,' he said. It was more curt than he had intended. 'But my time is short. And it was truly your husband with whom I wished to speak. About letters. Sent to Marlborough House from – well, from Ruthin. Close to here. And just before you and your husband were fortunate enough to find yourself in Wrexham as well.'

'*Vale,*' she said. Very well. A slight shrug of her resignation. 'Yet I hope you will forgive me if I sit?'

'Of course,' he replied, and instantly regretted not having accepted her invitation himself. He was now left standing like some supplicant at a royal reception.

'And when you speak of good fortune?' she went on, 'Then you must surely know about the establishment I ran in London also. Is that not what draws you here? Either repugnance – or, perhaps, attraction.' She laughed, then reached to the table by her side, picked up a small and beautiful damascene box, all black and gold tracery. 'But if you must stand, *señor* Palmer, there is one piece of hospitality you may not refuse.' She held out the box. 'Your favourite blend, I think. Wilsons, was it not? I now have my own supply.'

Indeed, he could not refuse. Not *Cigares de Joy*, perhaps, but the snuff certainly helped to clear his nasal passages.

'But let me tell you a story.' She took back the box, her own pinch of the Wilsons. 'About a girl,' she said, raising her proud head so she could stare him in the eye. 'A girl and the battle at Andoain. How she followed the soldier she loved to that place. How she found him. How they had hurt him, *los carlistas.*'

'Religious fanatics, are they not?'

'Men of God, *señor*? I saw our own side do some wicked things. In war it is the devil who drives. But I never saw such things as the *carlistas* did after Andoain.'

He was uncertain why she should now be telling him this tale, but he considered it might be relevant.

'Perhaps I will sit for a moment, after all,' said Palmer. 'Would you mind?' He gestured towards the brown leather armchair behind him. 'Wicked things, you say.' He unbuttoned his jacket, settled himself on the creaking cowhide. 'To you also?'

'To me also. Before I found Eduardo. No longer a man. Not in his body. Not in his head. But at least we were alive. Though sometimes I think the lucky ones were those who died. Somehow, I got him back to San Sebastián. Then here, to England. And how do you think a girl like me, after Andoain – after how they misused me – might survive in a place like London?'

'Crick returned here to Wrexham – for a while, at least?'

'A while. But I needed him. To protect me, *señor.*'

Palmer glanced again at the framed pencil sketch of her in her youth. Something about it.

'You never had the chance to answer my question – last time I was here. Did Eduardo draw the picture?'

She turned her head so she could see it also.

'He had a gift, I think,' she replied. 'But that all vanished as well – after Andoain. Now, there are *pesadillas.* How do you say? Nightmares?' Palmer nodded. 'Yes, nightmares,' she went on. 'He sees pictures. And they make nightmares for him. Sometimes the nightmares drive him.'

'Drive him – to what, I wonder? And does he see pictures in Mr Williams's coverlet too? Blood among the threads, you told me. Do *they* drive him?'

Faustina Blackstone did not reply. She simply picked at the arm of the chair with her carefully manicured red-tinted nails.

'He protected you, in London,' said Palmer. 'And eventually, your own establishment. Regent Street. Impressive.'

He protected you, Palmer mused. And now perhaps you protect him. You met Morrison. But did you, I wonder, later entice the poor fellow to the Horns Bridge? Did you – or your husband – arrange for Crick to lay in wait for him?

Palmer wanted to confront her with the accusations. The possibilities splattered across his mind like hailstones hammering upon the surface of a lake. But...

'I had some fortune,' she smiled, 'as well as some pain.'

'And it was there you met your husband-to-be? He knew about Eduardo, I suppose?'

She dropped her gaze, raised a hand to her forehead, covered her face. It must, Palmer imagined, be the strangest of *ménages à trois*.

'He knew,' she whispered.

'Does he know now? About the nightmares which drive Edward Crick? About the things they have driven him to do?'

'I have no idea what you mean.'

'Your husband was, by then...' He broke off long enough to blow his nose, a foghorn clarion note piercing the room's fog of deceit. 'At Marlborough House. But not visiting your establishment as a client, I am guessing. A bodyguard – to some prominent gentleman, perhaps. And might he still be fulfilling that duty, I wonder?'

He tucked the kerchief back in his pocket, and she offered to at least send for some tea – an infusion of peppermint and soothing herbs.

'I thank you, ma'am, but no.' He recalled once more the first occasion when he had taken refreshments there. 'I simply wish to establish the facts.'

'You sound like *señor* Morrison, *guapo*. You see mystery where no mystery exists.'

Guapo? What did that mean?

'You are right, *señora*. There is no mystery. Not about the letters. Letters from a certain lady in Ruthin to Marlborough House. To a person of importance. Letters which perhaps implied a lack of discretion. Or worse. Threats even. And your husband dispatched here to keep the situation under control. To make sure the indiscretion might not grow any worse.'

Her dark eyes flashed fire at him, and Palmer swore he could physically feel the flame's impact. Like a dangerous jolt of electricity. Her fingers no longer picked at the leather of her chair but, rather, gripped the rolled arm fronts, her knuckles white.

'And you?' she said. 'You have no part in this. Why? A man like you. These questions.'

'A part – in what, precisely?'

She shook her head, waved a gloved hand as though to dismiss him. He stood, began fastening his coat, knowing the interview was at an end.

'And where, precisely, might your husband be? Will he return later?'

'He has business. Along the coast. And I think we have said too much, *señor*. I am tired now.'

She fell silent and Palmer consulted his watch. It had stopped again, as it had already done since Chislehurst station. He took his leave as politely as he was able, though she entirely ignored his departure and rang for the child-like maid to escort him to the entrance hall.

He made his way back into town. Not a bad day for mid-October and he hoped it would hold fine for the weekend. So, his first stop? Mr Leadbeater's new shop on Chester Street. Leadbeater had made several fine contributions towards the collection of timepieces within the exhibition. Besides, was he not distinguished by holding the onerous responsibility for ensuring that clocks of St. Giles, of the Town Hall and of the Guildhall all told the same time? A most trustworthy fellow, therefore, to handle Palmer's necessary repair.

On Chester Street once more, he passed the engine house for the Prince of Wales Volunteer Fire Brigade – named, Mr Low had once proudly reminded him, in honour of His Royal Highness immediately following the prince's marriage. But now? Palmer could not help thinking that, in his own mind, the brigade's name was tarnished by the prince's immoral liaisons with so many of those ladies of intrigue listed by Reynolds. So many. Before, during and after his marital vows. Including Patsy Cornwallis West.

Back at the exhibition, he found the museum already closed, Bethan having taken herself off to the afternoon's recital. Mr Best, guest organist again, returned from Liverpool. A medley of sea songs. *A Life on the Ocean Wave.*

Palmer stopped to listen for a few minutes. All very appropriate. For, tomorrow, Friday, Ettie would be with him again. The invitation they had received from Major Cornwallis West.

'A regatta, of all things,' the major had told him. 'Along the Menai Straits to mark Trafalgar Day. You must join us, Palmer. Yourself and...?'

Ettie. How delightful it would be to see her again. Though there was a problem, of course. Should he tell her about the death at Chislehurst – or should he not? And there was the nagging new conundrum. The fellow who had died under the train wheels. Who had he been? Why try to kill Palmer? And how had he been able to follow Palmer from London? Or, rather, *had* he followed him – or was that simply Palmer's imagination again?

He wandered through into the industrial annexe. Mr Best was now teasing out the opening of Mendelssohn's *Hebrides* overture and Palmer stood in front of Mr Williams's coverlet, trying to digest the images, as he had also done so many times already. The serpent. The horned deer with the black-winged creature upon its back. The galloping horse. The viaduct at Cefn Mawr where Wicklow had hanged himself – or been hanged. Adam naming the beasts – and the image's reminder of the Tiger Inn where Maudie Meadows had been found dead.

He thought about the question from Faustina Blackstone. Why? A man like him. These questions. Blood among the threads. But his eye was drawn to the top left-hand corner of the patchwork. The suspension bridge. On the Menai Straits. And a chill shivered his spine.

Chapter Twenty-Four

'I know there is a link,' he told Ettie. 'And we should have come yesterday – if only you had not been so late.'

Would he be in time? Trepidation presently his constant companion. But in time for what, precisely? He was still unsure.

'My fault?' she said, though trying to keep her voice low, for they were not alone.

The L&NWR excursion train had pulled out of Wrexham's General Station long before dawn, at half-past five, and was scheduled to arrive in Menai Bridge at nine. Quite a haul, but at least the passengers were not required to make any changes and, for those blessed by Mr Low's beneficence – he had procured all of the available first-class tickets – there was this saloon coupé. Its very own water closet. Comfortably upholstered buttoned seats and banquettes. Lace curtains. Even a small stove to keep out the autumnal chill and allow them all to doff coats and hats, scarfs and gloves – for they had all been warned it would be cold upon the waters. But the carriage rather resembled a private family lounge. Pleasantly companionable but lacking privacy.

'I believe this may be a matter of life and death,' he whispered, glancing around at their fellow-travellers. A dozen or so, some of the ladies dozing, the carriage lamps dimmed, and a crepuscular stillness at their first stop, in Chester.

Then the stillness broken as the carriage door was thrown open.

'There shall be tea!' cried Richard Low, clambering aboard and bearing a blackened kettle. 'The fireman was a true diamond.'

'Life and death,' Ettie snapped at Palmer. 'As you told me last night, though you did not trouble to explain.'

In truth, she had been in no mood to listen. Her journey from Manchester had been disagreeable and, by the time he met her on the platform, Palmer had whipped himself into a state of agitation. She had been delivered to the hotel with barely a word passed between them. Met him again this morning still moderately mute.

'And where there is tea,' said Mary Louisa, eldest of Mr Low's daughters, and rousing herself with a yawn from her chair, 'there shall be breakfast.'

At her feet was one of the two large hampers provided to the party on its departure in the early hours from Roseneath House by Harriet the kitchen maid, and the grumbling cook, Charlotte.

'Allow me to assist, my dear.' Mary Louisa's husband, the parsimonious solicitor, John Bull, opening the basket and producing a bone china teapot.

'I considered it more apposite,' said Palmer, 'to wait until we were each somewhat rested.' He wanted to say, "in a better temper", but considered it might have been provocative. 'More – conversational,' he pressed on. 'But it was only when I saw the coverlet. Along the coast, she said – *señora* Blackstone. Her husband had work. Along the coast.'

'Perhaps, Neo, you should begin at the beginning.'

He would have done so had they not almost been hurled from their places. The ferrous furore of the couplings. The guttering of flames in the lamps. The screech of wheels as the carriages were thrust backwards by the new engine, now connected to haul them the rest of the way.

'Efficiency,' said Richard Low, glancing at his watch and steadying himself as they were now almost immediately jolted forward, the train pulling out towards their destination. 'And your arm, Mister Palmer. All healed now. No further problem with the Cauda Equina.'

He spoke in the manner of surgeons everywhere. Not enquiries. Simple statements of fact which brooked neither contradiction nor further complaint.

'A twinge now and again,' Palmer replied. 'When the weather is damp. But a pity, sir, that your father has not been able to join us.'

He reached for his own watch, to check that they were, indeed, running according to schedule. But, of course, the silver Hunter was now in surgical care as well, with Leadbeater.

'Papa?' murmured Richard Low's red-locked sister, Alison, still half-asleep. 'Despondent, Mister Palmer. But some engagement he could not postpone.'

For the next fifteen minutes or so, the family members fussed with the teapot, the boiled eggs, the slices of wholegrain bread wrapped in their waxed paper, the pots of fruit preserve and fresh butter. Palmer and Esther were treated like honoured guests. Tea was indeed served, and though it was still dark, Palmer calculated they had crossed over into Flintshire, though still following the upper course of the River Dee towards its eventual estuary.

'I have been studying the area,' he said to her, at last. 'Somewhere over there?' He pointed vaguely through the window next to them, the right-hand side of the carriage. 'Sealand. If we could catch sight of it, one would observe how flat it might be. For it was once entirely enclosed by the sea itself.'

'You may not distract me so easily, Neo. What do you take me for?'

He bit into his sandwich of raspberry jam. And winced. The tooth still bothered him, though his cold seemed somewhat better today.

Palmer glanced cautiously towards the members of the family, mostly now gathered at the opposite window, John Bull loudly admiring the virtues of the distant mountains above the Vale of Clwyd, more darkly outlined against the starlit sky and the highest of them, Moel Fammau, with a column upon its summit, just visible as a dim silhouette. Alison and Mary Louisa, meanwhile, were busy tidying away the remains of the picnic.

'Very well,' he said. 'I travelled to London, as you know. Well, to Chislehurst, in truth. To meet Reynolds.'

'And what manner of man might he be? In real life?'

Palmer smiled. The first time he had been able to do so for several days. The anxiety, he supposed. But at least he was now on his way. Riding, he believed, to... To what? Some gallant rescue? He raised his hands in a gesture which embraced the whole carriage.

'He is a mighty advocate for the power of steam,' he said. 'Trains. Boats, as well. Ships. But he is also, I fear, a revolutionary. Can you imagine? One of his older sons named Kossuth Mazzini. Another Ledru Rollin. Ledru Rollin Reynolds.'

She gave him a puzzled look and shook her head. He explained. Lajos Kossuth, the Hungarian who had fought so hard for independence from Austria. Mazzini, the Italian patriot. And Alexandre Ledru-Rollin, one of the leaders of the French Revolution in 'Forty-Eight. Reynolds had known each of them.

'And a passionate hatred,' Palmer concluded, 'for the principle of monarchy.'

'Then the Government must fear him.' Ettie lifted the final corner of her own sandwich from the serviette in her lap and popped it between her lips.

Of course, thought Palmer. How stupid! Reynolds would be under observation, surely. Like the Fenians. His movements, perhaps even the details of his diary, sure to be known. To Scotland Yard? To Military Intelligence? If so, they would have known about their planned meeting. And thus, the fellow in Chislehurst…

'Listen, my dear.' He set a hand upon her arm. 'You must not be alarmed. But there was an incident.'

He quietly and quickly explained the details, suffered her to stifle the gasp of horror when he came to the end of his tale.

'You think the rogue was some form of agent?'

Very possibly, but he had no chance to confirm her fear. First light, and they were passing at low speed through another station – Mostyn, read the name board. There were the lights of some very fine houses piercing the gloom on the landward side of the town. On the other, where the ground could now just be seen, sloping gently for a long way down towards the river, a flickering line of other lights from the distant Wirral peninsula, some miles away, on the farther margent of the Dee's glimmering navigation channel and mudbanks.

'And Mr Palmer,' said Richard Low. 'Do you have the details? The precise itinerary for the day?'

Palmer lifted his coat from the banquette and felt in the pocket for the *Advertiser*'s article.

'The competition regatta, early in the afternoon,' he began. 'One o'clock onwards...'

'Yes, but the parade of sail itself, sir. Shall we be on time?'

Palmer experienced another tremor of disquiet. He certainly hoped so. But yes, worth checking. He ran his finger down the list of competitions scheduled for later in the day, details provided by the Royal Welsh Yacht Club. Races for sailing boats with keels not exceeding twenty-five feet; for seventeen-footers; for rowing boat teams – gigs with four oars, and yacht tenders of the same capacity. And then, in a separate piece...

'Here,' said Palmer. 'A parade of sail and steam. *"To depart in orderly fashion from Menai Bridge and passing through the Swellies during High Water Slack and then returning. The parade to commence promptly, thirty minutes before HWS, a quarter-hour before eleven o' clock."* Should we arrive at Menai Bridge in a timely fashion, all should be perfectly fine.'

'There, you rascals,' Richard Low shouted to his youngest siblings, the girls all frills and flounces, both just weeks away from needing to be in ankle-length skirts. And the boy, a sailor suit, recently turned fourteen. 'You shall have your adventure, after all.'

As it became marginally lighter, he began to point out interesting features in the landscape, which triggered some sort of argument with Alison's husband, the physician, Doctor Davies. A dispute about the Hilbre Islands at the very mouth of the Dee, the origins of the name. Anglo-Saxon or Norse? Good-natured, but loud enough to allow Palmer to begin his explanation.

'The names,' he murmured, 'on Morrison's paper. He was pursuing a story about the involvement of... HRH.' He mouthed the letters rather than speaking them aloud. 'You understand?'

'Of course, Neo,' she hissed. 'Involvement with...?'

'Certain ladies of intrigue. A whole harem of them. And they seemingly included...' He looked up to make sure they were not overheard. 'Our very own Mrs Cornwallis West. Known to her closest friends as – Patsy.'

'And poor Mr Morrison – he came to Wrexham to investigate?'

There was a lighthouse, far away to the right. Point of Ayr, Palmer supposed.

'He initially, we think, came to speak with Rose Wimpole. But, of course, by the time he arrived, Widow Wimpole was dead. The snake – accident or otherwise – put an end to that ambition. By some curious coincidence – or not – an agent from the Directorate of Military Intelligence, once responsible for the protection of... HRH.' He mouthed the letters again. 'This agent happens to now be Master of the Wrexham workhouse. Frederick Blackstone. We know that the major's wife had been in correspondence with the Prince. Making a nuisance of herself in some way. If so, it seems logical that Blackstone might have been required to contain the situation.'

'To arrange – accidents?'

'There is another fellow at the workhouse – Edward Crick. A former soldier. And you remember how you saw the connection? Mr Williams's beautiful coverlet and the deaths?'

'A connection to Crick?'

'*Señora* Blackstone insists that the images drive Crick to – well, to certain nightmare visions. And the visions cause him... I am not entirely certain. Blood among the threads, she says. I believe that Blackstone uses Crick to do his bidding.'

'Then the fellow perhaps deserves our sympathy, does he not?' said Ettie. Dear girl.

'Perhaps. Yet there are victims, all the same. Those who knew about the affair, like Rose Wimpole and then Morrison. Two attempts, I now believe, upon my own life. And those involved in helping to conceal it. Wicklow and the maid, Maudie Meadows – from the hotel.'

'That young girl?'

'Indeed. Another loose end. To be... Yet it did not seem proper to write you about her death.'

But there the explanation had to stop, for the solicitor, John Bull, had come to sit alongside them. He wanted to know whether they had done much sailing, and they were forced to endure a lecture about the hazards inherent in navigating the Swellies. The mile-long stretch of turbulent waters between the Menai Suspension Bridge and the Britannia Railway Bridge. The narrowest part of the Menai Straits separating Anglesey from the mainland. The point where strong tidal currents around the island from east and west clashed together.

Deadly eddies and whirlpool devils. About how the recent removal of some of the dangerous rocks of the apparent channel had, in reality, made the passage even more difficult. Surely, the most treacherous single mile of navigation in the world, Bull claimed.

'And yet,' said Palmer, reaching for his snuff box, 'did Lord Nelson himself not sail an entire frigate through that same stretch? Is that not, in part, the point of today's excursion, sir?'

The solicitor replied with a reminder of Nelson's claim that a man who could navigate through the whole length of the Menai Straits might sail anywhere upon the seven seas. And Palmer wondered whether somehow he might himself acquire the gift of being able to navigate through his own labyrinth of mysteries. But he was now bored and, in the way of such things, his disinterest alchemically transmuted itself to disquiet, a certain dread about how this day might end. And he was grateful when the train made its second and only other stop.

Abergele. A quarter before eight o'clock. The hiss of steam. The guard upon the platform. The slamming of doors as he left each carriage, their own last in the line. He clambered aboard to extinguish the lights and Richard Low asked whether they might trouble the fireman for more water.

'Need to be quick though, see,' the guard told him. 'Only here five minutes, like.'

The surgeon scrambled for his kettle and jumped from the coach. Some of the others also detrained, simply to stretch their legs and, thankfully, John Bull among them.

'But now?' said Ettie. 'If you are correct – and it is a monstrous supposition, Neo – what does it all mean? If these accidents continue to occur...'

'It means, my dear, that their attempts to conceal the scandal are less than efficacious.'

'Is that not because you keep picking at them?'

Accusatory. Not for the first time, he thought there might be justification. Culpable. How much *was* he directly culpable for all this? He stared out of the window. Abergele. A name of infamous notoriety. Only eight years since the country's worst rail disaster. He could almost hear the explosion. The screams. See the yellow flames. Smell the sickly stench of burning flesh. Runaway wagons loaded with paraffin careering into the path of the Irish Mail train and its passenger coaches. Thirty-three dead, many charred beyond recognition. There was an echo of his first arrival in Wrexham. The journey with Morrison. Their discussion about that other disaster, on the Dee Bridge.

'Perhaps,' he said, finally. 'But Reynolds presented another possibility. That the letters from Mrs Cornwallis West to you-know-who might still be winging their way to Marlborough House. Amorous demands? Threats? Simple *billets doux*?'

'Good gracious. The girl. You remember, Neo? When you told me about the opening of the exhibition. About how you first saw the major's wife. You said there was a little girl swinging on her arm. Do you think...?'

'I have to admit that the same thought... But no, there seems no doubt that the children are, indeed, the major's. All the same, Reynolds suggested to me that if Patsy is still being troublesome — well, there was then *señora* Blackstone's explanation that her husband, and Crick, as well, have business along the coast. Work, she said. Her exact word. This very week. And I began to think, what if...?'

The family was back on board, Richard Low with another successfully procured supply of boiling water. And the remaining hour to their final stop allowed no opportunity for further speculation. Simply more anxiety on Palmer's part.

The train passed through the narrow valley south of Orme's Head and the carriage was plunged into darkness, into deafening cacophony, as they traversed through the iron tube bridge across the Conway River. In the open once more, and rubbing at their ears, everybody marvelled at the castle and the town walls, then at their first glimpse of Anglesey. Two more tunnels. The headlands of Penmaen-bach and Penmaen-mawr.

'There,' cried the surgeon, leaning across Palmer for a better view. 'The island. You see? Puffin Island. Priestholm.'

It stood like a proud jewel, in a setting of silver, just this side of Anglesey's main coastline.

'Ynys Seiriol,' murmured Ettie. 'In Welsh,' she explained. 'Saint Seiriol's Isle.'

She managed to convey a thousand years of Celtic mysticism within those few words.

'And that,' said Richard Low, pointing to the waters between, 'is Dutchman's Bank. Where the steamer *Rothesay Castle* ran aground. Loss of one hundred souls.'

Good gracious, thought Palmer. This is all just too dispiriting. One tale of woe after another. For the surgeon had then been able to recount a further half-dozen maritime disasters which had taken significant life along the Menai Straits over the previous century.

'Heavens,' said Ettie, and shivered. 'I feel as though somebody just walked upon my grave.'

'You see the lighthouse there?' the surgeon went on. 'More courses of brickwork below the low-water line than even the Eddystone.'

The lighthouse in question, white and black, stood in the channel between Puffin Island and Anglesey itself. But Dutchman's Bank did not seem so perilous today. The flooding tide was gradually covering the sand bars and there were boats away across the choppy swell. A couple of sloops. And a steam packet, twin-funnelled – from Liverpool, the surgeon surmised. A daily service, weather permitting.

More viaducts and tunnels, and they were soon passing through Bangor, before pulling into the station at Menai Bridge. Trains upon this line, Palmer knew, would normally then proceed to the iron tunnel atop the lofty Britannia Bridge, to cross the Straits and on to Holyhead. But, for the excursion train, Menai Bridge station, here on the mainland, was the end of the line.

They disgorged upon the narrow island platform separating the Bangor and Carnarvon tracks from those of the Holyhead to Chester line.

Across from them, the main station building, two storeys high on this nearer side, like a grand many-windowed private house. To reach it, Palmer – now even more impatient – hurried Ettie down into a brick-lined subway ahead of the other passengers.

'You meant to say,' Ettie blurted out, her words echoing, as they rushed through the tunnel, 'what if these agents of the Crown now think the best way to contain the scandal might be for the major's wife to suffer an accident of her own?'

'Precisely,' said Palmer. 'I believe Mrs Cornwallis West might herself be in danger. Today.'

Once more in the open, and at the side of the building, a flight of steps leading to a lower, circular driveway surrounding a lawn and pine trees, through which they could see, perhaps a hundred yards steeply below them, the waters of the Menai Straits flowing beneath the famed suspension bridge, just to their right.

He was so engrossed in the view, as well as his conundrum, that he missed the bottom step and Ettie grabbed at his arm to stop him falling flat upon his face.

'Clumsy,' Palmer muttered. 'Thank you, my dear.'

Outside the station building, upon the driveway, a pair of omnibuses, with tethered teams chomping at their bits. Several hansom cabs as well. And three dog carts also plying for hire.

'Perhaps we should take one of the dog carts,' he said.

Ettie negotiated the price in Welsh with a driver who spoke few words of English, and they were soon on their way around the lane and onto the bridge. A vertiginous drop below them to their left, with the equally high railway bridge a mile away, beyond the rocky outcrops and islets thrusting up through the stretch of water between – a stretch no wider than a substantial river. Perhaps forty yards across?

'Day, is good,' said the driver. 'Boats.'

'Yes,' said Palmer. 'That is it, then? The famous Swellies?' He could see no boats, truth be told. Not that way. Although in the other direction, to their right, there was a different view, through the metal meshing and the suspension bars, rods of iron, hanging from the monstrous mechanical chains above, chains of iron linkages supporting the whole structure. In that direction, towards more open water, to the north and east, there seemed to be vessels aplenty.

'*Pwll Ceris*,' said Ettie. 'And even in English, my father has always called it the Swillies – rather than Swellies.'

Her father. Ettie had already told him that Mr Francis had tried to forbid her from joining him for the regatta. But fortunately, she had defied him. Her nature, he knew.

'Is this road not perilously narrow?' he murmured, for there seemed barely enough width for the wheels of the cart, let alone the omnibus on which the Lows' family would surely follow.

189

He was almost tempted to close his eyes, to shut out the dizzying danger.

'Here it has stood, Neo, for fifty years already. No significant tragedy, so far as I am aware. You must learn not to be so timid.'

Palmer felt considerably relieved when the crossing was finally completed, and they swung down into the village of Menai Bridge itself, taking one more pinch of snuff to help clear his sinuses.

'Reynolds claims to have it on good authority,' he said quietly, his mind returning to the task at hand, 'that it was the prince's licentious behaviour which brought on the fever that killed his father.'

The narrow lane carried them past busy cottages and an ancient inn, but with frequent glimpses of the water just behind.

'You say so? Yet the thing which puzzles me, my dear, is this. If you truly feared for the life of the major's wife, would it not have been simpler to merely employ the telegraph service?'

'What? Attempt to condense all this into a few words? They would have thought me a madman. Mrs Cornwallis West already considers me as such. And I can only imagine the gossip such a message would have triggered.'

A shingle cove between some of the dwellings provided a landing place for smaller boats, a sailing canoe and a couple of gaff-rigged yawls. Oystercatchers wheeling and whistling overhead. Not far beyond, they turned onto a more substantial stone jetty – Davies's Wharf, read a sign on the warehouse. There was an iron pier, a piermaster's house. Across the Strait, a staggeringly beautiful vista – woodlands of autumnal sienna, saffron and sage, as far as the eye could see.

'Prince's Pier,' announced the driver, in barely intelligible English.

'Did he say *Prince's* Pier?' asked Palmer as they climbed from the cart. 'It seems I cannot escape the fellow. For pity's sake, Ettie, is that not one of your premonitions?'

But she did not reply, her attention turned to the pier, and the vessel moored at its end. Perhaps fifty feet in length. A paddle-steamer yacht with a tall, slender funnel amidships from the top of which hung a square yard arm, a furled sail and rigged headsails. At her bow, the name *Admiral* in gold lettering on a black plate, but the hull itself emerald green.

'At last, the first of my final guests!' It was the major, sporting the elegant blue tunic which Palmer and Ettie had last seen at its fitting stage in Mr Williams's shop – the same day Cornwallis West had saved them from those rogues on the High Street. The waxed Imperial moustache was the same, of course, but his oiled black hair was largely concealed beneath a naval cap. A loud-hailer in his hand. 'Welcome, Mister Palmer. And Miss Francis. A delight. Pure delight. Please, come aboard. And I trust the journey was comfortable.'

There were more pleasantries, Palmer and Ettie escorted down the gangplank. Introductions to some of the other passengers. A carnival atmosphere, a wine glass in each person's hand and *hors d'oeuvres* being served. Behind them, the rest of the Lows descended from their omnibus and made their way towards the *Admiral*.

Palmer glanced about, looking for the major's wife. But he could not see her. If he were honest, he rather feared the reunion. He could only imagine the scornful way she would greet him. And there, at the stern, was a highly varnished half-round companionway leading below.

'Hurry, please,' shouted the major through the speaking horn, then turned towards the deck crew. 'And prepare to cast off, gentlemen.'

Smoke began to billow from the funnel and the engine's pistons could be heard, thumping more loudly.

Palmer and Ettie moved to the farther rail, joined some of the major's guests to admire the other vessels already out upon the water. Another paddle-steamer yacht, the equal of the major's, perhaps even finer. The *Bethesda*. Upon her deck, a figure Palmer remembered from the exhibition's opening. A cadaverous and white-whiskered old fellow in a bath chair. Penrhyn. Lord-Lieutenant of Carnarvonshire, of course. '*Damn his eyes,*' Mr Low had said. '*Makes me ashamed to be a Scot.*' Somewhere over there, Palmer calculated, peering across towards the trees masking the mountains of the Snowdon range beyond, must be the quarries where he so badly treated his miners.

Beyond the *Bethesda*, a fine schooner, two converted former workboats, and a larger vessel, twin-masted and with her gaffs already raised, under sail. Yet the show stolen by the pride of the fleet.

'His Grace's yacht, I assume?' Palmer asked the man at his side.

'The *Lady Constance,*' the fellow replied. 'Ninety feet. Carvel-planked. She is a beauty, is she not?'

Lady Constance was also under steam today, her sails furled away, smoke curling from a bright yellow funnel. White hull and a huge red ensign fluttering from a flagstaff at her rear end. But it was not the cut of her jib which intrigued Palmer – it was one of her crewmen. A hulking fellow working near her stern, coiling a mooring rope. Something familiar about him. Could it be? It looked remarkably like Edward Crick. But why in Heaven's name would he be aboard the Duke of Westminster's vessel?

Palmer looked around for the major, found him with the helmsman at the wheel as the starboard paddles began to churn the water, reversing his yacht away from the pier. Cornwallis West seemed worried, as though not entirely comfortable or familiar with the process while, behind them, leaning casually against the companionway, stood a grizzled and whiskered old seadog, sucking on the stem of a corncob pipe.

'Steady as she goes, Major,' said the man – presumably the major's sailing master, or something of that ilk. 'The boy knows what 'e's about.'

'Forgive me, sir,' said Palmer, 'I can see you must be preoccupied. But I wondered – Mrs Cornwallis West is below, I assume. I thought I might pay my respects. Try to…'

'My wife? No, Mr Palmer.' The major waved his arm towards the *Lady Constance*. 'She is over there, with our daughter. With Her Grace.'

Chapter Twenty-Five

Fear gripped Palmer's heart. He could feel the rhythm of its beat change, become faster. Then, that other novel and not especially pleasant sensation, his first encounter with the sea.

'I had hoped for a word with her,' he lied, steadying himself against the rail. 'Perhaps later, then.'

'A pity,' said Major Cornwallis West. 'I thought she would be aboard to see us put the *Admiral* through her paces. Only purchased her recently, you see? The boat, of course,' he corrected himself with a hint of jocularity. 'Though, now I come to think of it...' This time he laughed out loud, and Palmer wondered what the respective prices must have been that the major paid for these two acquisitions.

'Still,' the major went on, 'our first significant adventure. I really hoped to impress the dear girl a little.' It sounded to Palmer as though this might be a rarity. 'But some fellow from the *Lady Constance* came in a tender. Message for my wife to join them.'

They had pulled away, backing into open water, where the major shouted into a speaking tube. There was a two-masted whaleboat, with an unstepped main and spars, afloat, tethered to the stern, but now pushed to one side by the *Admiral*'s backward motion.

'Stop, both,' he yelled, and the paddle wheel did indeed come to a halt, the vessel continuing its glide over a slight chop – though, to Palmer, the swell was exaggerated. His previous experience of boats? Family day trips with a friend of his father aboard a trading wherry on the Broads from Great Yarmouth. A friend who had done his best to inculcate in young Alfred a sound knowledge of all things nautical. Though this was – well, not the same, at all.

Across the water – the wide pool this side of the towering bridge – a band began to play on the Duke of Westminster's deck. A hornpipe, *Jack's the Lad*.

Spread about, for perhaps a quarter of a mile, out in the channel, the rest of their would-be flotilla. Boats of every shape and class and size. Sailing sloops and cutters, ketches and schooners, tacking or coming about with the north-easterly wind. Small steamers and fishing boats with sails of dusky red. Closer to the shore, several of the vessels weighing their anchors. And, all around, rowing boats with crews of four, or six, or eight, mingling with smaller canoes.

'You saw the message from the *Lady Constance*, Major?'

'His Grace would hardly have bothered... Mister Palmer, you have grown pale, sir. What troubles you?'

'You may think me foolish...' Palmer began and looked over his shoulder at the *Lady Constance*. But he had no idea how to proceed. Absolutely none. The words concealing themselves from him.

'Well, spit it out, man,' said the major. 'Time and tide, you know?' He bent once more to the speaking tube. 'Ahead. Starboard.'

The pistons pumped faster, the paddles engaging on that one side again, but this time pulling them in an elegant though bumpy turn towards the bridge.

'Mr Palmer,' said Ettie, appearing at Palmer's side, 'believes your wife may be in danger over there, Major.'

'Again?' The major laughed, then plainly decided he should explain. 'Riding accident,' he said, his smile now suppressed. 'Just last week. A carelessly loose girth. And over there? Yes, Mister Willcox has already warned me.'

The old seadog straightened himself from the companionway, wagged his pipe at them.

'Draught too deep for t' Swellies,' he growled. Strangely, to Palmer's ear, the accent was pure Yorkshire. 'Unless the' know wha' them's about. An' tha'd best go full steam ahead now, Major.'

Cornwallis West jumped for the speaking tube.

'Full ahead, both,' he shouted.

'Not wise, it's not,' said Willcox, shaking his shaggy head. 'Not wi' new crew, an' all.'

'New?' said Palmer, wondering whether the queasiness in his stomach might soon settle.

Smoke from the *Admiral*'s funnel was blown on the breeze off towards the shore. Ahead of them, the *Lady Constance* was already approaching the bridge, the other steam-driven vessels beginning to space out behind her, most of the sailing boats circling or hove-to, waiting to bring up the rear, while the rowing boats were stroking away, taking advantage of the shallower waters on either side of the channel.

'Steamed up fro' Conway this morning,' Willcox explained. 'An' I knows 'er skipper. Rowed over, us did. See 'ow th' old bugger were doin', if tha'll pardon us French. Two of 'is boys not showed up. Too much ale, as like. So, 'ad to take on a couple o' wharf rats, sharpish.'

'One of them a big shambling fellow?' said Palmer. 'The other with a purple mark – here, on his neck?'

'Aye, that's 'em. But 'ow...?'

Ettie pulled Palmer away, shouting a curt thank you to Mister Willcox.

'This will not do, Neo,' she said, as they made their way forward through the other guests, in between the winter coats and capes, the hats secured to heads against the wind, while a liveried servant, somewhat unsteady on his feet, offered them drinks from a tray, which they declined.

'I suggested the danger to him,' she hissed, 'simply to see how he might respond. But he did not swallow the bait, my dear – thinks it amusing that she had an accident last week. Accident, Neo. Last week. The major knows nothing about all this. Nothing. And hardly the time or place to break the news to him.'

He knew she was right. But he was also taken by the scene ahead of them. The *Lady Constance,* with all her bunting aloft, passing beneath the suspension bridge but, just ahead, a small sailing yacht had overtaken the *Admiral,* her profile now framed against the open expanse beneath the road deck.

'Oh, Heavens,' said Palmer. 'Look, Ettie. What do you see?'

'My goodness, Neo...'

It was a precise echo of the image stitched by Mr Williams into that top corner of his coverlet. He needed no further words from Ettie to know she would see this as a further forewarning.

'Grand sight, is it not?' The solicitor, John Bull, had come to stand with them, Mary Louisa huddled alongside, linking her husband's arm and her free hand holding her bonnet in place. The breeze had brought colour to their respective cheeks.

Bull launched into yet another lecture, about the construction of the bridge's two main piers and the archways linking those towers to Anglesey on one side, the mainland on the other.

'One hundred and fifty-three feet in height...' Bull was saying as they passed into the structure's shadow.

'Forgive me, John,' Palmer interrupted him. 'But we must speak with the major.'

Smiles and greetings from the rest of the family. Yes, all enjoying the adventure.

'What are you thinking, Neo?' said Ettie as they worked their way back towards the stern.

Above them, the underbelly of the bridge, high, dizzyingly high over their heads.

'The Bard's words?' he replied. '"*There is a tide in the affairs of men, Which, taken at the flood, leads on to fortune.*" You remember?'

'Perhaps time for us to seize the day, Neo?'

'Those wretches might be at their mischief even as we speak.'

Back at the boat's wheel, Mr Willcox instructed the helmsman – and Major Cornwallis West – that, as soon as they'd cleared the bridge, they must steer a course to starboard towards the church, towards Church Island, so they might avoid the Platters Rock. And then...

'Forgive me, Major,' said Palmer. 'I fear I may have blundered. I had not imagined the *Lady Constance* would be upon the water so early and Mr Low placed a duty on my shoulders. A duty on his personal behalf. A note that His Grace had asked him to see delivered. And before the commemoration at Lord Nelson's statue.'

It was a lie, of course. But Palmer remembered a similar ruse being employed in one of Maryatt's stories. And now they were making the turn to starboard, emerging from beneath the bridge to a vista of staggering beauty – Willcox pointing out the stretch of water on their left which presently covered the infamous Platters. Its backdrop, thickly wooded slopes, alive with autumnal shades of amber, red and yellow.

To their right, a sequence of rugged islands, the closest bearing an equally rugged chapel. The farthest, away ahead of them, with a house of some sort and, just beyond, the Anglesey extremity of the second bridge.

'Then I fear,' said the major, 'you have left your mission too late to be fulfilled, Mr Palmer. His Grace is likely to be displeased. Yes, indeed. Displeased, sir.'

'Wi' respect, Major,' said Willcox, 'us could rig t' lugger an' catch 'er. At wust...'

At worst, it seemed, they could come alongside the *Lady Constance* as soon as they reached the open water beyond that second viaduct. The major fulminated though, in the end, he saw that perhaps there may be an advantage for him, also.

'Very well,' he said. 'I will detail one of the crew to go with Mr Willcox. If you would care to provide him with the note in question...'

'Alas, Major,' said Palmer, very much aware of the dishonesty causing his voice to quake so badly, 'Mr Low charged me with delivering the packet in person.' He patted the breast of his coat for emphasis.

'And where my Alfred goes,' Ettie insisted, 'there go I also, sir.'

Palmer protested, of course, though he realised it would be easier to sail into the teeth of a gale.

'Perhaps there is merit in your venture, after all, Mr Palmer,' said the major. 'And you might be so good as to ask my wife to return with you to the *Admiral*. Please tell her I insist.'

Another impossible task, Palmer decided. And he could only imagine the reception he would receive from the major's wife. But he would not try to catch that particular trout before he had cast his fly.

'Really, Esther,' said Palmer, 'I should prefer you to remain here with the family.'

'Let you go on your own, Neo? Truly?'

And that seemed the end of the matter. Her tone allowed no further response. Orders were already being given to ready the smaller boat and Willcox repeated his instructions to the helmsman – the course to set which would help them clear the Swelly Rock, the transits beyond, and to be followed until, finally, the pyramid stone on the mainland shore marking the point where they should swing to starboard once more, to take them safely under the Britannia Bridge.

The lugger was soon secured alongside, her mast stepped and Mr Willcox aboard, loosening sail ties and checking that his twin halyards were ready.

'Come on lad,' he called up to Palmer. 'Get tha' self down 'ere, m'love. An' then yon lass.'

He sounded doubtful about the whole venture, but he made no more objection as Palmer swung himself out onto the boarding ladder. The lugger rolled alarmingly as his foot found the gunwale. He stepped back instinctively, still gripping the ladder's side ropes and, more by good fortune than anything else, steadied himself on the boat's main thwart.

Bringing Ettie aboard was somewhat more difficult, but he admired her ability to maintain her modesty while her boots accurately found each downward teak tread in turn. A duck to water, indeed.

'Sit tha'selves,' cried Willcox. He gestured towards the thwart on which they each balanced. 'But mind t' fingers an' th' eads.'

They seated themselves on either side of the main mast and marvelled as the old seadog sprang into action, like a man half his age. Unbelievably nimble. Agile as a monkey. He cast off and shoved them away from the *Admiral*'s hull. The small mizzen sail went up but then they had turned in entirely the wrong direction, facing back towards the suspension bridge, into the wind. Willcox had to almost push them aside as he hoisted up the gaff and mainsail, moved astern to grasp the tiller and swing them, at last, in pursuit of the major's paddle steamer. Before them, the second bridge. Three tall towers rose from the water and supporting the long box-like tube of the railway tunnel.

Within minutes, it seemed, they had overtaken the *Admiral*. Like flying, Palmer imagined – the whaleboat unconstrained by the elements or even, it seemed, by the normal channels with this heightening tide. He had almost begun to enjoy himself. Almost. Though not quite enough to make him forget the task he faced.

A small dark bird, swallow-like in shape, grey-backed, a flash of white, danced back and forth around them. Willcox turned his head to study the wispy clouds above.

'Foul weather afore t' dark – stormy petrel,' he explained. 'Never see 'em inshore wi'out squalls comin' after.'

Music still wafted back from the *Lady Constance. A Life on the Ocean Wave* again. Ragged singing from the *Admiral*. But Palmer could hear no joy in the sound. He turned to look at Ettie and could tell from the look in her eyes precisely what she was thinking. The same thing she always thought. The petrel, an omen of ill-fortune.

'Mr Willcox,' he said, surprised that his earlier queasiness had now passed, 'the rest of the parade...'

They had heeled sharply to starboard, closing with the span of the railway bridge closest to Anglesey, while all the other vessels still sailed towards the span nearest the mainland. To their right, the island with its white house and a flag staff, a Union Jack flapping in the wind.

On board the *Lady Constance*, the tune had changed. *Rule Britannia*, in honour, perhaps, of the bridge under which she was now steaming. On her decks, the Duke of Westminster's guests singing the words. Patsy Cornwallis West must be among them, though Palmer could not see her. But he *could* see Edward Crick, plain as day.

Chapter Twenty-Six

'There!' Palmer stabbed a finger towards the *Lady Constance*. 'The companionway thing. In the middle. See?'

Ettie turned to look in the right direction, shaded her eyes but, by then, the Duke of Westminster's sleek white vessel was passing behind the limestone slabs of the farther tower. Moments later, Willcox's sloop cantered merrily between the piers of the northern end.

'Both of them?'

Palmer shook his head. His tooth ached like the devil, and the cool wind funnelled under the bridge made it worse.

'Crick alone, I think. I could not see Blackstone. But he must be there.'

'To what purpose, Neo? What can they hope to achieve on a boat full of people?'

'Their plan? I have no idea. Yet purpose they must possess.'

'They wharf rats tha' mentioned,' yelled Willcox from the tiller. 'New 'ands for t' duke. Tha' knows 'em?'

His voice bounced back at them from the soaring stonework before they sprang headlong, faster than Palmer could say the word *spectacular*, out into the broad waters beyond. Away to their left, a hundred and fifty yards distant, the *Lady Constance* swung towards them, towards the ghost-grey statue of Admiral Lord Nelson on the shoreline ahead.

'I hardly know how to answer you, Mr Willcox,' Palmer replied, one arm wrapped about the bottom of the mast. 'And I have not been entirely honest with you. For I believe the major's wife to be in some danger from those same two individuals. Perhaps mortal danger.'

Willcox played the boat's mainsheet, swung her in a neat half-circle.

'Mind th'eads,' he cried and, as Ettie and Palmer ducked down, he brought the boom across the boat. They came to an abrupt halt. Hove-to. Palmer knew that much about sailing, at least.

Willcox lashed the tiller, but studied Palmer carefully, though half-closed his eyes as he did so.

'Tha' seems a likely lad, Mr Palmer. Clever enough, like as not. But if tha's reet, us needs t' know tha' course.'

'Mine?' said Palmer. 'I have none. No chart. No compass to guide me. Except to get aboard the *Lady Constance*. And then...'

Willcox nodded his shaggy old head, fiddled with the sheets for his headsail and mizzen, repositioned the lugger, shouted for them to take care again, then – monkey-like once more – he jumped forward to the thwart and lowered the gaff, the mainsail's rings falling smoothly down the mast.

'Let's get us alongside, then,' he murmured, and he did so, using headsail and mizzen alone, rope fenders over the side until he'd bumped her gently against the iron boarding platform of the *Lady Constance*.

Above them, the band played more hornpipes, while a crew member held the boat steady and Ettie helped Palmer out of the lugger, onto the narrow staircase with its rope handrails. Willcox shouted that he would be heading back to the *Admiral*, and they waved to him. Palmer had begged him not to say anything to the major about their exchange in case his suspicions should be entirely wrong, and Willcox had reluctantly agreed.

Then Palmer and Ettie were up, past the lifeboat hanging from its davits, and towards the bow, now all hustle and bustle. Preparations were underway: a lectern carried to the foredeck and set in place just in front of the eight bandsmen in their scarlet braided militia uniforms; folding chairs fetched from the varnished wooden wheelhouse just behind the foremast; passengers beginning to gather; and a chaplain fussing over his prayer book.

'Mr...' The breeze ruffled the Duke of Westminster's profuse sideburns just as Palmer seemed to have ruffled his feathers. But at least he offered Ettie a polite bow.

'Palmer, Your Grace.'

Beneath his feet, he could feel the vibration from the vessel's throbbing engine slacken and stop.

'Yes, of course. Mr Palmer!' The duke shouted over the grind of her windlass, the rattle of anchor chains. He was resplendent today in a uniform, presumably of his own design, white, and in the naval style. 'We saw your approach, sir. Yet we are already somewhat overcrowded. It was my intention...'

'We are not here to intrude, Your Grace. I only bring a message from Major Cornwallis West – for his good lady wife, sir. To rejoin him?'

The duke harrumphed.

'You say so? It was the damnedest thing – how she came to be here at all. Still, Mr Palmer, the ceremony is about to begin. I fear your message may have to wait.'

Palmer looked about him, perhaps a little too theatrically.

'But the major's wife is still onboard?' said Ettie

'In the saloon with her daughter, ma'am. And my own family.' He peered over Palmer's shoulder towards the stern. 'The deckhouse. Or perhaps the lower saloon. Please feel free to join them. At least, until after the ceremony. But then, Mr Palmer...'

All around the *Lady Constance*, the rest of the flotilla gathered, each boat slipping its anchor, and the *Admiral* steaming along to take up her own station.

'Have no fear, Your Grace. We shall return to the *Admiral* as soon as may be.'

From somewhere, the report of a signal canon. The Duke of Westminster pulled a watch from his tunic pocket.

'If you will forgive me, Mr Palmer...' And he was gone, off towards the lectern.

'Now, Neo?' Ettie gripped his arm. 'What now?'

Palmer pulled away from her, ran after the duke.

'Perhaps one more thing, Your Grace – the new members of your crew...'

'New crew? Why do you bother me with this, Mr Palmer? Why, sir? You must ask the master – or perhaps the mate.'

Palmer wanted to tell him that if he wished to solve the mystery of how Mrs Cornwallis West had come aboard, he would find the answer with those same recent additions to his crew. But, this time, the dismissal was final, the duke at the wheelhouse, the shining brass bell hanging from its corner. He swung the white braided clapper rope, and the tolling *clang, clang, clang* reverberated across the water. A signal for the bandsmen to strike up *Rule, Britannia!* yet again, and for one of the sailors to hoist the Union Flag up the mast. It was also a summons for more of the duke's guests to make their way forward, emerging from the stern saloon.

'My goodness,' Ettie murmured. 'Just look at the dress.'

Among the women, eclipsing even Lady Constance herself, Mrs Cornwallis West. A dress of lustrous cream wool, a row of matching pearls, dozens of them, down the centre of the bodice, large blue anchors embroidered upon the skirts, and a hint of similar embroidery upon each breast, just visible beneath the matching fur-lined short cape.

'You?' she said, as those green eyes alighted upon Palmer's presence. He tipped his hat politely, yet she recoiled, as though he were her nemesis. 'And here, of all places.' The Irish accent stronger, somehow, upon the water. 'Truly, above your station, do you not think?'

She turned towards Ettie.

'I am astonished, my dear. Still with this dullard?'

Yet, Palmer thought, you have stopped in your tracks, ma'am. You could have simply walked by, remained with those of your own class. But you did not.

From the foredeck lectern, the Duke of Westminster bellowed through a speaking horn to open the ceremony while six coloured flags were hoisted up the mainmast's port spreader. Blue and white, yellow and red. Squares and stripes and crosses.

'England Expects…' His Grace began, and then, with a further nine flags, 'That Every Man…'

'Perhaps,' said Palmer, 'speaking of station, you would prefer to discuss His Royal Highness here. Or somewhere more private?'

He watched the colour drain from her face and knew that, today, at least, this was no simple fishing expedition. And there were more flags, sixteen, this time on the starboard spreader.

'Will Do His…' cried the duke, '…Duty.'

'Duty,' Mrs Cornwallis West repeated. '*His* duty. It was all I expected from him. Though, how is this any of your affair, Mr Palmer? Or of anybody else?'

Her words spat at him, punctuated by those of the speaking horn voice.

"*Assembled host… sacrifice… Admiral Lord Nelson…*"

'Affair, ma'am?' said Palmer. 'It seems the world was about to turn a magnifying glass upon the affairs of His Royal Highness. For good or ill. And some are now dead, on account of their part in the story.'

The languid eyes conveyed nothing. No surprise, either at his use of the word *affairs*, nor about the possible multiplicity of deaths. Did she already know more about this than Palmer had supposed? Did she understand that her recent riding accident may not have been an accident at all?

'Rose Wimpole again?' she said. 'The world knows her death for an accident.'

The Duke of Westminster's disembodied words once more: "*My grandfather, the first Marquess… Gibraltar Chronicle… first account of the battle…*"

'Rose Wimpole and others,' said Ettie. 'Mr Palmer's own life threatened. Not once, but twice. And you may despise him, Mrs Cornwallis West, but he has a well-founded fear that you, too, may now be in grave danger.'

Mrs Cornwallis West rubbed her gloved hands together – gently, as though she might be washing them with perfumed soap. She looked towards the bow, towards the assembled audience, then out towards the other boats, small and large. A veritable forest of masts and steamer funnels, folk standing, wherever they were able, to catch the duke's reading.

"*Yesterday a battle was fought…*"

She walked away from them, though slowly, towards the stern saloon, her head down in quiet contemplation.

"*…a victory gained…*"

'I was young,' said the major's wife. 'And we were often in London. For the season. You understand what I mean by the season?' Sarcasm. Of course Palmer understood. He had done *some* homework, at least. Patsy's family and the Irish aristocracy. 'Sixteen,' she went on. 'And you cannot, in your wildest dreams, either of you, imagine the entrances I made. The heads I turned. Whistler wanted to paint my portrait. Sargent, as well. Now, only my husband with his clumsy brushstrokes. But would you not have wished to paint me, Mr Palmer?'

He supposed he would, indeed, but he shook the thought from his head as Ettie pinched his arm. Hard.

"*...the death of the noble Commander-in-Chief...*"

'People dead, you say?' Mrs Cornwallis West set her hands upon the rail and stared out towards her husband's yacht. 'People of note, Mr Palmer? Deaths of note? I think not. For, had they been so, the authorities themselves would have been involved. Rather than – what *is* your station in life, sir? Museum curator, are you not?'

She laughed. A whimsical little laugh.

'I may not be the Prince of Wales, ma'am,' said Palmer, 'but...'

'Not fit to polish his boots,' she spat, and turned to glare at him. 'It was my mother who introduced us. And danger? I think not. He loved me. I know he did. Loves me still. I might have become...'

Princess of Wales? Eventually, the Queen Consort? Palmer himself almost laughed. Great Heavens, he thought, she harbours regrets that he chose Alexandra of Denmark over pretty little Patsy Fitzpatrick.

'*...and Lord Nelson's final words: Thank God! I have outlived this day and now I die content.*'

Applause from the foredeck, answered from the other boats, ripples of cheering voices, and the wind rising.

'Yet, your husband, Mrs Cornwallis West,' said Ettie. 'He is...'

'He is provincial, my dear. My mother's insistence. And there...' She turned to the rail once more. 'You see? The *Admiral*. That is the level to which my children are consigned. Whereas here, the *Lady Constance...*'

Did she know? Palmer wondered. About all Bertie's other women? But he was thinking more about her husband's words. *She is over there with our daughter*, he had said. And then His Grace. *In the saloon with her daughter.*

A different voice from the loud hailer. The chaplain. The beginning of a prayer.

"O Almighty God, the Sovereign Commander of all the world..."

'Forgive me, ma'am. But your daughter – where is she now?'

Chapter Twenty-Seven

He found her in the engine room. He found her with Edward Crick.

Palmer had charged his way rudely past a couple of nannies and their charges in the stern deck house, down a stairway, two steps at a time, into the lower saloon, along the passage between the vessel's state rooms and through a port-holed door to emerge, breathless and wheezing, out onto this iron grating.

'Daisy?' Mrs Cornwallis West had said. 'Below. With the other children. And that great hulking sailor – little more than a child himself. Though…'

He had not waited to hear more. And now, on the grating itself, he found himself surrounded by pressure gauges and dials, grey-lagged pipes and the gleaming brass eye of the engine telegraph with its wooden handle presently set downwards at *Stop*. Below him, the green, red and shining steel of the pistons, rising from the cylinder and drive shaft. All scrupulously clean, despite the pervasive odours of hot oil and steam, coal and furnace fumes. The pistons were still, but there remained a deep background throbbing hum.

'Crick!' Palmer yelled. 'She is only a child. For pity's sake, you were a soldier once!'

At each corner of the grating, an iron staircase ran down, just three or four grille treads, to gantries which sat along both sides of the engine.

Upon the gantry, Crick, in a seaman's white duck trousers and a white canvas blouse. He held the small girl, held her in his extended arms, out over the drop below. She was laughing. And Crick laughed too!

Above them, the engine room skylight was open to admit the morning wind and, upon the breeze which brushed Palmer's face, stirred his beard, the muffled opening words and tremulous trumpet notes of a hymn.

"Eternal Father, strong to save..."

Edward Crick slowly swung the girl back across the guardrail, set her down at his side, but retaining his grip on her shoulders.

Palmer saw no fear in the child's eyes. She lifted a hand to sweep a straggle of dark hair from her face – a face which was the very image of her mother's. And Crick? Palmer realised he had never before taken note of the man's features. A foolish grin settling now to the beginning of a snarl. He had previously thought of the fellow as bear-like, but now he saw he was wrong.

Some while ago, Palmer had read another of Reynolds's novels, *Wagner the Wehr-Wolf.* An illustration. The lycanthrope at the point of changing from broad-faced handsome human to barbarous beast. Yet there was, indeed, something lupine about Crick's face, the lower parts, around his jaw, prominent like a muzzle. The eyes were inquiring, more intelligent than he had expected, but a hint of yellow to the whites. The hair was wolfish as well, grey, salt and pepper, unkempt and straight sideburn whiskers.

'You,' Crick rumbled. 'Here.'

Neither a question nor even a hint of surprise.

Crick pulled the child closer to him, as though – as though he were protecting her. And she, in turn, reached up her hand to touch his. Palmer heard her say some words about Edward. Her friend, she said, and asked whether they should go and find her mama now.

'Well, Crick?' Palmer shouted. 'Daisy's mama?'

From above, the words of the hymn.

"O, hear us when we cry to Thee..."

Beyond the engine and the steam pipes which fed the machinery, the bulk of the box boiler and its twin flues. More iron stairs leading still further down into the yacht's belly – towards, Palmer surmised, the bunkers and furnace. And coming up these stairs towards them, two men. One, with a walrus moustache, a tidy uniform and cap. The other? Frederick Blackstone. Unmistakeable – though no longer in his workhouse master's smart bridge coat. No, today playing a different part. Shirt sleeves. The sleeves rolled up. A spotted sweat rag around his neck, barely concealing the purple birthmark. His face and arms were smeared with coal dust, black as his facial hair.

'What's this?' yelled the walrus moustache. 'Shouldn't be down 'ere, 'e shouldn't. Nor the girl neither.'

'I knows this gentleman, Chief,' said Blackstone, all very matter-of-fact. 'I'll escort 'im back topsides. Make sure 'e knows just how many dangers there are down 'ere. For him, and the girl too. Gets my drift, Mr Palmer?'

Palmer took the uniformed fellow for the vessel's engineer. But friend or foe? It mattered little, for there was Crick again, picking up the child once more – though less gently now, it seemed. Daisy squealed, the noise drowned by the hymn's closing words.

"…For those in peril, on the sea."

But more disquieting? Palmer saw that Blackstone had carefully slipped an object from the pocket of his moleskin trousers. String was tied about the lower trouser legs but, in his hand, a knife. A clasp-knife, the blade of which the rogue held at his side – the side away from the engineer but plain for Palmer to note. And they were now on the gantry, no more than a couple of feet from the girl. The threats as sharp as the gleaming steel.

'Back here, quick as you like, then, stoker,' said the engineer and cocked an ear towards the skylight. The speaking horn voice. His Grace, the Duke again.

"One more surprise still in store for our return trip. But now, ladies and gentlemen…"

'Steam up in five minutes,' cried the engineer. 'Jump to it!'

But, by then, Palmer was already being hustled back through the engine room door, past the state rooms. Blackstone's knife was at his neck and the child, Daisy – still in Crick's arms – had begun to sob, calling for her mother.

'You cannot hope…' Palmer began, convinced that, at any second, they would be intercepted by one or more of the other passengers. Though, as they entered the saloon, and the strains of further music, more singing, reached them, he understood the reason for this lower deck being so deserted. The National Anthem.

"God save our Gracious Queen! God save our noble…"

Beyond the deserted saloon, the staircase leading upwards.

'Right, Eduardo,' said Blackstone. 'The brat back to its mother. And the note?'

Crick grinned and produced a crumpled piece of paper from inside his canvas blouse, tucked it inside the sleeve of Daisy's coat.

'Then go,' Blackstone told him, and Crick obeyed. But, at the top of the stairs, he had to step aside. For there stood Ettie, all a-fluster and trying to fathom what might be happening. Crick, however, had his orders and pushed past her with the child, while Blackstone pulled Palmer towards him, let her see the knife at her sweetheart's throat.

'Better come down 'ere too, girlie,' he snarled.

Palmer saw her hesitate, look hastily out of the deckhouse windows and, for a moment, he thought she might just call Blackstone's bluff, cry for help. And had it not been for the incident at Chislehurst station, Palmer might have considered this to be desirable as well. Yet now? He breathed a sigh of relief when she complied with the instruction.

'Neo, my dear,' she said, 'are you hurt?'

'My pride alone,' he replied.

Blackstone took Ettie's arm, pushed her in front of them into another short corridor, beneath the stairs, past a couple of water closets, to a low bolted door at the end.

'Inside,' Blackstone told them.

They had to lower their heads and found themselves in a room, the floor of which sloped up away from them. They edged past a central mast-like post, seated top and bottom inside heavy grommets, rings of black iron. The rudder post, perhaps. Alongside, an access hatch in the floor, also bolted. But lining the room were large canvas bags, each stencilled with the name of a particular sail: *No. 1 Jib*; or *Staysail*; and the rest. Among them, neatly coiled ropes hanging from hooks. Furthest away, a three-rung ladder connected the upward sloping floor to a small skylight.

'You plan to keep us here, Blackstone?' said Palmer.

'Not for long. And now – those ropes, fetch 'em. Or else. See?'

He pointed across to the thinnest of the lines. Even in this confined twilight space, Blackstone managed to make the blade gleam, pressed the steel closer into Palmer's neck, nicked him so that he cried out, felt the trickle of warm blood. And Ettie did not argue, simply stooped beneath the deck beams and crossed to fetch the manila cord.

Behind them, the sail room door opened and Edward Crick rejoined them. He seemed to fill all the remaining space with his bulk, blotting out the rest of the already limited light.

'Tie 'em,' said Blackstone. 'The girl first.'

And Palmer watched, helpless, as Crick took a knife from his own belt, snatched the coil from Ettie's hands and expertly sliced away a length, which he used to bind her hands.

'The note?' Blackstone asked him. 'Still safe?'

'Safe,' Crick mumbled.

He cut another length of rope and began to knot it about Palmer's wrists.

'Just so long as 'er ma finds it,' said Blackstone, 'then the job's all but done. Should be enough to stop 'er annoyin' ways.' He turned towards Palmer. 'So, just these two. Couldn't 'ave worked out better, Mr Palmer.'

'You were expecting us,' said Ettie, 'were you not?'

But Blackstone simply sneered.

'Need to 'elp fire up the boiler,' he told Crick. 'Or we'll never get away. Watch 'em. I'll be back.'

'Watch…?' Crick began, and Blackstone regarded Palmer with a look of sheer contempt.

'Yes, watch 'em, you dullard. Though Mr Palmer don't 'ave the air of a ructious man, Eduardo. No, not ructious. Won't give you no trouble. Not if 'e knows what's good for 'im.'

And he was gone. Palmer heard the bolt slam into place on the other side of the door.

Ettie was right, of course. Neither Crick nor Blackstone had shown the slightest surprise when they'd seen Palmer aboard the *Lady Constance*.

'I fear we may have walked into a trap, my dear,' he murmured. 'A trap of my own making.'

Culpable, he thought. I am culpable. For so much. He tested the cord, but it bit too tightly into his flesh to allow any hope of escape. In any case, Crick crouched there in the shadows, knife still in his meaty fist.

'And did you?' Ettie snapped at their wolfish captor, and Palmer wondered whether she still felt sympathy for the man. 'Know we would be here?'

'Tina knows,' Crick told her, though he regarded Ettie strangely. Somehow, more gently. 'Stop Palmer, Tina says.'

Faustina, yes. *Señora* Blackstone. It had all been too easy, had it not? Letting it slip that her husband, and Crick, had business along the coast. Work, she had said. This very week. And Palmer had made the inevitable links: the Menai Bridge image on the coverlet; the Duke of Westminster's regatta; the certainty that Patsy Cornwallis West would be here – and in danger. All enough to bring him running, like a dog to a bone.

'Neo, tell me there is a plan.'

Yet he could not tell her. For there was none. How could there be? He assumed they would be left down here until Blackstone and Crick had made their escape. But perhaps Blackstone had some other purpose.

'Stop Palmer?' he said to Crick. 'Your meaning, Mr Crick – Eduardo?'

'Danger – Tina says danger,' Crick told him, and looked again to Ettie, almost as though he expected her endorsement. His words ponderous, deliberate, somewhat slurred, as though inebriated – though Palmer suspected this must be his condition. And Crick was pointing at him with the knife.

'A danger – to whom?' said Ettie, and Crick's features softened. 'And you must stop me also?'

Crick lowered his head, seemed even more confused than his natural state might have inflicted upon him.

They fell into a seemingly endless silence. Palmer's tooth troubled him again and he longed for the comfort of his snuff but then the door opened once more, and Blackstone returned. He carried with him a lantern, a heavy hammer, and a long iron spike. He bent to slip loose the bolt securing the hatch in the floor. He threw it open and the beat of the engine's heart, from forrard, was suddenly more immediate.

'Cut 'em free,' he shouted to Crick while he, himself, fumbled to light the lamp. 'It's time.'

'It would indeed be wise, Blackstone,' said Palmer, rubbing at his grazed wrists, as Crick also sliced through Ettie's bonds, 'to release us now, while you have time. I am sure there must be a small boat...'

'Released you both shall be, Mr Palmer,' Blackstone laughed. 'Now, get below – and take this with you.'

He passed him the lantern and Palmer stared aghast at the square of pitch darkness. Beneath his feet he could feel the engine come alive, its rhythmic pulsation vibrating through the vessel, ready for them to be under way.

'Down...?' Palmer murmured.

But Blackstone had the clasp-knife in his hand again. There would be no dissent.

'At least,' said Palmer, 'not Miss Francis. You cannot, sir!'

'Can we not, Mr Palmer? Now...'

Blackstone prodded him with the knife and Palmer moved to the hatch, peered down into a stygian darkness, which the lantern did little to dispel. A ladder, running alongside the rudder post. There was not much room down there either, the floor here sloping towards the bow of the boat. Beneath this floor must be the outer skin planking of the hull itself, for he could plainly hear – and almost feel – the sound of water slapping against the vessel. He heard Blackstone instruct Ettie to follow and, while she objected, she was soon descending the ladder as well, all skirts and petticoats, followed by Blackstone himself, who took back the lantern, and hung it from a hook on one of the beams.

Where the post met this lower floor, it was fitted with a broad-toothed cogwheel, and a heavy-duty roller chain inside an open-topped crank case, also leading forrard.

'Over yonder!' Blackstone instructed and gestured for them to move to the side.

Palmer wondered whether there was some escape route, but he did not believe so. The meagre light showed, perhaps ten feet away down the slope, a metal casing, which he guessed must house the propellor shaft. Around it and beyond, lumps of stone or iron, the ballast. But it was a sombre, gruesome space, a stench of stagnant water. Why were they down there? He sensed the moment when the propellor shaft began to turn, felt the shudder with the first rotation of the blades and heard the water churn below. There was a lurch, and the roller chain worked the rudder post. A turn to starboard.

'Back towards the bridges,' said Ettie. 'You plan to leave us down here while you make your escape, sir?'

'That's about right,' said Blackstone. 'Though, for now, we waits.'

'If we must wait,' Palmer replied, 'you might as well tell me what this has all been about.'

He knew that this manner of suggestion always seemed to work well in the penny dreadfuls, but would Blackstone be so obliging? Indeed, he was.

'I'm guessin' you already sees it, Mr Palmer. Or why else would you be 'ere in such a pickle? Always an eye for a pretty girl, our sporty young prince. Usually knows their place, they do.'

'But not this one,' Palmer jerked his thumb upwards. 'Not Mrs Cornwallis West.'

'Not even after the family marries 'er off to the major.'

'She sent letters?' Ettie suggested.

'Oh, 'ow she loves 'im. An' then the major's brat.'

'Demands?' said Palmer. 'Or threats?'

'Wants our Bertie to promise, when the girl's grown, that 'e'll make sure she marries well. Other stuff. So we gets orders…'

'Orders,' Palmer repeated. 'Marlborough House, you mean? It *was* the Prince of Wales, then – who arranged your place at the workhouse? So you could keep the major's wife under control?'

'Marlborough House?' Blackstone laughed, incredulous. 'What kind of fool is you, Mr Palmer? You seriously think the Queen's favourite son needs the likes of me to clean up after 'im?'

'And the note?' said Palmer.

'Tucked into the brat's coat. Warnin' like. So she thinks we can get to 'er or the girl any time we likes. Writ by the boss, in person. Though little will Mrs High-and-Mighty know we'll be long gone.' He laughed. 'Yeah, long gone.'

The boss? Palmer was confused. If not Marlborough House, and it certainly did not sound like Blackstone spoke of his wife…

'Then,' said Ettie, 'those you have killed – and you *have* killed, Mr Blackstone, have you not? Rose Wimpole. Mr Morrison. The others. And tried to murder Mr Palmer as well.'

'Scare 'em off, those was the orders. An' Tina thought...'

'She thought,' said Palmer, 'she would sow the seed in my mind – in the mind of others too, perhaps – that Crick had this obsession with the tailor's coverlet. That if things went wrong when you were "scaring them off" – then poor Crick would be your sacrificial goat. And they *did* go wrong, did they not?'

It was very much Ettie's theory and Palmer saw the enthusiastic nod of her head.

'Eduardo was only supposed to threaten 'er with the snake. Just got too close. Bloody creature went wild, like. The serpent, I means. Eduardo – well, lucky 'e didn't get bit too.'

'And Morrison?' said Palmer.

'Objected to my warnin' on the bridge. Eduardo 'ad to push 'im around a bit. Knocked 'is head. Set a pattern, so to speak.'

'Then there's Wicklow, the Irishman.' Palmer wiped blood from his neck with his kerchief.

'Wasn't one of us, see. The boss sent 'im. But got too big for 'is boots after 'e took your papers. Got greedy, like.'

'The maid from the Wynnstay?' said Ettie.

Maudie Meadows, Palmer recalled, and Blackstone laughed again.

'Believe me or believe me not,' he said, 'that one, it truly *was* just an accident. Those steps at the Tiger Inn. Nothin' to do with us.'

'Then tell me about Chislehurst,' said Palmer.

'Nothin' to do with me, neither, Mr Palmer. Oh, we put the frights on you after that first visit to see Tina. Eduardo, the Headless Horseman, eh? But Chislehurst? The boss again.'

'The boss?' Ettie and Palmer spoke those two words at precisely the same time.

But they were destined to receive no answer. The roller chain once more, the great cogwheel and rudder post turning the *Lady Constance*, swinging her to port. A shout from Crick above, but Blackstone was already in action. The iron bar. He hammered the thing down between the chain and the cogs until it stuck fast, a screeching noise of metal upon metal, the vessel's course, the rudder, now jammed and fixed.

Ettie knew what this meant, just as Palmer did.

'Neo,' she said, her voice rimmed with terror. 'Come!'

She grabbed his arm, tried to pull him towards the ladder. But Palmer's gaze was fixed upon Blackstone's blade, threatening them as the rogue himself climbed up through the hole.

'You cannot escape,' Palmer yelled after him and Blackstone paused on the topmost rung.

'But you and yon girlie won't be around to worry about it, Mister Palmer. By the time they sorts out this mess, we'll be in Ireland. From Ireland – well, who knows?'

He climbed up, slammed the hatch shut over their heads – and slid home the bolt.

Chapter Twenty-Eight

The collision was so violent, it threw both of them to the floor. They reached for each other. Ettie clutched the cloth of Palmer's sleeve. In that way they slithered together down towards the propellor shaft casing. And the ballast.

A rending crash, splintering timbers. Horrifying, as though the entire hull must shatter. Then a banshee howl as the keel of the *Lady Constance* screeched across the rocks upon which she had been driven aground.

Water. Frothing white water. Impossible that it should be flooding the bilge so fast.

They scrambled backwards, up towards the ladder, the hatch which offered them no escape. And the rats scrambled with them. Palmer could see them in the kaleidoscope light from the swinging lantern. He heard the scratch of their nasty little feet as they scampered over the frame ribs.

Palmer wrapped one arm about the foot of the ladder, his other around Esther. He felt her shudder, cringing away from the creatures – a dozen or more of them, all frantic, but seemingly more desperate to find an escape than to bother fellow captives. But how long would that last? Palmer had heard troubling stories about trapped rats. Could they smell his wound?

'My hat,' he said, realising it was missing and fearful that his head was unprotected from the vermin.

'You lost it when we ducked into the sail room, my dear.'

Her voice quaked. Terror. Or cold. For their feet were now fully immersed in the icy waters.

And all this while the chain chafed and heaved impotently against its cogwheel. Palmer could imagine the efforts of the helmsman up in the wheelhouse to free the steering. The propellor also, spinning for all it was worth, though now in reverse. He could feel it, the whole vessel straining to pull herself backwards, off the rocks. But without success.

'Somebody will come, Esther. Somebody.'

'Who, Neo?' It was no more than a tremulous whisper, and she flapped her hand towards one of the rats which had come too close for comfort. 'Who? The Lows are all on the major's boat. Here? His Grace too preoccupied with all this to even remember we are aboard. And Mrs Cornwallis West? Really?'

'Still...'

He freed himself from her and climbed the ladder to thump on the underside of the hatch.

'Help! Help!'

He kept shouting, thumping, for two or three minutes and the effort left him wheezing. There must surely be a solution to their predicament – but it would not come to him. Instead, his brain was filled with images of that other disaster. The Dee Bridge. He had thought of it this morning, when they stopped at Abergele. This morning? Only this morning? Indeed. But there had been the occasion with Morrison as well. Poor Morrison. Their shared journey to Wrexham, when Palmer had stared down into the murky, swirling eddies of the Dee and imagined the horror of those trapped in their railway carriage, drowning as it sank into the river's depths.

He shuddered, climbed down to embrace Ettie once more.

'Somebody,' he repeated. 'And you still believe Crick deserves our sympathy?'

She pressed herself into him but did not answer his question.

'How long?' she said, instead. Just that.

'They say,' he told her as gently as he was able, 'it is best to accept the waters, rather than resist them. A more peaceful end. It must be an inglorious thing, to perish with fear as our final emotion.'

She squeezed his arm.

'It has always troubled me, Neo. It is my confession. That, when we pass to the other side – how many countless thousands of the unknown will have gone before us, since the last of our loved ones?

How might we possibly find them, or be found ourselves? Among all those multitudes. Lost and lonely, for eternity. But we, Neo…'

'Together, sweet girl. We shall indeed take the road together. And our Lord God shall guide our steps.'

The *Lady Constance* lurched, a violent roll to starboard. The ballast rolled with it, a tumbling landslide roaring like thunder.

Palmer and Ettie fell from the ladder, down into the rushing torrent which swilled, first one way within the vessel's convulsion, and then the other. He felt her slip away from him, down into the brine.

He reached for her, found a hand, dragged her up, splashing and spluttering.

'Oh, Neo…' she gasped.

'I told you, my dear.' He nearly choked on his own sentiments. 'Together. Only together. Yet, your father…'

The words remained unspoken. Mr Francis would, of course, curse his name forever. Still, he thought about his mother as well. Ailing and in his sister Catherine's care, though he never imagined she would survive him. He just hoped she might, by now, be too insensible to receive news of her son's premature demise. This would be some blessing. God preserve her!

The waters had almost stopped swilling from side to side, but deeper now. Around their waists. Freezing them. Palmer's legs entirely numb and he dreaded to think of Ettie's condition. But ridiculous to ask.

'If we climb… onto the upper side of the ladder,' he said instead, his own teeth now chattering, '…we can at least… be out of the waters… a while.'

'Not… embrace… them?'

'Not… just yet… perhaps.'

A triviality, but he had noticed the rats were gone, scuttled back towards the bow of the *Lady Constance*. And the engine had finally stopped.

'The tide…' he said, with no expectation she might understand him. But something in his head. If the vessel had settled on the rocks at High Water then, surely, given time…

'But… there is… no time, Neo.'

She would, of course, have had the same thought. By the time the tide turned, receded, they would be dead with the cold. Nobody to find them.

'Still...' he said and pulled her up the ladder – which no longer hung down straight but leaned sideways at forty-five degrees towards the locked hatch. They clung to the upper side of the ladder, Palmer's arms about Ettie's shoulders, holding her in place, trying to keep her warm.

'John... Wesley,' Palmer began, 'tells us... the art... of dying... requires our... full attention.'

'A craft, Neo... to be learned.'

It was a brave attempt at humour, though his admiration for her was lost somehow in the realisation that the waters now eddied about his chest. Still rising. How could this be? He pulled Ettie up as far as he was able. It felt as though they presently both existed only in some dream world in which Palmer was separated from his body.

In this dream world, he thought he heard the voice of Mr Low's son, the surgeon, Richard.

'Yes, but the parade of sail itself, sir. Shall we be on time?'

His own reply came back to him, quoting from the newspaper.

'A parade of sail and steam. To depart in orderly fashion from Menai Bridge and passing through the Swellies during High Water Slack and then...'

And he listened again to the tedious voice of Low's son-in-law, the solicitor John Bull.

'The nature of the tides in The Swellies. The Slack there almost two hours before High Water itself.'

Palmer had miscalculated. The water rising further. But it did not trouble him too much. He was tired. Drowsy. The cold seemed to have left him. Only the arm supporting poor Ettie still with any sensation. That and the damnable tooth. It hurt now like the very devil.

If it was not for the tooth, he thought, I could sleep. Set down my burden.

In the way of dreams, his father read to him once more from *The Children of the New Forest*. The part in which old Jacob surrendered his responsibilities to young Edward.

'You will then have all the load on your shoulders which has latterly been mine.'

The load on my shoulders, he thought. But it was difficult to remember quite what the load might be. Somewhere, in his scientific brain, he knew what must happen next. The cold. It took only minutes. But he no longer cared. If it was not for the tooth...

Another voice. Pale. In the distance. The words coming to him disjointed, faint.

'Birmingham... and... Sandringham...'

Ettie. That ridiculous song. He felt a tear run down his cheek. Bless her. If Palmer was Marryat's Edward, then Ettie Francis must truly be his Prudence. The indomitable spirit of Prudence.

'Torrington... and... Warrington...'

Somehow, he managed to join her for the final line, their voices croaking almost together.

'She said... she'd sure to find it... in my... Bradshaw's Guide.'

Then the lantern guttered and died.

Chapter Twenty-Nine

There was a tunnel. And there was a pinpoint of light at its end.

Palmer expected, when he finally reached that radiant haven, he might see the face of Our Lord. Yet, as his numbed extremities returned to agonising sensibility, as his vision finally cleared, as the light grew wider and stronger, there was simply the walrus moustache of the vessel's engineer.

'You done this?' the fellow yelled, brandishing the iron bar.

Palmer shook his head, clenching his teeth to stop them quaking free of his jaw.

'So, explain what you was doin' down there.'

They were in the deck saloon, Palmer stretched out on one of the banquettes. He had been stripped only of his coat but wrapped in several blankets. A few of the duke's gentlemen guests were gathered around, each of them fitted with a life preserver, all cork blocks and leather straps. Some of them showed signs of injury, bandaged heads and one with his arm in a sling. A steward, as well, in a white jacket and serving tea from a small trolley.

'Esther,' Palmer croaked.

'The girl? Below. But this?' The engineer held the bar in front of Palmer's face, as though he might strike him with it.

'Locked... in.'

It seemed to Palmer entirely self-evident. How could they be the wreckers if they were themselves victims of captivity?

'Hosed down your own petard, maybe?' said the engineer. Palmer would have corrected his malapropism, but the man was in full flow. 'Hatch slammed behind you an' when we struck, the bolt slid home. Simple. Observed it before, I 'ave. A dozen times.'

Even with the dulled state of his brain, Palmer knew this had to be an exaggeration.

'Must... see her.'

He dragged himself up into a sitting position. He needed to think – and quickly.

The steward pushed the trolley towards the banquette.

'Does 'e get a cup, sir?' he asked the engineer, who merely shrugged his shoulders in response. The steward seemed to take this as an affirmative, however, and began to pour.

'And why, precisely,' Palmer murmured, 'would myself... and Miss Francis... wish to damage the boat?'

He took the proffered enamel cup in his shaking hands and looked up to catch the condemning glances, the muttered accusations among the gentlemen passengers, before the Duke of Westminster blustered his way into the saloon. He must have been in the doorway, though Palmer had not noticed him there.

'A very good question,' he yelled, aiming his prominent nose in Palmer's direction. 'A good question indeed.'

There was oil smeared down the front of his fine white uniform and among the sideburns beneath his chin. His cap was missing. For the first time, Palmer was conscious of muffled hammering somewhere below and forrard, a mechanical sound, though not the engine. And, beyond the *Lady Constance*, a train whistle from above them, on the railway bridge.

'Your stoker,' Palmer said to the engineer. 'The rogue I saw you with... in the engine room.' He patted tingling fingertips to his neck. 'With the mark, here... him and Crick...'

'What *is* he talking about?' ranted the duke. 'Stoker? Crick?'

'Two men unaccounted for, Your Grace. Pierce the stoker. One of the hands, an' all. That big cove, too. Jones? The stern tender gone.'

'Not Pierce... His name is Blackstone. The other... Crick.'

'And why, Mr Palmer, should this Blackstone – if that truly *is* the fellow's name...'

'Anarchists, Your Grace,' Palmer replied, the lie curling readily from his lips. 'I had my suspicions... The newspaperman who died in Wrexham... Morrison. He was investigating. And when we were on board the *Admiral*, I imagined… well, that I saw them. Old Willcox brought us across…'

'Yet you said nothing,' murmured the duke, his fury now seemingly spent.

'I was not sure… and you were busy with the ceremony.' Palmer sipped at the tea. It was hot. And sweet. Restorative.

The duke harrumphed, most likely trying to recall their earlier conversation.

'And in the engine room,' said the engineer. 'You didn't think fit…'

'The wretch had a knife, sir. You could not see it… But Blackstone made its presence plain… to me, at least. And there was the girl. Remember? Mrs Cornwallis West's daughter. She is safe, I trust?'

'The Penmon lifeboat took off all the women and children,' said the Duke of Westminster. 'A mercy they were with us for the parade of sail. But all safe. And when we get her afloat again…'

'Afloat, Your Grace? She is capable of repair?'

'A competent crew, Mr Palmer. One of the sails over the side and lashed tightly over the hole in her hull. The pumps all working to slow the water coming in, lessen the level somewhat. A couple of the lads down there this minute. Shoring to be put in place. And Mister White here, gone below to dislodge this object from the rudder. High tide shortly, and then…'

'How we found you,' said the engineer. 'Needed to check, I did. See if the shaft were damaged. Though, truth be told, I was convinced as 'ow you must 'ave been involved, like.'

'Well, you were wrong, sir.' Palmer swung his legs from the banquette, pushed himself unsteadily to his feet. 'We seem to have been unfortunate enough to stumble into their scheme. And now, I must see Esther. Then – Blackstone and Crick? They must be stopped.'

'She is in good hands, Mr Palmer,' said the duke. 'Mr Low's son – the surgeon – below and taking care of those who suffered injury in this – this…'

Words failed him.

'Richard?' said Palmer, setting his hand against the back of the banquette to stop himself from falling. All his earlier nausea had returned. And a cough. 'Here?'

'The fellow from the major's yacht,' the duke replied. 'What did you say is his name – Willcox?'

'Yes, Willcox.'

'Brought the young sawbones across. And since then – well, been helping my men. With the – what do we call it again, Mr White?'

'Fothering, Your Grace,' said the engineer.

'Indeed. With the fothering.'

'And Willcox, still on board?' Palmer demanded. He was, indeed. 'Then, if you would be kind enough to provide some dry clothes, sir,' he said, 'and I might make use of Willcox's services, perhaps you would allow me to attempt to apprehend them – Blackstone and Crick. Bring them to justice, Your Grace.'

'You ain't fit to go anywhere, sir,' the engineer told him. He was still brusque, but at least he had lowered the iron bar.

'And apprehended they shall be, Mr Palmer,' said the duke. 'Though that, sir, is surely a task for the authorities. There shall be no corner in which they might hide themselves.'

'Yet, the birds... have flown,' Palmer replied. 'And bound, they said... for Ireland. Then... somewhere beyond. I suspect they are well-rewarded for today's mischief.'

'Anarchists? Rewarded?' the duke was incredulous.

Very sharp, thought Palmer, but chose to ignore his own *faux pas*.

'At least allow me to try, Your Grace. Attempt to follow them. Perhaps alert the police...'

It was agreed, though the engineer confirmed that neither Blackstone or Crick had been seen for at least a half-hour – or considerably longer.

'But if they've headed back towards Menai Bridge,' said the engineer, 'with the tide still on the last of the flood – and rowin' against a couple of knots...' he glanced out at the ensign flying from the stern. 'Wind freshenin' from the west...'

Palmer descended to the lower saloon, found Richard and satisfied himself that Esther was in good hands, but likely to suffer no lasting damage from her ordeal. He hoped not, but how could he be sure?

'You wish me to wake her, Mr Palmer?'

Palmer declined. Better, he decided, if the sweet girl should not worry herself with this decision which, he had already determined, was foolhardy in the extreme. Still, he accepted the clothing brought by the duke's valet. He changed in one of the water closets, a precarious operation in that confined and carbolic-scented space. Goloshes, duck trousers, canvas smock, oilskin jacket – and his battered derby, now returned to him. The crocodile leather of his wallet seemed appropriately to have largely protected the contents, though the notes inside were all very damp. His coin purse, on the other hand, was missing entirely – presumably lost down in the bowels of the boat. And his snuff? He dreaded to think about the contents, but at least the precious ivory box, the oriental fisherman carving, appeared undamaged. Sweet Ettie, he thought. I hope she will forgive me for abandoning her.

By the time he was back on deck, Willcox was there to meet him, his boat still tied alongside. He had, it seemed, already been told some version of the recent events.

'Anarchists?' said Willcox, as the freshening wind filled their sails. The lugger heeled to starboard, speeding back towards the suspension bridge 'Or Fenians. T' latter, I reckons. Trafalgar Day, an' all.'

He settled into some lengthy Yorkshire pearls of wisdom while he flitted about the boat. Opinions about Irish convicts with the temerity to escape from penal colonies in Australia. About the death of Bakunin the anarchist.

'An' good riddance to 'im,' said Willcox.

And damnation to the Turks for their atrocities during the Eastern War. But Palmer's attention was entirely turned to the waters around them, scanning each boat for any sign of Blackstone and Crick. Yet there was none.

Several vessels still clustered about the *Lady Constance*, Penrhyn's *Bethesda* among them. Shouts, back and forth. Assistance offered. Towing lines being rigged to help her off the Cribbin rocks.

Ahead, the various other craft of the flotilla, the schooners and cutters, the fishing boats and sailing canoes. But as they cleared the bridge's central span, there lay the town with its wharf and pier. At the pier, a significant vessel, a large paddle steamer, her decks busy. Black funnels. A flag flying from her mast, white cross on a scarlet background. And the Penmon Lifeboat rafted alongside, her charges being escorted up the steamer's boarding stairs – though no sign of Patsy Cornwallis West.

'Packet boat,' said Willcox, and reached inside his coat from whence he pulled a spyglass. 'From Liverpool. The *Prince Arthur.*'

As he spoke, the steamer gave a long blast on her foghorn.

Almost ready to sail, thought Palmer, then glanced at the open, closer waters, where the *Admiral* waited its turn to use the pier, though one of its own tenders missing.

Willcox trimmed his sails, swung towards the town, and they came in sight once more of that shingle cove Palmer had noticed earlier, on his arrival in Menai Bridge with Ettie. And there, pulled up on the hard, was an abandoned rowing boat.

'Your glass, Mr Willcox?' he said. 'Can you see the name painted on her transom?'

Willcox could, indeed. *Lady Constance.*

Rowing hard towards the beach, as well, that longboat from the *Admiral.* Sitting in the tender, some of the major's guests – as well as Mrs Cornwallis West herself with little Daisy.

Willcox – all his sails now furled, except for a corner of the jib, and the gaff lowered – ran them aground neatly in the cove, where Palmer almost tumbled over the bow in his anxiety to get ashore. The stones pressed painfully through the soles of his borrowed goloshes.

'Madam,' he yelled. 'Mrs Cornwallis West.'

'You,' she said, while the crewman helped her onto the shingle. Palmer had to assume she had persuaded the Penmon Lifeboat crew to deliver her back to her husband. 'And danger, sir? You are a buffoon, Mr Palmer. It seems the only danger we faced was from the helmsman's incompetence.'

'Then you should look inside the sleeve of your daughter's coat, perhaps.'

But he did not wait for her to make the discovery. If Blackstone and Crick had abandoned the tender here, then where had they gone? Blackstone had mentioned Ireland. Did that mean Holyhead? He pressed through some of the locals who had gathered for news of what had happened, but he brushed aside their questions. Had he himself been there? Had he seen the *Lady Constance* go aground? Had anybody died?

On the lane behind the cove there were carts and carriages, fishermen carrying creels of their catch up towards the town centre, a busy inn, the Liverpool Arms, a couple of porters helping travellers with their luggage off towards the pier.

Perhaps they had not come this way at all. He turned back towards the bridge, thinking that he should check the road from there to Holyhead itself.

He had almost climbed the hill in that direction when the four-wheeled growler passed him. It may have simply been the coincidence in which neither Palmer nor Inspector Wilde believed. It may have been the cab's horse, a grey mare which sneezed violently as it trotted past. It may have been the quantity of travelling chests loaded so precariously upon the cab's luggage racks. It may have been the cabbie himself, singing loudly as he plied his whip to the mare's withers. But Palmer chose that moment to turn his head towards the growler's window. Could it be? He looked again, though by then the cab had passed him.

Yet now he was certain. The passenger's outline – the unmistakable *mantilla*. Faustina Blackstone.

Chapter Thirty

'Perhaps one last favour, Mr Willcox?' Palmer was frantic. And he was shivering. He had, without doubt, caught a chill. Or perhaps worse. 'There must be a telegraphic office here in town?'

It transpired there were two, one in the Davies's warehouse, the other at the post office.

'And the police?'

Yes, of course. A police station as well.

'Look,' he said, with the familiar tingling sensation in his sinuses, 'I have to purchase a ticket. You see? They are about to sail and by the time I can alert the skipper, she will be underway. I doubt he will believe me, in any case. Is there some way...?'

There was. The police would be informed that the *Lady Constance*'s wreckers were aboard the *Prince Arthur*. The police would then telegraph Penmon and they, in turn, would alert the old semaphore station on Puffin Island. The station was still just in operation and should signal the paddle steamer. After that? The electric telegraphic linkage would continue – from Penmon by submarine cable to Great Orme's Head, onwards through Voel Nant to Hilbre, Hilbre to Bidston and, finally, by yet another cable under the Mersey to Liverpool.

'And might you, Mr Willcox, ask the Lows to look after Miss Francis? Perhaps she might wait for me in Wrexham. With luck, I should be back there tomorrow. Or the day after.'

Willcox promised to deliver that message also.

'Good luck t' you, sir.'

Palmer thanked him once more, and ran.

He had to scream at the City of Dublin Steam Packet Company's ticket vendor, who had technically closed the booth by the time Palmer raced towards the wharf. And the transaction itself was not without its difficulties. A fiver for a five-shilling fare? Did he have no less? And the note itself somewhat waterlogged. By the time Palmer had the change and the deck ticket in his hand, the same growler was driving back out through the pier gates and, as he himself turned through them onto the dockside, he was in time to see Crick upon the vessel's footbridge, just disappearing with an enormous trunk on his back.

'Wait! Wait!' Palmer yelled as the crew began to loosen the bridge's securing ropes, ready to haul it upright.

He attracted strange looks from many of the passengers as he scrambled aboard, the bridge raised behind him and another blast on the steamer's foghorn. The mode of his present attire, he knew, would hardly help him remain inconspicuous. Even the young man at the purser's office window – who must have seen some strange passengers in his day – looked him up and down in a most suspicious way.

'My friends are already on board,' Palmer told him. 'Cabin ticket, I imagine. Two men and a lady. A foreign lady. And am I speaking double Dutch, sir?'

The purser apologised, stopped staring at him and hurriedly began to scan his ledger. Just one cabin with three occupants. The Fredericks and their manservant listed as the occupants of cabin number twenty-three. Palmer thanked him for his efforts. The Fredericks? Yes, of course.

The office was located in the covered passageway between the promenade deck's general lounge and its second-class tearoom. Alongside the window, a wooden notice board with the *Prince Arthur*'s sailing schedule, its ports of call, each with an arrival time indicated by a small clock face and, beneath, the name of that particular destination shown on a rotatable roller. Leaving Menai Bridge at one-forty – and the timepiece above the window confirmed they were no more than five minutes late in their departure time. Arrival at Liverpool, five-thirty. Stops *en route* at Beaumaris and Llandudno. A separate notice, next to the board, advised that embarkation and disembarkation at this latter location could only be undertaken using the pier an hour either side of high water and, otherwise, passengers would be transferred by boat, depending on the sea's state. Alongside the schedule, a plan of the vessel, from which Palmer deduced that the cabin in question would be two decks below, and towards the bow.

He must bide his time, however. So, he stood out on the deck, sneezing, trying to picture how any confrontation with *señora* Blackstone and her husband – Crick as well – might possibly be played out. How to act? Palmer hoped the *Prince Arthur*'s captain, once appraised of the villains now on his ship, might clap them in irons and that he, Palmer, would need do nothing but simply observe their incarceration.

Ten minutes to Beaumaris. A cluster of windmills on the high ground behind the town. A score of additional excursionists waiting there upon the iron girder and timber pier. A quarter of an hour later, and they had followed a meandering course eastwards. Such a course that Palmer thought they must have a pilot on board to guide them through the navigation channel.

They were presently steaming across open waters, the wide bay of the Conway Estuary, towards the Great Orme. Puffin Island lay more than a mile away to port, like a humpback whale surfacing for air. There was also the channel between Puffin and Anglesey. There, the black and white lighthouse they had seen this morning from the train. Indeed, was Palmer not on board the same steam packet they had observed on its outward passage?

Surely, it must be so. Though the seas which earlier in the day had seemed so benign were presently becoming rough. A freshening breeze upon his face helped to keep his stomach from total rebellion. And he even ventured to open his snuffbox, pleasantly surprised to find the contents still dry.

He could see the semaphore station's signal masts like harpoons thrust into the whale's flesh – but no sign yet of an actual message being sent. He grew impatient, pacing back and forth through the covered passageway, pushing apologetically through the passengers, from one side of the ship to the other. He hoped the scenery might offer some distraction, for there was no denying its beauty – the mountain ranges and hills of the mainland particularly spectacular.

After a minute or two, Palmer made his way to the port side once more. There! The distant signal arms moving, silhouetted against the clouds. He hoped that somebody on the bridge would see it more clearly and he looked up towards the wheelhouse, above this forward lounge. To his surprise, the steamer was changing course, turning towards the island. The message? Could its effect have been so immediate?

But no. As the *Prince Arthur* swung into the wind and slowed, there before them lay the pilot cutter, hove-to and waiting to take off the pilot himself. Excitement on deck as folk leaned over the rail to watch the bold fellow make his leap from ladder to lugger. Then, up went the steam packet's sails. One after another, from stem to stern.

It took a few minutes before she had resumed her original course, heeling – though hardly at all – to starboard, the up and down motion of the vessel suddenly exaggerated by their increased speed. The bow rose upon one wave and slapped down hard upon the next.

'Forgive me,' Palmer called to a portly seaman making his rounds of the promenade deck and checking all was secure. 'Might you confirm that the message from the signals station is actually for this vessel?'

The man studied Palmer from the crown of his bowler to the toes of his goloshes. Yes, a strange sight, to be sure.

The sailor glanced towards the island.

'An' if it was,' he said, 'that'd be a matter for the skipper – would it not?'

'Is it common on this vessel to rebuke your passengers – *paying* passengers – for asking a perfectly reasonable question? What *is* your name, sir? And you shall escort me to your captain at once – or...'

Palmer's tirade lost a little of its ferocity by the sneeze which punctuated his words at this point.

'...Or I shall know the reason why.'

Still, it must have had some effect, for the fellow, though mumbling curses all the way, complied by leading Palmer onto the upper deck. It was now largely deserted as the passengers took shelter and refreshments below, or simply succumbed, wherever they were able, to bouts of *mal de mer*.

From the upper deck to the bridge, where the captain – evident by the deference shown him by the three other officers gathered about him, as well as his battered cap – studied a piece of paper. Next to him, a wooden bucket swung back and forth at shoulder height, suspended by a length of rope from a beam of the wheelhouse roof.

'What the devil...' said the captain, his accent Irish. He flicked the paper with his fingertips, then spun towards the doorway, his face contorted with anger. 'And Tiptree,' he yelled. 'What now? And who the hell is this?'

The seaman began to explain – until Palmer cut across him.

'My name is Palmer, Captain. And I believe I might shed some light on your message.'

It took a few minutes, for the skipper chose this moment to vomit into the bucket. Palmer's own stomach heaved. He was shocked – and little wonder. A seasick skipper seemed incongruous. But then he recalled, appropriate to this very anniversary, to this very day, that even Admiral Lord Nelson was frequently himself a martyr to seasickness. It made his quality somehow the greater. Besides, nobody else upon the bridge treated the incident as anything but entirely normal. Palmer hastily made sure he had eradicated any hint of surprise from his face, kept his own innards under strict control.

'Knew about the *Lady Constance* running aground, of course,' said the captain, and wiped a sleeve across his beard. 'From the lifeboat crew. And the women they brought to the pier. But anarchists? And this?'

He showed Palmer the paper. The message was brief, to say the least.

POLICE BELIEVE THREE SUSPECTS ON BOARD STOP
WILL ARREST LIVERPOOL STOP

'You *will* clap them in irons, Captain, I suppose?' said Palmer.

'Where do you think you are, Mr Palmer – aboard a man-of-war? Unless I am advised there is some threat to my ship or its passengers and crew, sir, I shall have the purser try to ascertain precisely *who* these suspects may be...'

'I have explained, Captain, that I was a victim of their criminality. The purser already confirmed the number of their cabin. I really must insist, sir...'

The explosion was inevitable.

'You will leave my bridge, Mr Palmer.' The captain was incandescent with rage. 'And if you have anything to say on this matter, I suggest you save it for the authorities in Liverpool.'

Chapter Thirty-One

Liverpool? They were still more than three hours from Liverpool and Palmer's rancour grew with every minute since his abrupt dismissal by the *Prince Arthur's* seasick skipper.

Did the fellow not comprehend the danger of having such felonious wreckers aboard his ship. What if…?

He stood at the stern rail, nauseous, and watching the wake churn away westwards as they began to round the bulk of the Great Orme. Its summit was shrouded with misty rain clouds.

Palmer forced himself to remember that causing harm to the steam packet could not be part of the Blackstones' plans. They would, of course, want to show Liverpool a clean pair of heels if they hoped to escape to Ireland. Ireland and beyond? Was that not what Frederick Blackstone had said? And why should they not believe themselves safe to do so? Surely, they must suppose Palmer and Ettie to be dead, while the disappearance of Crick and Blackstone from the *Lady Constance's* crew might pose something of a mystery, but hardly cause for a manhunt.

How likely was it that any of them would have seen the semaphore message *and* been able to interpret the signals? Not likely at all. Not even vaguely likely. No, if anybody was going to act, it must be Palmer himself. Act in some way which would prevent the miscreants being able to disembark with impunity and slip unheeded past the authorities.

He moved to the leeward, starboard side and vomited a thin stream of yellow bile out onto the wind. Then through the second-class tearoom, packed with sheltering passengers, to the water closets, where he washed his pallid face and stripped off the oilskin jacket. The derby as well. He left both items on a chair and would collect them later. Back at the counter, he ordered tea, sipped at the mug, steadied himself against the steamer's motion.

'Is it always this rough?' said a young woman with two small children sitting at a table close to him. She seemed terrified, looked up from his seamen's smock to his face. 'Are we safe?'

'Why, madam,' he said, as confidently as he was able, even adopting some approximation of a West Country accent to complete his performance, 'this is simply the slightest swell.' He slammed down his mug as though he had been at sea all his life, tugged at his forelock and bade her a pleasant journey.

Beyond the tearoom and the water closets, past the purser's office, he took the passageway around the side of the general lounge – a passageway which allowed the day trippers to wander safely along a visitors' platform through the wonders of the engine room. It was similar to the engine room of the *Lady Constance*, though significantly larger in scale, significantly noisier. But there was the Chief Engineer in spotless white overalls, tapping the multitude of dials on his control gantry and enjoying his own brew, a pipe of tobacco, while the *Prince Arthur* remained on this steady course.

Palmer climbed the few steps which took him up and over the shaft driving the paddlewheel on this side of the vessel and he paused to admire the gleaming steel of the huge connecting rods and piston rods, their *dunder-dudder-duh, dunder-dudder-duh* as they rose and fell, rose and fell. He admired the mechanics – but he recalled, as well, how close both he and Esther had come to death after their encounter with Blackstone in a place very like this one. It filled him with dread. He knew that, if he wanted to make sure the Blackstones were apprehended, he could not do so without putting himself yet again in harm's way.

The noise in here was different from the engine room of the *Lady Constance*, as well. The engine itself, with its heat and steam and oil, but the commotion of the paddles, only inches away on the farther side of the hull's fabric. To make the point more obvious, on the farther side of the raised driveshaft housing, there was a window, a large porthole through which an observer could see the frothing, swirling waters, white and seafoam green, boiling around the wheel's centre-boss, revolving arms and rim. The image drew him, with hypnotic and

236

dreadful fascination, in the way he had heard those with susceptible minds could be drawn towards the edge of vertiginous heights and then feel compelled to throw themselves into the void.

He drew away, bending his wavering will to the task he had now set himself. He would make for their cabin, confront *señora* Blackstone and her husband – Crick as well – and hold them to account for what they had done. He would make sure to leave himself plenty of room for escape and, should they threaten him, he would find some way to summon the captain once again.

There were holes in his plan – he knew that. But it was the best he could do. And he could not help recalling the knives carried by both men. Still, one step at a time.

And his next steps took him beyond the engine room, beyond another of the *Prince Arthur*'s beautifully varnished portals, out into a short corridor. To his right, prominent in the white iron wall of the hull, a tall watertight hatchway – though red-stencilled with the words, *Inspection, Authorised Personnel Only.* And with a further porthole window, though the door not quite fully closed, its locking latch in the open position.

Palmer's eye was caught by movement through the water-splattered glass, outside. He pressed his face to the window, caught an image of a triangular platform, bollards, ropes and belaying pins. And two men, somewhat indistinct. They seemed to be leaning over the rail. Crew members, inspecting the paddlewheels, as the door suggested? He supposed so, almost turned away, but then one of the fellows stood upright, turned towards his companion. It was Crick, without a doubt.

The other – Blackstone, Palmer was sure – pushed Crick back towards the guardrail. He seemed to be urging Crick to look down, perhaps at something below. Crick did so. And Palmer was astonished to see Blackstone quickly bend, grip his companion's knees, heaving the larger man up and over the railing. Crick bellowed with rage. But he did not fall. Not entirely. Somehow, he managed to grip one of the stanchions. Palmer could see only his fingers, his wrist, the sleeve of his coat – and Blackstone, kicking at the fingers.

A moment's hesitation. Though only a moment. Conflicting images screaming in his brain. Turning. Turning fast. Like actions seen through the viewing slots of a zoetrope.

Let Crick fall! The number of Palmer's enemies greatly reduced! And Palmer could simply walk away, revise his strategy – for what it was worth.

But Ettie's voice, as well. *'Then the fellow perhaps deserves our sympathy, does he not?'* And had Palmer himself not always preached that benevolence brings more lasting justice than revenge?

Only a moment, and he pushed open the door, assailed at once by the wind, by the suddenly darkened sky, and by the roar of the paddlewheel within its broad arched housing – to which this three-sided grating was attached.

'Stop!' he screamed. 'Stop!'

Blackstone turned. He looked into Palmer's eyes and took a step backwards.

'No,' he said. 'It can't…'

There was a flash of lighting. And Palmer recalled the tailor's coverlet. Almost the last image at the top. He saw himself as Blackstone must see him. The white smock. The white duck trousers. The white face.

But there was Crick, heaving himself up by the stanchion and guardrail wires.

'Mark of Cain!' he bellowed. It was directed at Blackstone. Yet if Palmer's ghostly appearance had caused Blackstone some momentary pause, he had plainly now conquered his demons. He leapt forward and gripped Palmer around the throat.

Palmer felt the fingers squeezing at his windpipe. Two hands, his chin forced upwards. He could see only the storm clouds through half-closed eyes. Distant thunder. Or perhaps simply the outcry of blood rushing in his brain. The last of the air in his lungs was driven out as Blackstone slammed him into the iron wall at his back. He tried to push the fellow away. A feeble effort. But he managed to force one of his own hands up between Blackstone's wrists, found his face, the wet pliability of the man's lips, the cavern of his nostrils.

Blackstone bit the hand. He bit it hard. But Palmer's scream of pain was choked off, throttled just as Palmer himself was being throttled.

His other hand groped along the cold white iron of the wall, felt for the rack of coiled ropes he had seen there.

'Eduardo,' Blackstone spat at him, 'outlived... 'is purpose.'

Palmer felt the grip on his throat tighten still further. But at least his fingers had found the ropes, dragged out one of the belaying pins from which they hung.

'An' so... 'ave you,' said Blackstone, releasing his right hand from Palmer's neck just long enough to swipe the belaying pin from Palmer's hand.

But the momentary relief, the temporary reprieve from that terrible double-handed embrace, allowed him to draw breath. A brief instant, before Blackstone swung him around, smashed his body into a tall cowl ventilator. Something pressed into Palmer's thigh. It hurt like the very devil. The snuffbox, he realised. The pocket of his duck trousers.

Blackstone still pinned him by the throat but was fumbling in his own pockets. For the clasp-knife, Palmer knew. And after that...

'This time...' Blackstone snarled, '...no mistakes.'

There was another flash of lightning.

Blackstone's head turned briefly towards the sea.

And Palmer's fingers found the snuffbox, flicked the lid open.

The knife's blade gleamed. But before it could strike home, Palmer had pulled forth the box and flung the contents in Blackstone's face. Most of it blew away on the wind but enough of the powder found its way into the rogue's eyes to make him recoil. He yelled and staggered – into the arms of Edward Crick who had, an instant earlier, swung himself back over the guardrail.

Palmer coughed, wheezed, struggled to regain his breath, rubbed at his own throat in an effort to soothe it. But now? What now? He was far from certain that Crick might even have the capacity to realise Blackstone had been trying to dispose of him. And Crick looked, more than ever, like Reynolds's wolf-man.

For Palmer, the moment froze.

'Lord,' he murmured, 'have mercy upon me.'

He looked at Blackstone and Blackstone glanced at Crick.

'Eduardo,' he grinned. 'Faustina will...'

But he got no further.

'Mark of Cain!' Crick repeated, then in one swift movement he had gripped the lapels of Blackstone's coat, lifted the fellow off his feet, then another hand to the broad belt of Blackstone's trousers. He hoisted him into the air, like a circus strongman.

Blackstone lashed out with the knife, blood spurting from Crick's neck.

Crick howled – just like a wolf – and he hurled his burden over the side. Blackstone screamed too, all the way down until he hit the water.

Palmer looked into the choppy sea, but Blackstone was already gone. He remembered about Crick just in time to see the big man stumbling back through the hatchway.

Palmer rushed after him, saw Crick making his way along the passage leading forrard but he, himself, turned the other way, back into the engine room.

'Man overboard!' he screamed. 'Man...'

There was the porthole, the viewing window for the paddlewheel.

Pressed against the other side of the glass, staring at him. Blackstone. The eyes wide open, lustrous. The mouth agape, like a fish. Then the wheel's arms took him once more, dragged the body away.

'Man overboard!' he shouted again. 'Here!' Palmer pointed. 'In the paddlewheel.'

But, by then, the Chief Engineer was yelling into a speaking tube and the ship was filled with the protracted ringing of an electric alarm bell. Three long rings. And then, three long blasts of the *Prince Arthur*'s horn.

Palmer knew he should wait, show the crew where they could find Blackstone's corpse. But there was still Faustina – and Crick. He turned, back past the porthole, and now the revolving wheel of Frederick Blackstone's afterlife had brought him full circle. Except that, somehow in that maelstrom, his trousers were gone. Simply the long white legs of his undergarment.

It cannot be, Palmer thought. For the image was strangely reminiscent of yet another scene from James Williams's coverlet. The image of Jonah's lily-white legs protruding from the whale's jaw.

Chapter Thirty-Two

'Of course!' Faustina Blackstone spat at him, hatred in her eyes. 'It had to be you, *señor* Palmer, did it not?'

She sat sideways on one of the bunks, and Crick – a wounded wolfhound – sprawled at her feet, his coat abandoned, and his shirt soaked with blood, one hand clamped to his neck. She stroked his head.

'I apologise profusely for the disappointment, madam,' Palmer croaked, his voice-box bruised and sore. 'I imagine you thought me dead aboard the *Lady Constance*.'

He stood in the cabin's doorway. His back ached like fury from being so badly slammed about. For some reason he had found himself compelled to knock before he entered. Inside, dark wood panelling and two narrow bunks, white linen, lace curtains at the porthole window. Travel chests stacked in the corner, and the contents of a smaller valise strewn across the floor.

'May Our Lady damn you to hell, *señor*. Poor Eduardo. Look at him. He spoke one thing to me. One thing only. The Hand of God, he said. Sent to save him. You? The Hand of God?'

'He did not think me so when he left us to die in that stinking hole.' It hurt him to speak, as though somebody had flayed the inside of his throat with a scourge.

'It was not part of my plan. No part. I knew about it only when Frederick told me what he had done. Here, on this ship.'

Palmer was convinced she must be lying.

'And this pretence of concern – your husband made it plain that Crick had outlived his usefulness.'

She wore a winter riding habit of deep purple wool, heavy jacket, skirts, and slender pearl-buttoned breeches tucked into her boots.

Once again, her dress, her features, her composure belied her age. And her age belied the seductive allure of her scent. Orange jessamine swept the air clean of the ship's other odours.

'But we have stopped.' Her head came up, startled. The *Prince Arthur* had indeed fallen into stillness, this wallowing inertia. 'And the alarm – for my husband?'

The ship vibrated more gently, strangely silent – except for three further long bursts of the electric bell. Recovering the body, Palmer supposed. To free the paddlewheel.

'Yes,' he gasped. 'Overboard. I am afraid...'

'And he stabbed Eduardo, *señor*? Or was that you?'

'Has Crick not told you himself?'

A violent roll to port. Palmer had to steady himself against the doorframe, the vessel now entirely at the mercy of the swell.

He saw that her left hand was tucked inside her coat, as though she was clutching at her stomach. Was she wounded also?

'The girl?' she said. 'The girl who was with you.'

Palmer saw Crick's hand move towards the jumble of contents from the spilled valise and pick up a framed picture. It was the pencil sketch Palmer had last seen hanging on the wall of the Master's Parlour at the workhouse. Faustina Blackstone as a young girl.

'Tina,' Crick groaned.

Palmer recalled how the fellow had spoken her name earlier, and Faustina took the picture from Crick's trembling fingers.

'He is convinced that your *novia* is me – though made young again. What do you think, *señor* Palmer? When you make love with her, will you see my face?' She laughed, the cackle of a mad woman, then tossed the picture carelessly onto the bunk. 'Yes, that is the gift I shall leave you, I think.'

It was monstrous. Yet Palmer felt himself bewitched. A curse cast upon him. A curse he feared might truly come to pass. He fought hard to dispel the vision she had sequestered into his brain.

'You see?' she screamed.

Her left hand was still hidden within the folds of her coat, but with the other she gestured towards herself, the wrinkled fingers shaking as though she suffered some attack of the palsy. Yet that one trembling hand as fluent as she was, normally, with two.

'And not part of your plan?' Palmer murmured. The woman must be more deranged than he had first imagined. 'Yet I was your quarry today, was I not? Lured me here. You, *señora*. Not your husband, wretch though he was.'

'It seems, then, that I succeeded. For there you stand. As large as life – is that not what you say?' She laughed. 'Though if I had wished to entice you here, it might simply have been to beg a pinch of your snuff, Neo.' Another smile. 'Is that not the way she says your name? Neo?'

She pronounced it in the Spanish fashion. *Nay-oh*. But how did she know that?

'I am afraid your husband…' He paused, swallowed, tried to moisten his words. 'Your husband… consumed the very last of it.'

'A pity,' she said.

'But Esther in safe hands. No thanks to any pity from you. Nor from Crick and your husband. *Your* actions which brought her so close to the valley of death.'

'Me?' she raged. 'Me? Or perhaps you, *señor*. Chasing shadows that are not your concern, like some *Quijote*.'

He had thought the same thing himself, so many times. But now he sneezed, the chill tightening its grip upon him just as Blackstone's hands had done – though, remarkably, his toothache, at least, seemed to have subsided. The *Prince Arthur* lurched again suddenly, caught by yet another swell. And the swell brought back his nausea. The cabin became a capricious carousel of dizzying colours – scarlet and purple plum, varnished teak and linen cream. Faustina Blackstone still spoke, but her words were merely distant reverberations in his ears. And the white perfection of her perfume had turned to black berries of cloying revulsion.

'But Crick,' he wheezed, and slid down the wall, sat upon the cabin's floor. 'He must know, surely, that you and your husband were simply using him this way?'

'Where else would he go? Poor Eduardo.' She began again to stroke his head. 'If I told him to leap into the sea, he would do so. But Frederick always wanted to follow his own path. It was my intention to leave Eduardo in Liverpool. Too old to travel further. Somebody would care for him there. Somebody.'

'Care for him, *señora*? Then you must be mightily relieved you no longer need trouble yourself with that task. Do you not see?'

He held out his hand in Crick's direction. Life was visibly ebbing from the man's body. Slumped entirely now and the crimson stain upon his shirt spread all the way to his waist. The face more ashen, Palmer thought, than perhaps even his own. But the woman seemed oblivious to Crick's obvious fate, regarded Palmer as though seeing him for the first time. Was this simple theatre?

'You, *señor* Palmer – Neo – why are you here?'

He despised her familiarity, though it was a good question. His desire to solve the mystery of Morrison's death was long behind him. His desire to increase his standing in the eyes of Ettie's father blown away entirely by the mortal dangers to which he had this day exposed her. His desire to somehow protect Patsy Cornwallis West from harm evaporated now in the fog of the woman's own hubris.

'The blood, it seems,' he said, at last, looking at Crick's own vital fluid leaking away.

'The blood among the threads,' she laughed. That same demented and gibberish chuckle.

'Is that not the thing you told me? The coverlet. Its hold upon Crick. More than just the remnants of his uniform within its design, I think. Did you intend the same just now?'

'Eduardo says it tells the past and the future. Both. All the things we cannot see.'

As though in response, Crick groaned, tried to push himself up from the floor. Palmer did the same, concerned that there might be more life, more aggression, left in the fellow than he had imagined. But Crick's effort failed, and he sank down again, Faustina Blackstone whispering words of comfort to him.

'Madam,' Palmer sneered as he pulled himself upright once more. 'Such a performance. Now you claim the coverlet has some mystical power. At least your husband was honest in his confession – that you were simply trying to make sure the incidents you arranged as *warnings* to those coming too close to Mrs Cornwallis West's secrets – that Crick should be your sacrificial goat should things go wrong.'

Yet he knew the coverlet had drawn him in the same way – or, rather, in a way he could not quite explain. He saw it now, as though he stood before it, the patches of black and red, the shades of ochre, the whites, and occasional splashes of blue. He remembered the coverlet images which had nothing at all to do with Blackstone's schemes and yet which had seemingly come to pass regardless. The death of Maudie Meadows on the steps at the Tiger, among others. More recently, that bizarre porthole picture of Blackstone's legs like Noah and the whale.

She glowered up at him, a malignant grin upon her lips. But then the smile disappeared. She cocked her head to one side as, deep within the *Prince Arthur,* the engines and the paddlewheels got the vessel under way once more.

'They have found him,' she said, and suddenly seemed vulnerable, afraid.

'I expect so,' said Palmer. 'And I also expect we shall find out more. Soon.'

It seemed to pacify her. She sat back against a pillow.

'You were thinking,' she said, 'of the things in the coverlet which happen of their own accord. And you see, Neo? You happened as well. The Hand of God. But what now?'

'Now? Liverpool – the authorities. No escape, madam.'

He wondered whether she told him the truth. What *had* been the original plan? For Blackstone and Crick to use the parade of sail merely to frighten the major's wife? And for *señora* Blackstone to join them later and then make their getaway? It was the most obvious scenario.

'Yet you have no proof of any crime on my part,' she said. 'None. Am I responsible for whatever my husband might have done? Or dear Eduardo, here? And by the time we reach Liverpool...'

'There shall be affidavits. From myself. From Esther. Your husband's own statement to us – of your involvement.'

He thanked Heaven the woman had not been there to hear it. For it was thin. Thin, indeed.

'Then it shall be your word against mine, Neo. I shall deny all knowledge, *cariño.*'

He wished she would drop the pretence at intimacy.

'Perhaps,' he said. 'But by then the whole story will be in the newspapers. I imagine that whoever put you up to all this – that they might not be too pleased. According to your late husband, they must have a long reach. Even as far as… And where would that have been, *señora*? It was clear from his words to me there must be some destination beyond Ireland itself.'

For the first time, he saw doubt in her eyes. Blackstone had mentioned the word *boss* several times. But not Marlborough House. If not the guardians of the royal indiscretions, then…?

'America,' she said. 'New York. Connections there. A new life, *señor*.'

The *Prince Arthur* had eased into a more regular movement now – one that helped to settle Palmer's stomach. He wondered where they had reached, but there was little to be seen through the lace curtains at the porthole. The dark motion of the sea, the flash of whitecaps.

'And the stop in Ireland?' he said.

'For the payment we are owed. Our reward, if you like. From our – our benefactor. Is that not the word? And there could always be a passage to New York for you, as well, my friend. *Dios mío*, it seems you need a benefactor also. Look at yourself. Look deep, Neo.'

He abhorred her. Yet, far more profoundly, he loathed his own attraction to her, his deeply hidden desire that, somehow, this game between them might continue forever.

'Truly, an evil creature, are you not?' he barked.

'Be *simpático*. Kind. I could also arrange a reward for you, Neo. Our benefactor would be generous. I could be generous also, Neo. Be kind and tell me… You will let me go?'

The thought of Faustina's generosity – the form it might take – appalled him.

'Some cowardly accommodation?' he growled. 'Betray all those whose deaths are upon your hands?'

'Then go, if you like, to the captain. Or join me. It is your choice, *señor* Palmer. But I promise you, there shall be no arrest.'

Crick chose this moment to mutter something incoherent, then began to cough, a dribble of blood running from the corner of his mouth. And a smell, a terrible smell, filled the cabin.

'He has lost a great deal of blood,' said Palmer. 'I must fetch a doctor – see if there is a doctor on board. A medical officer perhaps. If I might have your parole…'

He glanced back through the doorway, along the passage from the direction he had come earlier. A trail of blood there, also.

'Poor Eduardo,' she said. 'Such a long journey we have made together. But he is beyond the help of any doctor now. Time for his misery to end, I think.'

The old, faithful hound, he thought. A cruelty to keep it alive any further. More humane to...

'But why have you done this?' she went on. 'The great detective. The hero. Who would have thought? You want a confession? Like one of those foolish stories from your friend Reynolds?'

'Reynolds. Yes, my visit to old Reynolds was interesting, to say the least. Some fellow tried to push me under a train, *señora*. You know, I take it? But no, a confession is not necessary. You can save that for the police – and for your priest, I suppose.'

'You seek to redeem me, Neo?'

'I leave redemption to our Lord Jesus Christ, madam. All I need to satisfy myself at this point might be an explanation. Your benefactor. The boss your husband spoke about. If not the Department of Military Intelligence, then...?'

Before she could answer, there was more commotion out in the passageway. A knocking upon one of the cabin doors. A door opening and an enquiry to whoever the occupant might have been.

'Forgive the intrusion,' came the voice which, even at this distance, was familiar. Tiptree, thought Palmer. Was that not the name of the seaman who had escorted him to the bridge – and then been scolded by the seasick skipper for his pains. 'Nothin' to be alarmed about. Just checkin', like, that all's well.'

Another voice. Names being read from a passenger manifest or some such thing.

'Close the door,' hissed Faustina Blackstone. 'Close it!'

He turned to see that her left hand was no longer hidden inside her riding habit. Now it was extended towards him, and it held a small pistol, a pocket revolver.

'Too late for that, *señora*, I believe,' he told her. For, out in the passageway, Tiptree and his companion had made a discovery.

'Look 'ere,' Palmer heard Tiptree exclaim. 'Blood! That's blood, ain't it?'

Palmer took the risk, praying the woman would not shoot. Not yet. He stepped out of the cabin. Portly and bewhiskered Tiptree, indeed, with a ship's boy behind him, carrying the ledger. Palmer was forced to brace himself, one hand on each of the corridor's varnished walls, against the pitch and toss of the ship's motion. But these two seemed impervious, riding the thing as though fitted with their own personal gimbals.

'You!' said Tiptree. 'Is this...?'

'We have a badly injured man in this cabin, Tiptree,' said Palmer. 'And if you are searching for the identity of your man overboard, you shall find the answers here, in cabin...' He glanced at the brass numbers on the cabin door. 'Cabin twenty-three. Perhaps you might be good enough to fetch the captain. And remind him of my words. Criminals.' He lowered his voice and mouthed the final word. 'Anarchists.'

Tiptree and the young fellow muttered to each other.

'An' you, sir?' said Tiptree. 'Want me to...?'

'Nothing,' Palmer replied, and rubbed at his still tender throat. 'Best if you both go now. Bring your skipper.'

Palmer watched them retreat down the passageway, murmuring to each other and many backward glances. He stepped back into the Blackstones' cabin.

'I could have shot you, Neo,' said Faustina.

'As I could simply have gone with Tiptree. Left you here for the captain and his men. And what would have been the point of shooting me? Precisely the evidence they would need to send you to the gallows. You are correct, of course. My own affidavit, Esther's as well – they might not be enough for a conviction, but I am happy to leave matters in the hands of the law, señora. And Crick – is he...?'

She looked down into Crick's eyes. They seemed to be staring back directly into her own. Yet they were lifeless now. The fellow was plainly dead. And if Palmer had thought he might see some genuine emotion from Faustina Blackstone, he was destined to be disappointed. But she set down the revolver, at least. Her face showed no expression as she took Crick's huge head in both her hands, moved it sideways so that it now rested against the bulkhead behind.

For a moment, Palmer considered making a grab for the weapon, but he decided against such an action. No, he would leave matters to the skipper, beat a hasty retreat, if necessary.

'Poor Eduardo,' she said again, as she had done before. 'I often wondered whether it was a cruelty – when I helped him after Andoain. Then, I thought it was God's will, that I should save him. I had prayed to Our Lady that I might be able to do so. All that time, when those devils were…' She picked up the revolver again, the barrel pointed loosely in Palmer's direction. 'All that time, *señor*. It was not myself I prayed for while they did those things to me. It was for Eduardo – that I might find him, save him.'

Her eyes were fierce, defiant, as Palmer had seen them so many times in the past.

'He is at peace now, at least, madam. But has it been worth it? For it all to end like this?'

'Each story has its own life, does it not? The beginning of mine was sweet. Even the war, when it brought Eduardo to me. Not so sweet later. But I still had him with me. And then England. Hard, once more. At the start. Though I found fortune again, Neo. More money, at the time, than I could spend. But then, debts. Favours needed. And, with the favours, yet more debts.'

'Debts – to Marlborough House? To the Prince of Wales?'

Had Blackstone told him the truth? Palmer recalled his words. *'You seriously think the Queen's favourite son needs the likes of me to clean up after 'im?'*

Faustina waved the revolver at him.

'Move away from the door, Neo,' she said. 'And close it. You think the captain will come? I think not. He does not know about Eduardo. He has simply one dead passenger on his hands. The rest of us, he will leave here until Liverpool. And, at Liverpool – well, we shall see.'

Palmer closed the door, as instructed. He was tired. Exhausted. He tested one of the travelling chests for stability. A solid wooden trunk upon which he sat himself.

'But running the *Lady Constance* aground. Why? The risk to all those people…'

'Frederick,' she said. 'He hated them. The Governors at the workhouse. Their airs and graces. Their privilege. And what did you say about us – to the authorities, to the *capitán*, here? Not about the major's foolish wife, I imagine.'

'No. Not about Mrs Cornwallis West. I told them there were dangerous anarchists on board.'

She laughed.

'Then you were correct, I suppose. Anarchy. A fine word. Do you not sometimes think, Neo, that perhaps the purpose of God is to create chaos, rather than order? Frederick certainly believed in chaos, in anarchy.'

'Yet, you say you had a benefactor. If not the Prince of Wales or his household…'

Who had Blackstone meant? The boss? Vulgar American word, of course.

'Could you not see, Neo? I suppose it does not matter now. But Mrs Cornwallis West's own mother. You have met her?'

He had, of course. Mrs Olivia Fitzpatrick. Ironically, at the shop of James Williams, the tailor. And seen her, also, at the Exhibition's opening.

'What nonsense is this? You expect me to believe that the mother would put the lives of her daughter – her granddaughter as well – at such risk?'

'*Señora* Fitzpatrick will go to great lengths to protect her daughter's reputation. Her daughter's – and her own. It is said she once enjoyed an affair with our dear prince also. And the major's wife is very much her mother's daughter.'

'With the Prince of Wales? The mother?'

He was shocked. How little wonder the world seemed so debauched when those in the highest echelons of society set such low standards of morality for the rest to follow.

'Of course. The mother disgraced and banished from court. An aristocrat by birth, though forced by her family to marry some country *padre*, the Reverend Fitzpatrick. Forced to leave Ireland.'

'And move here?'

'Some big house in Cheshire. Years later, the daughter disgraced and forced to marry Major Cornwallis West.'

'Forced? He is the Lord-Lieutenant of Denbighshire.'

'But still not the aristocracy to which mother and daughter believe themselves to belong, Neo.'

'This beggars all belief. And why journey to Ireland?'

'She will not deal with us so close to her home. But her own family is powerful and wealthy. Before she married, she was Olivia Taylour, daughter to one of the most powerful men in your House of Lords. Her father is dead now. But an agent in Dublin acts for her. Perhaps for the family, as well.'

'But your husband. Military Intelligence. Marlborough House. Your establishment on Regent Street.'

'It is true, we both served the Prince of Wales also. In our very different ways.' She smiled at some memory. 'And His Royal Highness has already done much to help the major. Complicated, no? The mother also one of the prince's conquests.'

'The mother *and* the daughter. Beyond belief.'

'And at Regent Street the mother had met me. She knew her daughter's impetuosity.'

'Married her to the major to avoid further scandal. But then needed to have her watched?'

'Especially when she began writing her foolish letters. Demands. Assurances that her children, at least, should rise above what she saw as her own dull little life.'

'The mother used her influence at Marlborough House,' Palmer suggested, 'to get yourself and Frederick installed at the workhouse – and a handsome stipend to go with it, I suppose.'

'But we took our orders from her. From Mrs Fitzpatrick. Our task to scare off unwanted attention. Like that prying Wimpole woman. And in case anything should go wrong, yes, there would be Eduardo. Why not? Frederick said. Deranged. Mutilated. Obsessed with the coverlet. Its images.'

'And the fellow at Chislehurst?'

She shrugged her shoulders.

'I know nothing about Chislehurst.'

'The last time I saw the woman – Mrs Fitzpatrick – we were attacked. Ettie and myself...'

He had wondered about that day many times, wondered about the two drunken drovers and how they could have known to intercept him there, on the High Street, at precisely that moment. To deliver their warning to Ettie. And he had thought often about the tailor's apprentice, running past the churchyard gates. Yet he had never been able to make the connection. It made no sense that the lad should have been dispatched with a message to the Golden Lion by Williams himself, nor by the major – or, indeed, even by the major's wife. But the mother? Yes, he supposed that might fit. Just about, if she had some agent there, as well. The proprietor perhaps. Always easy enough to find a couple of handy louts to do their bidding.

'Attacked?' said Faustina Blackstone. 'It seems that you, at least Neo, are a cat with seven lives.'

'Seven? No, madam, it is...'

More noise outside the cabin. The sound of feet thudding along the passageway. Many feet.

'Twenty-three, you say?' came the captain's muffled voice.

An affirmative from one of his crew.

The motion of the *Prince Arthur* seemed to have eased, Palmer's nausea easing in equal measure.

'They are coming for you, after all – Faustina,' he said, simply. The first time he had ever called her by that name. But that produced no emotion from her, either. There was still venom in her eyes. 'I will make sure, at least,' he went on, 'that your husband receives a decent burial. And Eduardo as well, of course.'

He turned to look at Crick's corpse, and marvelled that, in death, his features also seemed softened, as though the memory of the young and more handsome soldier shone through. And even Faustina Blackstone's orange jessamine no longer cloyed in his nostrils. Somehow the clocks, time itself, had been reversed.

The woman had reached down, picked up the sketch from the bunk.

'This,' she said, 'they shall never take from me.'

She turned the revolver's muzzle, pressing it to her eyeball – and pulled the trigger.

Chapter Thirty-Three

The telegraphic message from Ettie contained just two words. Two curt words.

YES STOP

Palmer could sense the rage, could understand it – more or less.

He settled himself into his seat at Chester General, thankful that, for now, he was the only occupant of the carriage. Through the window, the darkness was punctured by the lights of the train at the opposite platform, the train from Liverpool on which he had so recently travelled.

All the noise and bustle, the familiar station smells, as they waited to depart. All the noise and bustle in his brain. It was not his fault, and after all his tribulations he had expected a modicum of sympathy in her reply. His own message to her had been necessarily brief. But was she incapable of reading between his lines?

ARRIVED LIVERPOOL STOP SAFE STOP
BLACKSTONES DECEASED STOP
DETAINED FOR INQUEST MONDAY STOP
STAR AND GARTER HOTEL STOP WAIT FOR ME STOP

It was a difficult request. Ettie's father would have expected her back in Manchester, to her duties as his honorary housekeeper.

No, things had not gone according to plan when the paddle steamer finally docked at the Princes Landing Stage. Palmer's second encounter with the captain had been difficult enough. But then the interrogations at the dockside and, afterwards, at the local Bridewell. The requirement for him to remain in the city. Problems finding accommodation, given both his disreputable appearance and the limitations – as well as the condition – of the currency he carried.

The Star and Garter was hardly the most salubrious place he had ever stayed.

Next, news that the inquest was postponed. Until today, Tuesday. Just this morning – though it felt like a lifetime ago. But yesterday he had sent a second communication to Ettie.

INQUEST POSTPONED STOP
RETURN WREXHAM TOMORROW TUESDAY NIGHT STOP
WAIT STOP

From that message, no reply at all. An angry silence.

The delay had provided one silver lining, however. A telegraphic message to Mr Low with a request for an advance of his salary, the money to be paid to the telegraph office in Wrexham and subsequently the telegraphic transfer to Liverpool. The wonders of this modern age! Some decent clothing purchased and a new rain napper for the autumn weather here in this unfamiliar and windy second metropolis of the Empire was inclement, to say the least.

He had also sent a message to Willcox. To the Liverpool Arms at Menai Bridge in the sure knowledge that the old seadog would be a patron. To thank him. To advise him that all was well.

Palmer also found a decent dentist, who recommended trying to save the tooth by removing all the decay with a foot-operated drill and then filling the cleansed hole with an amalgam. It was painful, though it seemed to have done the trick. His jaw still ached but the nagging pain was gone. Sadly, his chill was not.

Still, one day more, he thought. Just one day more. Was this too much to ask? Was it his fault – the postponement?

Postponed, it became clear, to allow a solicitor to travel all the way from London. A government solicitor – that was all the fellow would reveal. With the temerity to instruct Mr Palmer on the way he should respond at the inquest. Indeed, at almost every question put to Palmer by the Borough Coroner, Mr Aspinall, this government solicitor – Badger both by name and nature – chose to answer on Palmer's behalf.

He had therefore been permitted to make only the most banal and cautiously worded statement – between fits of sneezing and repeated requests from the coroner that he should speak up, for his throat remained weak.

Yes, he had been a passenger on board the Duke of Westminster's yacht, the *Lady Constance*. She had run aground, and foul play was suspected, two of her crew – Palmer recalled the men quite clearly – had disappeared from the vessel.

Later, at Menai Bridge, Palmer had seen the same two men boarding the steam packet. He considered it his civic duty to alert the authorities.

No, he did not know for certain they were anarchists, but he could think of no better way to describe them. And in a moment both spontaneous and perhaps impetuous, he had purchased his own ticket. It was possible, he had believed, the captain might have needed him to identify the miscreants. Indeed, he had spoken to the captain – and Mr Aspinall confirmed there would be a written statement from the captain later in the proceedings.

The captain, Palmer said, had promised to deal with the matter when they reached Liverpool. But, by chance, during the journey, Palmer had been passing through the ship and observed the very same men. Fighting, it seemed.

There was a deck plan of the *Prince Arthur* upon an easel, and Palmer was required to show where this altercation had occurred. And yes, one of the men had fallen or been pushed overboard, the other injured, pushing his way past Palmer and bleeding profusely.

The alarm raised – man overboard – before Palmer followed the wounded man, a trail of blood, to cabin number twenty-three, where there was a woman. Yes, foreign, by the few words she spoke. And no – he had been instructed by Badger to lie – he was not previously acquainted with the lady.

He had stepped back out of the cabin again to summon help and there had encountered members of the crew. Palmer had sent them to fetch the captain and there had been the sound of a gunshot. He had discovered the wounded man now seemingly dead upon the floor, and the woman on her bed, a revolver in her hand and an awful wound to her face, her eye. Her left eye, so far as he recalled. He had believed she must be dead also.

There had followed various reports from *post-mortem* examinations of the three deceased, identified by the purser's ledgers as being Mr and Mrs Frederick, and their manservant, Edwards.

'Am I not perjured,' Palmer had whispered to Badger, 'by my failure to identify them correctly?'

'Might as well be hanged for a sheep as a lamb, sir,' the solicitor smiled.

Finally, the captain's rather vague account, which somehow managed to neither support *nor* dispute Palmer's version of events.

And the verdicts? Further police investigation sought – to establish whether these three persons might, in fact, be anarchists. But so far as the three cases were concerned – one death by misadventure, drowned having fallen overboard from a steam packet; and one wilful murder by some person or persons unknown. The last? *That the deceased shot herself with a revolver and was killed thereby. There is no evidence to show the state of her mind at that time.*

No mention of suicide, therefore. Palmer was not sure how much note the Almighty might take of coroners' verdicts, but he hoped it would be enough to save her from whatever purgatory her own Catholic faith promised her. At least, he thought, she shall not be denied a Christian burial. His own Primitive Methodism tended rather towards that more liberal view within the scriptures. Romans, 8:35.

For I am persuaded, that neither death, nor life, nor angels, nor principalities, nor powers, nor things present, nor things to come, nor height, nor depth, nor any other creature, shall be able to separate us from the love of God, which is in Christ Jesus our Lord.

And with that conclusion, Palmer had been free to leave. Not quite free, however, for there was a last dire warning from solicitor Badger. Not one word to any person beyond that prepared statement. Not a word. Matters of national security at stake, Badger had insisted. And Mr Palmer would not be wishing to bring down the wrath of government upon his head now, would he? Beyond this, he refused to be drawn.

Of course, Palmer still had the inquest into the death of the fellow at Chislehurst hanging over him.

But all for another day and, after settling his account at the Star and Garter, he had been just in time to catch the mid-afternoon train to Chester. And now…

He heard the stationmaster's whistle blow and the engine's first slow *chuff, chuff, chuff,* when the carriage door was flung open and a gentleman came running alongside, gripping the edge of the door itself with one hand but the other encumbered by a leather brief-bag. Not enough momentum, therefore, to haul himself aboard.

Palmer to the rescue, leaping across to take the fellow's extended arm, to heave him upwards, allowing him to get first one foot, then both, onto the step, before clambering safely inside, the door slamming itself shut behind him. It was an action not without cost to Palmer himself for his body still throbbed from his encounter with Blackstone. Still, the man's gratitude was ample reward.

'My eternal thanks,' he gasped in a voice so deep as to be bottomless. He fingered the brim of his top hat, seemingly surprised to find it still in place. 'I should hate to have been forced to wait for the next one.'

Elegantly dressed, shoes polished like mirrors. Tall, ramrod straight. Profuse moustache and sideburns. A military man, surely. His age? Well past fifty, but nowhere near sixty.

'Indeed,' said Palmer. 'Not another until half past eight, I believe.'

'Twenty forty-three, to be precise.'

'You served with the army, sir?' Palmer enquired.

'Canada mostly. Crimea, of course. Then back to Canada. Fenians, you know? Raids across the American border. Had to be stopped.'

'Not with the Thirtieth, I suppose?' Palmer recalled how their band had led the parade at the opening of the Exhibition. And how they had thrilled him as a boy in Thetford. Yes, the Thirtieth had fought the Irish Republicans in Canada, he was sure.

'Royal Canadian Rifles,' the man corrected him. 'After we settled with the Russians at Sebastopol, I served with the Canadian Militia. Hope to be back there before too long. Canada, I mean. Only police actions these days, of course. No more major wars now, I don't think.' The gentleman made a bridge of his fingertips, as though in prayer, and gazed up at the varnished ceiling. 'You will know the psalm, of course? *"He maketh wars to cease unto the end of the earth; he breaketh the bow, and cutteth the spear in sunder; he burneth the chariot in the fire."* Do you not agree, sir? We are at the end of wars?'

Palmer tentatively suggested that the War in the East and, only a few years before, the conflict between France and Prussia – that these might suggest an entirely different conclusion.

'I have to say,' he told the gentleman, after a brief interlude of sneezing and blowing his nose, 'that I hold a contrary view. So long as there are manufacturers whose wealth depends upon the continuous production of arms, so long as there are generals who can be persuaded to use them, and so long as there are politicians who can be bribed to ensure those spent weapons are replaced with the latest shining model, we shall never see war's end.'

And hence their conversation continued until the train slowed for its passage across the Dee Bridge. He recalled how this had all started. Here, with Morrison. Their discussion about the disaster, almost three decades earlier. Poor Morrison. Palmer felt he had betrayed the man somehow but shook himself back to the present.

'You must forgive me,' he said. 'How ill-mannered I have been. Please allow me to introduce myself. Palmer, sir. Alfred Palmer. And might you be travelling to Wrexham for the Exhibition, by any chance?'

'Great Heavens!' said the gentleman. 'Extraordinary. Mr Alfred Palmer, presently in the employ of Mr Low?' Palmer was confused but confirmed that he was, indeed, that same Alfred Palmer. 'Then you, sir, are the very inspiration for my journey.'

He truly sounded astonished at the coincidence, but then his voice dropped to more of a growl.

'Yet I sent instructions,' he said. 'To your Inspector Wilde. Requiring that you should be detained in Wrexham pending my arrival. It is plain the fellow could not have directed you accordingly, sir, else you should not be here upon this train and nor would you have been on board the Duke of Westminster's yacht or, indeed, upon the *Prince Arthur.*'

At Thetford Grammar School, before he had discovered that being a perfect scholar was the best defence against the beatings, he had just once attempted to keep his adventurous ambition alive by devising a clever – or so he thought – system of cheating. He had been hauled before the entire school, the shame far worse than the pain of

Porter's cane. Incredibly, he felt the same level of mortification now, the colour firing his cheeks in the face of the man's ire.

'You would be Sir Patrick MacDougall?' he stammered and fought to overcome his foolishness.

'The same, Mr Palmer. The very same.'

'And if you have travelled all the way here from London, sir, if you already know about the *Prince Arthur*, I am forced to assume you must also know about the role in this sorry affair played by one of the government's own former agents – by Frederick Blackstone. And in Chislehurst...'

'Disley,' said Sir Patrick.

'I beg your pardon?'

'The fellow's name was Disley, Mr Palmer. Thomas Disley. And while it may be true that he sometimes undertook certain tasks for the Department, the attack upon your person at Chislehurst was certainly not one of them.'

'And I should be relieved by that, sir? But – Department? Military Intelligence, I must assume.'

'I have the honour to be the Department's director. My precise rank is Deputy Quartermaster-General.'

'Deputy to whom?'

'This is military intelligence, Mr Palmer. There *is* nobody to whom I play second fiddle. Not in the department. Though the Quartermaster General himself is nominally responsible for my own *and* the Topographical Department. A recent innovation. Before that – well, it matters little, I think. I know not whose bright idea it might have been to mask our intelligence activities as though they were merely a matter of administration, supply and demand, and therefore within the remit of a quartermaster, but...'

'Then, this Disley... If he was not acting for your department, and you have taken the trouble to arrange this *coincidence*...'

No, he thought. I do not believe in coincidence either. Though it was excruciating to try and imagine the network which must be at play to enable Sir Patrick to connive at their encounter. The precise time. The precise train.

'If not,' he pressed on, 'then I am forced to assume the rogue was under instruction from some other person of prominence. Such as...'

'Say no more, sir. For I understand that His Royal Highness has been mentioned in connection with this affair.'

'And is he not – connected?'

'My goodness, no. Or, rather, perhaps not in the way you imagine. Between ourselves, Mr Palmer, I rather fear for our poor nation when Her Majesty eventually shuffles off this mortal coil. And such a coil it is! Life is knotted and complex, do you not think? All noise and confusion. It is the reason I so admire Canada. The open space. The simplicity. But His Royal Highness is, as they say, the clay with which we must work. And, therefore, his reputation must be preserved. You understand me, sir? A matter of national security.'

'Do I detect a threat, Sir Patrick? And your solicitor, Mr Badger, lectured me at some length about national security.'

'Not my solicitor, Mr Palmer. Different department entirely. And is a threat necessary? Do you not love your Queen? Your country?'

Palmer was not quite certain. His country, yes, of course. But he found he rather shared old Reynolds's views on the monarchy. Still...

'In the England that I love,' he replied, 'one should be able to expect that those responsible for the violent deaths of others might be brought to justice. Do you know, sir, how many such deaths have occurred during this *affair*, as you call it. Let me tell you...'

Sir Patrick MacDougall listened with consummate patience to Palmer's concise summary. All the way past Balderton, Pulfordsen and Rossett.

'An interesting tale, sir,' said Sir Patrick when Palmer had finished, 'but one in which I know at least a *few* of the details to be incorrect. You see, dear Faustina may have misled you. Freddie was never more than a minor operative for the Department. Whereas Faustina herself – well, you may be able to imagine the intelligence to be gathered in an establishment such as her own. A shame, for her life to end that way. But I suppose...'

'You could not have allowed her to stand trial,' said Palmer. 'Could you?'

'I prefer to think that it was her grief at losing poor Crick which drove her to such an end.'

'You are a hard man, sir.'

'Perhaps. And yes, we provided references for them – Marlborough House to be precise, the household of our good Prince Bertie – for the workhouse posts. But that was indeed at the request of your Mrs Fitzpatrick and, from what you say, it would have been Mrs Fitzpatrick…'

'Then should it not be Mrs Fitzpatrick brought to justice?'

'You have only Faustina's word for any of this. And I can assure you Mr Palmer, the word of Faustina Blackstone…'

Had Faustina told him the truth, about Patsy's mother? He had no reason to disbelieve her. Yet what did he truly know of Mrs Olivia Fitzpatrick? He recalled the last occasion when he had seen her. In the tailor's shop, with her daughter. *'Palmer?'* she had said. *'The ubiquitous Mr Palmer?'* Ubiquitous. It seemed she had known far more about Palmer than he had known about her. And then there was that reasonable chance that it had been Mrs Fitzpatrick who had dispatched the apprentice boy, perhaps with a seemingly innocent message, but a message which had somehow triggered the drovers' attack. Yet proof?

'You see, Mr Palmer? All your principal players have left the stage. Not a shred of evidence against the lady.'

They pulled into Gresford Halt, where the platform's sulphurous lamplight barely pierced the rain and left the station's impressive building shrouded in a bilious yellow glow. Palmer remembered Morrison's words when they had stopped here, all those months before.

'Here, Mr Palmer. Draw your last salubrious inhalation here, if you will. For beyond Gresford you shall find nothing but pit wheels and coal dust, the stench of mediocrity.'

'Mr Palmer?' Sir Patrick MacDougall tugged at Palmer's sleeve. 'Did you hear me, sir? Every detail. Every detail of your involvement shall vanish. Believe me, such shall be our cleansing that, within a short while, there shall be no remaining record of you ever having been in Wrexham or anywhere near. Nor anybody else associated with the case.'

'My…'

'Miss Francis shall, I am sure, be guided by you, Mr Palmer.'

'I rather think she had hoped we might settle there. In Wrexham.'

'And perhaps, given the passage of time, when we are certain the prince's reputation cannot be sullied...'

'But Crick,' said Palmer, remembering Ettie's sympathy for the fellow. 'He was, by all accounts, once a fine soldier, Sir Patrick. His burial...'

'Of course. And there, we are on the move again.' He wiped a gloved hand against the glass, and he peered at the slowly passing nameboard. 'Gresford,' he said. 'The next stop your own, Mr Palmer, I believe. I thought I should have to stay. But this seems to conclude our business. With luck I shall find a decent room in Shrewsbury.'

'You will not stay to see the Exhibition?'

'I think not. It has already been necessary to dampen enthusiasm, to distract attention. Have you not read *The Spectator*?' He delved into the leather brief-bag, pulled out his copy. 'This week's edition,' he smiled. 'Let me see...'

He turned the pages and handed the folded publication. Half of page eleven, Palmer saw. He explored further. All of page twelve, half of thirteen. He cast his eyes over the opening lines.

That art should se nicher *in a region we associate chiefly with coal and slate... when one gets out of the train in Wrexham... and sees what an ugly and uninteresting place it is.*

Palmer remembered that Morrison had used almost the same words, on this very same train, over three months earlier.

'Your department,' he said. 'You arranged this?'

'A simple reminder, sir. That our reach is not only long, but also incredibly wide.'

Chapter Thirty-Four

'Not a word,' she scolded him. 'Not a single, solitary word. Either to ask after my own health. Nor to express the simplest of affections. Nor to invite me to join you in Liverpool – to support you in your tribulations, Neo.'

Palmer patted her arm, knowing just too late that she would find the gesture condescending, make her even more vexed with him. But he wanted to take one last look at the train, the silhouette of Sir Patrick MacDougall framed in the carriage window like some cameo on a piece of dark jasperware. It was all nonsense, of course. How could the fellow have been considering an overnight in Wrexham when he carried nothing but a brief-bag?

'He must have been staying in Shrewsbury all along,' he said. 'Waiting for word that I had left Liverpool.'

'Who? And Shrewsbury...?'

They were shrouded in clouds of smoke and steam as the train began its onward journey and Palmer led her along the darkened platform, his free hand clutching both the handles of his own recently purchased portmanteau as well as this damnable edition of *The Spectator*.

'I shall explain,' he told her, as they sheltered beneath his rain napper and waited for a hansom, 'but, first, I must try to seek forgiveness for my trespasses by so belatedly enquiring after your own condition, my dear.'

'Perhaps you should have realised, sir, if you truly knew me well, that the abruptness of my reply to your inadequate message should have assured you that I must be quite recovered.'

'I see that now. Had you still been incapacitated, you could surely not have expressed so much anger within so little diction.'

She called him a buffoon, and her annoyance seemed only marginally abated, but she told him her own tale, all the same. She recalled little of her arrival at Menai Bridge, but Richard Low had seen her safely to the Liverpool Arms, where the proprietor's wife lent her clothes.

'I sent a message there, at least,' he said, before realising how foolish was the disclosure. 'To Willcox. Yet it never occurred to me...'

'No, that much is apparent. But at least there I also had a room for the night. A room with a fire. The rest of the Lows had returned to Wrexham that same evening, but Richard had taken a room as well, so that I should not be abandoned entirely. We took the following day's train together.'

'He stayed?' said Palmer. 'He stayed the night?'

At last, a free cab, and they clambered aboard.

'Your hotel?' he snapped at her before she could reply.

'Yes, the Liverpool Arms. And you must wipe that vexed look from your face, sir. Before tonight's dinner.'

'Dinner?'

'Have you forgotten, Neo?'

He racked his brains. Then mumbled yet another apology. It felt like a lifetime past. Yet here it was. Tuesday. The twenty-fourth. And a dinner. Organised through the liberality of Mr Medlicott who was kindly providing the refreshments. A hundred guests and held in honour of those who had chiefly been responsible for the Exhibition.

'The invitation dinner,' he murmured. 'And yes, entirely forgotten. But perhaps...'

Ettie tapped on the roof of the hansom, instructed the cabbie to take them to the Exhibition.

'I should rather not be there either, my dear,' she said, her tone still tetchy. 'All this to absorb. Much of it makes so little sense...'

'We shall be too late by far, of course, to take our places at the table. But I *did* promise Mr Low. And we should at least be there for the speeches. The only problem is that I do not have the invitation with me and you, my dear, presumably are not in possession...'

'Mr Low, at least, was kind enough to ensure we are both on the guest list – though why I should have been so foolish as to wait for you...'

'*Which* Mr Low, precisely?' he snapped. 'Senior or junior?'

'Richard,' she told him, as though she savoured the name, 'was gentle, Mr Palmer.'

Palmer felt a dark pit of jealous embers open at his feet, and Esther had discovered a poker to rake through the ashes of his anguished soul.

'Gentle?'

He pulled out his kerchief, tried to clear his nose, though in truth he hoped the action might help hide the confusion he knew his face must display.

'You truly are a buffoon, Neo.'

And without another word of Richard Low, she completed her tale. By the time she was safely ensconced at the Liverpool Arms, the whole town of Menai Bridge had seemed awash with the word anarchists. No mention of Blackstone or Crick. Her inner sense had told her not to mention them either. She had discovered, of course, that Palmer had taken passage aboard the *Prince Arthur*. And the following hours – until she received his absurd message – had been an agony of fear for his safety.

'I still have no idea what drove me,' he said, quietly. 'And thoughtless, entirely thoughtless, to leave you in such turmoil.'

'There was a brief account in the *Western Mail* yesterday. You saw it?'

Indeed, he had. A tragic sequence of events aboard the steam packet. Three dead. A woman and two men. Police investigation. Inquest to be held. But remarkably few details.

'Yet nobody has noticed they are missing? The Blackstones?'

'It is the strangest thing, Neo. By Sunday evening, at Mr Low's – did I tell you, that old Mr Low insisted I should move out of the hotel and await your return at Roseneath?'

No, she had not mentioned it earlier and he felt the embers stirred once more. Had Richard Low arranged this also?

'In any case,' she pressed on. 'Sunday evening. And news that the Blackstones had absconded from the workhouse. Absconded, according to the story, with a considerable amount of the finances. Vanished without trace. The police alerted but, so far...'

The long arm of military intelligence, thought Palmer. He glanced through the cab window and saw they had arrived in Regent Street, the flags and turnstiles outside the archway.

'I still refuse to believe it,' she said, after they had surrendered their coats, and Palmer's bag – though not *The Spectator* – at the cloakroom. 'Can this man have so much power, such control of our fate, that he can simply cause historical fact to vanish, the clocks to run in reverse?'

The dining tables had been set in a lengthy line down the broad centre of the entrance hall outside the exhibition gallery itself and they were presently being cleared, the guests stretching their legs or coming and going from the lavatories, while the luxuriously bearded surgeon, Dr Eyton-Jones, in his scarlet robe and mayoral regalia, stood at the centre of the arrangement, shuffling through a sheaf of papers, presumably his oration. Palmer rather feared it would be a lengthy one.

'I have never believed,' he said, 'time to be a fixed entity. Our attempts to constrain it, with the invention of clocks and measurements, are entirely artificial. Time is fluid, I think.'

'The way,' she murmured, 'time passes quickly or slowly depending upon our humour?'

'The perfect example. In this regard, therefore, time is very much on Sir Patrick's side. And yes, he made it perfectly clear. Not a word of these events must pass either of our lips. Not a trace of our entanglement on the pages of any publication.'

'Yet many more than simply ourselves embroiled in this web, Neo. What about that fellow on board the *Lady Constance*? The engineer who found us down in that foul hole.'

'I suppose, Ettie, that His Grace will want as little attention as possible to the day as a whole. His reputation tarnished. It could all have been a disaster of much greater proportion. And we never mentioned Blackstone by name, so far as I recall.'

Now they were noticed. Mr Low striding from the other side of the room.

'Laddie,' beamed the old fellow, though his face was creased with concern, 'I cannae say how pleased I am to see ye' safe. But such calumny. I can scarce believe it.'

'Anarchists,' Palmer replied, while shaking Low's hand. 'Yes, who would have…'

'Anarchists be damned, laddie. I mean *that!*' He had seen *The Spectator* in Palmer's hand. 'Ye've read it, my dear?' he said to Ettie.

She had not. She apologised. She had been rather occupied with other matters. Did it concern Saturday's events?

'It does not, Esther,' Palmer told her. 'It concerns the Exhibition.' He lowered his voice in the hope Mr Low might not catch this particular sentence. 'Though it might indeed relate to our earlier discussion.'

A long reach. A wide reach. A *rapid* reach.

The dinner gong rang, an urgent demand for the guests to resume their seats.

'Shall we find you a place at table?' said Mr Low. But Palmer declined. There were chairs here, along the wall. They would answer perfectly.

In truth, he was exhausted. The day's proceedings. All that had transpired. And he rather feared a bout of sneezing or coughing might disrupt the gathering – easier to slip away unnoticed from here, should the need arise.

'In that case,' said Low, 'I shall join ye' both here.'

And he did.

'*The Spectator?*' Ettie murmured, as the mayor, finally satisfied that all were seated once more, proposed a loyal toast. The queen, the Prince and Princess of Wales – the entire royal family, in fact.

'About the Exhibition,' Palmer whispered, as the harmonium's opening bars to the National Anthem brought them all to their feet. 'I shall be amazed if the speakers may restrain themselves from raising its scurrilous critique.'

The singing itself was led by the voluptuous Mrs Jacques, whom Palmer recognised from so many of the Exhibition's previous concerts – as, indeed, he recognised many of the other badly discordant dignitaries, and their wives, naturally. Inspector Wilde, Hancock from the *Advertiser* and Bethan Thomas there, as well. Each of them acknowledged his presence, Wilde and Hancock with enthusiasm, Bethan with the briefest nod of the head.

Palmer stumbled his own way through the familiar lyrics and searched for a first sight of Major Cornwallis West – and for Patsy. Ah, there. Guests of honour near the farther end, the head, of the table. He found her staring back at him. Those same languid eyes. The same venom.

But as the anthem went from verse to verse, with the guests knowing less and less of the words, he found himself reminded of Reynolds. The Prince of Wales? Or, as Reynolds had said, the Prince of Wastrels. His Royal Hellspawn. He knew he was now cursed to recall these titles every time he heard the National Anthem for the rest of his life. Yet, where would he spend those years? Not here in Wrexham, it seemed. For he had already determined he could not risk ignoring Sir Patrick's dire warning. If he stayed here, in time there would be questions. Inevitable questions. And if there were questions…

Besides, there was a task he must perform. A task in Manchester.

Chapter Thirty-Five

Palmer knew he was being forced into a conspiracy of silence but here, at the end of the invitation dinner, there was a conspiracy of an entirely different stamp. A conspiracy of excessive refinement, of extravagant gentility. For they all must have read *The Spectator* article, yet it received not a mention. Not verbally, in any case. Only through inference.

It must have been difficult in the extreme. The mayor's opening words were uncontentious enough. A toast to the army, to the navy and to militia volunteers. Praise for the glories of British dominion. Simple enough for a man who, besides his present medical notoriety was also a distinguished essayist and, previously, Surgeon-Major with the Denbighshire Hussars. But when it came to his main theme – celebration of the Exhibition and its organisers – his speech was delivered almost through gritted teeth, the sheets of paper in his hands trembling with suppressed annoyance. So many things he *could* have said. So many parries and ripostes he *should* have made to *The Spectator*'s biting thrusts. Yet just too urbane to sink to the journal's level.

'And this remarkable edifice,' he was saying, 'given the time available...'

The words instantly triggered Palmer's recollection of the article's bile about the structure – and he could see the guests fidget and squirm as they remembered the same sentences, looked about them at the construction flaws to which they could no longer close their eyes.

...the Exhibition building, an ill-shapen, lop-sided structure...

There was a great deal of harrumphing, of thumbs thrust tetchily into waistcoat pockets, of sour face. Yes, Morrison might have written this. Except that Morrison...

'Aye, nothing wrong with the place,' Mr Low grumbled.

'We have been blessed by those who have attended in such numbers,' Dr Eyton-Jones read from his notes, 'our visitors, as well as the fine folk of this remarkable town.'

But this was not quite the way in which *The Spectator* observed matters.

...flat, dull, dirty – and crowded with people who are exceedingly unbeautiful...

'Fine folk, indeed,' snapped Mr Low. 'Indeed, they are, Mr Palmer.'

Palmer agreed and, at the table, there seemed to be much discomfort among the ladies. Much polite coughing.

'Yes, a fine town.' The mayor emphasised the point with a stab of his finger towards the roof.

...the visitor will probably be attacked by a profound melancholy...

'All have praised the quality of the entertainment offered within these walls.'

...people have different ways of enjoying themselves, however, and this may be the Welsh way...

'And even those few – those very few – critics of our Exhibition have been forced to admit that the collection on display here is remarkable for its quality and variety.'

Well, thought Palmer, even *The Spectator* had made this point at least, almost half a page devoted to the many especially noteworthy exhibits. Yet there had been a sting in the tail here also.

After a very short time the Exhibition grows so much upon the previously desponding visitor, that he makes up his mind it will take him at least a week to appreciate thoroughly the art treasures which are displayed in the unlikely and uncongenial town of Wrexham.

'There will be those,' said the mayor, 'who may seek to condemn the paucity of financial reward for our efforts...'

Palmer could recall no direct reference in the article to financial probity, but there was implication in so many of the phrases used by the author. That perhaps the high costs incurred did not tally with the lesser standards achieved.

...a roof covered with dirty strips of awning...

He glanced up. Yes, the roof. And other features. Once one's attention had been drawn to the defects of the structure, it was impossible to ever again put them out of sight. For anybody inside the town or beyond, anybody who had questioned the wisdom of the Exhibition's cost – and there were many such people – *The Spectator*'s words would be grist to the mill.

'Four thousand pounds, laddie,' murmured Mr Low, standing to acknowledge the tribute presently being made to him by the mayor. 'Aye, that's what we're likely to lose.'

Further tributes to Mr Chaffers – whose duties as the exhibition's General Superintendent had been so admirably undertaken – and, of course, to Major Cornwallis West. An entire eulogy of the principal art treasures themselves. And surely, the mayor suggested, the entire enterprise must be justification for a permanent museum and gallery within the town.

'Permanent museum?' Mr Low whispered in Palmer's ear, while the mayor proposed the toast of the evening, to Medlicott himself, without whose beneficence, said Dr Eyton-Jones, such an excellent occasion would not have been possible. 'Aye, laddie, a fine thing that would be.'

The presentation of a silver platter. Then Mr Medlicott's own thanks and a toast to the ladies, without whose presence the evening would not have been complete.

'A fine thing indeed,' said Palmer as the proceedings concluded and the company began to retire. 'And I wish I could be here to see the dream become a reality. But sadly, sir, I now fear I may not remain even until the close of the Exhibition itself.'

Ten o'clock and he knew this exchange would have been better undertaken after a good night's sleep. But *carpe diem*, he said to himself. *Carpe diem.*

Low seemed stricken, his fingers disappearing within those fulsome white whiskers as he rubbed at his chin.

'Ye cannae leave us now, Mr Palmer. Do you not see how we're under attack? Typical of *The Spectator*, mind ye', not to name the rogue who penned that filthy piece.'

Palmer knew it was too great a leap, to assume somehow that the attack might be his own fault, a warning shot arranged by Sir Patrick

MacDougall and his agents. A persecutory delusion, surely. Though he could no longer be entirely certain. He simply understood that his life, now, would be less complicated, easier, if he was anywhere other than Wrexham.

'You shall have Bethan to help you, sir,' he said. 'She is competent beyond belief.'

Low glanced at the cloakroom, where Bethan was being helped into her coat. She seemed even more incapacitated than usual, but he found that he had grown very fond of her. He would miss her.

'Bethan, my dear,' Low called to her and she joined them. 'I've some bad news, I fear. That our friend Mr Palmer plans to abandon us.' Palmer thought he saw some slight dismissive movement of her poor shoulders, a look of total *ennui* upon the face turned upwards to peer at him.

'*Rargian fawr*,' she laughed. What the devil. 'Never here any'ow, he's not.'

'And when, laddie?' said Low.

'It seems we shall need to leave almost immediately. I shall, of course, repay the advance you so kindly arranged. But then I must escort Miss Francis back to Manchester. Tomorrow, if that might be possible. I should like the opportunity, of course, to bid the family farewell.'

'He'll be back,' said Bethan. 'Can see it, I can.'

'I doubt it, Miss Thomas,' said Palmer. 'Levinstein shall be glad to see me once more at my post, I hope. I doubt he shall ever release me again.'

He watched as Ettie bent down to embrace Bethan Thomas and he wished he might have been able to do the same.

'And yes,' said Ettie as she stood upright once more. 'I see it too, Bethan. I think he *will* be back.'

'You're sure, laddie?' said Mr Low.

'Certain, sir. I have a duty to perform – in Manchester. But before all the lights are extinguished, I should like to take one last look at Mr Williams's coverlet.'

They parted company with further promises to say their final farewells tomorrow, and Palmer led Esther towards the tables, beyond which the doors to the Exhibition Hall remained open.

'Well?' Inspector Wilde gripped his arm. 'Coincidence?' It was almost a whisper. 'The Blackstones missing. Crick as well. Three dead on board the steam packet to Liverpool. That's what the papers say. Three. And you, Mister Palmer. Supposed to be detained here in Wrexham until...'

'Never fear, Inspector. I have already had the honour of meeting Sir Patrick.'

'I'm well aware of that, sir. But you could have been killed, I'm told. And then, where would we have been?'

'As you see, Inspector, I am perfectly well. Apart from this annoying sniffle. And Miss Francis also. But we shall not be here to trouble you further, you may be pleased to know. We leave for Manchester tomorrow. And I doubt we shall ever return.'

'That would be a great pity, if you don't mind me saying so, Mister Palmer. But you've still not told me. A coincidence? The Blackstones and those three on the *Prince Arthur*.'

'But naturally!' Palmer laughed. 'What on earth else could it have been?'

'I thought, Neo,' said Ettie, when Wilde had left them, 'you told me the inspector doesn't believe in...'

'Of course, he does not, my dear.'

They excused themselves as they passed more guest, but there was Hancock, blocking their path.

'You have solved it, Palmer,' he exclaimed. 'Tell me you have solved the rest of your puzzle and may now be ready to tell the tale.'

Guilt. Palmer had promised the fellow, had he not? To share whatever he discovered?

'I fear the whole sorry story is entirely beyond solution, old boy,' he said. 'A complete dead end. None of our clues leading to a *dénouement*. Isn't that true, my dear?' He turned to Ettie for support.

'Sadly,' she said, and offered Hancock her most sympathetic smile.

'But the Blackstones' disappearance?' he insisted. 'And the steam packet. Two men. A woman. You were there, sir. Will you deny it was them?'

He was incredulous, but Palmer could see that his mood was rapidly turning to anger, hoped he might assuage his frustrations.

'I understand that the papers will have the story tomorrow, Mr Hancock. There was a reporter at the inquest. He took all the details. And the names of those poor unfortunates aboard the *Prince Arthur*? Formally identified. Their names in the purser's ledger – though I cannot now recall them. But definitely not Blackstone. If you should like the details I was compelled to give to the inquest, I am happy to oblige, dear fellow.'

'Under oath, Mr Palmer. You gave those details under oath?'

'Indeed, I did.'

'And no mention of the Blackstones? Or Crick?'

'None.'

Hancock gazed into Palmer's eyes. Then at Ettie. Hopeful. Then the gaze she offered in return extinguished whatever feelings he may once have had for her. He nodded his head and stood aside. Palmer knew he would have to write to him, try to make amends. And, in his haste to escape, almost collided directly with the Cornwallis Wests.

'Mr…' said the major, both animated and confused at the same time.

'Palmer, sir.'

'Of course. Of course. Palmer. And what do you think of all this, Palmer? *The Spectator*, of all things. I had thought we should do so well – for the entire county. The Exhibition. The Eisteddfod. But now…'

But now he finally recalled how he knew Palmer at all.

'Palmer,' he said again. 'Great Heavens, it is good to see you. The very thing. Willcox told me you pursued the villains who scuppered the *Lady Constance*. Anarchists? I believe His Grace intends to offer you some reward. And quite right, too. Good grief, my dear,' he said to Patsy at his side. 'Can you believe it? Palmer pursued the devils. Forgive me, but I assume…'

The major's wife said nothing, stared through him as though he did not exist.

'Yes, major,' said Palmer. 'A long story but the two rogues from the *Lady Constance* were the same who died aboard the *Prince Arthur*.'

'I should very much like to hear the entire yarn, sir.' The major turned to his wife. 'What d'you say, my dear? Might we not invite Mr Palmer and his charming companion to dinner at Ruthin Castle?'

Palmer leapt into the breach before Patsy Cornwallis West might respond. He would spare her this much, at least.

'I regret to say we both leave for Manchester tomorrow, major. And, sadly, unlikely to return. At least for some time.'

'Shame. Shame.' But the major was already looking over Palmer's shoulder. 'Ah, there is Chaffers. I must speak with him. Perhaps, Mr...'

'Palmer, sir,' said Palmer, though the major had already slapped a farewell upon his arm and brushed past, leaving them alone with Patsy. He realised he would indeed be forgotten much faster even than he had supposed.

'You had some part in it, I assume?' she said, as soon as her husband was out of earshot. 'The note. What did you mean by it?'

'Some part?' Ettie turned upon the woman. 'Some part, you say?'

Mrs Cornwallis West, as beautiful as ever, statuesque, all pearls and silver thread embroidery glittering through her seagull grey silks. Yet the aquamarine eyes were no longer languid. They flashed, bright with animosity, though somewhat startled by Esther's assault.

'We almost died,' Ettie snarled. 'Both of us. Because we believed you to be in danger. Because we saw your daughter in danger.'

'And do you still believe, madam,' said Palmer, 'it was only a danger from the helmsman's incompetence?'

'The *Western Mail* reported one man overboard and two other fatalities, Mr Palmer. I truly hoped that one of them might have been you, sir.'

Palmer was speechless. Is there any other creature on this planet, he wondered, capable of wishing hurt upon another of its kind simply for the sake of the hurt itself?

'Anarchists,' Ettie reminded her. 'Your husband said as much, did he not? You believed Mr Palmer to be one of them?'

'I have no idea *what* Mr Palmer purports to be, my dear. And I care even less. But he knew about a certain note within my daughter's coat...'

'I told you about the note,' he said, still reeling somewhat from her wish to see him dead.

'And you must therefore have played some part in it being there, must you not?' she said.

'Wait.' Palmer had an epiphany. 'I was just speaking with Inspector Wilde. He is still here, I think. At the cloakroom, I imagine. Esther, would you mind? Fetch him, perhaps?'

'Fetch him – why?' said the major's wife, a hint of caution in her voice as though she were given pause to think afresh.

Palmer set a restraining hand on Esther's shoulder.

'Perhaps, my dear, in a moment. And why, Mrs Cornwallis West? Because at every turn you have reported me to Inspector Wilde. Yet when I chatted with him just now… It seems you did not relate this latest suspicion to him. About the note.'

He saw the doubt now in those green eyes.

'I have friends in higher places than Inspector Wilde.'

'Enemies as well, I think.'

'You speak in riddles, Mr Palmer.'

'Do I? Will you not show me the note – you have it, I suppose?'

'The note is none of your concern.'

'Very well,' he said, over the chink of glass and porcelain, as he stood aside to allow one of the caterers to collect the abandoned tableware. 'Esther, if you please, the Inspector…'

'Wait!' Patsy barked at him. 'There is no reason, but…'

There was a final look of defiance, a pause before she delved into her purse of silver chainmail and produced the crumpled piece of paper, handed it pointedly, not to Palmer, but to Esther.

'You see, Neo?' said Ettie and showed him the writing. The hand seemed too elegant for Blackstone, and certainly so for Crick.

> *Final warning. No more begging letters.*
> *We can reach your children.*

'If I didn't know better,' said Palmer, 'one might almost take this for a woman's hand. And a woman of some refinement. An older woman, perhaps.'

He watched her attempt to resist the temptation, though it was too strong, and her eyes were drawn to study the paper afresh, doubt clouding them somewhat.

'You daughter,' said Ettie, with true compassion. 'She has recovered from the ordeal?'

Patsy Cornwallis West glowered at her, affronted by the impudence of the enquiry, perhaps. Yet she softened, looked up from the piece of paper, answered in a civil enough fashion.

'She remembers little. More, I think, about the *Lady Constance* running aground. The excitement of the lifeboat. But twice she has asked me about the bear. Big Bear, she calls him. She says he frightened her.'

There was something in her voice. Palmer's second epiphany.

'And you have seen such a creature before, perhaps?' he said and saw the instant reaction. She recoiled a step, for he had struck another nerve. He was certain. 'But where, I wonder?'

He decided it could not possibly have been the workhouse. So where, indeed? Yet there was no chance to satisfy his curiosity. He should have expected it – her ability to rally in the face of adversity. He almost admired it.

'Truly, Mr Palmer,' she said with renewed defiance, 'I believe you should be writing penny dreadfuls. A fine dumb show it is, that you make of your innocence. But I think we both know how you have persecuted me. I should have liked to see you pay a heavy price for your ambuscades, though I suppose I should take some crumb of comfort that I shall never have to look upon your absurd face again.'

She pushed past them without a backward glance.

'A thoroughly unpleasant woman,' said Ettie.

'She is destined to have an unhappy life, I think,' Palmer replied. 'Especially if she does, indeed, ever discover that her mother played a part in this business.'

'And do you think so, Neo – that she might have seen Crick before?'

'Now I am certain of it. A man of that description, perhaps. If I were forced to guess, perhaps somewhere in company with Blackstone. And what an irony if it had been coming or going from her mother's house.'

'Then you believe what she told you – the Spanish woman? About this all being a scheme of that creature's own mama? A less than subtle attempt to prevent the precious Patsy from drawing further attention to both of their dalliances with...'

He looked into her eyes and remembered that, in his travelling bag, there was the portrait of Faustina as a young woman – the portrait sketched by that gallant English volunteer in the Carlist War. Sketched by Edward Crick. Sketched when he was still whole and unbroken. There was a resemblance, that much was certain. But would Faustina's curse be effective? Would he indeed think of Faustina during their moments of intimacy together? No, he would not.

'Mrs Fitzpatrick?' he said. 'Either she, or the Prince of Wales himself. Perhaps both. Or neither. How shall we ever be certain? I have done no more than satisfy myself that the Blackstones and Crick were the perpetrators – even if they were not themselves the instigators.'

There was an attendant, beginning to close the wide iron doors into the Exhibition Hall.

'Wait!' Palmer shouted. 'Might you give us ten minutes, sir? Ten minutes and no more?'

The fellow grumbled, of course. Did they know what time it was? Did they? But he grudgingly conceded the ten-minute extension when Palmer graced his outstretched hand with a silver halfcrown. The Queen's head, Victoria in her own youth, ribbons in her hair.

'I wonder,' he said, as he led Ettie through to the industrial annexe, 'what Her Majesty must think of him.'

'Her favourite son, is he not? Whatever sins he may commit, I suspect she would turn a mother's blind eye to them all.'

'Well,' said Palmer, 'there you have it.'

Mr Williams's coverlet hung just as he had first seen it, though it somehow seemed darker than previously. The lights had been dimmed, naturally. But it was more than that. The darkness seemed to emanate from the patchwork itself. Blood among the threads?

'You see?' He pointed to the top left corner. 'The bridge at Menai.'

'Did I not warn you, Neo? My letter, before you left to come here?'

'I still have it,' he replied. 'Nightmare visions, you said. Fears for my safety. But nobody welcomes a wiseacre, Esther.'

He saw from the twinkle in her eye that, despite his disparagement, Ettie knew it was she who had scored the *touché*. Palmer knew better than to pursue the point further, allowed his eye to follow all the other images, most of them with their own reminders of a particular episode from the story – from the journey they had taken together. There was just one of the larger sections which seemed to bear no relationship to the rest. The top right. Some intricate structure, oriental perhaps. Like a pagoda.

'And that?' she said. 'Do you think it might be the permanent museum, of which the mayor spoke so emotionally? A permanent museum for Wrexham?'

'That would be a glory indeed, Ettie. Perhaps a reason for us to return, after all.'

'Bethan Thomas says we shall do so. And she is a woman, Neo, with a certain power for prophecy.'

'As do you, Ettie, as I recall. As do you.'

He would need to write to Reynolds, of course. Sadly, he would say, the puzzle remained in pieces. No demonstrable malfeasance for the authorities to prosecute. And, therefore, sadly, nothing for the newspaper to savour. But perhaps when they were next together…

For the Widow Morrison there would be a very different letter. A further apology for the loss of her husband's papers and his conclusion, following the completion of Inspector Wilde's thorough investigation, that her husband's death had, indeed, been a tragic accident.

'Yet did you not tell Mr Low you had urgent business in Manchester, my dear? You have become quite the dissembler, I see. Shall you not be stripped of your entitlement to preach the Lord's Gospel?'

'I have been forced to take the view, Esther, arising from the words of the National Anthem – an implication that those in service to the Crown must somehow be working in the name of the Almighty. Therefore, if those same servants of the Crown require me to dissemble, it must also be in the name of the Lord, must it not?'

She laughed.

'Yet, in this case,' he went on, 'there was no dishonesty. None, whatsoever. Business in Manchester, indeed. For, you see, I did not entirely waste my time in Liverpool, and nor were you as far from my thoughts as you plainly imagined.'

He reached into his inside pocket and drew forth a small box.

'Surely,' she said, with a slight gasp, 'you did not?'

'A jeweller with the unlikely name of Wolf, my dear. And there was certainly a ravenous, lupine quality about the way he devoured my limited capital.'

He opened the box and displayed the diamond. This time, a more sustained sigh, before she pursed her lips and became playfully pensive.

'Such difficult choices to be made,' she said. 'I rather fancied that Richard Low might also have been contemplating – or, indeed, poor Hancock...'

There it was again, his absurd jealousy, though now without any depth whatsoever.

'Esther!' he scolded her. 'Should you choose to inflict yourself upon either of those ill-fated fellows, that is entirely your own affair. But you must know that I shall be in Manchester asking Mr Francis for your hand long before either of them may know we are even gone. Now...'

She reached up to kiss him. On the lips. The strangest of sensations. And Palmer's analytical mind began to wonder at the chemical reaction taking place in that most bizarre example of human behaviour. Life as a chemist, he supposed, still held its own mysteries to be resolved. Its own adventures. And, as he had told Faustina Blackstone, adventures might abound upon every page of a history book.

'Well,' she said, 'I suppose there is always the chance *neither* might have asked me. And then where should I have been? Yes, I suppose it might be a case of beggars and choosers, Mr Palmer.'

She lifted the ring from the box and set it upon her finger. She was humming a tune. A familiar ditty. That one about *Bradshaw's Guide*.

'How does that final verse go?' he said. 'Like this?' And he sang.

'Yet while we both were searching, I squeezed her little glove,
And suddenly discovered that I was deep in love,
I proposed and was accepted, and now she is my bride,
And together we amuse ourselves with Bradshaw's Guide.'

'Is there not some innuendo in that last line, Neo?'

'I suppose there may be, my sweet. Though at least we have lived to tell the tale.'

Except, of course, they could not tell it. Not ever.

The End

Historical Notes and Acknowledgements

Wrexham would have to wait a further 120 years before it was blessed with its first permanent museum but, by then, the town's history (Wrexham has recently been granted city status) had been wonderfully researched and recorded – by Alfred Neobard Palmer.

Palmer was born in Thetford in 1847. He was a Primitive Methodist who had worked for a while as a teacher before becoming an analytical chemist in Manchester where he met – and in 1878 married – Esther (Ettie) Francis, daughter of the city's Caernarfonshire-born Chief Surveyor. They moved to Wrexham in 1880, where Palmer worked for a mineral water company and then for the Brymbo Steelworks, at which he was the chief chemist until ill-health – which seems to have dogged most of his life – caused him to leave and set up his own private practice, still as an analytical chemist, on Wrexham's Chester Street. His first local history book – the first of ten – about the town and its surrounding areas was published in 1883. He died in March 1915 and was buried at the cemetery on Ruabon Road where he has a prominent, though often neglected, memorial headstone. Just behind the cemetery, at 46 Bersham Road, a blue plaque marks the house – "Inglenook" – in which he lived with Ettie. They had no children.

And so, as I said, at the outset, Palmer could not – so far as we know – have been in Wrexham for its great 1876 Art Treasures Exhibition. But the Exhibition itself, with its Industrial Annexe, and the 1876 National Eisteddfod held in Wrexham, plus the Horticultural Show and many other events depicted in the novel are all factual and, I hope, accurately portrayed. The novel is, as much as anything, my own small tribute to those events – as well as to Palmer himself. I was lucky enough to find a copy of the Exhibition Catalogue and the day-to-day details are richly reported in the regional newspapers for 1876, all of which are wonderfully available in online archives.

Those details include the closing ceremony on Monday 27th November 1876, at which great tribute was paid to the work of Major Cornwallis West in helping to bring the Exhibition to Wrexham. It must have been a huge undertaking. The sureties which must have been given against the safe return of so many priceless artefacts. The logistical problems of packing and delivering so many substantial artworks. So much more beside. And yes, in his closing remarks, yet another promise of a permanent museum.

But the archives also include the article which appeared in *The Spectator* on 28th October 1876. It's easy enough to find. Acerbic and supercilious.

For other sources, I also owe a huge debt to Elen Phillips, Principal Curator of Contemporary and Community History at the St. Fagans National Museum in Cardiff for answering my increasingly bizarre questions about the Tailor's Coverlet – so often and so erroneously known as the Wrexham Quilt.

The background story of the First Carlist war is one with which I was already familiar. A distant ancestor, Francis Crook Ebsworth, served with the British Auxiliary Legion and is buried in San Sebastián. He was one of around ten thousand military volunteers who fought in Spain from 1836 onwards on behalf of the Liberal faction and Queen Isabella II against the reactionary conservative supporters of her rival Carlos de Borbón – and therefore *carlistas*, or Carlists. Almost a third of the British volunteers, like F.C. Ebsworth, died there – although only half of those in combat, the rest through illness or at the hands of their Carlist captors, who treated them as heretics. There are some strange echoes of the Spanish Civil War which would take place a hundred years later.

The circus episode is fiction, although there were always frequent circus visits to the town. Sometimes two different circus shows in the same month. In 1876 it was W & G Pinder's Grand Continental Circus – though that had been back in April. The decade saw visits to the area by Wombwell's Menagerie; Franconi's Circus; Fossett's Circus; Ginnett's Circus; Hutchinson and Tayleur's Great American Circus; Powell and Clarke's Paragon Circus; and several others. In

1870, it had been the Manders Star Menagerie, with its legendary lion tamer, the Great Maccomo. So, the Pinder Continental Circus and Lion Show is simply a composited invention to suit the story.

So far as the Wrexham Poor Law Union workhouse is concerned, in practice, the Master and Mistress there, from 1864 until 1884, were Luke and Elizabeth Ralph. Their tenure of that institution is well-recorded – for example, by Graham Lloyd and Annette Edwards for the *Wrexham History* website – and, needless to say, bears no resemblance to the roles played by my fictional Frederick and Faustina Blackstone. For more general background on this theme, I went to Peter Higginbotham's *Workhouses of Wales and the Welsh Borders*.

And what about "Patsy" Cornwallis West? I stumbled across her story a while ago when I'd been reading bits of research surrounding the swings and roundabouts of British monarchs – the fact that, while we are sometimes lucky enough to have a worthy heir to the throne, we're just as likely to end up with somebody as dissolute as Edward VII, known to his harem of mistresses as Bertie. They included Patsy herself, of course – and probably her mother as well, Olivia Fitzpatrick. Indeed, it's likely that Olivia had earlier also enjoyed a relationship with Bertie's father, Prince Albert – who, of course, has always been presented to us as the "honourable and devoted" husband of Queen Victoria. All of this – plus the scandals which continued to surround Patsy until her death in 1917 – is lovingly and carefully detailed in *Patsy: The Story of Mary Cornwallis West* by Tim Coates.

Incidentally, Patsy's efforts to secure beneficial marriages for her children were hugely successful. The oldest – "Daisy", who appears briefly in the story – married Prince Hans Heinrich XV von Hochberg. Her son, George, married the American heiress, Jennie Jerome – Churchill's mother and another of Bertie's mistresses. That one was all a bit weird since, by the time George married Jennie (then the widow of Lord Randolph Churchill), he was only the same age as her son, Winston. And the youngest, Constance, actually married Hugh Grosvenor, the Second Duke of Westminster – son, of course, to the duke who features somewhat in this story.

And what about "Bertie" himself? This serial philanderer and playboy eventually succeeded to the throne upon Victoria's death and reigned for only nine years, until his own death in 1910. Those who enjoy studying such things cite at least fifty-five mistresses and, in a strange twist of fate, the great-granddaughter of one of them, Alice Keppel, is Camilla Parker Bowles – who, of course, became the mistress and later wife of our present king, Charles the Third.

On a lighter note, I have become a great fan of George W.M Reynolds – and am now a member of the Reynolds Society. He was a remarkable man. A socialist – though he would probably not have recognised the word – as well as a prolific journalist and writer.

During his lifetime he was more widely read than Dickens or Thackeray. He is credited with publishing perhaps forty novels and a batch of short stories, as well as editing at least eight journals and newspapers. He died in 1879 and, in his obituary, the trade magazine *The Bookseller* called Reynolds "the most popular writer of our times".

The background tale of the exiled French imperial family in residence at Chislehurst has been well covered elsewhere – especially since the young Prince Imperial, Louis Napoléon, would die in a Zulu ambush three years later, a tale which lies at the heart of my third novel, *The Kraals of Ulundi*.

The regatta and parade of sail through the Menai Straits is purely fiction, though *Black's Picturesque Guide Through North and South Wales* gives a good account of the excursions through the Swellies and other traffic along the Menai Straits in 1869. I was fortunate enough to acquire a copy of the *Tide Tables for the British and Irish Ports, 1876*, as well as a more-or-less contemporary version of the Admiralty Chart 1464, *Menai Strait* – although I owe a huge debt to the outfit Rib Ride at Menai Bridge, with whom I enjoyed some memorable days testing out the account on that fabulous stretch of water.

Welsh speakers and others may bristle at the spelling of place names and personal names (like Owen Gwynedd, rather than Owain), but I have chosen to use those which were commonly in use in 1876 itself. As usual, I apologise for any other errors in the historical background, as opposed to the fictional plot. But it may be worth noting that I was inspired to write this one after working on a non-fiction guidebook. It's called *Wrexham Revealed*, a pocket-sized companion for those wishing to undertake self-guided walking tours of Wrexham's history. But it was in the process of compiling the guidebook – it took almost four years because of the pandemic – that

I came across the Art Treasures Exhibition and so much more which appears in the pages of this rather unusual (for me) crime story of Victorian Wrexham.

The Music Hall ditty *Bradshaw's Guide* was written, published and performed by Fred Albert (real name, George Richard Howell) early in 1876. It became an instant success and by mid-1876 *everybody* knew it. Fred's self-penned satirical songs were hugely popular, and he became known as "an infallible mirth-maker". There is no surviving recording of the song, but the lyrics are widely available, and the Special Collections Archive Department at Kent University were able to provide a rare copy of the sheet music. I owe a huge debt, therefore, to the inimitable Monika Evans for helping me reconstruct its performance.

As usual, I owe a great deal to my "ideal reader", best friend and constant companion Ann, who is also foremost among my literary critics as well as tolerating my endless ramblings about plot lines and character developments. And this time I was lucky that Pauline Vickers agreed to act as a further beta reader, supplementing the historical advice I've enjoyed from Jonathon Gammond and the formal editing process by Nicky Galliers. Finally, my thanks to cover designer Cathy Helms at Avalon Graphics, as well as to Helen Hart and her team at SilverWood Books for assisting with the technical publishing processes.

I hope you've enjoyed the story and, if you want to keep in touch, I send out regular monthly newsletters, as well as always being happy to chat and answer questions.

My website is: davidebsworth.com. You can also sign up for the newsletter there.

I'm on Facebook – my personal page, dave.mccall.3, plus my David Ebsworth author page, @EbsworthDavid – and occasionally Twitter: @EbsworthDavid.

And if you liked the book, a short review is always welcome.

David Ebsworth
April 2023

Milton Keynes UK
Ingram Content Group UK Ltd.
UKHW010629080923
428287UK00006B/162

9 781800 422612